Eleven Miles to Oshkosh

Eleven Miles to Oshkosh

JIM GUHL

The University of Wisconsin Press

The University of Wisconsin Press
1930 Monroe Street, 3rd Floor
Madison, Wisconsin 53711-2059
uwpress.wisc.edu

3 Henrietta Street, Covent Garden
London WCE 8LU, United Kingdom
eurospanbookstore.com

Printed in the United States of America

This book may be available in a digital edition.

Library of Congress Cataloging-in-Publication Data

Names: Guhl, Jim, author.
Title: Eleven miles to Oshkosh / Jim Guhl.
Description: Madison, Wisconsin: The University of Wisconsin Press, [2018]
Identifiers: LCCN 2018011135 | ISBN 9780299319106 (cloth: alk. paper)
Subjects: | LCGFT: Fiction.
Classification: LCC PS3607.U4732 E44 2018 | DDC 813/.6—dc23
LC record available at https://lccn.loc.gov/2018011135

This book is a work of fiction. The settings and many location names are real, including businesses, street names, and other places that existed in the years 1972 and 1973 in the Fox River Valley of northeastern Wisconsin. Shattuck High School has been represented based on the author's memory of the place. Descriptions of individual homes are fictitious. All characters and their actions are fictitious and not intended to represent actual individuals or events. The negative portrayal of law enforcement agencies and individuals is, likewise, fiction and not intended to reflect on actual people, behaviors, or events.

For my parents

JACK and **MARY**

with love and thanks for everything,

especially a wonderful childhood

Eleven Miles to Oshkosh

1

As near as I could tell, every cop in Wisconsin was there. Hundreds, thousands, maybe a million of them. Firemen and paramedics came too, from all over the Fox Valley, standing like toy soldiers along the winding narrow road through the cemetery that led to the gravesite. The parked police cars stretched even further, lights flashing, as they lined up in a row along Main Street and halfway down Tullar Road in Neenah. That's how they did things when a police officer was killed on the job in Winnebago County. The officer's name was Deputy William S. Finwick. My mom called him Billy. To me he was Dad.

Mom clung to the sheriff's elbow as he guided her to a metal folding chair in the shade of a large oak tree. My sister, Sally, and I sat to her left. Grandpa Asa was on her right. That was it—our whole family—or what was left of us anyhow.

The last chair was for Pastor Olson, who we knew from Christmas Eves at Ebenezer Lutheran. I liked him. He wasn't one of those television preachers. Instead, he was quiet and seemed to actually care about my grieving mom.

Once the bagpipe player started up, Mom sobbed and pressed her face against Grandpa Asa's shoulder. Pastor Olson touched her hand, but nothing helped. She couldn't even look at the flag-draped casket being carried forward by six men in Winnebago County Sheriff's Department uniforms. The casket moved ahead slowly, like an empty canoe in a slow-flowing current. Along both sides, those thousands of officers all saluted with their white gloves. The bagpipe player followed behind, getting louder and louder as the procession came near. When Dad's casket finally reached us, the funeral men guided it gently on the platform over the grave and backed away. That's when I started crying, too.

Pastor Olson said some things but, to be honest, I don't remember the words. When it was over, our small family gathered around Mom and someone got her a glass of water. By the time we were ready to go home, most of the officers and other folks had left. Except for the cars and trucks on Highway 41, the cemetery was quiet again, and I could even hear the robins singing in the oak trees.

The funeral man drove our car up the narrow road and helped Mom get in the front passenger seat. Grandpa Asa got behind the wheel. Sally and I climbed in back. As we started out toward home, I looked out the window and saw two men standing in the shade of an especially large burr oak. The men were dressed in blue coveralls. I thought they were mill workers until I saw each one leaning on a shovel. After we passed, I turned around to look at them again. They were walking toward Dad's grave.

2

My brain said that school would be better this year. How could it not? I had shaken off that miserable freshman label and moved on to the rank of sophomore. That *had* to make a difference.

I banked into the turn onto Reed Street and stood on the pedals. Then reality set in. Just like last year, there they were again. Dirtballs, grits, and stoners, all huddled around their favorite spot outside the chain-link fence that marked the property line at Shattuck High. *Jeez!* It was like they had never left, standing around in knee-torn pants and faded denim jackets. Their morning routine hadn't changed one iota — smoking cigarettes and weed, acting tough, looking around for easy targets — like me.

I tightened my grip on Ike's handlebars. (Ike stood for Eisenhower, which was the name of my red Schwinn Typhoon because it was built like a World War II tank.) I lowered my head and worked up a grimace as I accelerated toward the goons. The bike racks stood on the other side of the smoking herd, just beyond an opening in the chain-link fence.

"Here comes Minnow," I heard one say.

I recognized the guy with the scraggly brown hair as Larry Buskin and knew him to be the leader of that gang of mindless thugs. He considered me an easy mark, but who didn't? That was the problem with being me. I was *always* an easy mark. Hiding from dirtballs was practically a part-time job for me — ever on the alert for an escape route — always turning to run away.

"The toll is a quarter," said Larry. He and five others stepped out to block my path as they waited to grab Ike's handlebars.

After Dad's murder, I had sort of hoped they would lighten up. *Cripes!* Hadn't summer been bad enough already without more of the same old "let's pick on Minnow" crap? Believe it or not, a little part of me wanted to fight back this time. That's right—me—the little shrimp who was afraid of everything.

Have you ever seen a movie called *The Great Escape*? Did you see the part where Steve McQueen dodges the German Nazis on a motorcycle? That's who I wanted to be. But in my movie, instead of jumping the barbed wire fence, I would slam my front wheel right into Larry Buskin's crotch as he groans and falls backward in the mud. Then I would leave a black tire track right down his chest like a zipper, and one of the dirtballs would say, "Hey, I guess we better not mess with Minnow anymore."

Yep, there was a tiny molecule of courage inside me, and if you had an electron microscope, maybe you could have found it. Unfortunately, the biggest part of me was still the *scared of everything* part. And that part of me said, when your name was Del Finwick and your nickname was Minnow and you weighed eighty-four pounds in high school, it was time to run away—again.

I hated it, of course. I hated being scared of everything. And I hated it even worse that the whole world knew about it. My dad used to try to give me pep talks, trying to pump confidence into me like a blood transfusion.

"Stand up to them," he would say. "What's the worst that could happen? A bloody nose?"

Now with Dad gone, who was I supposed to listen to? Mom? Yeah right! She needed all of her energy just to get out of bed and turn on the coffee percolator in the morning.

Larry Buskin and the other Nazis hadn't moved. They stared me down, and I quickly recognized that I wasn't Steve McQueen, and Eisenhower wasn't a motorcycle. As usual, I had sixty-five cents in my pocket for my school lunch and not a nickel to spare. Option one was to pay the twenty-five-cent toll and skip lunch. Option two was to make a run for it. Either way I was still a stupid coward.

I chose option two, did a quick U-turn, and zoomed back onto Reed, where I ducked behind a line of yellow buses.

"I'll find you, Minnow!" Buskin yelled. "This will cost double tomorrow!"

"Crap," I said out loud. *Now what?* The school bell was set to ring in ten minutes, and I still needed a place to park Ike.

I kept my skinny legs pumping until I was completely out of their sight. Then I took a right turn on Division and spotted Randy Schnell stepping out his front door with a sack lunch in one hand and a notebook in the other. Unlike anyone else I had seen that morning, Randy Schnell was a good guy.

"Hey, Randy," I said.

"Hey, Minnow."

"Can I park my bike behind your house?"

"Sure," he said. Randy showed me where I could lock Eisenhower to his apple tree. I grabbed a Macintosh for my pocket and we walked together to the front entrance of Shattuck High. Five minutes till homeroom bell and I had already dodged the grits for the first time in the new school year, knowing that it would not be the last.

❁

In case you're wondering about the whole *Minnow* thing, the name was nothing new. I had been the smallest kid in my grade since kindergarten and had been branded with the name ever since. I was fifteen now, but getting pegged as a seventh-grader was normal. Being picked last for every sports team on earth was so common it was practically part of my DNA.

Have you ever heard of a poem called "The Charge of the Light Brigade"? It talks about how I felt on my first day as a sophomore at Shattuck High. The poem was written by a British guy named Alfred Lord Tennyson about a million years ago, and my favorite part went like this:

> Theirs not to reason why,
> Theirs but to do and die.
> Into the valley of Death
> Rode the six hundred.

The six hundred were the soldiers. They were probably just a bunch of ordinary guys with swords, leather scabbards, and sixty-five cents for lunch money in their pockets, but because of jerks, like a stupid king or army general, they all get sent to be killed in battle. Just like me they didn't have any good options either. Unlike me, they at least had the guts to fight.

❁

Shattuck used to be the only high school in Neenah, but shortly before I showed up, a new one was built across town. After that, Shattuck was just for ninth and tenth graders, but that was still over a thousand students, all piled into a building built before my grandpa Asa was even born. On the other side of Neenah the juniors and seniors all switched over to the brand-new school, named Neil Armstrong High after the astronaut. (Our nickname was the Rockets—pretty clever, weren't we?) Unlike Shattuck, the new building was modern and nice and, according to my sister, Sally, hadn't even been vandalized yet.

If you thought it sounded a little weird to split the two schools by grade instead of just making one Neenah East and the other Neenah West, then you didn't know much about the town religion—high school basketball. The holy grail, of course, was the Wisconsin state basketball championship, and we had been chasing it for a long time. Can you imagine what would have happened if Neenah had split the upper classmen into two completely separate schools? Talk about destruction of the talent pool. *Good grief!* We would have become another Hortonville.

I found both my homeroom and my locker within minutes, a minor miracle considering that Shattuck was designed like a maze. Then a second good thing happened. Steve Hawkins showed up in my homeroom.

"Hi, Del," he said.

"Hi, Steve."

Steve was a pal and a science nerd like me except he stood six feet tall. He had blond hair that hung down to his eyes like the fringe on a lamp shade and wore black plastic Buddy Holly glasses, which made him look even goofier. All the cool kids had already switched to wire rims.

Steve was always making sketches in his notebook, and most of them were pretty funny. My favorite one was a picture of Richard Nixon riding an atom bomb like a bull and wearing a cowboy hat. The other thing Steve did was invent stuff. He had about a hundred thousand ideas for inventions sketched here and there in his notebook, and *one day*, he said, he was going to build every one of them.

Our homeroom teacher, Mrs. Willison, had one of those big smiles that was all teeth and gums, and she wore a dragonfly pin on her blue sweater. At the front of the class she wrote her name in perfect cursive and explained a few rules about behavior and tardiness that we had all heard fifty-seven thousand times before. We sat through the announcements, stood for the Pledge of Allegiance, and for a few minutes that morning I actually thought the year might be okay.

Things kept being okay for three whole hours. Then, in the hallway, between third and fourth periods, something happened that ended my dreams of world peace.

I was flowing with the stream of bodies toward geometry class when I approached a flight of stairs. On the second step stood two dirtballs, plugging up traffic, shooting their mouths off, and basically looking for trouble. The Neanderthal on the right didn't worry me. It was the tall, weasel-faced goon in the Budweiser hat that I was watching. His name was Leon Dinsky. I knew him as the scumbag who had made a career out of *spotting out* nerds and other unsuspecting weaklings in the hallways between classes.

"Hang onto your books!" someone yelled. I clamped down.

For those not trained in tenth-grade terrorism, spotting out was the time-honored tradition of slapping a kid's books out of his arms and then kicking them down the hallway during the mad scramble between classes. The practice had grown rampant at Horace Mann Junior High, and a few creeps, like Dinsky, had kept it going at Shattuck.

I kept my head down and muddled along with the flow, trying to make myself invisible. I was just a couple yards away, nearing the moment of truth, when the unexpected happened. Dinsky didn't pick on me. Instead, he set his snake eyes on the person behind me. At first this came as a relief. Then I saw who he had chosen to destroy.

The girl was small and pretty, wearing a pink blouse and matching ribbon in her hair, and she was absolutely, absolutely, absolutely just minding her own business. On top of that, she was a brand-new student to Shattuck High. Maybe you're wondering how I knew that. How, in a collection of over a thousand kids, could I tell right away that she was an innocent rookie? Well, let's just say she stood out from the crowd. Yep . . . she had a distinctive feature from every other kid in the entire ocean of students who attended Shattuck High. Dinsky's target was a black girl.

Dinsky lifted his arm over his head. "Welcome to hell!"

The announcement was followed immediately by a karate chop of the girl's books such that the entire stack, complete with papers, notebooks, pens, and pencils, was driven to her feet in a scattered pile. Leon smiled like some zit-faced jack-o'-lantern.

"Good one, man," said his chubby pal with the silver front tooth.

They nodded and yukked it up as if causing mayhem and misery was a hobby for which they had both taken lessons.

"Watch this," said Dinsky.

The six-footer reached back with his long right leg and kicked all the girl's books and papers like he was attempting a fifty-yard field goal. From there, it was over. The foot shuffling of the migrating masses spread the girl's books and papers to the outer reaches of the halls. At first her face showed shock. Seconds later, tears streamed down both cheeks.

But wait. Here's the worst part—I did nothing.

The black girl slumped to her knees. The river of people flowed around her. The girl's books, papers, pens, pencils, and everything else drifted away with the current of shuffling and kicking feet.

She was right behind me—I did nothing.

As usual, my stupid survival instincts had taken over. Instead of helping the girl, I just lowered my head and burrowed through the crowd until I landed at a desk in room E132. I tried to justify my behavior. *I couldn't be late for class. I got stuck in the flow of people. I was too small to do anything about it.*

Through it all, I knew the truth. I did nothing. I did nothing. I did nothing. Any kid with a milligram of courage would have helped that unsuspecting black girl. What I should have done was punch Dinsky in the nose and live with the consequences. At the very least, I should have helped her gather up her stuff.

So, there you have it. Other than my size, that was the other reason folks called me Minnow. I was never the predator and always the prey. I was scared of everything and never fought back. I, more than anybody, should have helped that little black girl in the hall with her books kicked every which way by those two crumbs. I, more than anybody, knew how she was feeling. But what did I do? Not one damn thing.

3

When I sat down for a breakfast of Froot Loops the next morning, I was alone in the kitchen. Just as well. Worthless cowards weren't supposed to talk to anybody.

The thing that happened between Dinsky and the black girl kept running through my head like a bad TV movie that I couldn't turn off. I saw myself, the despicable coward, watching it all happen. The enemy attacked and I ran away. The United States Army tracked me down and tossed me in the brig, where I ate stale bread and drank warm water. That I would be executed after my court martial was a foregone conclusion. The only question was whether I would die by hanging or firing squad. I wiped my nose, chewed my Froot Loops, and drank my glass of Tang.

Do you want to know what else I kept asking myself? How come I didn't inherit some guts from my dad? *Jeez!* He wasn't afraid to go after creeps a hundred times worse than Dinsky and Buskin. He wasn't afraid to tackle a felon. He wasn't scared one bit about searching for the very same Highway 41 Killer who ended up murdering him. That's right: in a way, it was Dad's own bravery that killed him — that and the sheriff dumping him onto the graveyard shift to work the highway all by himself.

So, how come I didn't get any of those traits of bravery from my dad? How come I was born the pansy? I took biology. I knew how genetics were supposed to work. *What a rip-off!*

After a few minutes of feeling sorry for myself, I looked around. Where was everybody? My big sister, Sally, must have been locked in the bathroom doing whatever she did for almost an hour every morning. I poked my head around the corner and spotted Mom in the living room, smoking a Lucky Strike with one hand and sipping coffee with the other. I set my gaze on the kitchen window. A thick fog had filled up the neighborhood like spilled milk during the night, and I couldn't even see the Johnsons' house next door. Yep, the day was starting off gloomy all around.

The only sound came from the radio on the kitchen countertop. I took a breath between gulps of cereal and listened as the news announcer talked about air strikes, ambushes, and more soldiers coming home dead from Vietnam. Cripes, even I was getting sick of hearing all the rotten news. On top of that, according to my calculations I was just three years away from being sent there myself. Then again, who would take me? The army probably filtered out the shrimps and the cowards, and heck, I was a member of both groups.

The radio announcer switched to the presidential election coming up. Nixon was ahead of McGovern by about a thousand light-years. I guess everybody thought old Millhouse was doing a stellar job or something. Never mind that we were still bogged down in that stupid war and that the commies in Russia had about nine million A-bombs aimed at us.

A pair of car headlights rolled up our gravel driveway with a crunching noise. The car door slammed shut.

Ding-dong!

I waited to see if Mom would answer but she didn't move. Apparently the commercial for the Veg-o-matic was just too exciting to take her eyes off the TV. I went back to eating Froot Loops and checked the second hand on my watch to see how long it would be before Sally yelled at me.

Ding-dong!

Her scream came from the top of the steps. "Del, open the door! Jeez! Why do you have to be such a retard?" Twelve seconds. *Hmm.* Quicker than usual.

There was never any question about who was on the front porch. Every morning, Sally's boyfriend, Kevin, picked her up in his piece of crap Pinto on his way to Armstrong High. Kevin Muldoon always started the day with an insult aimed at me. I yanked the door open and waited.

"Hey, Minnow—did you get promoted to rat yet?"

"I hope you didn't injure your brain thinking up that one, Mull-goon. We wouldn't want to wreck your future as a turd inspector at the sewage plant."

I returned to the kitchen and left the idiot drooling on the welcome mat. Mom never even noticed his arrival. Her attention was now welded to the *Today Show*, where Barbara Walters was talking about the latest trends in women's fashion. *Women's fashion? Gee whiz.* I would be happy if she would just get out of her pajamas once in a while. Needless to say, my mom was still a basket case after Dad's death. It didn't help that the doctor now said she might have early symptoms of something else.

Sally came out of the bathroom, finally, with a towel wrapped around her head. She glared at me while dropping a couple of Pop-Tarts in the toaster. "Would it kill you to invite Kevin to sit down?"

I ignored her. If she wanted to hang out with Mull-goon, that was her business. I wasn't about to babysit the moron.

Mom finally hollered out from the living room. "You're on your own for supper tonight, Del. Marge and I are going out for cocktails in Oshkosh."

Great! Her first social activity in a month and it was some stupid shindig aimed at getting drunk and smoking even more cigarettes.

"Better take the lake road," I said.

"Why?"

"Highway 41 Killer's still out there."

You see, my dad wasn't the only one shot dead on the side of the highway. Two other times men had been found lying alone in the ditch next to their cars. One was two years ago and the other just five months before Dad was murdered.

My real motive behind that suggestion to Mom, however, was keeping her from getting busted for drunk driving on the way home. There were a lot more cops patrolling the highway than on the lake road following the west shore of Winnebago. I grabbed sixty-five cents for my lunch out of the loose change bowl in the kitchen and made my escape out the back door.

Riding Ike through the mist was sort of fun in a science-experiment kind of way. Microscopic water droplets piled up on my face as I cruised through the gunk. Sounds seemed twice as loud through the blanket of fog. From the crest of the bridge I heard water tumbling over the dam, the low rumble of paper mills, and a train whistle in the distance.

A strange confidence surged through me as I locked Eisenhower to Randy Schnell's apple tree once again. Parking there had saved me a lot of headaches and probably my lunch money. By the time fourth period was over I realized that I had avoided grits and dirtballs all morning long.

The best part of my day, however, was when I learned that the black girl was in my English class. I watched her all period long, wondering what her name was and how she ended up moving to Neenah in the first place.

She never smiled, but otherwise she seemed to have recovered from the Dinsky incident. *Gosh*, how I wished I could rewind the tape from yesterday. Yep, things would have turned out differently. I for sure would have helped her collect her books and stuff. Maybe there was even a way I could have popped Leon Dinsky without getting myself killed.

Was it really in me? Maybe I just didn't have enough bravery to do anything. Some people were probably *born cowards*, I figured, and maybe I was one of them. I hoped it wasn't true, but if it was true, I hoped it wasn't permanent.

The bell rang and I watched the black girl gather her things and stand up, straight-backed and proud. She walked sort of like that skinny black girl in Little Rock, Arkansas, who had to go up against the governor and practically the whole world just to attend a better school. I decided that I would find a way to meet her. I didn't know how, but one way or another I would learn her name and she would learn mine.

❀

After school I didn't go straight home. It was hot and sunny, so I rode my bike down to the lighthouse at Kimberly Point. I had planned it out in advance, bringing my dive mask and swim trunks with me in a plastic bag. I changed in the bathroom of the lighthouse and put on some beat-up tennis shoes to protect my feet. Looking around for bank fisherman, I spotted only two guys. One man was bottom fishing by the downstream corner of the park. The other was casting a spinner a short distance to my south. This was good news. I had the whole stretch of shoreline, a hundred feet on each side of the lighthouse, to myself and sure as heck didn't want to catch a number 4 treble hook in the neck.

Before going in the water, I looked east across the choppy waters of Lake Winnebago. All the way, across eight miles, I could see High Cliff. The shoreline rose sharply to the height of the bluffs. I knew all about that place and had ridden Ike there more than once to explore the cliffs, caves, and Indian mounds. A narrow white spire marked the ruins of the old lime kiln chimney that still stood below the cliffs. To the south, the shoreline almost disappeared to nothing as the thirty-mile length of Lake Winnebago swallowed it up like an endless sea.

I walked carefully into the greenish-brown water until I was waist-deep. Then I spat in my mask and smeared it around to keep it from fogging. As I lowered myself in, the chill shocked me worse than usual.

I shook it off and pulled myself to the bottom with an underwater breaststroke.

The waters of Lake Winnebago and the Fox River, which it fed, were almost as murky as chicken broth. The only question was whether visibility would be ten inches or ten feet. The view beneath the surface was almost never any greater than that. On this day I was fortunate enough to be able to see four feet in front of my mask before the clouds of silt and algae caused everything to disappear behind a curtain the shade of green olives. The bottom of the Fox River by the lighthouse was my own private place where nobody else ever went. I knew the fish, rocks, and buoy anchors. To me it felt like my own private property and I didn't even have to pay taxes. As far as I knew, I was the only idiot who explored the bottom of the Fox. The pollution and algae scared most would-be swimmers away. And diving for lost treasure? Well, it just wasn't done.

What I was after were fishing lures, sinkers, hooks, and other gear lost by fishermen who snagged them in the rocks. The trick to finding these plums was learned through experience. I shouldn't tell you the secret, but I will. Here it is. *Look for the trail instead of the treasure.* In the case of the Fox River bottom, that meant looking for the fishing line, usually clotted up with algae, and following the line to the lure. In a matter of seconds, I was on the trail of my first stray fishing line until it reached a dead end in the crevice between two rocks. I shoved one of the rocks aside and it made a deep, metallic *thunk* to my submerged ears. There it was, a blue-and-silver Little Cleo, almost new with just a little rust on the hook. I shoved it in my plastic bread bag, took a breath of air, and dove again.

As I searched for the next line, a sheepshead swam in front of me just beyond the length of my arms. The fish wasn't afraid, just playing a game with me. Around the back side of a bowling ball–sized rock, I found a coppery walleye lying in the gravel. It bolted at the sight of me, seeking a new place to ambush a minnow. I knew every type of fish in the lake and river, and they were many. Once I saw a spotted gar with its whip-thin body and alligator snout. Another time I saw a weird-looking paddlefish with its bucket-sized mouth and canoe paddle bill. A lamprey eel once slithered under my leg, and I was glad that the bloodsucker didn't latch on. What I really wanted to see, but never had, was the biggest monster of them all, the sturgeon. With its prehistoric face, ridged back, and shark-like pectorals, it would be a shocker for sure, especially if I happened upon a seven footer. I knew it would be scary and that maybe I would freak, but I knew they were in there and I really, really wanted to see one.

I had been in the water for almost an hour when I stumbled out with my bag of goodies. I shivered as I dumped the load onto a wooden picnic table. It had been a good take. For starters, I had two Cleos, including one old one with the naked lady stamped on the back side. I also had a Gypsy-King, a gold Rapala, a red-and-white Daredevil, and at least a dozen hooks and lead sinkers of various sizes and shapes. Between these and the others at home, I had accumulated enough to fill a Hughes candy box, and hopefully make some serious cash.

The sun was a big gold coin over the river as I stood on Ike's pedals by the hospital and climbed the bridge for about the millionth time. At least three dozen sailboats clung to their moorings by Riverside Park, and the big, seventy-five-foot lake cruiser, *Pilgrim*, lay asleep at her dock. I knew I would never cross Lake Winnebago in that gleaming hull, but nobody could stop me from dreaming about it.

My legs churned like an egg beater as I bombed past the mansions of the paper barons on Wisconsin Avenue. I zoomed by the stack of tiny pram sailboats where I had once taken lessons, then whipped a right turn onto Pine Street. On a whim I decided to treat myself to some baseball cards and a pack of Twinkies at Mertz's at the corner of Lauden and Congress. I slid two quarters on the counter and the old man returned a dime for my pocket. For the third day in a row, I parked my bike in Randy Schnell's backyard and helped myself to an apple. Not a single person gave me any crap as I walked through the big oak doors and jostled toward my locker. The prospects of surviving until the weekend were looking pretty good.

I walked into English class right at the sound of the third-period bell. The desk next to the black girl was open and I quietly slid into it, checking to see if she saw me. I felt almost invisible. Her serious face and dark eyes stared straight ahead. Her super curly black hair seemed to defy gravity, puffing out except where a blue bandana held it in place. She sure wasn't like any of the other girls in school and was the first black person I had ever seen close up. Her skin looked like liquid chocolate. Her nose turned up a little like a miniature ski jump and her cheeks were a pair of perfect, round pitcher's mounds. Those eyes never wavered as she kept on looking straight ahead. They were bright and dark at the same time and her mouth was . . .

"Mr. Finwick, are you with us?"

"Huh?" My head snapped around and my eyes landed on the not-smiling face of Mrs. Borger.

"I asked you a question, Mr. Finwick."

"Could you repeat it, please?" I was pretty sure that Mrs. Borger already hated me, and the current situation wasn't helping matters.

Her face tightened up like a knotted rope as she looked over the top of her glasses. She cleared her throat for effect. All eyes were on her. "What is the rhyming scheme in the Shakespearian sonnet form of English poetry?"

Heads snapped around and all of a sudden every eye was on me. I gave a quick glance in the direction of the black girl. Even she was looking at me now, apparently concerned for my survival.

"Mr. Finwick? Do you have an answer? This *was* in your reading assignment." Mrs. Borger pushed her glasses to the top of her nose and stretched her long neck like she was the Queen of Sweden or something.

I squinted my eyes and looked toward the ceiling. Around me the giggles and snickers began to rise. I mined my brain for the answer that I had seen somewhere. Then, very slowly, I spoke: "a b a b c d c d e f e f g g."

Silence filled the classroom as all heads whipped back around to Mrs. Borger, who now looked at me with her mouth hanging slightly open. Apparently, the Queen of Sweden didn't like to be shown up.

"That is correct, Mr. Finwick," she said without smiling.

I glanced at the black girl, who was trying very hard not to smile but losing the fight, and for one very brief microsecond, she looked at me in a way that made me feel very, very good.

The remaining forty-eight minutes of English class were spent by me trying to work up the courage to talk to her. The bell rang and the commotion began. It was now or never.

"Hi," I said. (That was my opening line after forty-eight minutes of thinking about it.)

"Hi," she said.

"I'm Del Finwick."

"I'm Opal Parsons."

She paused and smiled, but only with her eyes. Then she was gone.

❀

My mom and sister were still asleep on Saturday morning when I snuck out the door with my Hughes candy box full of fishing lures, an empty pickle jar, and a folded-up card table. The box and jar fit neatly enough in Eisenhower's front basket. The card table posed another problem. Lacking any better ideas, I ended up carrying the thing by holding it with one hand alongside Ike while steering with the other. It wasn't easy, and Fox Point Shopping Center was two miles away, but, with rest stops every few minutes, I finally made it there by eight in the morning.

The flea market at Fox Point was really just a ragtag operation with nobody in charge. A few dozen tables had been set up in the parking lot in two rows, back-to-back. The usual arrangement was a car or pickup truck backed in to the spot so the merchandise could easily be moved from the trunk or truck bed to the tables. People were selling all sorts of assorted junk. They had record albums, dishes, old coins, radios, used clothes, antique door knobs, and pumpkins just to name a few. I was the only one who came by bike and the only one selling fishing lures.

I set up my table and organized my stuff by category. In the first row I had my spoons and spinners. In row two, my various plugs and plastic worms. Backing up the display were the accessories, such as sinkers, hooks, swivels, and bobbers. My prices ranged from a nickel to fifty cents.

An old, bald-headed man at the table next to me was set up with antique milk and pop bottles. I thought they were pretty neat and told him so. I had found a few old bottles on the river bottom myself and had a genuine interest. The old man's bottles were mostly small, but the best one was a gallon-sized, clear job with green letters that said *Eskdale Dairy* on the side. It was clean as a whistle, with a built-in metal handle and everything.

"How much for that one?" I asked.

"Two dollars," he said. "But I'll give you a discount if it's still here at noon."

Things started off slow, but by nine o'clock, customers started rolling in at a pretty good clip. Like any boy in Neenah, I had done my share of lemonade stands and door-to-door wreath sales, but this was different. I was sure glad I went to the bathroom before leaving home because the bargain hunters just kept coming.

It was weird listening to people insulting my stuff as if I wasn't even standing there. "Looks like a lot of junk to me," said a father to his son. "You're better off going to the hardware store."

A gray-haired man in coveralls walked up with a rusty toaster under his arm. "Used fishing lures?" he said. "Bunch of crap."

Well, crap or otherwise, *some* people seemed to like my stuff. By ten o'clock I had sold an Abu-Reflex and all but two Little Cleos. At 10:15

a lady in pink pants gobbled up my red-and-white daredevil with plans to give it to her husband for his birthday. Five minutes later, a man in a sweater vest offered a buck for two Rapalas and every sinker on the table.

All this time I kept stuffing the money into the glass pickle jar that I had washed out at home and brought along for the purpose. I was rolling in dough and wishing I had more merchandise to put out.

Meanwhile, the old man with the milk bottles was scratching his head in amazement at my success. "Looks to me like you've found yourself a vocation," he said with a smile.

By eleven in the morning, my merchandise was pretty well tapped out and all I had left was a plastic crayfish, a half-dozen swivels, and a cork bobber the size of my fist. It was time to pack things up. I looked over at my friend with the milk bottles who was still trying to make his first sale of the day. I picked up the gallon-sized Eskdale with the metal handle and admired it once again.

"I'll let it go for a dollar and seventy-five cents," he said.

I pondered the beauty, and glanced at my jar that now brimmed with almost eight dollars in bills and coins.

"Would you go for a buck-sixty-five?" I asked.

He took a step back, as if appalled by my offer. I felt a little embarrassed, not meaning to insult the old guy. At last, he shot me a wink and a smile.

"You drive a hard bargain," he said. "But I'll go for it."

I handed him a paper dollar, two quarters, a dime, and a nickel.

"Good doing business with you," said the man. "My name's Wilbur."

"I'm Del," I replied. "Good doing business with you, too."

"Will we see you here again?" he asked.

"Most likely," I answered.

I took it slow going home with the Eskdale bottle perched next to the candy box and pickle jar in Eisenhower's front basket. Every bump in the road had me slowing down. Every railroad crossing brought me down to a walk. I think my left arm may have stretched a few inches with the weight of the card table hanging from it, and, in the end, it took me twice as long to get home as getting there.

My heart was still pumping when I got to my room. I stashed the pickle jar of cash in my sock drawer and placed the Eskdale gallon milk bottle with the metal handle on top of my dresser next to the other two bottles in my collection. One was a bright-blue medicine bottle and the other an old greenish pop bottle with bubbly glass, both of which came out of the Fox River while diving for lures. The Eskdale was the first bottle that I had actually paid for.

From my bed I could see all three as they sparkled and glowed in the sunlight that poured through my window and, as far as I was concerned, they were as valuable as any of Captain Kidd's treasures.

❁

I was the first of my friends to arrive behind the bleachers of the Neenah High School football field that Saturday afternoon. Even though the team was almost all juniors and seniors from Armstrong, the games were still played on the field behind Shattuck. I heard trombones, drums, and tubas playing something that sounded like a reenactment of the end of the world. Just last week the marching band did a halftime show that re-created the first moonwalk. (When your new school was named for Neil Armstrong and your mascot was the Rockets, it was apparently the thing to do.)

Having already scoured the gravel behind the bleachers for money and coming up with zilch, I sat down by the chain-link fence and ripped open a frozen Milkshake bar on a stick. It cost me thirty cents at the concession window, but with my recent success at the flea market, I figured I could splurge. Just then, something hard drilled me in the back of the head.

"Ouch!" I said. Without turning around, I could tell it was Mark by his shadow with the untucked shirt and gangly legs. He was also the most likely guy to thwack me in the head with a stone, although there were others. Mark stepped up and sat next to me.

"How are things, Delmar?" He pulled out a pack of Red Man and placed a pinch of the soft tobacco under his lower lip. "Have a chew?" He reached out with the pouch.

"Maybe later," I said. "And I was better before you put a lump on my head." I rubbed the spot with my index finger and checked for blood but came up empty.

It was weird that Mark was one of my best friends, considering that he was neither a weakling nor a nerd. He was strong and athletic and a year older than the rest of us because he was held back a year in grade school. Heck, he could probably have been quarterback of the JV team if he had bothered to try out. But Mark was funny that way. And I'm pretty sure the reason he didn't go out for football was because his dad wanted him to do it. There was definitely something weird going on between him and his dad.

Other than bringing a certain cool factor to my small group of friends, Mark was also the only one who actually knew anything about girls. He had gone out with a bunch of them and even French kissed some. I knew all of this because Mark told us everything. I reckon 10 percent of my sex education came from Mr. Ward in Health class and the other 90 percent came from Mark.

"Did you meet any new girls this week, Delmar?" That's another thing about Mark. Other than my great-aunt Martha (now dead), he was the only one who ever called me Delmar.

"I met a girl in English," I said.

Mark turned his head slowly in my direction and his eyes widened. "Details?"

"It's nothing really," I said. "I just talked to her a little bit. That's all. She seems nice and . . ."

"And what?"

"And she's colored."

Mark's head turned again in my direction, but it really snapped this time.

"You're going out with the black chick?"

"No! I just met her."

"Holy shit, Delmar. You got more guts than I thought."

"I *said*, I just met her, and I would appreciate it if you didn't say anything to Steve."

Mark looked at me for a long time like he had just learned that I was an Apollo astronaut or something. "All right—but you better keep me in the loop, okay?"

"Sure. Whatever," I said.

"Hey, Minnow! Hey, Mark!" It was Steve.

"Hey, Steve," I said.

"Hey, dork," said Mark. "You score any chicks this week? Delmar's got 'em lined up around the block."

I gave Mark my "I'm gonna kill you" look.

"Lighten up, Delmar. It's a compliment." Steve was oblivious.

"Let's go," said Steve. "The national anthem's coming up. Mr. Glannek's going to sing it and a bunch of us are going to boo him."

Mark waved his hands over his head in mock excitement. "Holy crap, we wouldn't want to miss that, now would we." We got to our feet and started walking. I saw my chance, grabbed a stone from the gravel and nailed Mark in the back of the head.

Typical of Mark, he said nothing and just kept his cool as he walked on. Several seconds later, he reached his hand around behind his head like he was going to rub it and flipped me the middle finger.

Except for the part where we all booed Mr. Glannek, the football game went pretty much like all the others. Kids goofed around. Adults watched the game. Neenah lost. We all went home.

5

On Monday morning before homeroom, Steve was buzzing around like he had swallowed a whole can of Folgers. I knew without asking that he had concocted some sort of invention again. It was as predictable as the seasons. About once every three months, his geekiness got the better of him. Last spring he dreamed up the Moto-Surf, a motorized surfboard on wheels. We even built a prototype and I had to admit it was pretty cool. We started with a six horse go-kart engine and a used surf board that Steve bought from a mail-order place in California. (That cost him fifteen bucks just for shipping.) We painted the thing banana yellow and rigged it up with roller-skate wheels, foot brakes, directional signals, and a cable-actuated throttle control. It was neat—or was, at least, until Steve crashed it into a parked ice cream truck on Chestnut.

"I've got an idea! You've got to hear it!"

I looked at the clock. Two minutes before homeroom bell. "Sure."

"Remember how Menasha screwed us last year by making that big white letter M out of salt on our football field the night before homecoming?"

"Yeah."

"And remember how the salt turned the grass brown and everyone could still see the brown M for the rest of the football and track seasons?"

"Yeah."

"I've got an idea on how we can get 'em back."

"Okay." At this point I was calculating the odds of Steve ending up in juvie before the first snowfall.

Steve looked left and right to see if anybody was listening. Then he leaned in so his nose was just inches from my face. I leaned back until my head hit a metal locker door. CLANG!

"Okay, here it is," he said. "You know that fake volcano we made by mixing vinegar and baking soda in Earth Science?"

"Yeah."

"We bury a tank full of baking soda in the Menasha football field, and another tank full of vinegar and then somehow we get them to mix together and we have a pipe leading to the center of the fifty-yard line and the eruption will come right out of the ground at some critical moment and screw everything up for Menasha's homecoming ceremony."

He looked at me all proud and goofy like he had just won the national spelling bee. I was speechless. (And probably stone-faced, but I couldn't see my own face). I was also changing my calculation on Steve. Maybe he would have to make a stop at the nuthouse for a few weeks before going to juvie.

"It's great, right?" he said.

"Pretty good," I said.

"Are you with me?" he asked.

"I guess so."

At this point in the conversation, Steve literally started twitching. I don't think I had ever seen a bigger smile on anybody's face, ever, and that includes scarecrows and clowns. It was even bigger than when he announced his invention of Rocket Shoes. (Nobody died and Steve's feet have fully recovered from the burns, in case you're wondering).

"All we have to do now is work out the technical stuff. That's where I need your help. Will you help me, Minnow?"

The bell rang. "Okay," I said. We blasted into homeroom.

❋

I got to third period as early as I could in hopes of nabbing the desk next to Opal Parsons again.

Opal Parsons, Opal Parsons, Opal Parsons . . . She had such a groovy name I couldn't stop repeating it in my mind. I had even looked up opal in the Encyclopedia Britannica and found out that it was a fluorescent gemstone from Australia, which made the name even better. *Opal Parsons. Cripes,* that was about fifty times cooler than Delmar Finwick . . . and seven million times better than Minnow.

I watched the door as she walked in looking real serious and holding her books tight to her chest. I couldn't blame her for being unhappy after what happened on her first day.

"Hi, Opal," I said.

"Oh—hi." Her voice leaked out sort of quiet as she looked back at the door.

"Is something wrong?" I asked.

She shrugged her shoulders and opened her English book. Then she glanced again at the open door.

"Are you looking for somebody?"

"Not really," said Opal.

"Is Leon Dinsky giving you more trouble?"

Her eyes got as large as ripe plums and twice as dark. "What do you know about it?"

"I saw him slap the books out of your arms on the first day of school. I was standing right next to you," I said. My eyes sagged.

"Oh," she said. "Is he your *friend*?"

"No."

She studied me like a puzzle. I think she was trying to decide if she trusted me or not.

"Believe me," I continued. "Dinsky is *not* my friend. I can't stand the jerk."

"Then why didn't you help me?"

There it was. The question that defined me. *Why didn't I help her? Why did I walk away? Opal Parsons needed my help. I was right there, and I did nothing.*

"I'm sorry," I said. "I guess I was afraid."

As soon as I said the words, I regretted them. What did I expect? Pity? Compassion? *Good grief.* Opal was the one who had been attacked by the creep. *I was afraid. I was afraid. I was afraid.* My God—they might as well carve the words into my tombstone right now. It was the one and only thing I was good at—being afraid and running away. I dropped my eyes toward the floor. Then my face followed. Then my whole head sagged like it was held up by a thread.

The bell rang. I wanted to die.

Then something touched the back of my hand and my eyes told my spinning brain that it was her small, smooth hand.

"I wish you would have helped me," she said.

I nodded.

Opal leaned over and whispered. "But at least you told the truth."

Time stopped. Albert Einstein was right about relativity. I know, because third period English on that day with Mrs. Borger went on for at least a month. Through it all, the clock refused to move. I heard the words. Something about similes and metaphors and cadence and verse. I was just thankful that she didn't call on me again.

At the end of class she told us that we would be reading one of six different books from classic American literature. She said that we would be preparing written papers as well as oral reports presented to the class and that we would work in teams of two.

"If you know who you would like to partner with, let me know. Otherwise I will assign a partner for you at our next class."

Opal leaned toward my ear and whispered again. "Do you want to be my partner?"

"Okay," I said. My heart sped up.

Opal walked to the front and told the teacher right away. Mrs. Borger nodded, wrote it down, looked at me, and smiled—slightly.

❋

When the final bell rang, I didn't go straight home but rode through downtown Neenah past the old shopping district and the big red-brick Bergstrom Paper Mill, and down by the bars where the workers drank beer after their shifts. I clunked over the railroad tracks and zigged left off Main onto the side streets before locking Eisenhower to a light post in front of an old apartment building.

A man in a plain white T-shirt with a spider tattoo on his hand sat on the concrete steps out front with a six-pack of Old Mil.

"Are you sure you belong here, boy?"

"Yes, sir. I'm visiting my grandpa."

"Who's your grandpa?"

"His name's Asa."

The man nodded and let me pass.

The hallway at Emerald Gardens Apartments smelled like dead mice. The single light bulb glowed so dim I couldn't tell what color the walls were. Maybe gray or brown, I wasn't sure.

I found apartment 118 and banged on the door.

"Who is it?" Grandpa's voice sounded like he had a throat full of gravel.

"It's Del!" I yelled it loud because Grandpa's hearing wasn't so good anymore.

I waited for several minutes before the door creaked open. Grandpa stood there with the support of a wooden cane. He had been tall and strong once. I had seen pictures of him when he worked at the Neenah Foundry making manhole covers and sewer grates. He smiled his usual crooked smile. "How we doing, Del? I didn't know you was coming or I'd have cleaned up."

"I'm okay, Grandpa."

"Come on in. You want some ice cream?" Any visit to Grandpa Asa included ice cream. If you said yes, you got a bowl of ice cream. If you said no, you got a bowl of ice cream.

"Yes," I said.

"You scoop it up. There are dishes in the sink. Get some for me too."

I came face-to-face with a pile of dirty dishes that filled every bit of the sink and most of the countertop. The open cupboard doors revealed empty shelves. As I lifted some pans, a cockroach skittered to a new hiding place. It took a while to find the soap and a usable wash rag, but I finally got two bowls and spoons cleaned and filled with vanilla ice cream from the freezer. I handed one to Grandpa. He had plopped himself back down in a soft blue chair.

"How's your mother?" asked Asa.

"She's okay," I said.

"Is she still smoking cigarettes?"

"Yes."

"Those things will kill her one of these days," said Asa. He looked at me. "Are you smoking cigarettes?"

"No."

"Good."

We both clanked away at our ice cream and I carried the empty bowls back to the sink and returned to sit across from Grandpa Asa.

"I need your help with something, Grandpa."

Grandpa looked at me suspiciously. "Well . . . Let's hear it."

"Do you remember my friend Steve?"

"The kid with the motorized surfboard?"

"Yep."

"Yeah, I remember him. Good idea man but a bit of a nut isn't he?"

I nodded. "He has a new idea."

"Well, spit it out."

"We want to build an underground, artificial, baking soda and vinegar volcano on the fifty-yard line of the Menasha High School football field so that we can explode it at their homecoming ceremony in a few weeks and ruin everything for them. I was wondering if you could help us get the stuff."

For a full minute, Grandpa stared at me with half-closed eyes like I was a werewolf or something.

"Is this some sort of retaliation for the salt letter M on our football field last year?"

"Yes, sir."

"You could get suspended for this if you get caught."

"Yes, sir."

"And you expect me to help you with this cockamamy idea?"

"Yes, sir. I mean—we could sure use your help."

"Have you told your mom?"

"No."

"Good."

Asa started flipping through a copy of *Popular Mechanics* magazine like I wasn't even there.

"Will you help?"

"I guess so," he said without looking up. "It's not like I've got anything better to do."

"Thanks, Grandpa." I got up to leave. Then I remembered something else. I stopped and looked at Asa but didn't know if this was the right time to ask for another favor.

"What is it?" he asked.

"Could you show me how to shoot Dad's 12 gauge?"

That got my grandpa's nose out of the magazine. His eyes got a wild look.

"Who are you planning to shoot?" he asked.

"Nobody."

"Then why do you want to learn how to use a 12 gauge?"

"Duck hunting on Poygan."

"By yourself?"

"Dad was going to take me this year. It's all right though. I reckon I can do it by myself. I've rowed the skiff before."

"That's pretty big water for October. You dump the skiff and you're probably dead." Asa's face turned serious.

"Maybe you can go with me."

"I don't hunt anymore."

"Yeah, I know. But maybe you could go with me anyhow."

"Could I even climb into the skiff?"

"I could help you."

"I don't know. I'd have to spend a whole day outside of my beautiful home here at Emerald Gardens."

Both of us smiled.

"Does your mom know?"

"Nope."

"Good. You sneak out of there with the shotgun and I'll pick you up in front of Governor Doty's cabin at six o'clock sharp."

I nodded.

"You got any shells?"

"No."

"I'll get us some. You just be at Doty Cabin tomorrow with the 12 gauge."

6

I got to English class early the next day and found Opal already in the room with her nose in a book.

"Hi, Opal," I said.

"Hi, Del," she said. "I'm halfway through *The Scarlet Letter.* Have you started yet?"

"No. I haven't even bought it, but I'm going to Bookland tonight. My grandpa's taking me out to learn how to shoot the Winchester Model 12 shotgun, and we'll be driving right by." I watched Opal closely. I thought she would be impressed by what I said about the shotgun. I waited.

"You're learning to shoot a gun?"

"Yes."

"Why would anybody want to do that?"

In a split second my thoughts came off the rails. They quickly vacated the pride section of my brain and moved toward the defense department. I tried to come up with a response but the puzzle pieces were scattered and I had nothing.

"Um . . . well . . ."

"After what happened to your father, why would you even want to touch a gun?"

"You know about my dad?"

"Del, everybody knows. I'm very sorry."

I lowered my eyes.

Opal continued. "Just because your dad was murdered by someone with a gun doesn't mean you have to start using one."

"Opal! This isn't about that."

"What?"

"This is about duck hunting."

"Duck hunting?"

31

I nodded.

"Well, I guess that's different. It doesn't sound like much fun though."

"What do you mean?"

"Don't you have to sit in a swamp?"

"Gosh. Being in the swamp is the best part."

"Huh?"

"It's hard to explain."

"Try me." The sparkle in her eyes was back.

My thoughts returned cautiously to the pride department of my brain. Then I just started yakking.

I explained in some detail how ducks, beginning with the mallards, teal, shovelers, woodies, and pintails, funneled in great flocks through the Mississippi and Central flyways toward their wintering grounds to the south. I went on to tell her that in late October the great migration shifted to bluebills, goldeneyes, canvasbacks, buffleheads, and ringbills. And through it all, some twenty species or more, not counting geese, swans, gallinules, and snipe, peeled the sky at speeds that sometimes exceeded fifty miles an hour. Most importantly of all, I explained that hundreds of thousands of these birds, maybe millions, would be passing through the region where we lived. How we were the lucky ones who lived by the great waterfowling lakes of Winnebago, Poygan, Rush, and Butte des Morts. I explained that it was a spectacle and that the Poygan Marsh in particular held a magic almost beyond description. I told her how in the near darkness of predawn as the herons screeched and the owls moaned, if you lay back in the skiff and listened hard, you would hear the whistling of unseen wings that told you the first flock of ducks had taken flight and that the show was about to begin.

"Besides, it's a tradition in our family," I said. "And they taste good. I mean, you eat chicken, don't you?"

It was Opal's turn to go slack-jawed. She just looked at me strangely with a sort of crooked, half smile. "I had no idea," she said at last.

I shrugged and produced a half smile of my own. "Well, okay then— now you know."

"But, how did you learn all that if you never shot a gun before?"

"I've gone out with my dad for the past three years," I said. "This year he said I could carry a shotgun."

"By yourself?"

"I asked my grandpa to go with me."

"And for three years you went with your father just to watch?"

"Absolutely."

"You know what I think?" she said.

The school bell rang and Mrs. Borger rose to her feet.

"What do you think?" I whispered.

She whispered back. "I think I'd like to go with you sometime." Her smile glowed like a crescent moon. And for the first time, I wondered if a scrawny kid called Minnow could someday have a girlfriend—for real.

❀

After supper I told my mom I was going to Doty Park, and it wasn't even a lie. I went into the garage and found the Winchester right where I had stashed it behind a stack of scrap lumber. It was in a brown leather case, but anybody could tell that there was a gun inside by the shape of it. I took off through the backyards and found Asa parked in his turquoise-colored Chevy Apache pickup just outside Doty Cabin.

"Put the shotgun behind the seat," he said. "You drive. It hurts my hip to work the clutch."

"I can't, Grandpa. I'm only fifteen. I don't have my license yet."

"Don't speed then." Grandpa got out and slowly hobbled around to the passenger side.

"But, I don't even know how to work the clutch," I complained.

"Do you want to fire that shotgun or don't you?"

"Yes."

"Okay—I'll talk you through it. Now, get in."

I put the Winchester behind the seat and got in on the driver's side. My eyes scanned the chrome knobs and the numbers on the speedometer that went up to 100. My fingers found the indentations in the steering wheel and I tested my grip of the shift lever. Grandpa Asa explained how driving a truck with a clutch could be a delicate procedure, sort of like setting the hook on a walleye.

"You've got to take up the slack real slow as you lift your left foot off the pedal. There's a spinning disk connected to the engine and another disk connected to the transmission. When you lift up your left foot on the clutch pedal, those disks come together and start gripping each other. You have to let up the pedal slowly and let it grab on gradually, like the walleye. When the truck starts moving pretty good, then you set the hook by releasing it the rest of the way while giving it some throttle. After that, you're on your way."

Guess what. Hooking a walleye was a hundred times easier than getting that stupid truck going in first gear. *Gee whiz!* On the first five tries the thing bucked like a mule and died.

"Dammit," I whispered.

"If you're gonna swear, say it like you mean it," said Asa.

"Dammit!"

"That's better. Now try it again, but take it real slow and let the disks slip together for a long while before they grab. Just let the truck start rolling real slow until I tell you different."

I tried again and lifted my foot up from the clutch pedal very slowly until the truck started to creep along.

"Let up on it another quarter of an inch and give it some more throttle," said Asa.

I did as he said and the truck gained more speed.

"Okay, set the hook."

I lifted my left foot all the way off the pedal and the truck chugged right along as smooth as could be.

"Give it some gas," said Grandpa Asa.

I did.

"Now shift to second gear by working the clutch all over again."

I pushed in the clutch pedal and Grandpa showed me how to shift the lever into second. We were on our way. I wasn't a kid anymore. All I needed was a leather jacket and a haircut like James Dean. Then I saw the stop sign coming up, and a half minute later we were right back to square one.

It took a while, but we made it over the bridge and through downtown Neenah on Wisconsin Avenue. I even stopped at Bookland to buy my paperback copy of *The Scarlet Letter*, by Nathaniel Hawthorne, for sixty cents plus two pennies for the governor. Then it was back on the road toward the foundry and beyond, where we chugged past corn fields and patchy woods. The sky blushed pink in the west by the time we got to the spot marked by X-shaped crossing signs at the railroad tracks on Dixie Road.

"Park the truck just this side of the railroad crossing," said Asa.

I put the passenger-side tires on the grassy incline of a ditch, turned off the ignition, and handed the keys to Asa.

"What's next?" I asked.

"We'll walk alongside the tracks until we're out of sight behind that sumac bush. You carry the gun and the shells. I'll try to follow with my cane."

I walked as slowly as I could, but Grandpa Asa still fell behind. I waited and offered my arm for support. Between that and his cane, he finally made it behind the brightly colored leaves of the sumac. A low rumble came up from the direction of Oshkosh to our south.

I looked at Asa. "A train's coming, Grandpa."

"Get down under the bushes," he said.

We tucked ourselves under the red leaves and waited for the train to pass. It was a Soo Line train. I could tell by the approaching red-and-white locomotive engines up above the embankment. The whistle blasted twice and the rumble got louder and louder. The train had three engines, hissing and popping as they moved by ahead of the long string of railroad cars. *Clickity-clickity-clickity.* They drummed out a rhythm as the rails sagged and rose beneath the shiny, steel wheels. Boxcars, hopper cars, tankers, and flatbeds all rolled on for our inspection.

At last, the red-and-white caboose passed through and Asa gave me the signal that we could come out from our hiding spots. When all was clear, Grandpa Asa pulled a cardboard cereal box out of his coat pocket.

"This is your target. Put it on that bush over there."

I did. Then I unzipped the case and held the Winchester across my chest with both hands. The heavy 12-gauge shotgun had once belonged to my dad's dad, Oscar Finwick. It was a long-barreled, no-frills, pump-action job with none of that foo-foo checkering on the stock. All 12-gauge shotguns are big and powerful, but this one was bigger than most. It felt like a sixty-pound barbell and I could barely heft it.

Asa showed me how to work the safety and the trigger. "Do you remember the three safety rules?" he asked.

I rattled them off. "Be sure of your target. Treat every gun as if it were loaded. Always keep the muzzle pointed in a safe direction."

"Good."

He helped me slide a single shell in the chamber and I shut it with a clang. Asa backed up a few steps as I tried to shoulder the ungainly thing. The Winchester was so big that I couldn't even reach the wooden forearm with my left hand. Instead, I held the gun at the steel section just beyond the receiver but short of the forearm piece.

"Hold it tight," said Asa. "Safety off, then aim. Squeeze the trigger when you're ready."

It all sounded so easy. I hoisted the enormous thing and tried my best to sight down the plane of the barrel. It was impossibly long and heavy. I couldn't keep it steady. Up and down, left and right, the thing wobbled in my grip. Finally, I saw the cardboard box in my sights and gave a steady tug with my trigger finger. All at once, the whole world turned upside down.

The blast was so powerful that my brain heard it as a giant thunderclap two inches from my head. It left both ears ringing like crazy. My feet instinctively scrambled for balance as the blast launched me backward and the gun skyward at the same time. Somehow, I kept a grip on the barrel and stock but the gun had pivoted to almost vertical and I found myself aiming up at the purple sky. *Hang on*, I told myself as the thing reached its apex before dropping back down. I found my footing in a place several feet behind where I had started. I had done it.

"Are you okay?" asked Grandpa.

"Yes."

"You were wobbly."

"I know."

"The recoil almost knocked you off your feet."

"I know."

"You want to try another shot?"

"Sure."

Step by step, I went through the whole procedure again and took aim once again at the cereal box in the bushes. I forced myself to put all of my strength into gripping the gun. I was steadier the second time before squeezing the trigger. The blast and recoil weren't as bad either and I actually kept the gun from flying up in the air. I put it back on safe.

"Let's take a look at the target," said Asa.

The box had been shredded. I looked at Asa for a reaction. He just raised one eyebrow and nodded.

"Pretty lucky . . . considering. But, I'm not sure if you've got the arm strength to aim and control the thing. If I had a 20 gauge you could hunt with that, but I don't. It's either the 12 or nothing."

"I can do it."

"I'm not so sure." Asa folded his arms—a bad sign.

"I could practice lifting and aiming it every day, before and after school."

"Not a bad idea," said Asa. "Okay, we'll try it. But if we get out in the marsh and that barrel flips up above your head when you shoot, then we're done until next year."

I didn't squawk. Asa was right and I knew it. If I couldn't control the Winchester, there would be no duck hunting season for me. Opening day was less than two weeks off. Somehow, my biggest concern curved back around to Opal. After all my big talk about duck hunting and the Winchester Model 12 shotgun, I wasn't sure how I would tell her that I was too weak and scrawny to hunt with it.

7

I had set my alarm clock ten minutes earlier than normal and woke before it went off. I flicked the switch so it wouldn't buzz. The house was quiet but I peeked out my bedroom door to make sure nobody was awake. Then I pulled the Winchester out of the closet, laid it on my bed, and unzipped the case.

"Here goes," I whispered.

With the shotgun at ready position across my chest, I looked toward the ceiling and spied an imaginary green-headed mallard against the white overcast. I hefted it to my shoulder, an action that came with a grunt. *Holy Moses!* Even unloaded, the thing weighed a ton. I shifted my feet, then swung the gun left to right at about 45 degrees so I wouldn't scrape the ceiling and aimed down the shooting plane of the barrel. I pretended to pull the trigger and whispered the sound of the blast.

"Pow."

I brought the Model 12 back down to ready position. There was no sense kidding myself. I was wobbly. Laying the shotgun back on the bed, I shook out my arms before going through the exercise again.

The second time I didn't aim the shotgun over my head. Instead of imaginary ducks, I aimed at the dark rectangle of my partly open closet door and my mind shifted to the faceless man who had killed my dad. I could see him there as a silhouette in that closet darkness. I put the plane of the barrel right on the center of his chest and held it firm and steady for a long time, never shaking a bit, before lifting it off my shoulder.

Yep, an angry fire still smoldered inside of me, and I had felt it flare up before. This time was different. This time was the hottest blaze yet. White hot. For the first time I actually thought about killing—and I didn't mean ducks.

I laid the gun back on the bed and let my heart beat down.

Mom's voice echoed up the stairs. "Del, are you awake?"

I took a long, deep breath. "Just getting out of bed," I said. "I'll be down in a few minutes."

I slid the Winchester back into the leather case and shoved it under the bed with a flannel shirt draped over the top. Before going down for breakfast, I took one more look at the dark opening of my partly open closet door. The silhouette of the man was gone.

✳

It was a Wednesday and it bummed me out because I didn't have English class, which meant I wouldn't be sitting next to Opal Parsons. I had survived Phys Ed and was on my way to American History, my last class of the day, when a familiar scene appeared up ahead. Dinsky again, with that idiot, dink friend of his. They stood at the intersection where the west wing branches off from the main building and I could just tell they were looking for more trouble.

"How 'bout that red-haired kid?" said Leon. "I'll spot him out. Then you kick his stuff."

The goon just laughed and bobbed his head up and down like an idiot. I recognized the red-haired kid as Jay Finley, a boy I had known since Horace Mann. He was really smart and just an all-around good guy. Unfortunately, he had no idea that he was walking into a trap.

"Hey, Jay!" I yelled.

He didn't hear me. I forced my way through the crowd to get closer.

"Jay! Jay Finley!" I waved my arm over my head. "Wait a minute."

He looked a little annoyed but he at least tried to maneuver toward me. I plowed through the crowd and finally reached him.

"Hey, Minnow. What's up?"

"Don't go that way," I said. "Dinsky is waiting to spot you out."

We both looked over at Leon Dinsky. He was pissed. His face burned red as he yelled at me. "Mind your own business, you little prick!"

Jay made a quick left with me right behind him and we both wiggled through the crowd like a couple squirrels running from a bobcat. It wasn't much, I guess, but at least I had done *something* that time. I thought about my reading assignment. In *The Scarlet Letter*, the woman who committed adultery had to wear a bright-red letter *A* so everyone could scorn her. I felt like I needed to get a certain letter off my own shoulder, only mine was a *C*. I hadn't actually gone face-to-face with Dinsky but at least I had done *something*, and I figured it was a start.

Now, if only I could do something about the damned bastard who murdered my dad.

✻

Steve and I both had study hall for sixth period, but we agreed to meet at the Science Resource Center instead. Mrs. Schwartz was used to seeing us. We picked out a table in the back where we sat between the periodic chart of elements and a poster showing the lifecycle of a frog.

Steve was twitching again. He started unfolding the master design, but I gave him the stop signal and checked to make sure Mrs. Schwartz wasn't watching. She had her nose in a file cabinet. I nodded my head and Steve continued. The plans for the volcano were drawn in colored Magic Markers on brown paper that had once been a Red Owl grocery bag. Not exactly the stuff of real engineers, but good enough for a couple of tenth-graders.

Like I said before, Steve was a danged good illustrator. The drawing showed a cutaway view of the Menasha High School football field at the fifty-yard line with a big "M" in the middle. A thick, horizontal line separated the aboveground parts from the underground parts. The aboveground parts included details like school buildings, clouds, trees and goal posts. He even had a black crow sitting on a telephone pole. On the field, the drawing showed stick figures representing a whole army of people, two of which were wearing capes and crowns on their heads. They stood right above the volcano tube at the fifty-yard line. The below ground parts included the workings of the volcano, which had two big oval shapes that were side by side and some smaller squares, lines, and circles in between. Steve had also drawn in a few worms and bugs below ground, just for effect.

"Do you have any questions?" asked Steve.

"How does it work?"

Steve pointed at the oval shape on the left. "This is the vinegar tank," he said. "Right next to it is the baking soda tank. That's where the chemical reaction will happen. The pipe that runs up to the fifty-yard line is called the conduit. The lava goes up the conduit and shoots up in the air all over the field and the unsuspecting victims."

I was following so far. "But how does the vinegar and baking soda get mixed together at just the right time?" I asked.

"That's the tricky part," said Steve. "We'll need a pump to push the vinegar into the baking soda tank. And to drive the pump, we need a motor and probably a battery to power the motor and some kind of switch to turn it on at the right time. Once the vinegar gets pumped into the baking soda the chemical reaction should take care of the rest."

"Holy crap!" I said. "This is complicated."

"No kidding."

"Do you know how to get the stuff and put it together?"

"Not really."

I shrugged. "My grandpa can help us."

We folded up the plans and I put them inside my geometry book. I glanced over at Mrs. Schwartz. She still wasn't looking.

❄

Before going to see Grandpa Asa after school, I rocketed over to the lighthouse at Kimberly Point with my swim trunks and diving mask. After my success selling fishing lures at the Fox Point flea market I was determined to replenish my supply and get back there with another batch of lures. I already felt like Rockefeller with the money from last Saturday. If I could make another eight bucks . . . *Wow!*

The trick was to get as much diving in as possible before the water got too cold. It was the third week in September. Swimming season at the Neenah Rec Pool had wrapped up weeks ago. I locked Ike to a park bench and did a quick change in the lighthouse bathroom.

The only problem (other than maybe freezing to death) was the fishermen. A half dozen of them all stood casting for white bass and walleyes up and down the rocky shore. My only opening was way down by the old Council Tree monument where the Indians and the early explorers used to meet. Well, I figured if it was good enough for Chief Four Legs it was good enough for me, so I tightened the laces on my tennis shoes and waded in.

I thought I was prepared for the shock, but I wasn't. The cold water bit into my legs like muskellunge teeth. For a few seconds I stood there, knee deep, wondering if I really wanted to do this. On the one hand, I needed more lures. On the other hand, I wasn't crazy about freezing my *you-know-what* off. A slimy, flat rock made the decision for me. My feet went out from under me and suddenly I was in all the way with what must have been a pretty impressive splash.

I worked as fast as I could, using my special technique of following old fishing lines to the prize. Being pretty far into the mouth of the river, the current was stronger than usual and I had to hang onto rocks to pull myself along the bottom without getting swept away. It paid off, and right away I was picking up Spinno-Kings, Little Cleos, Mepps Spinners, and plastic worms. I even found a Black Bucktail with a silver spinner blade as long as my thumb. I figured it must have been lost by the cigar-smoking guy I had seen wearing a straw hat. Nobody else threw lures that big. The treble hook was huge, and I shivered at the thought of something like that getting jerked into my head while diving beneath the surface.

It had been a pretty long spell in the cold water and my whole body was numb. When I finally stood up, I was chest-deep, shivering like a human tuning fork and looking toward shore for a place to get out. Suddenly, my eyes landed on something that made me drop back in up to my neck. A Winnebago County patrol car with Sheriff Heiselmann himself standing outside.

What's he doing here? I wondered.

I just watched as the sheriff looked left and right and then walked over to a black Cadillac where another man had pulled into a parking place and rolled down his window. The sheriff leaned over and talked to the guy for a few seconds. Then he stood up again and looked left and right, up and down the street.

Somehow my brain still worked even though the rest of me was frozen. Thoughts raced through my mind like minibikes on a dirt track.

Why is he acting so nervous? What's he up to? Who is that man in the black Cadillac?

At the same time, my whole body was a Popsicle and getting colder. I couldn't stop shaking but lowered myself nose-deep in the cold, green water and continued keeping watch.

The man in the Caddy had a square head and black hair. Between puffs on a cigarette he said something that made Heiselmann smile, but then the sheriff stood again and looked left and right on the street. Whatever he was up to, he sure didn't want anybody watching. I took a breath of air and lowered myself to eye level. Then the Cadillac Man handed a yellow envelope to the sheriff. Heiselmann took it quickly and looked left and right again before walking back to his car. That's when the Cadillac Man decided to get out of there. He tossed his cigarette butt out the window, backed up from his parking spot, and drove away. As he left, I noticed a big, melon-sized dent in the rear bumper on the driver's side.

The sheriff stood alone now and again he looked left and right on the street. He looked in the envelope and took something out. Whatever it was, he was flipping through it like the pages of a book.

Is that money?

I was pretty sure. He shoved it into his pants pocket, ripped up the envelope, and tossed the little pieces into a trash can. Heiselmann looked left and right one more time. Then he got in his car and sped away.

By the time I got out of the water, I was shaking like my mom's old washing machine, and it wasn't just from the cold. I didn't even look through my bag of fishing lures. As quick as I could, I changed back into dry clothes and unlocked my bike. I don't know why, but something told me to go look in that trash can where the sheriff had ripped up the yellow envelope. I rode up to it and stopped. I looked left and right. Then I went in head first and picked out every single scrap from that ripped-up yellow envelope and put all the pieces in the plastic bread bag with my lures.

On the ground I spotted the cigarette butt that the Cadillac Man had tossed out the window. I picked it up and read the word *Winston* in blue letters before tossing it back down and wiping my hand on my pants.

I jumped on the pedals and rode Eisenhower as fast as my legs could crank. I sailed past the big red-brick paper mill and past the millworker taverns and over the tracks. My heart hammered like an engine that had run out of oil as I skidded to a stop in front of the Emerald Gardens apartments, where I locked Ike again to the light pole. The same man with the spider tattoo was sitting there again on the concrete steps, drinking from a quart-sized brown bottle this time.

"You here to see Asa again, boy?"

"Yes, sir," I said.

He nodded and I walked by. I pulled the brown paper with Steve's volcano plans out of my geometry book and knocked on the door at apartment 118.

8

The next morning, before breakfast, I thought some more about Sheriff Heiselmann and what the heck he was doing with that Cadillac Man by the lighthouse. After a night's sleep it seemed sort of dumb all of a sudden. What difference did it make if he was talking to somebody at the park? It was all part of Winnebago County, wasn't it?

Anyhow, I still had the scraps of yellow paper and I decided to try to put them together. I spread them out on my bedroom floor and noticed lines of ink on the outside of some. I arranged the puzzle pieces to make the envelope into a rectangle again and stuck them all together with Scotch tape.

I don't know what I was expecting to find—maybe an address or a phone number, I supposed. What I got were doodles. That's right, little pictures like people make when they're bored while talking on the phone and need something to do with their hands. The doodles were pretty good. I had to admit that at least. In one corner of the envelope some-one had drawn a little house with smoke coming out of the chimney. In another corner he had sketched a sea gull and a crescent moon. Under-neath that he had a picture of a sailboat. And off to the side, a basketball player shooting a layup.

"Doodles," I said out loud.

I dropped the taped-up envelope into my Eskdale gallon-sized milk bottle along with a red rock I had found by the railroad tracks. The fishing lures went in the Hughes candy box, same as always.

❁

School came and went and, except for the tuna casserole served up by the cafeteria ladies, things were okay. I had locked Eisenhower again to Randy Schnell's apple tree and managed to avoid Leon Dinsky all day long. I sat by Opal Parsons in English class and found out that she was all the way done with *The Scarlet Letter* and itching to get going on the report. Meanwhile, I had barely cracked chapter 3.

I couldn't dive for lures or read after school because it was Thursday and I had Hoot Owls to deliver. The Hoot Owl Shoppers Guide was sort of a miniature newspaper where ordinary people advertised things they were trying to find or get rid of. In Neenah, it seemed like everybody was trying to buy or sell something—dogs, cats, cars, trucks, sewing machines, drum sets, bean bag chairs . . . you get the idea. Anyhow, every Thursday, I delivered 232 of them on my route that covered about a third of Doty Island. With good weather, I could get it all done in three hours by carrying them around on my bike. It took a little longer in the wintertime.

In case you're wondering, nobody ever got rich delivering Hoot Owls. They paid a penny a paper, so once a week I got a little orange envelope with two dollar bills, a quarter, a nickel, and two pennies inside. I know, I know—but when you were fifteen years old and your allowance was fifty cents a week, you took what you could get.

I had finished rolling and banding the entire stack of Hoot Owls and, as usual, my hands were black from the ink. I loaded half of 'em in my canvas delivery bag, slung it over my shoulder, and took off on Eisenhower.

Like always, I started out by riding along the Fox River by Doty Park where Neenah got named in the first place. The naming of Neenah was a pretty good story, and I've heard it about two hundred times, including every time my grade-school class toured Governor Doty's cabin. Mr. Doty was chatting with some Winnebago Indians near his cabin and wanted to know their word for the land on the other side of the river.

"What do you call that?" he said, pointing across to the other side.

The Indians must have figured him to be a slow learner, because why else would a grown man be asking how to say "water."

"Neenah," they said, which was, of course, their word for water. Mr. Doty wrote it down and the future city of Neenah had its name. That story, told by Doty Cabin tour guides, was usually good for a groan from fifth-graders.

Once past Doty Cabin, my Hoot Owl route took me along the riverbank where I could chat with fishermen along the shore and find out what was biting. I mostly cared about walleyes, white bass, smallmouths, northerns, and mooneyes. Bullheads and sheepsheads were too plentiful to worry about. After updating the fishing report, it was time to get back to work.

The route followed Park Drive on the east end of the island. I zigged and zagged through the numbered streets starting with Twelfth and working my way down to about Sixth before I had to fly home again to reload my satchel with more papers and my stomach with a glass of milk. Then I started up again where I left off and kept pedaling and tossing and pedaling and tossing until I got down by the hospital and kept going west past the sweater-knitting factory, railroad tracks, and the YMCA. One thing I'll say about my Hoot Owl route is that it covered a pretty good slice of every sort of people, from the rich to the poor, who lived in the city. And I'll tell you something else. If you kept your ears and eyes open, you could pick up some local gossip too. That's how I found out that there was an Indian living in a hiding place just beyond the train tracks.

On that particular Thursday I had three goals on my Hoot Owl route. The first was to find Opal Parsons's house. She had told me it was on Fourth Street, and I planned to keep an eye out for her. The second was to locate Leroy Kazmynski's place. He was a Green Bay Packer player, brand new on the team, and Mark told me he lived on Second between Forest and Lincoln. I planned to ride slow and look for clues. My last goal, of course, was to get done before dark so I could spin over to the Menasha locks and see what the fishermen had caught and if any boats were passing through. Those were my goals, and I struck the jackpot on two out of three.

Finding Opal's place was easy enough. All I had to do was read the names on the mailboxes. I found *Parsons* painted in white letters on a black mailbox and knew it had to be hers. Instead of riding by and tossing the Hoot Owl from the sidewalk, I took the extra time to stop and walk right up on the porch. Through the screen door I could hear the TV going, so I knew somebody was home. Now, anybody who knew me even just a little realized that I wasn't the type who horned in on other people's business. But finding Opal's house seemed sort of like spotting a shooting star, and if there ever was a time to stop and take a chance, well I figured this was it. My knees shook, but it wasn't from being scared. I was nervous, and there's a difference. I walked right up to that screen door, tapped with my right hand, and held out a Hoot Owl with my left.

After just a few seconds, a black lady poked her head around the corner of what must have been the kitchen. She studied me, wiping her hands on a dish towel. The lady wore a blue uniform dress that had a patch with her name, Ellie, stitched in the middle of a white oval. Her face looked tired and her eyes cautious, like a deer's eyes. They were big and black like Opal's, and her skin was the color of cocoa powder a little lighter than Opal's. I know I shouldn't have been paying such close attention to skin, but black people were rare in our part of Wisconsin, and Opal's mom was only the second I had actually seen up close.

"Can I help you?" asked the lady.

"My name is Del Finwick," I said. "I've got your Hoot Owl, ma'am, and I'm also Opal's friend from school."

The scared look washed off her egg-shaped face and a friendly smile showed up instead.

"Yes, she tol' me 'bout you." The lady had a different way of speaking, and I was pretty sure it didn't come from northeastern Wisconsin.

"We're doing a report together on *The Scarlet Letter*. I was wondering if she was home."

"She at piano practice," said Mrs. Parsons. "But I'll tell her you stopped by."

"Thank you. Nice to meet you."

"Nice to meet you too, Del."

As I tossed Hoot Owls onto porches on Fourth Street I felt all warm and happy on the inside. A river of confidence flowed through me and my pride swelled up like a lake after the snowmelt. I had talked to Opal's mom and she was nice. In fact, it felt almost like she was happy to see me. I don't know what I had expected, but it sure wasn't that.

My focus returned when I saw the sign for Second Street. It wouldn't be as easy to figure out which house belonged to a Green Bay Packer. Everybody knew that NFL linebackers weren't the type to paint their name on a mailbox. I rode my bike slowly from house to house looking for a clue.

At the side of an ordinary, white two-story, I spied an Arctic Cat snowmobile parked on a trailer. On a hunch, I coasted Eisenhower up to it. The name *Kazmynski* was permanently burned into the trailer by an arc welder and then painted over.

Jackpot! Wait until Steve and Mark hear about this.

If I had a plain piece of paper and a pencil, maybe I could have made a rubbing on the bumpy name on the trailer like my mom did on her great-grandmother's gravestone.

Wait a minute.

I did have the stump of a pencil in my right front pocket. I dug it out. I just needed a piece of paper and took a chance by lifting the lid on a trash can beside Leroy Kazmynski's house. About a million flies buzzed out and it smelled so bad I put the lid back on. Then I remembered the pink insert inside each Hoot Owl. I grabbed one of the sheets. It only had writing on one side so I lined it up over the name on the trailer and started rubbing with the side of my pencil.

Just then, a lime-green Dodge Charger rumbled up the driveway. *Oh-oh!* Kazmynski's giant head and gorilla shoulders filled up the whole inside of the car. I lifted the pencil and paper off the trailer, stood up with quivering knees, and waited for him to squish me like a lake fly.

He stepped out of his car and scowled. The bone over his eyebrows stood out like a small log. His jaw and chin were made of iron. Between all of that and his dark hair and beard stubble, Leroy Kazmynski was one of the scariest guys I had ever seen. His shadow on the garage door was a picture right out of *Famous Monsters* magazine.

"What are you doing?" he asked.

"Sorry. I was just copying your name to show my friends."

"You mean like a gravestone rubbing?" He smiled.

"Yes, sir. And here's your Hoot Owl."

He took it, looked at it, and tossed it in the general direction of the trash can. I said nothing.

"Would you like something with my name on it, son?"

"Yes, sir."

"Wait here."

I took a deep breath of air like when I've been underwater in the river too long. *Holy smokes!* Kazmynski could have booted me off his driveway or even called the cops. He didn't even get mad—yet.

He came back out on the porch with a football and a black marker. I held my breath as he wrote his name on the side and handed me the ball. It was the real thing, with the NFL insignia stamped into the side and everything.

"Thanks." I could barely squeak out the word.

"No sweat, kid. It's a practice ball."

"Cool," I said.

Leroy Kazmynski walked through his front door and closed it with a thud.

Somehow, I must have finished delivering the rest of my Hoot Owls but I don't remember a single thing except that I got an autographed football from Leroy Kazmynski and a smile from Opal's mom.

9

Gym class had never been my favorite, but in the fall of 1972 it was worse than usual. We were learning the fundamentals of football and that meant getting assigned to a position on the field. Mr. Reckler started with the biggest and tallest kids and worked his way down. By the time he got to me, it was like he was staring at the worthless prize that just fell out of a Cracker Jack box. He only had one thing to say.

"Get on the line and block someone."

Things went downhill from there. On a good day I lined up across from someone fifty pounds bigger than me. On a bad day, I blocked Thor Knudson, who probably should have been listed as his own species, a cousin to the mountain gorilla.

Before I wised up, the plays went like this. The center hiked the ball to the quarterback. Knudson gave me a two-handed shove. I flew backward and landed flat on my back and banged my head into the ground. It didn't take long before I learned to dive left or right at the snap of the ball before he could touch me. Reckler yelled at me every play.

"Block him, you yellow-belly!"

As a matter of survival I ignored him.

The second thing I hated about gym class was getting my lunch money stolen. When it happened, it was while I was in the showers. After the third theft, I quit showering altogether. That's when Larry Buskin took the direct approach and started looking for me between Randy Schnell's house and the school instead. Usually, it went something like this.

"Hey Minnow, how's it going?"

"Good."

"Can I borrow a dollar?"

"No."

"That's not very friendly."

I would cover my head with one arm and my stomach with the other before Larry punched me hard in the ribs and ripped the lunch money out of my pocket.

My answer to all of that was to sneak into school by a different route every day. It was either that or wait for Mark to show up and walk in with him. Like I said before, Mark was tough and he could have been a good bodyguard when it came to getting past Larry Buskin. The only problem was that he was almost always tardy. Mark just didn't care if he was on time or not. Even when the school gave him a note from the principal to get signed by his dad, he didn't care. The bottom line for me? Three days a week I snuck through Larry Buskin's ambush. Two days a week I got punched hard in the ribs. One day a week I lost my lunch money. I could live without lunch once in a while, but let me tell you, those twice-a-week punches from Larry Buskin couldn't go on forever.

❀

It was the last Friday in September, and I had taken another punch to the ribs from Larry Buskin, even though I had saved my lunch money by hiding it in my shoe. After school, my head hung low and I didn't even feel like riding my bicycle, much less ride it fast. As I crept past the sailboats in the harbor and the fancy mansions on Wisconsin Avenue, I didn't even look at them. One way or another, I had to do something about Larry Buskin.

Instead of taking a right turn on the bridge to the island, I rode through downtown Neenah, past the red-brick mill and the taverns and across the tracks. I locked my bike to the light post outside Emerald Gardens. For the third time in a row, the same man sat on the concrete step out front, but this time he wore a blue sweatshirt and drank from a flat bottle that was still inside the brown paper bag. He nodded his head without saying anything as I went inside, walked down the dark, smelly hallway, and knocked on the door to apartment 118.

Grandpa Asa and I had vanilla ice cream, of course, but this time we sprinkled wild hickory nuts and maple syrup on top. The only sound was that of our spoons clanking and when we finished, I put both bowls in the sink.

"Grandpa," I said. "Can I ask you a hypothetical question?"

"I reckon."

"Suppose there was a big kid who was trying to get the lunch money from a smaller kid and the smaller kid wouldn't let him and the big kid kept punching him in the ribs and sometimes getting the money anyhow."

"Go on."

"And suppose the smaller kid had taken about as much crap as he was going to take but he knew he would get his butt whipped if he fought the bigger guy. Do you know what I'm saying, Grandpa?"

"Maybe."

"What do you suppose the smaller kid should do?"

"Fight him."

"And get his butt whipped?"

"Maybe."

"What do you mean, maybe? The smaller kid would need a dozen rabbits' feet in his pocket to win a fight like that. The odds against him would be a million to one."

"So he needs to get lucky, is that it?"

"Yes."

"Are you familiar with the concept of making your own luck?"

"I guess so."

"Are you familiar with a product called Eaglewing steel-toed boots with a reinforced shank?"

"I think so. Don't the mill workers wear them?"

"That's right."

"What good would new shoes do?"

"Well, a kid isn't allowed to bring a weapon to school, but I don't think they can tell him what kind of shoes to wear, can they?"

"No."

"If I was your friend, I would get a pair of those boots and then I wouldn't wait to get punched in the ribs before using them."

"You mean I should kick him?"

"I'm still talking about the hypothetical kid," said Grandpa. "I didn't say nothing about you."

"Sure . . . but should the hypothetical kid kick the other kid?"

"Does he want to win?"

"Yes."

"Then an Eaglewing to the shins is his best option. A direct hit from the steel toe should drop the guy. After that he can break his nose."

"What if he misses the shins?"

"Then he'll get creamed."

"Oh."

"And your friend better practice first so he gets the feel of aiming and what it means to kick as hard as he can, because that's what it will take."

"Okay."

"Are you going to tell your friend to do all that?"

"Yeah, but there's just one small problem."

"What's that?"

"He can't afford Eaglewing steel-toed boots."

"What size shoes does he wear?"

"Four."

"Well, you stop here tomorrow afternoon, and I'll have a pair of those size 4 Eaglewings that you can give to your friend. You understand?"

"Yes, sir."

I just stood there looking at my grandpa Asa. My brain was all mixed up just thinking about it all.

"If I was you," said Grandpa, "I would tell that hypothetical kid to not tell anybody about the Eaglewings."

"Okay, I'll let him know."

"Now, let's take a walk to my pickup truck out back. I've rounded up some supplies for the Menasha homecoming game and I think you should take a look."

10

I switched to riding the bus. I said I would never do it, but I did. I stashed Ike in the garage and started riding the stupid bus to school.

I know, I know. It was just like me to run away again, right? Well, if that's what you want to believe, you go right ahead, and you're at least partly right. I *did* have enough of getting punched in the ribs and collecting bruises of every color and losing my lunch money on top of everything. And when Grandpa Asa found out that size 4 Eaglewings with steel toes had to be ordered special, and it pushed the timetable for me fighting Larry Buskin out by at least three weeks, maybe I *did* say enough was enough. So fine—go ahead and give me one more patch with the letter *C* on it. But if it was you who was getting pounded in the ribs and skipping lunch, then I dare you to say you wouldn't have switched to riding the bus too.

Okay, fine—there was one other reason for parking Eisenhower in the garage and switching to riding the school bus. I got to sit by Opal Parsons for ten minutes every morning. Okay? Are you satisfied now? Well, all right then . . . now you know.

❋

It was the Friday night before duck hunting opener and Grandpa Asa said he wanted to see for himself whether or not I could heft the Model 12. Besides that, neither one of us had said anything to Mom yet about our hunting plans. I was waiting in the garage when Asa drove over.

"You been practicing?" he asked.

"Every morning."

"Let's see you handle the gun."

I brought the shotgun out of the corner and pulled it from the leather case. Before lifting it I took three long, deep breaths of air to prime my lungs with oxygen.

"Pretend there's a duck directly overhead," said Asa. "Pick up the shotgun, point it nice and steady for five seconds, and bring it back down."

I grabbed the Winchester, and my fingers were a steel vise. (That's a metaphor I learned from Mrs. Borger.) I scrunched up my whole face and didn't even grunt as I hoisted it vertical and steady as the flagpole at the VFW. I counted to five and brought it back down. Rock solid. My best one ever.

"Pretty impressive," said Grandpa Asa. "Now, do it again on a duck coming in from north to south. Swing the gun around and track that greenhead nice and steady, right across the sky."

I did it. It wasn't perfect, but pretty good. Asa clenched his jaw and nodded like a true believer.

"What are the three big rules of gun safety?" he asked.

"Be sure of your target. Treat every gun as if it was loaded. Always keep the muzzle pointed in a safe direction."

"Okay, let's go hunting. Now we've just got to notify your mom."

"She might freak out," I said.

"We'll see."

We both walked into the house through the kitchen door. As usual, Mom was puffing on a Lucky and watching television in the living room. I heard the theme song from *Petticoat Junction* as we stepped in the room and stared at her.

"What?" She flicked an ash onto a dinner plate.

"Grandpa's taking me duck hunting on Lake Poygan tomorrow," I said.

"Whatever," she said with a backhanded wave of her left hand. "Make your own lunches." Her eyes left us and found the TV screen again.

Asa and I walked back into the kitchen.

"That was easy," he said.

❉

We arrived at my dad's uncle Kermit's boathouse at 4:15 a.m. Like most of my relatives, Kermit was already dead. Dad had inherited the duck shack on Lake Poygan, so I didn't really know who owned it anymore. Maybe Mom, I supposed.

I unlocked the doors and started loading decoys, life jackets, our extra gear, and lunches into the skiff. I tossed a blanket in there in case Asa wanted to sleep. Then I took a brush cutter out behind the shack and snipped a bunch of willow branches and tossed them in the skiff too.

The duck hunting season would officially open at noon. You might think starting out before 5:00 a.m. was crazy, but to get a good spot on Poygan meant getting out there early—really, really early. There were hundreds of hunters and only a certain number of good spots. Every hunter had to set up in the weeds, because that was the law. Dad and I had always gone to an area of smaller lake weeds only a foot or two tall and concealed the rest of the skiff with willow branches. My plan was to do the same thing again except for one change. I would be sitting in my dad's seat and Grandpa Asa would be sitting in mine.

We stood on the small dock in front of the boathouse and looked out on the big lake. Almost everything was black except the stars and the moon and the red lights of a radio tower far away. The air smelled like a swamp. A few small waves hit the rocks on the shore, sounding like a little girl's clapping hands.

"The really serious hunters are already out there," I told Asa. "Can you see those lanterns shining from the cane near the center of the lake?"

"Yes."

"Dad told me that the early birds get set up twenty-four hours ahead of time. That means some of those guys have been on the water since noon yesterday."

Asa nodded.

"Let's get started," I said, helping Grandpa into the skiff. It wasn't easy for him with his two bad hips. He made it though, butt first and sliding backward into the stern. I got in the middle, pushed off from the dock, and started rowing.

It was a little bit scary to be way out there in the darkness, with nothing but some old cedar planks between us and the cold, black water of Lake Poygan. Dad had always told me that those planks were probably sawed by steam-powered mills, most likely in Oshkosh, even before the Great Depression. Same thing with the old wooden duck decoys at our feet, all carved by Uncle Kermit's dad with tools that had funny names like "drawknives" and "spokeshaves." Even the lead decoy anchors and their keel weights came from a time when things were made by hand. Uncle Kermit told me once that the weights on our decoys were molded by pouring molten lead into the round, metal shell from the bell off his bicycle handlebars. I took a pause from rowing and we studied the sky. The stars blazed brighter than ever.

"That Orion's sort of a show off, isn't he, Grandpa?"

"Why do you say that?"

"I mean, look at his fancy belt with the three bright stars all in a perfect row. Then hanging from his belt he has his sword and his shield out front. He's sort of like those TV wrestlers."

"I reckon," said Asa.

On the other side of the sky, I could see the Big Dipper.

"Did you know that a person doesn't need a compass if they can find the Big Dipper in the sky, Grandpa?"

"Is that so?"

"Yep. The last two stars on the pan side of the dipper point right at the North Star, which is called Polaris. And do you know that Polaris is so far away from earth that the light we see now was sent to us from the star about three hundred years ago?"

"Imagine that. Where's that blanket? I think I'll take a little snooze."

I handed Asa the blanket and started rowing again. I don't know why I got so excited about stuff like the moon and stars. I guess I just really liked everything about duck hunting, and that even included the night sky.

It took forty minutes or more of pulling on the oars, but I finally got us across the open water and into the shallow weeds. I dropped anchor to keep us from drifting, then poked the willow branches into the muck around the boat. The final step was to hang Asa's old railroad lantern. I clamped the L-shaped bracket to the edge of the skiff and hung the lantern like a noose hangs on a gallows. When I lit the wick, the small, blue light grew until it finally glowed bright yellow to mark our spot on the lake.

A sliver of pink started showing itself on the eastern horizon. With Asa snoring peacefully in the other end of the skiff, I pulled my hat down tight over my ears, adjusted my gloves, and lay back to look at the sky again.

If you were paying attention, you already heard me talking to Opal about the magic that happens very early in the morning on the Poygan Marsh. Here's a list of the sounds I heard before the sun cracked the edge of the earth.

Green heron somewhere — *kuk-kuk-kuk-kuk*
Small fish jumping — *splash*
Big fish jumping — SPLASH!
Barred owl — *hooo-cooks-for-yoooooo!*
Wood duck somewhere — *teereeee! teereeee!*
Train whistle far away — (you know the sound)
Coots playing — *splish-dabble-splash*
Geese somewhere — *honk-honk-gahonk*
Unseen ducks overhead — *wheey-wheey-wheey-wheey*
Motorboat — *rrrrrrrrrrrrrr*
Sunrise — "Wow!"

Like I said before, on opening day of duck season nobody was allowed to shoot before noon, so there was plenty of time to look around, relax, read a book, and just wait out the morning. I looked around for hunters. A few other skiffs were set up in the shallow weeds like us. Other hunters had their heads poking up in the big swamp, and at least one guy was set up right next to the shore.

Grandpa Asa made a grunting noise and sat upright. "Do you want something to eat?" I asked. "We've got sandwiches, chips, pop, apples, and some cookies."

"I'll take a cookie," he said. I tossed him two.

I pulled a transistor radio out of my pack and worked the dial until I found the Saturday morning auction program. Just like with the Hoot Owls, the radio auction show was all about people buying and selling stuff they probably didn't need, but since it was an auction, well that made it sort of fun. People got their competitive juices flowing when somebody outbid them for some stupid thing like a used lawn mower or an old guitar and, of course, they called right back in and bid higher again. Well, the funniest part was that they couldn't even see the stuff they were buying in the first place. It was good entertainment for an hour for me and Asa.

As the morning wore on I had plenty of time to read, so I cracked open *The Scarlet Letter* and plowed through the middle third of it. *Holy smokes!* All of a sudden I was glad I didn't live in the 1850s.

As we got closer and closer to noon, Asa used his cane to stand in the skiff and look around. The wind had picked up a little and our willow branches rustled. Otherwise, everything was peaceful and calm.

"When do you think we'll hear the first gunshot?" I asked.

"I thought you said that nobody could shoot until noon."

"Some of these guys get an itchy trigger finger," I said.

"Doesn't surprise me."

"Last year a hunter couldn't resist shooting a nice, fat mallard about twenty minutes before official shooting time. You know what happened after that?"

"No."

"Lots of other hunters got the itchy trigger finger too and at quarter 'til noon everybody was blasting away."

"Is that what you're going to do, join in with the mob?"

"Nope. Dad always waited. I won't even load the shotgun until five minutes 'til."

The morning wore on and at 11:00 we put our eighteen decoys in the water. After that we ate our lunch. At 11:45 I pulled the Winchester Model 12 out of the case. Then at 11:47—BOOM! The first shot rang out.

It was as if General Grant gave the "commence firing" order at Gettysburg, and wouldn't you know it, all that noise caused ducks, hither and yon, to jump up and start flying. So did I load up the Winchester? No, I did not. It didn't matter what every other Tom, Dick, or Harry did, our rule was that we load the shotguns at 11:55 and start shooting at noon.

When the minute and hour hands on my Timex overlapped, I lifted the Model 12 a little higher on my chest and got ready.

"It's time," I said to Asa.

"Go get 'em, boy," he said.

Guess what. It was a whole lot harder to hit a flying duck than a cereal box alongside the Soo Line tracks. I knew I was supposed to lead them, but *jeepers*. It was like shooting at jet fighters, they were so fast. After the first hour, I think I was zero for infinity. Then a blue-winged teal came within my range. I hoisted up the Winchester and held it at about 45 degrees and tracked in front of that speedy duck and pulled the trigger.

POW! . . . *Splash.*

"Good shot!" yelled Asa.

Holy smokes! I was a duck hunter—for real. I rowed us out and re-trieved the dead bird.

Things quieted down as the sun plowed across the sky and started sliding back toward the horizon. A group of hunters on the marsh blasted away at a high-flying flock, and a lone mallard fell somewhere in the middle of the weedy mess. I watched one of the men gliding on swamp skis through the soupy sludge, his shotgun slung over one shoulder. He retrieved the duck and skied back through the swamp grass to his hunting blind and raft of decoys.

"That's so cool," I said. "Did you see him glide right over that muck?"

"That's Sheriff Heiselmann and his group," said Asa. "I recognized their voices and saw his truck at the boat landing."

A half hour passed. I kept my mouth shut and so did Asa, but we both watched and listened as Heiselmann's group horsed around, using language that didn't belong anywhere—not at home, not at school, and especially not on the Poygan Marsh. They must have been drinking beer or something, because every once in a while we saw them toss bottles into the lake. Asa just shook his head.

We both heard the sound at the same time. I thought it came from geese at first, but the call had a rough, scratchy wheeze and whistle to it.

"Swans," said Grandpa Asa.

My eyes scanned the horizon and there they were, to the west. Two of them—huge, white birds sliding though the sky with a slow, sweeping wingbeat that sort of made me think of a time before humans walked the earth, more majestic and wonderful than anything ever created by man, that's for sure.

"Just look at 'em," I said.

"They're getting rare," said Asa. "It's against the law to shoot them. You know that, right?"

"Yes."

I couldn't keep from smiling. It was Poygan magic all right. In they came, right over the marsh. Closer. Closer. Closer.

"They're going to go over Sheriff Heiselmann's group," I said.

Asa said nothing.

"You don't think they'll shoot 'em, do you, Grandpa?"

Asa said nothing. We both watched and listened. Watched and listened. Watched and listened.

All three men in Heiselmann's group popped up in their blind and their shotguns went vertical as they blasted away like crazy with flames shooting out of the muzzles. Both swans lurched in response to the noise and the impact. Frantic now, they beat the air with their huge wings and tried to pull themselves higher into the sky. I thought they were going to survive, I really did. But then a final shot rang out and the impact broke the wing of the lead swan causing it to tumble and spiral down at an angle until it crashed in the middle of the swamp.

The Heiselmann gang hooted and laughed their fool heads off.

"That son of a bitch," said Asa.

One of them, and I'm pretty sure it was the sheriff, got on his swamp skis with his shotgun slung over his shoulder and started out toward the crippled swan. He wobbled and nearly fell and his buddies laughed and hooted all over again. Eventually he got going on a pretty steady glide and stopped.

"Oh no!" said Asa.

I looked at him but his eyes weren't on Heiselmann. He was watching the sky again. The surviving swan had circled back.

"It's returning to its mate," said Asa.

My gut twisted as I watched the surviving bird set its wings and glide in toward its crippled mate. At the same time, I could see Heiselmann working his gun, trying to get it reloaded quickly. He brought the shotgun to his shoulder.

BOOM! . . . BOOM! . . . BOOM!

The sound rang out and echoed back from the wooded shore. The flying swan, as before, pounded its wings hard, gaining altitude once again in a second attempt to escape. Climbing, climbing, climbing, the surviving swan hammered its wings against the air. And once again the sheriff tried to reload, but the second swan was out of range, fleeing for good into the empty sky.

Heiselmann kept going and caught up to the crippled swan in the middle of the swamp. The next thing we knew, he was beating it to death with the barrel of his gun. He reached down and came back up waving a long, white wing feather, then stuck the feather in his cap and shuffled back to his buddies, who laughed and drank more beer.

"He killed that swan for the fun of it. Did you see that?" I asked and looked at Asa.

"Yes. I did."

My thoughts drifted back to the afternoon when I had seen Sheriff Heiselmann taking the yellow envelope from the Cadillac Man. He had been doing something illegal, all right. Anybody who would kill a swan just for fun had to be crooked, right through to the core.

✳

When we got home a note on the kitchen table surprised me, saying that Mom had gone to a movie. Anything was better than watching her lie around the house, so I felt happy. There was no sign of Sally either. She had disappeared, as usual, to wherever seventeen-year-old girls go on Saturday nights.

I only had the one small blue-winged teal to pluck and clean, and Grandpa Asa instructed me along the way. When I was done I popped it in the refrigerator.

"We'll have roast duck for dinner tomorrow," I said.

"You better get a chicken to go along with it," said Asa.

Do you think I thought about Heiselmann killing that swan when I went to bed that night? Yes, I did. In fact, the picture played over and over again in my mind. And do you think I thought about Opal Parsons? Yep, I thought about her too—but only about a million times.

11

Have you noticed that I haven't had much to say about my mom? Maybe, by now you're getting the idea that she just hangs around the house smoking cigarettes, drinking coffee, and watching television all day long. Well, if that's what you think—you're right. And knowing that, you probably think she's not a very good mother. And if that's what you think—you're wrong.

When I was a little kid, my mom held our family together just like the thread that keeps the scraps that make a quilt from coming apart. When nobody would lead my Cub Scout den, my mom said she would do it. And when my sister, Sally, wanted to try out for the school play, my mom volunteered to make the costumes and run the stage lights. When I was just five years old and had my tonsils taken out, guess who was there when I woke up? And when my throat was too sore to eat sandwiches and toast, guess who made me Jell-O with banana slices and marshmallows mixed in? My mom, that's who. And when Dad needed to give a speech at the Rotary Club, guess who wrote it for him and helped him practice? That's right, and it was a dang good speech too. He got a standing ovation, if that tells you anything. And did I say that she was a great cook? She once made a batch of lasagna that was so good that her friend Mrs. Larrusso asked for the recipe. Mrs. Larrusso was born in Italy, if that tells you anything. So if anybody thinks I don't have a great mom, well they don't know anything about anything.

My mom came down with something called multiple sclerosis, okay. It's just a stupid, bad-luck thing that hit her, sort of like polio in the olden days. I read all about it, too. When multiple sclerosis hits, there's nothing anybody can do to fix it. It creeps up on a person slowly, but it's bad—understand? Sure it was hard on our family, and I even complained and felt sorry for myself sometimes, but that's nothing compared to how it changed everyday life for my mom.

She started out having blurry vision. Well, lots of people get blurry vision, so she didn't think anything about it at first and just blamed it on her eye glasses. About a year later, she started getting dizzy spells and stumbling and even falling down. That's when Dad took her to see a doctor. The doctor wasn't sure, so he sent my mom to a specialist. And when the specialist wasn't sure, he sent my mom all the way to the Mayo Clinic in Minnesota. That's when we found out that Mom had multiple sclerosis—for sure.

Here's the good thing about multiple sclerosis: people can live with it for many years. Here's the bad thing about multiple sclerosis: it never gets better.

Okay, so now you know.

And if you're wondering why our house is messy most of the time and why we don't eat eggs and sausage every morning and why we don't even have lime Jell-O with sliced bananas anymore, well, now you know.

And if you're wondering why my mom didn't go over to Grandpa Asa's apartment once in a while and help him clean up that dump even though he's her own father, well now you know that too.

Mom just got sick, that's all. She's like Lou Gehrig of the Yankees. They didn't keep him out of the Hall of Fame just because he got sick, did they? No, they did not.

That's how it was with my mom. And if anybody wanted to argue with me about that—well they could just come on over to our house on Fifth and pay a visit. I'll be the one wearing the Eaglewing steel-toed boots with the reinforced shank.

12

I finally finished reading *The Scarlet Letter*, and Opal was itching to get started on the report. We were scheduled to give our presentation in just a week.

"Where should we meet to work on it?" she asked.

"How about the Science Resource Center?"

Opal rolled her eyes. "Is that the only place you ever go? This report has nothing to do with science, you know."

I shrugged. "I like it there. Have you seen the jar with the pickled tape worm?"

"That's just gross."

Even though Opal didn't like the Science Resource Center idea, I sure didn't want to go to the regular study hall and get pelted by pencil erasers for an hour.

"How about my house?" asked Opal.

I was paralyzed. Her house? I stood rigid and mute like a totem pole.

"Could you come over at 5:30 on Thursday? You can join us for supper." Opal smiled.

"Thursday? I've got to deliver Hoot Owls on Thursday."

"How about six then?"

"Okay, I guess that will work."

"Great! I'll tell my parents that you're coming. I hope you like southern cooking."

"Southern?"

"Didn't I tell you? My mom and dad are from Alabama."

The bell rang and kids settled into their seats.

"You'll be there, right? Six o'clock on Thursday?" she whispered.

I nodded.

For the next ten minutes my brain flew around like the Tilt-a-Whirl

at the Winnebago County Fair. *Can I get my Hoot Owls delivered by six?*
Southern food? What the heck is that? Crayfish and Frogs?

❀

I set a new record for delivering 232 Hoot Owls in an hour and fifty
minutes. As it turned out, you could save quite a bit of time by not stopping to check with the fisherman behind Doty Cabin and by skipping
the Menasha Lock and Dam and by not sniffing around for the houses
of Green Bay Packers players on Second Street. The time was three
minutes before six when I ditched my delivery satchel and grabbed my
notebook and copy of *The Scarlet Letter*. I tiptoed through the house
and snuck back toward the kitchen door leading to the garage. I almost
made it too. My hand was actually touching the screen door handle
when Mom picked me up on radar from the living room.

"Where you going, Del?"

"Riding my bike." It wasn't a lie.

"Where to?"

"A friend's house." Still not a lie.

"Which friend?"

"Just a kid in my English class." Still not a lie.

"Try not to get run over by a truck."

My mom actually *does* love me. She just has a weird way of expressing
it sometimes. I dashed out the screen door. The spring twanged and the
door slapped shut. I was gone.

You're probably wondering why I didn't want to say too much to my
mom about going to have supper at Opal's house. Well, first of all, it's
just good policy for any kid to avoid specifics when it comes to those
where you going? and *what are you doing?* sort of questions. I mean, a kid
has to think for himself sometimes, and parents don't need to know
about *everything*. And big sisters? Well, they don't need to know *anything*. Besides, did you really expect me to tell my family that I was
going off to eat southern food with the only black family in Neenah?
Hey, Martin Luther King Jr. achieved a lot, but America still had a long
ways to go. Don't get me wrong. My mom believes in equal rights, but
that doesn't change the fact that she was raised by Grandpa Asa, if you
know what I'm saying.

I pulled up to Opal's house, and instead of dumping Eisenhower in
the yard or behind some bush, I used the kickstand and set Ike alongside the lamppost out front. In the reflection of a window, I saw my hair
going in about twenty-seven different directions, so I licked the palm of

my hand and flattened it out. I heard some pots and pans clanging inside, and some interesting smells made their way to my nostrils. My stomach felt hungry and a little bit sick at the same time as I approached the front door. I banged three times, but not too loud. Then I waited with my arms hanging down properly at my sides.

Opal came out of the kitchen smiling. "Hi, Del."

"Hi."

"Come in. Supper's almost ready."

We walked into the kitchen. Was I nervous? Yes, I was nervous.

Mrs. Parsons turned on a friendly smile as she greeted me with a big metal spoon in her hand.

"Hello again," she said.

The cautious look from our last visit was gone. Happy wrinkles in the shape of bird's feet sort of sprayed out of the corners of each eye. Her nose had that same little upturn as Opal's. Mrs. Parsons wore the same blue uniform I had seen before with the name *Ellie* stitched on the white oval patch on her shoulder, but a white apron covered most of the front with strings that tied in back.

"Hello, Mrs. Parsons."

"You get all them papers delivered?"

"Yes, ma'am," I said. "Got them done in record time."

"Good. I hope you hungry. We havin' fried chicken."

I listened hard to her accent and felt a little bit like I was meeting someone from another country or something. The closest I'd ever been to Alabama had been a family vacation trip to Illinois when we visited Abraham Lincoln's house and tomb.

The door to the garage swung open and Mr. Parsons walked into the kitchen. He was a big, stocky man with a large, round head with short hair that looked like black carpeting. A few white hairs showed up on the sides, each one as curly as a spring. His skin was darker than Opal's or Mrs. Parsons, and he had deep wrinkles in his forehead. I watched as he wiped his hands on a greasy rag.

"Daddy," said Opal. "This is my friend Del."

Mr. Parson didn't smile. He flashed his eyes quickly across my face, and just nodded his head without saying anything at all. His mouth sort of tightened up. Then he turned his back and went to the sink, where he spent several minutes washing his hands over and over again with a bar of Lava soap. At last he turned around and studied me some more, smiling very slightly.

"Del must be short for somepin," he said.

"Delmar."

Mr. Parson's eyebrows shot up and he launched into a look of admiration.

"That's a fine name," he said. "Is dat a family name?"

"Yes, sir," I said. "My father had an uncle named Delmar. But he died so I'm the only Delmar now. I usually go by Del."

"Have a seat, Delmah. Glad to make yo quaintance." At last, he smiled for real.

"Glad to meet you too, Mr. Parsons."

We all sat down with one of us on each side of the square table.

Mr. Parsons looked at me. "Would you do us de honah of leading us in grace, Delmah?"

"Sure," I said, and everybody bowed their heads, folded their hands, and closed their eyes.

Do you remember how I pulled a rabbit out of my hat when Mrs. Borger asked me about the rhyming scheme in a Shakespearian sonnet? Well, now I was in a similar fix. I tapped into a hidden corner of my brain and pulled out some words my dad used to say at Sunday dinner. That's right. Our family used to say a prayer at dinner every Sunday even though we've pulled it back recently to just Thanksgiving, Christmas, and Easter. Anyhow, I had the words and the problem wasn't saying them. The problem was trying to say them *southern*.

Well, I gave it a run and started out in the conventional way by thanking God for the good food we were about to receive. Then I tried to imagine how to embellish the prayer to meet the expectations of a family from Alabama. I went on to give thanks for warm weather, our homes and families, the warm furnaces in our homes, our clothing (especially coats and gloves, since winter was coming soon), our cars (so we don't have to walk outside in the cold), our . . .

I glanced at Opal and her eyes were as big as the bottle caps off an old-fashioned milk bottle. She gave me the *cut it off* signal, and I brought the prayer in for landing.

" . . . In Jesus's name we pray. Amen."

"Amen," said the others. Mr. Parsons gave me a worried look.

Everything on the table was hot and steaming. Mrs. Parsons had served the chicken in a big dish surrounded by chunks of something that looked like yellow squash. There was a dish of cooked spinach with chunks of tomatoes mixed in. Mrs. Parsons had another name for it, but I knew cooked spinach when I saw it. She had a bowl of corn and a bowl of some sort of pale beans.

I ate some of everything and it tasted very good—mostly. I went light on the spinach with the tomato chunks but made up for it with corn.

All the while we ate, Mr. and Mrs. Parsons peppered me with questions about Neenah and the region. Since they were new to the area and interested in learning, I gave them the whole pitch, or at least as much as could fit into the time it takes to eat supper.

I told them about how the Winnebago Indian tribe lived in the area for centuries and how a French explorer named Jean Nicolet came through the Great Lakes all the way to Green Bay and made friends with the Winnebago people. I talked about how Nicolet was actually looking for China and how he wore fancy silk clothing and liked to fire off his pistols to impress everybody. And it worked too, because the Winnebago Indians prepared feasts of beaver meat to share with him and his men. I talked about how they guided Nicolet and his men right up the Fox River and had another beaver feast on Doty Island, where our families now lived. I paused and then cleared my throat to let everyone know that something important was coming up in the story telling.

"Did you know that your home could possibly stand on the very place where the beaver meat feast took place?"

Mrs. Parsons spoke for the whole family. "We had no idea."

"Well, it's possible," I said. "And did you know that there was a raging whitewater rapids on both sides of this island that we live on?"

"We didn't know dat one either, Delmah," said Mr. Parsons. "You certainly know yo local history."

I paused and swallowed a scoop of corn. I looked quick at Opal to see if I was going to get the *cut-it-off* signal again. She just smiled. I could have stopped there. The Fox Wars were next on the timeline but I wasn't sure it was a good dinner topic.

Mr. Parsons solved the puzzle for me. "Tell us more," he said.

So I did. I told the Parsons family that the Fox Indians were a fierce group who had built fortified villages on Little Lake Butte des Morts. The Fox tribe wanted control of the fur trade, and for a few decades they achieved it by controlling the river. Well, of course, the French didn't like it, so they teamed up with other tribes and set out on a plan to knock the Fox tribe down a notch or two. Guess what. They did more than that. When it all came to a head in the 1730s, the French and their allies killed off almost the whole entire Fox tribe.

"Do you know that Little Lake Butte des Morts got its name from that massacre?" I asked.

Nobody said anything.

"Do you know what Butte des Morts means in French?" I asked again.

"What does it mean, Del?" asked Opal.

"It means Hill of the Dead," I said.

They all stopped chewing their food, and Mrs. Parsons even set down her fork.

"I had no idea," said Opal.

"That's right," I said. "There was already a hill that the tribes used to bury their dead over the years. After the massacre, another hill had to be started up."

"What happened to the other Indian tribes?" asked Mrs. Parsons.

"It doesn't get much better," I said.

"Go on," she said. Her eyes were wide with interest.

I told them about the old council tree on the point near the lighthouse and how that was where the Winnebago Chief Four Legs was lied to by the government and bullied by General Leavenworth. I told them about the Black Hawk wars and how, in the end, the Winnebago, Fox, Sauk, Ottawa, Miami, and Potawatomi all got pushed right out of Wisconsin.

Only the Menominee tribe held on to part of their territorial land, thanks to their leader, Chief Oshkosh. The chief was stubborn as a boulder and would not be moved. In the end they still lost most of their land, but Menominee County, Wisconsin, was eventually named and that land reserved for their home.

Mrs. Parsons leaned in toward me. "Are the Indians still there?" she asked.

"Yes, ma'am, just an hour north of Neenah. It's one of the prettiest counties in the state."

"Well, I'll be."

"Do you want me to go on about the logging boom?" I asked.

"We better work on our report," said Opal.

"But I would like to hear 'bout it," said Mr. Parsons. "One way or another, I'm sure it had somepin to do with all the paper mills that have sprouted up round this town, and that's how I make my living."

"Do you work in one of the mills?" I said.

"I work in most of 'em," said Mr. Parsons. "I'm a machine technician for Pearson & Greene. We make some of the huge papermaking machines dat you may have seen. You ever toured a mill, Delmah?"

"More than one," I said.

I wanted to learn more, but Opal kicked me in the foot, so I excused myself and followed her to a card table in the living room. The paper and pencils were already laid out along with her copy of *The Scarlet Letter*.

13

wasn't very optimistic about Steve's volcano idea. For starters, I figured it wouldn't work. How could it? We were combining Steve's plans made on a Red Owl bag with Grandpa Asa's collection of used junk. To me it was about as likely to work as flying to the moon in a garbage can. The other problem, of course, was that we might get caught. But like I told Steve, I signed up to be part of it and wasn't about to back out, no matter what.

For two weeks we had been collecting baking soda and vinegar. Every couple of days, each of us stopped in at Red Owl or Food Queen and picked up a few boxes and bottles. It put a pretty good dent in my money supply, and we didn't have anywhere near the amount we needed for the big volcano eruption on Saturday afternoon. Grandpa Asa caught wind of this and got pretty concerned.

"You mean to tell me after all my scrounging to get tanks and such, you boys couldn't come up with the groceries?"

"We're running out of money, Grandpa," I said.

On Friday, after school, Steve, Mark, and I all met in the parking lot behind Emerald Gardens. I was amazed to see about a hundred yellow boxes of baking soda and a couple dozen jugs of vinegar under a canvas tarp in the back of Grandpa Asa's pickup truck.

"Where did you get them, Grandpa?"

"Never mind. Let's just say that there are some ladies out in Winneconne who won't be canning pickles or baking bread for a few days. I also picked up thirty little bottles of red food coloring to mix with the vinegar. You want this thing to blow off in Rocket red, don't you?"

69

Mark gave my grandpa a gentle punch in the shoulder. "Good work, sir."

Grandpa nodded like an army sergeant who had just completed a dangerous mission. He had a serious look on his face, and I got the feeling that he was in on this volcano prank even deeper than I was.

Steve was more excited than anyone—all jumpy and squirrelly to the point that I thought he might pee his pants. "We're finally ready," he said.

"Not exactly," said Grandpa Asa. "That business with the pumps and batteries is too complicated. You're going to have to use a gravity feed system to mix everything together."

"What?" Steve's attitude went from supercharged to hopeless in two seconds. His shoulders sagged.

At the same time Mark perked up. "That's actually good. Gravity is simpler."

"Two problems." Grandpa scowled.

We all moved in closer to listen.

"The first problem is that you guys need to make a deeper hole. Those two tanks will have to sit on top of each other now."

"You mean we need to dig a hole six feet deep?" Steve was pulling at his hair. "Holy mackerel."

"Don't worry about it," said Mark. "What's the other problem, mister?"

"The trigger," said Asa. "We need a trigger to open the valve. It's going to take a lot of extra work, but I think you boys will just have to cut a trench in the field and lay a pipe in there with a length of rope inside to some hiding place. You'll need to rig it such that a pull on the rope opens the valve on the vinegar tank."

Steve spun around like he was having a nervous breakdown or something. "We don't have time to do all that!"

"Don't sweat it, Steve," said Mark. "What else, mister?"

"You're going to have to get rid of the dirt," said Asa. "Once you fill in around those tanks, you will still have a lot of extra dirt and it has to go somewhere. You guys are going to have to figure out all this stuff on your own."

Mark and I nodded. Steve looked like he might throw up.

"Okay," said Grandpa. "Let's get those tanks loaded with baking soda, vinegar, and food coloring. We've got one hour to put this thing together, then we'll cover it all up in the back of the truck. I'm going to leave the key right on top of the front tire. Then I'm going to bed. I don't even want to know what happens after that."

We all nodded.

"One more thing," said Grandpa Asa.

"What's that?" asked Mark.

"Anyone gets caught, he takes the heat on his own. Nobody rats out the team. Agreed?"

"Agreed." We all said it together.

Steve, Mark, and I met at one o'clock Saturday morning back in the parking lot of Emerald Gardens, just like we had planned. It was easier than I thought to sneak out of the house. Mom and Sally were both sleeping. I had propped the screen door open the night before so it couldn't make any noise, and I avoided the creaky third step going down the stairs.

Riding Eisenhower over the bridge and across town in the middle of a cold night was pretty weird. Water poured over the dam and threw a mist up over the river. The paper mills churned out steam just like always. Not a single fisherman stood against the fence and the railroad bridge looked like a black prison fence that separated the mills from the rest of the world. A big, almost full, moon hung up in the sky like it was watching me. A planet right alongside the moon glowed brighter than any star. Jupiter, I figured.

We all arrived behind Emerald Gardens at about the same time. Steve came on a bike and Mark on foot.

Mark took a quick peek under the tarp to make sure everything was still there. "You okay driving, Delmar?"

"I guess so."

"Do you even know *how* to drive?" asked Steve.

"I've driven it before," I said. "Plenty of times."

Steve and Mark didn't need to know about my troubles working the clutch. Steve sat in the middle and Mark on the other side. I jumped behind the wheel, stretched my legs, and shifted my butt to reach the clutch and accelerator pedals. It started right up with a loud roar.

"Cripes, you want us to get caught right here in the parking lot?" said Steve.

"Relax," said Mark. "A little less gas Delmar. You know how to drive a stick, right?"

"Yes."

I clunked it into first gear and took off the parking brake. Then the moment of truth. I released the clutch pedal slowly with my left foot just as I gave it some more gas with my right. The truck barely inched forward at first, then came up to speed. I shifted into second and we were off.

"Lights," said Mark.

I pulled the chrome knob on the dashboard and turned on the radio. Buddy Holly sang "Oh Boy" as we chugged past the taverns, around the bend by the red-brick paper mill, through downtown Neenah on Wisconsin Avenue. The light turned yellow at Commercial Street and I didn't want to downshift so I squealed the tires on the left turn.

Steve grabbed the dashboard. "You trying to kill us?!"

I held the steering wheel in a death grip.

"You're doing fine, Delmar," said Mark.

Crossing the island was a snap. I had to slow down for a few mill rats coming out of the bars as they dragged the soles of their work boots on the pavement. Other than that, I just kept it in third gear. I hit all the lights. The Tayco Street drawbridge came next.

"If the bridge goes up I'm jumping it," I said.

"Five bucks says you'll chicken out," said Mark, and we both waited for Steve's reaction.

"Can we just get there without dying, please?"

Mark socked him in the thigh and Steve socked him back.

We rolled up and over the bridge and hung a right. Zigging and zagging through Menasha's streets, we spotted the football field just ahead with their stupid GO BLUE JAYS signs plastered all over the fences. We parked the truck away from the street lights and got to work.

❀

It was weird being down in the bottom of the hole. Mark and Steve had dug the first three feet but, as the skinny kid, the deep parts belonged to me. The only sounds were my own breathing and the shovel scraping the dirt. I felt like one of those African diamond miners in National Geographic as I lifted another bucket of dirt over my head. My only light was Grandpa Asa's railroad lantern, hanging from a spike hammered into the inside wall of the hole. It burned kerosene with a flaming yellow wick inside a glass bubble that had a wire cage around it. It was pretty cool, except that it stunk up the hole and burned my arm a couple times.

"That's deep enough," said Mark.

I pushed the shovel up and out, followed by the lantern. Then Steve and Mark reached down for my upstretched arms and together pulled me straight up the shaft. Even in the dim light, I could tell I was a mess—covered nose to toes in sticky, brown clay. I flopped on the grass, filled my lungs with clean, cool air, and looked at the sky full of stars.

Steve and Mark let me rest and took over from there. They dropped the tank assemblies in the hole. Everything fit perfectly, with the volcano tube just below the height of the surrounding grass of the field. Somehow, Mark had rigged up the trigger with a metal rod that lined up alongside the tube. Then they filled in the sides with dirt and packed it all down. Mark gave it one final stomp and placed the circle of grass turf back over the top. Other than a small opening from the sunken pipe and a mound of extra dirt, the Menasha High School football field looked exactly like before. Even the white stripe marking the fifty-yard line went right over the top of our hole once the turf was back on top. The volcano was loaded and ready to blow in less than ten hours. Other than a stray cat and a couple of cars, we hadn't seen a single living creature the whole time. If I hadn't been so worn out I might have even smiled.

"We're out of time to rig up a trigger rope," said Mark.

"But, we have to," said Steve. "It's the only way to set it off without getting caught. Holy moley!"

"I'll figure something out tomorrow," said Mark. "Right now, we've got to get rid of this dirt and get out of here."

That was good enough for me. I trusted Mark and knew he wouldn't chicken out. One way or another, he would come up with an idea to set off the trigger. Together, we dragged the tarp with the extra dirt and just dumped it next to the bleachers, hoping nobody would notice. The return trip to Emerald Gardens went smooth. I worked the clutch on the first try and didn't even have to squeal the tires.

It was past four in the morning when I slipped through the door and snuck up the stairs, avoiding the third step. I shoved my muddy cloths in the corner of my closet behind my box of fossils and camping junk and then crawled into bed. My alarm clock was set for seven-thirty, just three hours away.

❀

The next morning was a blur, and I felt like going back to sleep right there under the kitchen table. My head bobbed up and down so much that I thought I might drown in my Froot Loops. Then I saw Mom's pot of coffee steaming on the stove. I poured some in a cup, tasted it, and nearly puked.

How can she drink this crud?

I mixed in a scoop of sugar and gulped it down like dirt-flavored Kool-Aid. In ten minutes I was wide awake and hammering toward Menasha. I hid Eisenhower behind some bushes about a block from the football field, since the bike had a Neenah license plate on it. No sense tempting fate with Menasha's version of dirtballs. Steve was easy to find in the bleachers, staring straight down the fifty-yard line.

"Hi, Steve."

He said nothing. His face looked pale, like he was under a voodoo spell or something. I punched him in the arm.

"Oh . . . hi, Minnow." He didn't even look at me.

"What's wrong?" I asked.

"It's going to fail."

"Why?"

"We have no way to pull the trigger."

"Mark said he would come up with something."

"He's not even here."

I looked around as the bleachers filled up. The band was playing and the gray-haired soldiers from the VFW were marching slowly onto the field with their white rifles and the American flag.

"He's usually pretty reliable about this sort of thing," I said. "I'm not worried."

"We should have done the thing with the pipe and the rope," said Steve.

"Mark will come up with something," I looked all around but couldn't find him.

When the Blue Jays band played the national anthem and referees did the coin toss, even I started to get nervous. I kept looking and looking, but Mark was nowhere in sight.

The first quarter ended with Menasha leading by a touchdown. They scored again with six minutes to go in the half, and it looked like it would be all blue and white for their homecoming. "The Rockets will crash and burn," I heard one smart aleck yell as he walked in front of the visiting bleachers. Steve chucked a crunched-up popcorn bag at him and the guy flipped us the middle finger. I took another look around and saw Grandpa Asa hobble up to the fence by the far end zone.

"There's my grandpa," I said. "He came to see the volcano."

"He's going to be ticked off when he finds out we didn't rig up the trigger like he told us," said Steve. Now we were both hanging our heads.

"Hey, nerds."

I looked to my left just as Mark slid into the seat next to me.

"You made it!" I said. Steve looked up and his eyes showed a glimmer of hope.

"Did you rig up a rope?" Steve asked hopefully.

"Nope."

"We're screwed," said Steve.

"Halftime starts in ten minutes," said Mark. "I want you guys to just keep your eyes on the fifty-yard line."

"You've got a plan?" asked Steve.

"Just watch the fifty-yard line." Mark jumped down off the bleachers and disappeared.

Steve and I looked on hopefully as the ref blew the whistle for half-time and both teams ran off the field. The Blue Jays marching band had assembled and the homecoming king and queen were announced as they waved to the crowd from the Menasha sidelines. My eyes flashed in three directions at once: to the sidelines, to the fifty-yard line, and over to the end zone, where Grandpa Asa stood alone with his cane.

The band members took their positions on the field. If it was going to happen, this was the time. I looked again toward Grandpa and could see him craning his neck. The announcer's voice rang out over the loudspeaker.

"Ladies and gentleman, please welcome the Menasha Blue Jays Band with their medley of Big Band tunes, beginning with a Glen Miller favorite, 'The Chattanooga Choo Choo'!"

The band started marching to the beat of the drums and the blast of about three dozen trumpets, trombones, and tubas. In their blue-and-white uniforms they pumped their feet in unison. Then, from their positions in the center of the field, the group broke up into a bunch of curving lines until they made the shape of an old steam locomotive. The crowd cheered, clapped, and whooped as the band members forming the wheels walked in a circle to give the thing the look of motion. Two people even walked back and forth with a big silver bar between the wheels to act like piston rods that drove the wheels. Even I had to admit that it was pretty cool.

We gaped at the spectacle from the perspective of knowing the precise location of our volcano buried in the dead center of the field. Suddenly, our eyes landed on a late-arriving band member in a poorly fitting uniform carrying what appeared to be a small tree branch that he played like a clarinet.

Steve squinted his eyes. "What the heck?"

"It's Mark," I whispered.

Mark took an awkward position at the top edge of the locomotive, like a wart on the top of a perfectly straight line. He stood tall and proud like the rest, his head arching back as he pretended to play music out of that ridiculous stick of wood.

I was frozen in my seat, not knowing whether to laugh, scream, or cry. Steve twitched like a little kid who needed to pee. Then, altogether as a unit, the band began marching toward one end zone and in a split second we realized that the movement would take Mark directly over the top of the trigger to the volcano. He was at the forty-five yard line, forty-seven, forty-eight, forty-nine.

"Now," said Steve. "Pull it."

Mark dropped to his knees, tossed the tree branch to the side and dug around for the trigger. Other members of the band bumped him and swerved around him. A tuba player tripped on his legs and fell over sideways as the crowd gasped. He scrambled to his feet and ran to find his place in the formation.

"What's going on out there?" asked a man's voice behind us.

"That boy is doing something on the ground," answered his wife.

At that point in the show everybody had noticed that something wasn't right, and a murmur rose up from the crowd. With everyone moving around him, Mark just stood there watching. No instrument, no marching legs, just Mark, all by himself—watching.

"Did he pull it?" I asked.

"Nothing's happening," said Steve.

I don't know what I expected exactly. An oozing puddle? Maybe a bubbling pile of foam? What came out of the ground was a perfect miracle. A geyser. A pink one. It gurgled and sputtered at first in shots of foam three or four feet tall. Then it was like someone flipped a switch as the stream blasted into the sky as tall as the goal posts.

To our amazement, people in the bleachers clapped and cheered.

"They think it's part of the show!" I yelled to Steve, who hooted right along with the crowd.

The marching Blue Jays panicked. Their formation came unglued as band members responded to the unnatural disaster unfolding before their eyes. At first, the locomotive changed shape as the kids nearest to the geyser moved out of the way and a giant dent appeared on the top edge that had just been so perfect and straight. Then as the pink spray splattered their perfect blue-and-white uniforms, a few of them took off at a sprint, leaving their instruments on the field. More kids ran for cover and, soon enough, the Chattanooga Choo Choo split in half. The music fell apart too, and sort of simulated the sound of a train coming off the tracks. A lot of screeching and groaning was followed by a few screams and, finally, dead silence as everybody watched. It was perfect.

I heard the lady behind me paging through her program. "I don't think it was supposed to happen this way," she said. Steve snorted in laughter, nearly sliding off his seat.

Eventually, the geyser died down and shrank into a sort of ordinary volcano after all. Lava flowed up and then out in a puddle matching the bright-red color of the Neenah Rockets symbol. The mess oozed out over the giant letter *M* on the field.

Recognition of the prank came gradually, starting with curses and growing into a thunder of boos and jeers.

"Oh-oh," said Steve. "Where's Mark? He better make a run for it." We searched the crowds of people on the field and found one still standing alone.

"There he is," I said. Not only had Mark set off the eruption. He had stayed on the field and watched the whole thing.

Mark picked that moment to make his getaway. He started by walking toward one end zone but it didn't take long before a few Blue Jays from the trombone section spotted him. Mark took off at a dead run and the chase was on. A roar went up from the bleachers on both sides of the field and a few adults on the Menasha sidelines even joined in the pursuit. The last thing we saw was Mark throwing off his Blue Jay hat and jacket as he disappeared between houses.

"Holy smokes," said Steve. "Mark is my hero."

I looked over to where Grandpa Asa still stood behind the other end zone. His crooked back had straightened. His head was upright and his crew cut glistened in the sunlight. Gosh, if he had a uniform and a pearl-handled revolver, he could have been General Patton himself. I half expected to see a salute.

Steve and I couldn't keep from smiling. I punched him in the shoulder and he punched me back. My mom once said that there are certain moments of pure joy in a person's life and that they usually lined up with wedding days and the birth of children. For Steve, Mark, and me, this had to be one of them. Even if I were to strike it rich and become the King of Siam with twenty wives, nothing was likely to top the pink geyser on the fifty-yard line at the Menasha High School homecoming game.

❋

Believe it or not, Mark escaped. Like I said before, he was a natural athlete, so by dodging between houses and never stopping, he shook off all those angry Menasha guys until he got all the way to the Dairy Queen in Neenah, where he could cool his jets and catch his breath. Mark called me later that afternoon to let me know that he made it home safe. He also wanted to talk about the volcano. We all agreed that it was the coolest thing ever when it actually turned into a geyser and the biggest achievement so far in all of our academic careers. I called Steve to let him know that Mark had escaped. I called Grandpa Asa too. He was as proud as the rest of us and agreed that Mark deserved most of the credit.

14

When Dad was still alive, Sunday had always been a family time. Mom would make a big pot roast for the midday meal, complete with potatoes, carrots, peas, and apple sauce. Dad would carve up the steaming roast, and we would joke around about who got stuck with the "butt piece" on the end. We had good conversations too. Dad shared funny stories from when he was a kid, and Mom talked about the latest gossip in the neighborhood. Sally usually came up with something funny from school, and I even chimed in with a few zingers.

As I sat alone at the kitchen table, it finally hit me that those days were never, ever coming back. Gosh — Sally was hardly around anymore, and Mom slept later and later every day. I flipped to the last page of the Sunday comics and decided not to bother with Dick Tracy. My stomach groaned and I checked my watch. Quarter past noon and not a peep from Mom. I fixed a peanut butter sandwich to go with my glass of milk.

The phone rang and I jumped all over it. "Hello, Finwick residence."

"Hello, young man. This is Sheriff Heiselmann. I'm calling to check on your mother. Has she been doing better since the funeral?"

Holy Hell! Now what?! My thoughts all drifted off to images of Heiselmann smirking alongside the Cadillac Man and of dying swans falling out of the sky. The idea of hanging up the phone and pulling the plug from the wall crossed my mind. Instead, I decided to tell a lie.

"My mom's doing lots better now," I said.

"Good. That's real good," said the sheriff. "Can I speak with her, please?"

"She's sleeping right now," I said.

As soon as I said the words, guess what. The stairs creaked.

"Who is it, Del?" asked my mom.

I thought about lying again but ended up blurting the truth.

"It's Sheriff Heiselmann. He says he's just checking to see how you're doing."

"I'll be right there."

I set the phone down and snuck into the living room to listen. The last thing I wanted was for Sheriff Heiselmann, the enemy of my dad, to be sweet-talking Mom all of a sudden. When I heard her say, "Oh, you're too kind," I got pretty worried. Then I heard her abruptly say, "Gotta go now. Thanks for calling." The phone clunked back into the receiver cradle and I felt better again.

Back in the kitchen I sat down next to Mom. "Why is he calling you?" I asked.

"I don't know," she said, looking directly at me. "I don't even like the man."

"Neither do I."

"Neither did your father."

Satisfied, I grabbed my peanut butter sandwich and wandered upstairs to my room and opened a *Green Lantern* comic book.

About thirty minutes later I snuck back down the stairs. Mom's eyes were glued to the TV, watching a rerun of *F Troop*. I just wanted to get out of the house, but wasn't sure where to go.

The phone rang again. I hesitated for a second, then picked it up.

It was Mark. "Hey Delmar, you want to meet me for a bottle of pop or something?"

Did I ever? Three seconds later, I bombed out of the garage on Eisenhower.

Since Mark preferred walking to riding a bike, I met him on his end of town at the Red Owl. He was already sitting out front on the bench with two bottles of Royal Crown and a large box of Milk Duds.

We yukked it up about our success with the volcano in Menasha.

"How did you get one of their band uniforms?" I asked.

"I just walked into their band room with everybody else and grabbed one off the rack."

"No kidding?"

"Nobody even said a word." Mark's smile was a mile wide.

"Good job setting off the trigger too."

"Did you see how the Chattanooga Choo Choo broke into pieces?"

"Yeah," I said. "That was tops."

We clinked RC bottles and finished them off. I bought us two more for the road, and we walked in the direction of the lake.

At the Fresh Air Camp we stopped to skip stones and look out at the water. A couple of fishermen were motoring in off the reefs, so I walked over to check their stringer. They had seven decent walleyes and weren't afraid to show them off.

"Where did you catch 'em?" I asked.

"Mansur."

"That's a good reef," I said.

The man nodded and smiled. Most people went to Stevens Reef, which anyone could find from the red buoy, or Haystack Reef, where they could line up the radio tower with the notch in the trees. Finding Mansur Reef took some doing. In ten minutes their Alumacraft was trailered up and gone. Mark and I had the gravel beach to ourselves again. At least a dozen other fishing boats glistened in the distance, and a pair of fifteen-foot snipes raced southbound with full sails, toward Fond du Lac.

"You want to take out a canoe?" asked Mark.

"We don't have one."

"I know where we can get one."

"Okay."

We walked through a couple of backyards along the shore. "That's Mr. Dunn's house."

"The school counselor at Horace Mann?"

"Yeah."

Mark rang the doorbell but nobody answered.

"Come on. He keeps a canoe behind his garage."

"What if we get caught?"

"Relax, Delmar. We're just *borrowing* it."

The beat up aluminum canoe wasn't much, but it floated. The paddles were right underneath, and in two minutes we were on the lake heading south along the shore. The sun broke through the clouds and all of a sudden the green water of Lake Winnebago looked like a trillion flashing diamonds. A pair of mallards took off quacking and passed right in front of me. I turned my paddle around and made like I was shooting the Model 12.

"Pow! Pow! Got 'em both," I said.

We paddled for over an hour, just talking about junk.

"Where are we going?" I asked.

"I don't care. All the way to Oshkosh, if you want. You pick."

"There's Blackbird Island," I said. "How 'bout we stop and take a look."

"Fine with me."

Blackbird Island was a tiny little clump of ground with a few willow trees in the middle. It took us maybe two minutes to walk around the whole thing. Then we just sat down, facing the bluffs on the east shore and watched the waves wash in. I felt like Huck Finn with my shoes kicked off and my feet dangling, half-expecting to see a steamboat roll by like they did a hundred years ago on Winnebago.

"Can I ask you a question, Delmar?"

"I guess." I sidearmed a skipper.

"Who do you suppose killed your dad?"

"The Highway 41 Killer. That's what everybody says."

"Yeah. I know that's all the talk. But who actually is the creep?"

I shrugged. My mind was on Sheriff Heiselmann and the Cadillac Man.

"That's just bullshit. Three murders in two years and we've got nothing. Are the cops even looking for the Highway 41 Killer anymore? Are they even trying to solve the crime?" Mark picked up a stone, weighed it in his hand, and threw it about a mile. We both watched it fly.

"It wouldn't surprise me if Sheriff Heiselmann knows something but isn't talking. I've got a hunch he might be involved, somehow."

Mark quit throwing stones and looked straight at me. "What?"

"Sheriff Heiselmann was my dad's boss. They didn't like each other. I heard Dad telling my mom once that he was getting yanked around pretty bad at work. That Heiselmann didn't like him looking into certain things."

"That's weird. But it's no reason to kill a guy."

"Yeah. I know." I looked at Mark and cocked my head. "I just don't trust the prick."

"Why not?" asked Mark.

"For one thing, I saw him acting strange one day when I was diving at the point."

"What was he doing?"

"Well, he kept standing by his patrol car, looking around to make sure nobody was watching. Then he went up to the driver of a black Cadillac, talked to him, and took an envelope from him. There was something in the envelope that he put in his pocket—money, I think. Then he ripped up the envelope and threw it in the trash."

"Son of a bitch, Delmar. You should have told me earlier. You should have saved the envelope."

"I did save it. I fished out the pieces and taped them back together, but all it had on the outside were a bunch of doodles."

"What do you mean doodles?"

"Just little drawings of sailboats, basketball players . . . stuff like that."

Mark sat down in the gravel and put his hands under his chin. His face got hard as he looked out over the water. I kept my mouth shut for a while.

He turned his head and looked at me again. "Is there anything else? What else do you know about the sheriff?"

"He killed a swan at the Poygan Marsh. Me and my grandpa saw it."

"What else?"

"He called our house today and I think he was trying to sweet-talk my mom."

"You're right, Delmar. He is a prick."

"Yup."

Mark got quiet again. He made a furrow in the gravel with his heel, then turned and looked at me again.

"Delmar?"

"Yeah?"

"Do you think your grandpa would let us use the truck again?"

"Maybe. Where are we going?"

"To the place where your dad was killed."

❋

A couple hours passed before we returned the canoe and made it back to where Eisenhower was locked up at Red Owl. From there I headed toward home, zigzagging through the side streets. Ike and I chugged north on Reed Street leading up to Shattuck High.

Wouldn't you know it—three grits stood there smoking on a Sunday afternoon, and from a distance I could see that one of them was Larry Buskin. He said something to the other two, flicked his cigarette, and started walking directly toward me. I picked up my speed, hoping to get past him, but in two seconds it was obvious that he would catch me unless I took drastic action. I angled Ike hard to the right, jumped a curb, and suddenly found myself making my own trail through the backyards. Buskin sprinted around a couple houses, trying to cut me off, but by the time he emerged onto Congress Street, I had fifty yards on him. At that point he gave up.

"You can't run forever!" he yelled.

I pounded Ike's pedals with something like nitro in my veins, hammering toward the island. By the time I got there the streetlights were blinking on. My stomach practically did a flip, it was so hungry. The garage door slammed shut, and the screen door twanged open. The kitchen was quiet. I opened the fridge in search of leftovers. Nothing. I peeked around the corner to the living room. There was Mom, sleeping on the couch in her pajamas next to an ashtray full of cigarette butts.

"Jeez," I said aloud. I was mad at Mom for having MS. I was mad at Sheriff Heiselmann for being a prick. I was mad at Larry Buskin for chasing me, and I was mad at myself for running away. My thoughts went to the Eaglewing steel-toed boots that Grandpa Asa had ordered. I needed them more than ever.

15

Grandpa Asa wouldn't let me and Mark take the truck to the murder scene, but he agreed to drive us there himself. From the reports in the newspaper and on TV we knew exactly where to go on the side of Highway 41 between Neenah and Oshkosh right next to a big billboard that advertised Fine Dining at some joint in Fond du Lac. The sun dangled low in the sky, and the clouds sprayed orange and pink. Grandpa parked the truck, and we all got out on the gravel shoulder.

All of a sudden, my dad's murder became very, very real again. I felt his presence in the cool breeze that cut through my jacket. Shivering, I pulled the zipper up all the way to my collar. *What had actually happened here? Did Dad see the person who shot him? What did he feel?* The cops said that the bullets passed straight through him. *Where were those bullets? How much of Dad's blood soaked into the ground?* A sick feeling sank into my gut.

"Over here," said Asa. "This is where the newspeople were standing."

Mark and I walked over. "What are we looking for?" I asked.

"Clues," said Mark. "None of them are going to be obvious, Delmar. Let's take our time and see what we can find."

I stood by the truck. Mark squinted his eyes and slowly turned in a full circle. He walked to the north, studying the gravel as hundreds of cars zoomed by. Then he did the same thing to the south. He came back to the truck and leaned against it with his eyes still almost closed.

"What do they say happened?" asked Mark.

"They say my dad pulled over to investigate an abandoned car. He was shot three times in the chest. When the other cops got here, Dad was dead on the roadside and the other car was gone."

"Did he call in a license plate number or describe the car to the dispatcher?"

"I don't know."

"Do they have any shell casings from the bullets?"

"I don't know that either."

"Was there any gunpowder residue found on your dad?"

"I don't know."

Mark looked directly at the billboard at the edge of a cornfield. "Those posts holding up the billboard could be a hiding place," he said.

"But they said it happened right by the car," I said.

"Wouldn't hurt to go look."

I looked over to Grandpa Asa, standing there with his cane. "Check it out if you want. I'll stay by the truck."

Mark and I jumped a fence and wandered over to the corn field.

"Let's walk the edge of the corn first," said Mark.

"Okay."

"You walk inside the first row of corn and I'll walk inside the second. Look for anything, even if it's just a piece of trash."

Side by side, we walked the corn. The wind made a rattling sound in the dry leaves and stalks. We shifted over to the third and fourth rows of corn and walked again. Still nothing. Mark signaled for us to walk over to the billboard. We waded into the tall grass and explored each wooden post that held up the sign. At the third post, Mark held up his hand to signal me to stop.

"The grass looks like it was flattened out here," he said.

I shot him an unbelieving sort of look. To me the grass didn't seem any different. "It's the same as everywhere else," I said. "Besides, the murder happened three months ago."

Mark pushed some of the tall grass to the side, and I had to admit that it did look like a matted-down spot underneath.

"Keep looking for clues," he said.

On our hands and knees we scrounged all around. For ten minutes we poked our fingers down to bare dirt, raking the ground for anything, but came up empty.

"Expand our perimeter," said Mark. He pointed with his finger in a larger circle around the matted grass.

We walked slowly in circles that got bigger and bigger as we moved out. I was getting frustrated at the whole idea that a couple kids could search the area any better than the cops. I kicked around in the tall grass with my tennis shoes, knowing that there was nothing there. Then I thought I spotted something small. I bent over and picked it up.

"I found a cigarette butt," I said, holding it up.

Mark hurried over and studied it with me. The whole thing was sort of old and gross, but we could still make out some of the details. The paper was brown around the filter and white further up. The word *Winston* appeared in blue letters on the white part just above the filter. Whoever had smoked it burned it down only halfway, and then pinched it off.

My mind flipped back to the day I saw Sheriff Heiselmann and the Cadillac Man together at the Neenah Lighthouse. I remembered picking up the cigarette butt that the Cadillac Man tossed out his car window. It had brown paper around the filter too, and blue letters that spelled out the word *Winston*.

"We better keep this," said Mark. "Keep looking, there might be more."

We looked and looked for another five minutes but found nothing else. Back at the car, Grandpa Asa was interested in the cigarette butt too.

"Now why would somebody sit under a billboard by the highway and smoke half of a cigarette?" he asked. We all looked at each other with the same idea that nobody wanted to say out loud.

"I have a better question," said Mark. "Why did a tenth-grade kid find this clue instead of the cops?"

"Tell you what," Grandpa Asa said. "I'll make a visit to the Sheriff's Department tomorrow and talk to the investigator assigned to your dad's case. I'll get the latest update. If we're not satisfied, then we can come back."

"Good idea, sir," said Mark. "Are you going to tell them about the cigarette butt?"

"No."

An hour earlier, I had figured that going to the murder scene was just a waste of time. I still wasn't so sure that a cigarette butt really meant anything, but it did seem odd that somebody smoked it just halfway down underneath a billboard on the roadside. And it sure felt like more than a coincidence that the cigarette was a Winston.

I didn't talk much on the way home from Highway 41. While Mark and Asa jabbered about my dad's murder and the investigation, my mind drifted off in a completely different direction. I was worrying about my mom. My still-breathing—not-dead-yet—mom.

16

Sunday morning came around again and I got an idea in my head that I should go to church and have a heart-to-heart talk with God. I had a bone to pick. If he really loved us, then where was he when we needed him? Some days I actually wanted to yell up at the clouds: *Can we get a little help down here, please?!*

But I wasn't just planning a crank call either. In many ways I realized that we had quite a bit to be thankful for, so I figured on including a long-overdue thank-you note. Thanks for giving me a best friend named Mark. Thanks for our good home on the island. Maybe I would even thank God for my little four-person family, even though it felt like we were hanging on by a thread.

I locked Eisenhower to a bike rack and walked up the stone steps to the big wooden doors outside Ebenezer Lutheran. Suddenly, a surge of angst hit me.

Do I really want to go in there? What does God want to see me for anyhow?

I almost chickened out as I thought it all through. Nobody in my family had been to Sunday church service in six months, and I wasn't actually sure that we were even welcome anymore. On top of that, I was supposed to be taking confirmation but hadn't attended a single class. I was just about ready to unlock Ike and dash home when I heard a voice, and it wasn't God.

"Good morning, Mr. Finwick."

My head snapped around. *Oh-oh!*

"Good morning, Mrs. Borger."

"I'm so glad to see you," she said. "I didn't even know you were a member."

"I'm not sure if I'm a member or not."

"This is a Lutheran church, Mr. Finwick. Everyone is welcome, and that includes you. Have you been here before?"

"Last Easter."

She didn't even flinch. "You'll join me this morning, won't you?"

My antennae went up in search of a way to wiggle out of the predicament. After all, I was having my doubts about coming in the first place and sure didn't want to sit with Mrs. Borger. *Holy Moses!* How was I going to escape this one? I glanced left and found the gray stone walls of the church. I glanced right and my eyes landed on a big, thick hedge. Blocking the sidewalk in front of me stood Mrs. Borger.

"Yes, ma'am," I said. "I would love to join you this morning."

She smiled—a rarity for Mrs. Borger. Then she grabbed my elbow like I was her date to the prom and together we walked through the big wooden doors.

It was tough duty being Mrs. Borger's church date, let me tell you. She made me visit with all sorts of old codgers. At first she introduced me as Mr. Finwick, but that made everybody squirm because they knew right away that I was the son of the murdered deputy.

Since I didn't want to be treated like a lost orphan, I whispered in her ear. "Maybe you could just introduce me as Del."

"Good idea," she whispered back.

The chitchat got easier after that—easier for a while, anyhow. Then I spotted Marsha Charboneau and Lynn McGivens from my geometry class. They smiled and acted friendly, but I could tell that underneath they were each splitting a gut. Yep—soon enough, everybody at Shattuck High would know that I was Mrs. Borger's church date at Ebenezer Lutheran Church on Sunday. I shrugged it off. Maybe I had bigger worries.

Once we got our programs and found a pew I finally relaxed a little bit. The choir sat in three rows at one side of the pulpit. Their gowns were bright blue and so shiny that they could have been metal armor. Then the music leader stood up in front, lifted his hands, and nodded to the organist. I wasn't expecting much. Then POW! Who knew that white-haired coots could belt it out like that?

They sang two hymns, and all of a sudden we were invited to stand and sing the last verse along with them. Mrs. Borger had the page already bookmarked in the red book, and we held it together, singing loud and strong. I was feeling pretty good by the end of it. Then those blue robes brought back a vision of my sins at Menasha High. I squirmed and shifted my eyes, but they landed on the stained-glass windows where Jesus Himself stared back.

When the music wrapped up, everybody settled into their seats and the pastor walked up behind the pulpit. He announced the chapter and verses from the Bible that he was about to read from, and I could hear a few people behind me flipping to find the right pages. Mrs. Borger opened her Bible and we followed along together. After the reading, the pastor invited everyone to bow for a moment of silent prayer, and that's when I decided to have my private chat with God. As near as I could tell, he just listened and didn't say anything back. We sang a couple more hymns and Mrs. Borger put the red book back in the rack.

"Time for the sermon," she whispered.

I nodded and settled in for what I figured would be twenty minutes of head-bobbing boredom. Well, guess what. It wasn't boring at all. Actually, it was really, really good.

Believe it or not, Pastor Olson talked about being in World War II. He told us about the terrible things he saw during the Battle of the Bulge. Fellow soldiers getting killed. Captured German soldiers being shot, point blank, because there was no way to take prisoners. Even when they weren't fighting, it was pure misery as they camped outdoors in the terrible cold. And then he talked about coming into the Buchenwald concentration camp, where thousands of men and women lay dead or starving. He told us all about the sickening sensation of hopelessness that he felt for the whole human race. Things were so bad, he said, that he almost lost faith in God.

"Why did God allow it?" he asked.

I was on the edge of my seat. I could hardly wait for the answer. It was a question just like the one I had just asked God about my mom. Then Pastor Olson looked at us sort of meekly. "I don't know why," he said.

Could I believe my ears? Pastor Olson didn't know. In his white gown, standing there on the fancy wooden pulpit behind the banner with the silver cross around his neck, how could *he*, of all people, not know? All I could think was—*Wow! That took some guts.*

The pastor went on to remind us of all the good that God stands for in the lives of people. He told us that God is a beacon of light for everyone to follow, and he encouraged us to not lose faith during times of pain, because through thick and thin, through all our sins and suffering, somehow God still loves us.

After that he led us in another hymn and a prayer and benediction. You probably won't believe me, but it's true. I was sorry when it ended.

For a second there I even forgot that I had a church date. Mrs. Borger looked at me and smiled. Then she took my elbow again and I walked her to the back. She went for the coffee. I went for the cookies. Then I looked around for the other reason I came there in the first place—to find the church ladies from Dad's funeral to ask them if they could help my family one more time.

❊

Since I was already nearby, I jumped on Eisenhower and spun over to Emerald Gardens to see Grandpa Asa and have a bowl of ice cream. We talked about this and that, and he showed me a copy of the *Post-Crescent* that had an article about the volcano at Menasha High. Then he showed me some letters from the opinion section, and I realized that not everybody thought it was such a funny prank. Some folks were pretty angry, and I was happier than ever that we never got caught—or not yet, anyhow.

I was fixing to ride Ike back home when he handed me a sack with a heavy box inside.

"They came yesterday," he said.

"What?"

"The Eaglewing steel-toed boots for your friend."

"Thanks," I said.

"Tell your friend to practice," said Grandpa. "He knows where to aim, right?"

"The shins?"

"Yep, right on the bone."

As I rode Eisenhower back home my mind drifted to the Battle of the Bulge and Buchenwald. Then I thought about Dad, shot dead for no good reason. And then, there was Mom, still messed up from MS, which was chopping her down a little bit more every day. I thought about Mark and his struggles at home. I thought about Opal and the loneliness of being the only black kid in the whole entire county. I thought about Grandpa Asa, getting old and weak just when we needed him most. And I remembered everything he told me about the Eagle-wings. Then I wondered how God fit into all of it, and I came up with the same answer as Pastor Olson. I didn't know either.

17

Tuesday was Halloween. The cafeteria, study hall, and library were deco-rated with fake cobwebs and the usual pictures of green-faced witches and Frankenstein's monsters. Guess what else happened on that day. We got caught. That's right. Somebody remembered seeing Steve working on his volcano plans and reported him to the principal. Well, as soon as word got out that Steve was caught, other kids started talking about how they saw me and him scheming in the Science Resource Center, and then somebody else realized that we had been seen together with Mark. Pretty soon half of the kids in school were bragging about how they helped get us captured.

We were hauled, one at a time, into Principal Baggert's office for interrogation and by the time Steve was done, he had spilled his guts about the whole thing, including the parts that involved Grandpa Asa. When I got in there, the principal had the whole story memorized, in-cluding the part about me driving the truck through Neenah-Menasha in the middle of the night. All I could do was nod my head.

After Baggert finished with me, he pointed to a chair outside his office where I sat down next to Mark and Steve. "What are they going to do to us?" I asked.

Mark looked at me calmly. "One week suspension for you guys. Two weeks for me. They'll probably call the cops on your grandpa."

After a few minutes of discussion with a counselor and the vice principal, Mr. Baggert returned with a grim reaper look on his face and called us all back into his office. He drummed his fingers on the desk like it was the countdown to our never-ending doom.

"Your delinquent actions have certainly cast a pall of disgrace upon our fine school, and I for one am disgusted with such behavior."

We said nothing.

"I spoke with the principal of Menasha High School about the three of you, and he encouraged me to let *him* select your punishment. You may be interested to know that he used the terms yardarm, shackles, and flogging in his recommendations."

"I'm pretty sure flogging is unconstitutional, sir?" Mark couldn't resist.

"Shut up!"

We did and the principal glared back at Mark.

"You of all people, Mr. Marmotti, should have learned by now to keep your mouth *shut* prior to the dissemination of your sentence. If I'm not mistaken, you have visited my office before."

"Yes."

"For what offense?"

"Stink bomb, sir."

"In the teachers' lavatory?"

"Yes."

"It gives me no pleasure, Mr. Marmotti, to inform you that you will all be punished for these acts in the form of suspension from school. For you it will be a period of two weeks."

Mark gave no reaction as the principal turned toward Steve.

"Well, if it isn't Mr. Hawkins, the inventor of the ridiculous contraption that showered such wrath upon Menasha's special day."

Steve tried not to smile but couldn't help himself.

"You think this is funny, Mr. Hawkins?"

"No."

"Your father is a dentist, isn't he, Mr. Hawkins?"

"Yes."

"Well, I'm certain that he will be thrilled to learn that his delinquent son has received a one week suspension from school."

"I'm more concerned about my mom, sir."

The principal lifted his eyebrows and grinned. Then he directed his attention toward me.

"Well, Mr. Finwick, I am especially troubled to learn of your role in this debacle. These events seem to me especially despairing considering the burden that your family has already endured due to the untimely death of your father."

"He didn't just die. He was murdered." I regretted it as soon as I said the words.

"Yes—of course. And for you, Mr. Finwick, as the pawn in this scheme, I sentence you to three days suspension from school."

"I wasn't actually a pawn, sir."

"Shall I amend your sentence to a week?"

"No."

"Very well. Three days it is." He lifted his index finger for emphasis and smiled like the devil himself. "In addition to your suspension you will have to endure the humiliation of knowing that your elderly grandfather is likely to be charged with a crime for which you are ultimately responsible."

I almost said something that I would have regretted. Luckily my mouth stayed shut.

"Mrs. Abraham is presently calling your parents," said Mr. Baggert. "They will be picking you up shortly."

I knew that was true for Steve and his parents. For Mark and me, things weren't so predictable. By 2:30 Steve was long gone. At five o'clock Mark and I were still sitting there. Things got pretty quiet with all the students gone and members of the faculty walking out the door one by one. The school secretary got up and pulled her coat out of a closet. She looked at us without smiling.

"Just go," she said. We did and she locked the door behind us.

❉

I told my mom about the suspension and what I had done to earn it. She just sighed, shook her head, and lit up another cigarette.

"Your father would be disappointed," she said.

Those words hurt even more than a Larry Buskin punch to the ribs. I swallowed hard and could feel the tears coming. Like a jerk, I clomped up the stairs and dumped my school stuff on the floor like none of it was my fault. Then I slumped in the corner and cried.

❉

Our suspensions were scheduled to begin immediately. When I woke up Wednesday morning I didn't know what else to do so I got out of bed at the usual time. Sally was in the kitchen getting ready for school.

"I hope you're happy, ruining everything for Mom and me," she said.

"What do you mean?"

"What do you think, you little brat? You got suspended from school for that idiotic fountain prank."

"It was actually a geyser," I said.

"Whatever! It was a dumb thing to do! There was a picture of it in the paper, you know. That's how bad it was."

I almost smiled as I thought about the picture. Somehow, the photographer had captured the perfect shot, with the geyser at its maximum height. The article in the *Post-Crescent* had even compared it to Old Faithful—a big compliment for sure. Anyhow, I cut out that page and had saved it in the Eskdale bottle on my dresser.

"How does my suspension affect you?" I asked Sally. I knew that I was lighting a fuse but couldn't resist.

"How does it affect me? You're clueless, Del. Everybody's going to be asking me questions about my stupid little brother. 'Why did he do it? Is your brother going to juvie? Why is your little brother such an idiot?' That's what my life is going to be like. And think about what you've done to Mom and Grandpa and our family's reputation. When Dad was alive, people respected us. Now, thanks to you, the Finwicks are the white trash of the neighborhood. Believe me, little brother, it affects me. Maybe you should have climbed into that hole you dug on the football field and just stayed there."

Her words didn't really bother me. Sally hardly ever said anything nice about me anyhow, so arguing with her was sort of like a game. She slammed the door and left. I dropped a Pop-Tart in the toaster, stirred up a glass of Tang, and poured milk on a bowl of Froot Loops. Then the phone rang. It was Mark.

"Hey there, you delinquent."

"Hi, Mark."

"I *really* need to get out of my house. You want to meet somewhere?"

"I was thinking about going fishing at the Point."

"Good. I'll be there in an hour."

❇

Mark didn't bring a fishing pole. For all I knew he didn't even own one. I dug around under some rocks and found a crayfish for bait so I could rig up my pole for bottom fishing with a bell sinker, a swivel, and a number 4 snelled hook. I speared the critter through the tail and hefted it out in the current. Then it was just a matter of propping the pole upright in the rocks and waiting for it to twitch. When it came to fishing by the Neenah lighthouse, I fancied myself the world's foremost expert.

"What are you going to catch on a crayfish?" asked Mark.

"Sheepshead or walleye," I said. "Most likely sheepshead."

"How did your mother take the news of your suspension?"

"Not very well. How about your dad?" I asked.

"Not good. He smacked me and cussed me out. Then he went downtown and got drunk."

"He hit you?"

"Nothing serious," said Mark. He lifted his hair from his face and showed me a purple lump on his forehead.

"Holy crap," I said. "What's going to happen when you go home?"

"Why do you think I got out of there?"

"You have to go home eventually."

"Not necessarily. I've got a place south of here."

"A place?"

"Yeah. Sort of a hideout. When you're done fishing I'll show you."

We fished for an hour. I caught three sheepsheads altogether, stomped the lucky stones from the biggest one, and threw the rest back. The needle was pinned on my curiosity meter and I couldn't wait to see Mark's hideout.

❋

"In here," said Mark. He looked both ways on Bayview before jumping the ditch and walking into a thick swamp of cattails, scrub brush, and willows. I hid Ike and my fishing pole, then jumped the ditch and followed him.

The walking was easy at first, but then it got as thick as the African Congo, and pretty soon we were ankle-deep in freezing-cold muck and black water. It was the darkest, nastiest swamp I had been in. That was saying something too, because I had explored them all, mostly, from the north shore at Plank Road in Menasha to the sloughs behind the golf course to the willows around the Fresh Air Camp. It seemed like I had spent half my life looking for frogs, snapping turtles, and old bottles. Besides, I learned long ago that swamps are the best places to go for avoiding contact with adults.

We were only three minutes in and our shoes were already bricks of black gunk. All of a sudden, things opened up into a small clearing just big enough for what looked to me like a makeshift wigwam.

"My second home," said Mark.

We crawled through the small opening on a floor made of leaves and a plastic tarp. A green metal cooler sat at one side, a rolled-up sleeping bag on the other. I looked it over once inside. Mark had bent about a hundred willow branches and joined them all together with knotted twine. Each branch made an upside-down U-shape so that, overall, the hideout was a miniature dome. In between the sticks, a sheet of plastic poked out here and there—Mark's attempt at a waterproof roof, I figured.

"This is cool," I said.

"Thanks." Mark nodded. He smiled with his eyes. I could tell he was proud of the place, not so much because he built it himself, which he did, but because he had figured out a way to escape his father.

"Is it waterproof?"

"Mostly," he shrugged. "You want something to drink?"

"What've you got?"

"Pop and beer."

"You've got beer?"

Mark shrugged. "It's easy to steal from my dad. You want one?"

"I don't know."

"Have you drank beer before?"

"A couple times," I said, and it was true. I had taken a few sips from Grandpa Asa but had never drank a whole one.

Mark moved a hunk of driftwood and lifted the lid on a metal box buried in a hole in the ground. "This is where I keep the good stuff," he said. He pulled out two cans of Old Style and handed one to me. We pulled the tabs and tossed them out the door.

"Here's to the volcano," said Mark.

"Here's to the *geyser*," I said, and we clanked beer cans together.

Mark took a long, large gulp. I took a sip and tried not to make a face.

"You can use this place if you need it," said Mark.

"Thanks." My mind was on the beer and how the heck I was going to drink it all. Mark took another long swallow from his can.

"The mosquitoes are bad in the summer," he said. "But this time of year, it's perfect."

I nodded and attempted another quarter-ounce sip without gagging.

"There's a muskrat trapper who pokes his nose back here sometimes, but I don't bother him and he doesn't bother me."

I nodded and coughed.

"I'll be staying here for a few nights," said Mark. "Just until my dad gets back on an even keel. After that I'll just use it for emergencies."

"Emergencies?"

"Yeah, he gets mad for no reason sometimes."

I nodded.

"When is your grandpa going to check with the cops about your dad's murder investigation?"

I shrugged. "Today maybe."

"Good." Mark took another drink.

I forced down a sip and nodded.

"Do you know where we could get a metal detector, Delmar?"

"Mr. Johnson has one," I said. "He looks for coins at Riverside Park sometimes."

"Can you borrow it?"

"Probably."

"See if you can get it. We need to go back to the crime scene and do some more snooping around." Mark inverted the beer can over his open mouth and emptied it. "How are you doing with that beer?"

"I'm not that thirsty."

"That's okay, Delmar. Just dump it in the swamp if you don't want it. It's no good for you anyhow. My dad's proof of that."

"Okay." I reached outside the wigwam door and poured my beer into the black muck of the swamp.

❉

After leaving Mark's hideout, we walked all the way through town to Emerald Gardens to see Grandpa Asa. It was barely past noon, but the man with the spider tattoo sat on his throne of concrete steps working on a six-pack.

"The cops were here," he said. "They talked to your grandpa. You know anything about that?"

"No," I said.

Mark and I walked through the dark, stinky hallway and knocked on 118.

"Door's open!"

We walked into the mess that looked and smelled even worse than usual. I kept an eye on Mark for his reaction, but he didn't even flinch.

"Hi, Grandpa," I said.

"Damn cops are onto me," said Asa.

"I know. We all got suspended. That's why we're not in school."

"Who squealed?"

"Steve."

"I figured he was the weak link. It was worth it though."

"What did the police say?" I asked.

"They told me to appear before a judge tomorrow morning. If they throw me in jail for a few weeks don't worry about it. Can't be any worse than sitting around this dump."

"Did you get a chance to check on the murder investigation?" asked Mark.

"Made a few phone calls," said Grandpa Asa. "On my first call, they connected me to somebody who claimed to be a detective. He said he was in charge of the investigation and had about as much energy as a road-killed deer. Sounded like he hadn't done a thing since finishing up at the crime scene the day after the murder."

"Did they find any evidence?" asked Mark.

"Hell no! No fingerprints, no bullets, no shell casings, no witnesses. I asked him if he had any suspects and he said they were investigating someone. I don't believe him."

"What about the autopsy report?" asked Mark.

"I didn't get that far yet." Grandpa looked out the window, then back at me and Mark. "You boys want ice cream?"

18

By the time I got home, I was hungry again. As I parked my bike in the garage, the smells of something good drifted out of the kitchen through the screen door and found my nostrils. Was Sally cooking supper? It had to be her because I knew for sure that it wasn't Mom.

I walked inside and found Mom sitting between two women at the kitchen table like a corn stalk between two boulders. Another lady was standing at the stove. They were the same three women who had helped after Dad's funeral. The two big ones, Mrs. Samuelson and Mrs. Weiden, wore flowered dresses with aprons and filled up their chairs completely. The skinny one, Mrs. Stevens, resembled a length of twine as her hips sort of shimmied like a kid with a Hula-Hoop while she stirred a big kettle of brown stuff and another steaming pot of something else at the same time. A loaf of homemade bread cooled in a basket on the counter. *Holy smokes!* I thought . . . *The church ladies! They came!*

"Hello, Del," said the biggest one. Her puffy, pink face glowed like the full moon and she had a voice like Popeye the Sailor Man.

"Hi, Mrs. Samuelson." I couldn't keep from smiling. The cavalry had arrived.

"We just stopped to say hello to Dorothy. Mrs. Weiden and Mrs. Stevens suggested that we bring a few things for supper. Do you like chili and corn?"

"Yes, ma'am."

Mrs. Stevens lowered her gaze and spotted my filthy clothes.

"You better get out of those pants," she said. "Kick your shoes off and run upstairs. Tell your sister to come down while you're at it. Supper's ready in five minutes."

I looked at my mom and noticed that she wasn't wearing her usual pajamas. I imagined her trying to chase away the church ladies but giving up and changing clothes after losing the battle. Mom gave me the signal with her eyes to do as I was told and go upstairs.

"I'll be right back!" I practically shouted the words. Mom gave me a suspicious look and I realized that I should have dialed back the enthusiasm.

I gulped the food like a half-starved lion—three helpings of chili, a full scoop of corn, and about half of the loaf of bread. Even Sally dove into the delicious meal, although she kept looking at me like I was guilty of some new crime. Mom did okay, nibbling here and there and managing to eat a bowl of chili. Through it all though, she kept glancing at her pack of cigarettes on the counter like it held the golden ticket to Wonka's chocolate factory.

"Your mother has agreed to help us with the church rummage sale on Friday," said Mrs. Samuelson, with a smile as big as the backyard. "Isn't that right, Dorothy?"

"Yes." Mom looked like a mouse in the shadow of a great horned owl.

"It'll be fun," said Mrs. Samuelson. "You'll see." She gave Mom a playful tap on the shoulder that nearly knocked her out of the chair.

Mom pretended to smile, then glanced at me again. It was a look that said, *I'll get you for this.*

"Dorothy's going to help us with the bake sale too, isn't that right, dear?"

"Yes."

"What did you say you would bring, Dorothy?"

"Peanut butter cookies."

"Goodness," said Mrs. Samuelson. "I can hardly wait to taste them."

I chewed and listened and glanced around the table. Sally had her eyes aimed at me like laser beams. *You better not rope me into this,* they seemed to say. I quickly shifted my eyes back to Mrs. Samuelson.

When the meal was done, after ice cream and coffee, Mom finally managed to shepherd the church ladies to the front door. I tried hard not to grin, but on the inside I felt like the shah of Iran.

"We'll see you in a few days, Dorothy," Mrs. Samuelson said.

"Yes, of course," said my mom. "Thank you for visiting."

"It was our pleasure." She hugged her like a wrestling bear. Mrs. Weiden gave her shoulders a gentle squeeze, and Mrs. Stevens simply waved her spatula on the way out.

The door was almost shut when Mrs. Samuelson pushed it back open.

"I almost forgot the most important thing of all," she said. Her eyes landed on me. "Good news for you, Del. I've spoken with Pastor Olson and together we're going to help you get caught up in confirmation class. We'll see you this Saturday at nine o'clock."

The chili and corn took a turn in my stomach. What had just happened? None of this was supposed to be about me. My mom looked me over with a *gotcha* smile that was rooted in a mixture of satisfaction and revenge. Mrs. Samuelson smiled and pulled the door shut with a clunk. Mom made a dash for her cigarettes.

❁

The next morning, Mom and I picked up Grandpa Asa and drove him to the courthouse in Oshkosh for his appearance before the judge.

"Be polite and respectful, Dad," said my mom to Grandpa. "Maybe they'll go easy on you."

He just gazed out the window as the choppy, gray waters of Lake Winnebago passed by. True to his nature, Grandpa Asa was neither polite nor respectful. He refused to admit anything and shot his mouth off to the judge every chance he got. It was almost like he *wanted* to go to jail.

"I have a good mind to find you in contempt," said the judge.

"What's stopping you?" asked Asa.

The judge banged the gavel hard on his desk. "That's a two hundred dollar fine."

Grandpa Asa stared him down. "I'm not paying a nickel," he said.

None of it worked out well for Grandpa. The judge tossed him in the Winnebago County Jail for thirty days, one day for his part in the Volcano incident and twenty-nine days for contempt of court. The sentence was to start immediately. The bailiff took him away in cuffs, just like one of the bad guys on *Dragnet*.

Mom looked right at me and seemed about ready to die. Her eyes were red and watery and her skin, a pale gray. "This is your fault," she said in a voice that sounded eighty years old.

I dropped my head and we walked to the car. Neither of us said anything all the way home. After we got there I ran to my room, shut the door, and fell in the corner like a bag of dirt. Maybe Sally was right about me. Maybe I should have crawled back into that hole on the Menasha football field and just stayed there. I was a juvenile delinquent all right, and now my elderly grandpa was paying for my crime. My thoughts went to movie scenes with dark cells, iron bars, and rats crawling on the floor. I imagined meals of stale bread, water, and no ice cream—ever.

I cried myself sick and finally puked in the toilet. Then I walked downstairs to talk to my mom. I couldn't see her but heard her quietly sobbing, so I changed my mind. I walked out the door and found my stack of 232 Hoot Owls waiting for me. Rain had started to fall. I sat on the cement under the porch roof and started rolling and banding Hoot Owls. It would be a long, cold ride.

19

I woke up the next morning wishing my life was just a bad dream, and quickly realized that it wasn't. Dad was still dead. Grandpa Asa was still in jail. Mom was lying in bed, and Sally was pretending I didn't exist. To top it off, I was cold, hungry, and facing day three of my suspension as a juvenile delinquent. I looked out the kitchen window. The slate-colored sky and drizzle fit my mood. A yellow school bus rumbled past my house and picked up some kids at the corner. It would soon be moving on to pick up Opal Parsons, who surely wouldn't be talking to *me* ever again once she learned I had been suspended. *Cripes!* Who the heck was I kidding, thinking she could be my girlfriend? Even her mom would hate me once she heard the news.

I opened the fridge and spied the pan of leftover chili. *Thank you, church ladies.* My stomach gave a little groan as I heated it up, stirring until it bubbled and splattered little drops all over the stovetop. I wiped up my mess, sat down at the table, and scooped the steaming chili into a bowl. In the cupboard I found some Saltine crackers, which I crumbled on top. I stirred up a glass of Tang, cut a thick slice of bread, and slathered it with butter.

Five minutes later I felt okay again. I slipped out through the screen door, careful not to let it slap shut. In the garage, I grabbed a shovel and a tin can out of the garbage and proceeded to dig up worms from the moist soil in the area that had once been Mom's flower garden. A few minutes later I was sailing across the bridge by the hospital. Just then the sun peeked out from behind the clouds.

I decided to fish for mooneyes, but I'm not sure why. They were neither big nor common. On top of that, they were only good to eat if you smoked 'em, and I wasn't set up for that with Dad gone. The dock behind the Neenah library was the best spot I knew of for mooneyes, so instead of turning left on Wisconsin Avenue, I wheeled right, behind the public library, and slammed on the brakes.

Dang! Somebody was in my spot. I stopped and just stood there, straddling my bike. Without even seeing his face, I could tell that he was poor. He wore a coat so raggedy that the collar was halfway torn off and the elbows worn through such that the cream-colored insulation was falling out. He wore a hunting cap with the flaps folded down over his ears, but it was in rough shape too. And for a fishing pole? *Shoot.* The man held nothing more than a willow stick with a string tied to the end, and it wasn't proper monofilament fishing line either. *Good grief!* The guy was fishing with kite string. With a rig like that, his chances of catching a mooneye were in the neighborhood of zero percent.

For a second I contemplated a U-turn. My cowardly instincts had always told me to get away from people like this man. Nothing good could come out of it. And what if he wanted to talk?

Just as I was fixing to jump on the pedals and peel out of there, the man looked directly at me. It startled me as he turned his gaze on me with dark eyes that reflected nothing back. His skin was dark too, like an Indian. *Holy smokes*, I thought. *He is an Indian.* My mind recalled the rumor I had heard on my Hoot Owl route about an Indian living on the island somewhere near the train tracks.

"Plenty of room for you," he said.

Great. I'll look like a jerk if I leave now. Not knowing what else to do, I propped Eisenhower up against a tree and slowly walked out on the dock.

"You can fish off the right side," said the Indian.

I shrugged my shoulders, acting cool like I didn't care one way or the other, and sat down just an arm's length away.

I dug into my bait can for a worm. It squirmed wildly as I cut it in half with my thumbnail and stabbed it twice through with the hook. I had left a half inch dangling—the perfect way to attract those fussy mooneyes. With a flip of my wrist on my spin-casting rig, the baited hook and bobber sailed out thirty feet and the sinker pulled it down to a preset depth of six feet that I had memorized from previous visits.

I watched the bobber with anticipation. *Come on, fish. I'm ready.* Five minutes came and went and I casted to a new spot. In the meantime, I kept an eye on the Indian. He twitched the bait occasionally. *Yeah, yeah. Nothing new there*, I told myself. Then the guy got a bite and pulled in a ten-inch mooneye by dragging the string in hand over hand. I redoubled my focus and cast my bait in a new spot. Well danged if he didn't catch another mooneye two minutes later on that same, crude fishing rig.

He looked at me and smiled. Then the Indian reached in his pocket and pulled out something that looked like a tiny white flake.

"Put this on your line right above the hook," he said.

He handed me the object and I could see that it shimmered like a pearl on one side, reflecting faint shades of pink and yellow. It was no bigger than the fingernail on my pinky and had a tiny hole on one edge. The thing looked like it was made from clam shell.

"Thanks," I said.

I may have been a stubborn mule about some things, but when it came to catching fish I used whatever worked. I tied the clam shell decoration near the top of my hook and cast the line back out to my spot.

Right away the bobber twitched a couple times and finally went under. I set the hook and cranked on the reel. With a splash, I pulled up the wriggling nine-incher, a shimmering bar of pure silver. The eye was a big golden circle around a black dot that took up practically the entire head of the fish.

My plan was to toss the mooneye back, but then I considered my new acquaintance. For everything I had learned about Indians, and that includes movies, books, and even a drive through the Menomonie Reservation, I had never actually known one.

"Do you want it?" I asked.

"Sure."

I dropped the fish in his metal pail. He responded with a nod, then stoically faced the river again.

I couldn't help but study the man. Close up, he was a puzzle—hard edged like stone around his eyebrows and chin—soft and curved like deer leather around the mouth and nose. With his eyes on the horizon he looked like a warrior. When he dropped his gaze to the water, it felt like maybe he could be my friend.

From that point I had a mission. I started by cutting the worms down to thirds to extend the life of my bait and even asked the man if I could fix up his willow branch with monofilament and a properly sized hook. He was happy to accept the improvements, and right away started getting even more bites. Between the two of us the bucket filled up, and by the time the clock tower at city hall rang noon, the man's pail was dang-near brimming.

"Time for me to go," I said.

He gave a little wave.

I was feeling pretty good as I picked up Eisenhower and prepared to wheel away. Then something nudged me to ask the man a question I had been wondering about.

"Where do you live?"

Without looking, he pointed across the water. "On the island," he said.

"I'm Del," I said. "What's your name?"

The Indian turned his head and looked directly at me. Those black eyes weren't empty any more. They blasted me with an electricity that was neither anger nor frustration, like the man was trying to figure me out.

"Why do you want to know my name?" he asked.

I shrugged. "No reason."

"Wolf," he said.

"What?"

"My name is Wolf."

As I pedaled across the bridge my mind was a whirlpool of questions. If he lived on the island, why hadn't I seen him? Where was his home, exactly? What tribe was he from? How long had he been here? I looked back over my shoulder and saw him stand up from his place on the dock, pick up the pail of mooneyes and his makeshift pole, and start walking.

I skidded to a stop on the other side of the bridge and ducked behind one of the spruce trees along the edge of Theda Clark Hospital. I would follow the Indian and figure out where he lived. For all I knew he could be on my Hoot Owl route. Curiosity burned inside me. I just had to know.

As Wolf walked across the bridge I watched through the branches. He turned into the park and walked along the river's edge before climbing and crossing the railroad tracks. I jumped on Ike and followed. At the top of the embankment, I caught sight of him just as he approached a pile of abandoned railroad ties. I watched from behind a clump of brush as he scanned the horizon and climbed into a hole beneath the pile.

"Holy smokes," I whispered.

As I skidded to a stop in my driveway, I was full of the excitement that comes with having a secret. On the one hand, it felt good to know that I did a good deed, helping Wolf catch a bucket full of fish. On the other hand, I had no business spying on the guy.

My thoughts skittered around like a pond full of water bugs as I pulled down the garage door.

❈

The sting of cigarette smoke hit my nose and eyes before I even opened the screen door. I let it smack shut so Mom would know I was back.

"Is that you, Del?"

"Hi, Mom. Should I heat up some leftover chili for you and me?"

"Sure," she said.

I almost had a heart attack, but in a good way. Mom was going to eat a meal with me? She walked into the kitchen. *Holy kamoly*, she wasn't wearing pajamas. Mom had dressed in a nice pair of gray pants and a navy-blue shirt and she even had her hair fixed up fancy.

"Mom!"

"What?"

"You look great!"

She tried not to smile but couldn't hold it back. "I told Mrs. Samuelson that I would help out at the church rummage sale today."

"Sounds like fun," I said.

She rolled her eyes, then pointed a finger at me. "Tomorrow it's your turn," she said.

"What do you mean?"

"Confirmation."

Now my eyes were rolling. I *really* didn't want to go to confirmation. It was worth it though—a fair trade. *Thank you, church ladies!*

❈

Mom was already gone when Mark called after lunch, itching to snoop around some more out on Highway 41. He hinted at us borrowing Grandpa Asa's truck. I actually thought about it for a second because I knew where the spare key was hidden under a rock. In the end I told Mark that if we went there, it would have to be on bikes. He grumbled but finally agreed. Then he reminded me that he wanted to use my neighbor's metal detector.

Crap! I thought to myself. First it was Mrs. Borger, then Mom and the church ladies, then Wolf behind the library. Now I was bugging Mr. Johnson to borrow his metal detector. All this dealing with grown-ups was practically killing me.

I rapped gently on the door. Mr. Johnson worked shifts at the Banta Mill and if he *was* home, I worried that I might be waking him up. I heard heavy footsteps on a wood floor—definitely not those of his wife. Mr. Johnson's eyes got big when he saw me.

"Why aren't *you* in school?"

"I got in a little trouble and they gave me three days off."

He nodded and gave me one of those *been there myself* looks.

"Would you mind if I borrowed your metal detector? A friend of mine is looking for something that was lost."

If it had been Mrs. Johnson I'm pretty sure she would have asked about a hundred questions. Who was the friend? What was lost? Where did we lose it? That and everything else that I didn't want to get into. Mr. Johnson, on the other hand, just shrugged his shoulders.

"Sure," he said. "Put it up against the garage when you're done." In case you haven't figured it out already, Mr. Johnson was a pretty good guy.

❋

Getting to the crime scene on Highway 41 by bicycle while carrying a metal detector was tougher than we thought. For one thing, it was almost an hour away from my house. For another thing, it was technically illegal to ride bikes on Highway 41, since it was a four-lane road. The hardest thing, though, was carrying that clunky metal detector that weighed about twenty pounds. Mark and I took the lake road toward Oshkosh, then zigged west on County G and bombed the last couple miles on the 41 shoulder to get to the billboard that marked the spot. We were gassed by the time we got there, so we ditched our bikes in the corn and flopped down in the grass until our hearts quit pounding. Then we got to work.

"We're looking for the brass casing from one of the bullets," Mark said.

He turned on the battery-powered detector and started swinging it side to side as he walked the grassy area along the highway. That sounded easy, but it wasn't. The ground was uneven, and the detector ring kept getting hung up in the goldenrod and milkweed plants. I started stomping down the weeds in front of Mark as he moved along. After a long twenty minutes we finally got our first beep signal. I dug around with my pocket knife and found the pull tab from a beer can that had been buried for about a thousand years. Then it was back to stomping weeds and swinging the detector back and forth again.

After a while, Mark worked his way out of the weeds and onto a patch of bare ground. Since Mark didn't need my help anymore, I decided to snoop around again where we had found the cigarette butt. I walked through the corn toward the big posts that held up the Fine Dining billboard. Just like last time, I got down on my hands and knees, feeling under the weeds with my fingertips.

I felt the object before I saw it. Something very smooth, unlike the hundreds of stones and pebbles that my fingers had touched. I picked it up and brought the thing close to my face. It was a black plastic button about the size of a quarter with four holes in a square pattern. When I held it up to the light and looked closer, I noticed that it had a white streak running through it. It had to be a coat button. I tightened my fist around it and walked back to the edge of the road where Mark had just clicked off the metal detector.

"Bummer," said Mark. "All that work for nothing."

"Maybe we should go further along the highway," I said.

"Maybe, but where do we stop?"

I shrugged.

"Let's try something else," said Mark. "The killer must have picked up all the casings. Let's see if we can find one of the actual bullets."

I sort of cringed at the thought. "The bullets that killed my dad?"

"They had to end up somewhere."

"But will the detector even find lead bullets?"

"Maybe not," said Mark. "But if they were the kind with a copper jacket, then it might still work."

"Where should we look?"

Mark squinted his eyes and scrunched up his face as he looked all around.

"If the person was hiding where we found the cigarette butt the other day, and he was shooting toward the road, then a bullet could end up on the other side," said Mark.

We both looked across the highway and saw the raised bed of the Soo Line tracks.

"I know it's a long shot," said Mark. "But, I think a bullet could be in that embankment."

"We came all the way out here," I said. "Let's try it."

Mark and I dodged traffic as we ran with our bikes across the highway. The button was still pinched between my thumb and finger. *Should I tell Mark about this?* I didn't know but something felt right about keeping the black button with the white streak as my own personal clue about my dad's murder. I slipped it into the front right pocket of my jeans and caught up with Mark.

We had been searching for over an hour, finding everything from rusty nails to bottle caps to aluminum chewing gum wrappers, but no bullet. On top of being tired and hungry, we were all scratched up from thistles, and the sun was getting low.

"Five more minutes," said Mark.

At that very moment the detector beeped again, and I started digging on hands and knees. On my first scrape with my jackknife blade, something shiny and copper-colored popped out from the dirt. Whatever it was, the thing was all bent up and smooshed, not round and pointed like a bullet.

"What is it?" I asked.

Mark studied it, up close to his face. "A bullet," he said quietly. He turned it over and over in his fingers. "It's all smashed up from impact, but it's a bullet."

We had found the needle in the haystack, as they say. So did we jump around and celebrate like the Packers winning the NFL Championship? Did we slap each other on the back and whoop it up? Nope, we didn't.

In my hand, I was holding the thing that had killed my dad. As you can probably imagine, I didn't feel anything like celebrating. I slid the bullet into my right front pocket alongside the button. My thoughts shifted all of a sudden to Grandpa Asa still sitting in the county jail. Mark and I rode home together but hardly even talked.

It was dark when I quietly closed the screen door and snuck upstairs. I dropped that bullet and the button into the Eskdale gallon-sized milk bottle with the metal handle. They lay in the bottom along with the cigarette butt and the taped-together scraps of yellow paper. And no, I wasn't going to show any of it to Sheriff Heiselmann.

20

Saturday morning started off good. Mom fixed me up some scrambled eggs and sausage patties. Could you believe that? Well, it was true. And she had bought us two cans of real orange juice concentrate, which I mixed up with tap water in a plastic pitcher. The next thing I knew I was eating a breakfast fit for the sultans of Zanzibar. The best part was that Sally stayed in bed and Mom ate with me and she sipped her coffee and didn't smoke any cigarettes while we just sat there and talked. Then Mom said the words that brought it all to a screeching halt.

"Your confirmation class starts today."

If you've never been to a confirmation class and have a choice in the matter, I have four words for you: Run-For-Your-Life.

Do you remember how, in Sunday church service, Pastor Olson talked about the Battle of the Bulge and wondered why God let it happen? Remember how I was on the edge of my seat, and couldn't wait to hear the answer? Remember how he had the guts to say *I don't know?* Confirmation class was nothing like that.

In confirmation class it was all a lot of memorize this and recite that. It was like all the mysteries about God had been already figured out and it was all just a matter of filling in the blanks on the mimeographed worksheets. Don't get me wrong. Mrs. Doppler was nice, and she was just following the workbook, but I'm pretty sure she had never seen Buchenwald or been on the Poygan Marsh at sunrise.

Anyhow, my first day in confirmation lasted three hours and I survived. I did the math. A person only gets about four thousand Saturday mornings in a lifetime. One of mine had just been yanked away from me and I wasn't ever getting it back.

Back home, I spent the entire afternoon working. Anybody with two eyeballs could see that our house and yard were heading for the toilet and something had to be done. In the olden days, Dad used to take charge of that sort of stuff. I figured that now it was up to me. I raked and bagged the leaves and piled them along the north side of the house just like Dad had shown me. Then I took down the window screens and sprayed them clean with water before storing them for the winter in the garage. In their place, I put in all the storm windows and, believe me, they weren't easy to hoist up that ladder and clip in position by myself. I washed them all too, with soapy water and a squeegee. It felt good doing all of that, and I went to bed as tired as an old, worn-out plow horse.

✳

My bedroom clock showed a time of one in the morning when a sound woke me up. I recognized the music right away as the Glen Miller album from my dad's collection and snuck down the steps to peek into the living room. My parents had always been good dancers, but the sight of Mom dancing alone with her arms wrapped around a pillow gave me a sad, hollow feeling. It was a sorrowful thing, watching her sway back and forth with her eyes closed and her head tipped a little bit to the side. My God, I had never realized how lonely she was until that exact moment. Mom moved in an oval around the couch, following dance steps she had probably memorized since her teenage years. The loose folds of her nightgown swayed with each step. Her stocking feet floated over the floor like two little white clouds.

Maybe I made a sound because when Mom's eyes cracked open they caught me on the stairs by the banister. She just smiled and gave a little hand wave of embarrassment.

"Don't stop," I said. "Keep dancing."

"You come here and dance with me, then," she said.

I walked down the remaining steps, and as I got close to her she took my left hand in hers and showed me where to put my right hand on her back.

"This one is a waltz," she said. "It's easy. Just follow the three step beat."

Together we synchronized our steps. One-two-three, one-two-three, one-two-three. It was easy, just like she said, and before long Mom and I were dancing that oval path around the couch and making little circular swirls along the way. When the waltz was finished another song came on.

"This one has four beats to the measure," she said. "Let me show you how to foxtrot." I don't mean to brag, but I caught on quick. At first we did the basic step, but then Mom taught me how to change direction and add some spins.

"My goodness, Del, you're a natural," she said, smiling.

"I never knew it was so much fun," I answered.

"Well, now you do."

Just to be clear, what made it easy for me was my mom. You see, Mom was no ordinary dancer. She was a wonderful dancer. I imagined in my mind how she and Dad must have looked on the floors of the big dance halls where they used to go with friends on Saturday nights. I could see them twirling and floating across the floor. That was before Mom got hit by multiple sclerosis, of course, and before Dad got dropped down to working the graveyard shift.

We danced to every song, Mom and me, on both sides of that record album. Then Mom put on another and we did it all over again. Whatever weariness I felt from hefting those storm windows was gone. As long as I was seeing that little smile I was happy to keep going and going. The chime on our mantle clock clanged three times, and Mom finally said that she'd had enough.

"Thanks, honey," she said. "I needed that."

"Good night, Mom. I needed it too."

❈

I slept late, skipped church, and ducked out with my fishing pole and a leftover smile still on my face from my private dance party with Mom. It didn't matter to me where I fished so I let Eisenhower lead the way, and he took me toward the old railroad bridge on Little Lake Butte des Morts, which I hadn't visited in a few months.

I parked Ike behind some bushes and listened hard for any sign of oncoming trains. Then I scurried out on the tracks until I was a hundred yards out from shore and shimmied down to one of the big concrete footings that supported the bridge and allowed the Fox River to flow underneath. Then it was just a matter of pinching on a split shot sinker, hooking up a worm, and chucking the whole works out into the current.

The bullheads came and went in schools, sometimes biting steadily and sometimes disappearing for a half hour at a time. During one of those lull periods, a slow-moving freight train rumbled out on the tracks and stopped dead. Any worries about having my fishing spot invaded by others went away after that. I caught a couple dozen bullheads and threw all but the three largest ones back in the lake. Once the train rumbled off, I took advantage of the opening and made a run for home, where I cleaned and fried the fish for Sally, Mom, and me for lunch. Sally turned up her nose, and made a peanut butter and jelly sandwich instead. But Mom ate the fish with me and I could see that, like me, she still had a little smile on her face from the night before.

After lunch the two of us sat together at the kitchen table. She sipped coffee and read her *Reader's Digest* magazine. I listened to the Packers game on the transistor radio and paged through all three hundred pages of my Herter's outdoor products catalog. I could spend hours salivating over the endless pictures of hunting, fishing, and camping supplies. From tents to duck skiffs to fish hooks of every size, they had it all. Along the way, I kept one ear glued to the play-by-play announcer. In the end, I ordered nothing from the catalog and the Packers beat the Bears by six with our great running back, John Brockington, leading the way.

Was it possible? Could our lives actually be shifting back to normal again?

❋

The next thing I knew my alarm clock was going off again. Monday morning. Time to think about school again.

After brushing my teeth and getting dressed, I pulled a box out of my closet. The size 4 Eaglewing steel-toed boots with the reinforced shank looked like a pair of living things. They even smelled alive. I pushed my thumb against the toe and it felt like solid granite. I knew what they could do because I had practiced in the garage, breaking boards and putting a few new dents in our trash cans. The boots came all the way up over my ankles, and when I pulled my pant cuffs down over the top nobody would even know that I was wearing lethal weapons.

At the bus stop no one paid any attention to me. Didn't they know that I was the kid coming back after a three-day suspension? The brakes screeched like always, and the red-haired, gum-chewing lady pulled the door open on the bus so we could all pile on board. I picked out an open seat and sat in the middle to save a spot for Opal Parsons. Two stops later, through the bus window, I saw her waiting in her light-blue jacket with a white headband around her puffy hair. She climbed on the bus. I waved and smiled. She looked right at me but didn't wave back—didn't even smile. She slid into a seat in the second row. Suddenly, I was staring at the back of her head, and there was no sense saving the seat anymore.

I knew that it might happen that way but had convinced myself that it wouldn't. Apparently, after a three-day suspension some people figured I had turned into a bad apple, not all the way rotten, but pretty bad and not worth keeping. Maybe I was on track to turn into a dirtball. Not too long ago an adult might say, "Hey, there's Del Finwick. He's a pretty good kid." Not any more—I was bad news all of a sudden—a kid to be avoided—a bad apple.

Even though the Earth still spun on its axis like it had for four billion years, my place in the universe of Shattuck High was on a whole new orbit. I droned through the day, neither listening nor speaking much to anyone. Luckily, I didn't have English class, so at least I could put off the humiliation of Opal finding a new place to sit on the other side of the room. I was behind in every class, and since nobody liked me anymore it didn't matter. I had a math test the next day but I just left all my books in the locker. I hung out in the study hall, where nobody studied, and never once set foot in the Science Resource Center, where Mrs. Schwartz used to smile at me just about every day. At last, the final bell sounded and I began my foot-dragging hike toward home, because I sure as heck wasn't about to ride the stupid bus.

21

Tuesday morning the gray sky delivered snow pellets and a cold, north wind. Breakfast consisted of Froot Loops and toast because we were out of Pop-Tarts. At least the jug of orange juice I had mixed up from concentrate was still partly full, so I gulped down a glass. Sally had already left for Armstrong and Mom was asleep. The announcer on WNAM reminded everybody that it was Election Day, and that folks should get out and do their civic duty. Lots of people had posted signs in their front yards, and it seemed like two-thirds of them cheered for Nixon and only a few for McGovern.

My mind drifted away from the election. In just a few hours I would be in English class with Opal ignoring me again. It would be a gut buster but I had to get through it. In the meantime I had made the decision to go back to riding my bike to school. There was no sense putting up with riding the bus if Opal wasn't even going to sit next to me.

While locking my bike to the apple tree, I wondered if it was still okay with the Schnells now that I had a suspension stuck to my permanent record. Randy sure wouldn't care, but his parents? Well, they were another question.

As I jogged around the corner of the Schnell's garage two arms grabbed me from behind and spun me. It was that dickface, Larry Buskin, and he wasn't smiling. His big hands grabbed the collar of my jacket, and he jerked me up and toward him. He pushed my head back with the crown of his forehead.

"Well, if it isn't my old pal, Minnow. Seems we've got some catching up to do."

His stinky cigarette breath practically gagged me and made me turn my head away. I struggled to bust free but with every twist, Buskin tightened his grip.

"Leave me alone," I yelled.

I made an attempt to sprint away from the goon but couldn't get any traction. As I continued to squirm out of his grip he just spun me around again like a puppet and locked me into a standing wrestling hold with my back toward him. I glanced down at the Eaglewings on my feet. They were ready. I was ready. It was time to make my own luck. All I needed was a straight shot.

I writhed and lurched, getting nowhere. In the meantime, he maneuvered my arms until he had me hooked with both elbows behind my back. Everything was backward. I was the good guy, yet Buskin had me in a bent-elbows lock like he was a cop putting me under arrest. I had seen the move a hundred times on *Mod Squad* but didn't realize until now how painful it was. *Jeez!* My elbows and shoulders were getting ripped right out of their sockets.

Dammit all! I'm supposed to be winning this fight.

"I need a couple dollars, Minnow. Are you going to help me out today?"

"No!"

"Just a buck then."

"No!"

I twisted and squirmed. *Dammit!* He just wrenched harder on my already pretzel-twisted arms. The next thing I knew I was off the ground and gasping for air. Suddenly, he released one of his hands and shoved it in my front pocket where I had my lunch money. He pulled out my dollar bill.

"Thanks, Minnow. I knew you'd come through for me. Next time just hand it over."

Buskin finished me off by spinning me around and tripping me with his leg as he slammed me to the gravel driveway. My back hit hard. My head slammed even harder as bright, twinkling lights appeared before my eyes. I sprang to my feet, ready to run but not sure which way. I tried to focus my eyes in the direction of the school as the flashing stars faded away. What I saw was two of everything, including two Larry Buskins trotting away. I dropped to my knees again, trying to gather what wits I had left. After a while, I made it back to my feet and shuffled like an old man into the main entrance of the school building, just barely making it to homeroom.

Mrs. Willison looked at me.

"Are you okay, Del?"

I couldn't answer. My head throbbed like I was going to throw up all over myself and the desk. I must have passed out because, when I opened my eyes again, my head was half-submerged in a bag of ice and two eyes stared back at me from about twelve inches away. Miss Puckett, the school nurse, had a very worried look on her face.

"How did this happen?" she asked.

"I fell on my bike."

"Are you sure? You hit hard on the back of your head and everything else is fine. That's not consistent with a bicycle accident."

"I fell on my bike." She frowned and turned quiet. No way was I changing my story. My thoughts went to Grandpa Asa sitting in jail. He sure didn't need to learn that my hypothetical friend was such a wimp that he got beat up and robbed while wearing the Eaglewing steel-toed boots. So much for the puny nerd who thought he could make his own luck.

22

The doctor said I had a bad concussion and sent me home for what was supposed to be a week of resting in bed. *Another whole week?* I had barely returned from my three-day suspension.

The double vision went away pretty quick, but my head hurt something awful. It felt like my brain was the bell in the Neenah clock tower clanging over and over again. On top of that, I couldn't eat anything without puking it back up, and when I finally could keep something down it was only a few soda crackers. By the time I could stand again without feeling dizzy, my body had skinnied up so bad that Mom had to punch two new holes in my belt just to keep my pants up. In my desperate desire to grow bigger and stronger, I was headed in the exact opposite direction.

Believe it or not, there was a bright side to getting thrashed by Larry Buskin. I found out that I still had friends. Mark had heard about it somewhere, and since he was suspended and living out of his hideout anyhow, he came over every day. It was good for him to get inside a warm house. It was good for me just to have somebody to talk to. Mark knew right away that I hadn't been in any bicycle accident.

"Was it Buskin?" he asked.

"Yes, but don't tell anybody." I said.

"I won't."

"And don't do anything about it."

"Why not? Somebody needs to thrash the creep."

"It's just something I have to figure out on my own."

Mark nodded. "You want me to get your bike?"

"Crap. I forgot about that." I gave Mark the combination so he could go get Eisenhower back from Randy Schnell's house.

Mom correctly assumed that Mark would be with us for a few days, so she bought a stack of TV dinners at Food Queen and rolled out a sleeping bag on the floor of my bedroom. Someone else rang the doorbell just before suppertime on Wednesday. I recognized the voice right away in the front hall. *Holy crap!* It was Mrs. Borger. Mom led her right up the stairs to my room and shut the door. Maybe she was going to yell at me for missing class. Maybe she was going to punish me with more stupid questions about William Shakespeare. She looked at me sternly in my bed, but then she flashed me a huge smile and even gave me a hug. I was pretty sure nobody at Shattuck had ever seen that side of her before.

"How is my church buddy?" she asked.

"Fine." I tried not to smile. She was still my teacher, after all.

"I heard about the *bicycle accident.*" She sort of half-closed her eyes like maybe she knew the truth. "Mrs. Willison tells me you got a pretty big bump on the back of your head."

I rubbed the bump to show her. "It's getting better."

"God is looking out for you," she said.

I wondered about that one. God could have done me a bigger favor by keeping Larry Buskin from pounding me in the first place. Mrs. Borger plopped a stack of worksheets on my bed as well as a brand-new paperback book called *To Kill a Mockingbird.*

"I'm concerned that you'll get behind in your schoolwork," she said. "I brought a few worksheets from me and your other teachers. The book is for our modern fiction unit. It won the Pulitzer Prize. You're going to find it interesting," she said.

I nodded and figured that was about it for the teacher visit, but instead of leaving, Mrs. Borger pulled up a chair, sat down, and started yakking. And do you know what she told me? She said I was one of the nicest and brightest young men in the entire tenth grade at Shattuck. I'm not kidding. She said it, and she knew about my three-day suspension and the volcano and everything. She said I had unlimited potential too, and that I could become a doctor or a lawyer or an engineer or maybe even a civic leader like Mr. Shattuck himself. She said I would make an especially good teacher because I had "a sensibility for the world around me," whatever that meant.

"I have high confidence in you, Mr. Finwick, and if I was a gambler, I would bet on your success. And if you ever need my help along the way, well . . . all you have to do is ask." I soaked it all up. Then she was gone.

As you can imagine, a kid doesn't hear stuff like that said about him every day. Those words would have puffed anybody up, and nobody needed puffing more than me. It was like a whole bunch of my worries washed right down the Fox River, through the Great Lakes, and all the way out to the Atlantic Ocean.

❀

Mark kept coming over every day, and on Thursday afternoon he even delivered my Hoot Owls for me, all 232 of them. When I tried to give him the money, he said I probably needed it more than him and that he was just glad to return the favor for letting him stay over for most of the week.

My last visitor came on Friday. Mark had gone somewhere, and I was just hanging out in my room reading *Ghost Rider* comics after finishing a stack of worksheets for Mrs. Borger. I heard Mom talking to somebody after a knock at the door. It clicked shut and my mom came up the stairs.

"There was a girl on the porch who says she's from your English class," said Mom, looking worried. "She wanted to see you but I said you were too sick. She brought you this." Mom held out a blue envelope and I took it.

"Why didn't you let her come in?"

"She's colored."

"Mom, her name is Opal Parsons. She's my friend."

Mom sucked her lungs full of cigarette smoke and blew a big cloud at the ceiling. Then she put a hand on her hip like she was fixing to give me a speech. I could hear the words in my head already. *There are hundreds of nice white girls in Neenah. I don't know why you're hanging around with Negroes.*

Mom's eyes went to the blue envelope. "Aren't you going to open it?"

"Maybe later," I said.

Mom made a scene, rolling her eyes and shaking her head before stomping down the stairs. Part of me felt angry, but then I remembered all her troubles. On top of that, she was Grandpa Asa's daughter, and I knew that was where her ideas about black people came from in the first place.

I ripped open the envelope. It was a homemade get-well card with a duck drawn in colored pencil on the front.

> Sorry I was mean to you on the bus.
> I'll save your seat in English. Get well soon.
>   Opal

It was time to take my headache pill, and I did, but to tell you the truth, I wasn't sure I needed it anymore.

❋

On Saturday morning I had a temporary relapse of my headaches right around the time that confirmation class was supposed to begin. Mom took the bait and let me stay home.

"Just don't get any ideas about fishing," she said. "If you're too sick for confirmation, you're too sick to go outside."

Mark came over again in the afternoon and we watched *Batman* on TV and played a few games of checkers and chess. He was looking around my room and his eyes landed on the Eskdale wide-mouth gallon milk bottle with the metal handle.

"What's in there?"

"Stuff."

"Like what?"

"Like the bullet, the cigarette butt, and the yellow envelope that Heiselmann got from the Cadillac Man at the point."

Mark pulled out the yellow envelope and studied it. "Maybe these doodles mean something."

"I doubt it," I said.

"You never know. Maybe the sailboats mean he's a member of the Neenah Yacht club. Maybe the basketball player means he has a kid on one of the local teams."

Then Mark held the envelope up to the light and squinted at the fine print along the edge. "Made in U.S.A. by Kensington Paper Company," he said.

"That's no help," I said. "You can probably buy them at a million stores all over the country."

"Maybe it didn't come from a store. Maybe the Cadillac Man works at Kensington Paper Company," said Mark. "I'm pretty sure they've got a mill in Appleton."

"What are we going to do, walk in the front door and ask them who stole a stupid envelope?"

"No, we're going to drive through the parking lot and look for a black Cadillac."

"Huh?"

"You sure we can't get the keys to your grandpa's pickup truck?"

"Not until he gets out of jail."

❁

I managed to sneak out of the house once on Saturday while Mom was getting groceries at the Food Queen. Something had been bugging me all week since I had helped Wolf catch mooneyes behind the library. From my garage I zipped west past the hospital, across First Street and through Island Park, where some old guys were reeling in bullheads along the fence bordering the Fox River. At the tracks I ditched Ike in the weeds and hustled over the embankment. A lightly trampled path led to Wolf's little cave underneath a pile of abandoned railroad ties.

I got down on my knees and poked my head inside. "Hello. Are you in here?"

Silence.

I took my almost-new spin-casting rod and reel and pushed it into the opening along with a small box of sinkers, bobbers, swivels, hooks, and even a couple fishing lures I had scrounged from the river bottom. Then I pulled a sheet of paper out of my pocket and read the note that I had scratched out at home.

YOU MIGHT NEED THIS MORE THAN i DO.

Good grief, I thought. The poor guy didn't even have a house. The least I could do was help him catch his supper.

23

Sunday morning came and, as usual, Mom and Sally slept in late. I sat down at the kitchen table with my Froot Loops and Tang. A stack of newspapers sat on the chair next to me, so I fished through them. Most of the news was about the reelection victory of President Nixon, and the picture showed him smiling and making the V-for-victory symbol with both hands.

Guess who else got reelected. Sheriff Heiselmann, and by a landslide even bigger than Tricky Dick's. Believe it or not, most people in our county really liked the guy. They had their reasons too. Heiselmann was always in the news helping out with civic causes. He volunteered his time for the Save the Clock Tower campaign. He went to schools and the Boys Brigade to teach kids about the dangers of drugs. He even started a fundraiser to feed starving children in Africa. *Gosh*—it seemed like everybody *except* me and Mark thought the sheriff was Mr. Wonderful.

Mom finally came down to the kitchen and she could hardly believe it when I told her I wanted to go to church again.

"It's required for confirmation," I said.

"Hmm . . . Are you strong enough to ride your bike?"

"Yes."

I got there fifteen minutes early so I could meet Mrs. Borger. I grabbed a cookie and looked around. A skinny, bald-headed guy with a white mustache pulled up next to me with a cup of steaming coffee. He had a white shirt and striped tie with a gold tie clip in the shape of a wrench.

"You waiting for Gladys Borger?" he asked.

"Yes."

"She's a nice lady. Always comes by herself. Are you going to sit with her again?"

"Yes, sir."

"Good. I think she gets lonely sometimes. Her husband's not the best egg in the basket, you know."

I thought that was an odd thing to say. "What do you mean?" I asked.

He pantomimed like someone drinking from a bottle.

Just then, Mrs. Borger showed up. She waved, hung up her coat, and scurried over to where I was talking to the bald-headed guy. We all exchanged greetings and I walked with Mrs. Borger down the center aisle. She held onto my elbow just like last time, and the usher directed us into the third pew just as the organist started playing and the choir joined in. Before I knew it, we had said a prayer, sung two hymns, and listened to some words from the Bible. It was time again for Pastor Olson's sermon, and I leaned forward like a bobcat—ears open and mouth shut.

Pastor Olson did it again. While the last sermon had been about how it's hard to understand God, this one was about how it's sometimes hard to even hear Him. This time, instead of talking about war, he talked about the death of his mom. Pastor Olson was just a kid when it happened, and he told us about the empty feeling and how he wondered if his life would ever feel normal again. And guess what. Through all of that grief, right at the time when he needed help the most, God was silent. Not a whisper, not a signal—nothing but stone-cold silence.

Then Pastor Olson told a story. It was about a girl who had lost her pet kitten in the big dusty hayloft of a barn on a day when fresh bales were being stacked inside. A half-dozen men from the hay crew scrounged and searched through the corners and top layers of baled hay, but they never found the little kitten.

"It took the small girl, herself, to finally find the trapped kitten," said the pastor. "And do you know how she did it? She waited until sundown when all the men were gone and the wind quit blowing and everything had gone quiet in the dead of night. Then she lay down perfectly still. All around her there was nothing but silence. And in that silence the girl did one thing and one thing only."

The pastor seemed to lean toward me from over the pulpit and I leaned in toward him. Then he continued.

"The girl listened." Something like a flash-cube went off in my brain. "Only by putting all her energy into listening did she finally hear the weak cries from that little kitten, trapped seven layers down in a gap between hay bales."

I know that Pastor Olson prepared that sermon for the whole congregation, but it sure seemed like that story was made just for me. He was two for two on sermons. I already knew that it was a great average for baseball players and figured that it was pretty darn good for preachers too.

I had another cookie while I waited for Mrs. Borger to drink coffee and chat with about five hundred different people in the fellowship hall. She sure was a nice lady—way nicer than I ever expected during the first week of school when it seemed like she hated my guts. After a good long time, the crowd cleared out. It was now or never.

"Mrs. Borger?"

"Yes, Mr. Finwick?"

"Remember when you said I could ask you for help anytime?"

"Yes, Mr. Finwick."

❋

Monday started off with me sitting next to Opal Parsons again on the bus.

"Are you feeling better? Did you get my card?" she asked.

"Yes," I said. I hoped my smile was enough to say the rest.

"I'm sorry I was mean to you. I was mad because of your suspension from school."

"I guess the volcano wasn't such a great idea."

"I told my dad about it and expected him to get mad at you just like I was. I expected him to call your volcano a dumb idea. Do you know what he said?"

"What?"

"He said it was an ingenious idea."

"He did?" I sat up a couple inches taller. Mr. Parsons? The machine technician? That was a pretty big compliment coming from a man like him.

"Yes. He saw the picture in the paper and loved it. He even taped it to the door on our refrigerator. And do you know what else he said?"

"What?"

"He said it took guts. He told me that there are millions of people who have great ideas but not many with the guts to act on them."

I felt my chest and shoulders rising.

"So I changed my mind," said Opal. "I'm sorry I got mad at you." She touched the back of my hand with hers. It only lasted a few seconds, but she really did touch my hand and there was nothing accidental about it. Maybe, to be honest, I should have told her that it was Steve who came up with the actual *idea* of the volcano. *Oh well*, I thought, *no sense getting all particular about everything.*

For the whole rest of the day it felt like I was riding a magic carpet from class to class. Everybody was nice to me, I handed in all my worksheets, and was caught up again on homework. I even came back to the Science Resource Center, and Mrs. Schwartz was so happy that she winked at me from across the room. It helped, of course, that I hadn't seen Larry Buskin all day. And in case you're wondering—yes—I *was* wearing the Eaglewing steel-toed boots with the reinforced shank.

When the last bell of the day rang out, I flew into Mrs. Borger's classroom, where she was grading papers.

"Are you ready, Mrs. Borger?"

"I guess so."

She packed up her papers and we walked outside to her yellow Chevy Nova. It was kind of a junky car, but then I remembered that teachers didn't get paid like Rockefeller, and the only thing that mattered was that it went down the road. I saw Barry Hattenkoff give me a funny look when I got in the car with Mrs. Borger, but I didn't give a rip.

We picked up Mark at Red Owl and drove past Banta Paper, through Menasha, out on Plank Road and finally north through the countryside to Appleton. At the Fox River, we zigged and zagged through the mill district until we were face-to-face with the tan brick buildings of the Kensington Paper Company. Just like all the rest of the mills, it faced the street on one side and hung out over the river on the back. That old Fox River sure worked hard. All that water power used up. All that wastewater dumped back in, just so we could have paper for writing and reading—even for going to the bathroom.

"There's the parking lot," said Mark.

"And *why* are we interested in the parking lot at a paper mill?" asked Mrs. Borger.

"It has to do with finding the person who murdered my dad," I said.

She looked at me, unsmiling. "Shouldn't the police be helping you instead of me?"

"The police aren't even trying, Mrs. Borger. We think there's something fishy going on. I know this sounds weird, but it feels like the sheriff doesn't even *want* to solve the crime."

"That's ridiculous; everybody knows it was the Highway 41 Killer."

"Who's that?" I asked.

"I most certainly don't know," said Mrs. Borger.

"That's the problem, ma'am, nobody does."

Mrs. Borger nodded her head. "And you think the *real* murderer is employed by the Kensington Paper Company?"

"Maybe."

"Would you like to tell me why, Mr. Finwick?"

"Not really."

"Would you like me to drive through this parking lot, Mr. Finwick?"

"Yes, please."

Mrs. Borger turned left and proceeded slowly down the first aisle toward the river.

"What are we looking for again?" she asked.

"A black Cadillac," said Mark.

We drove back and forth through the rows of cars and probably passed a couple hundred, but not a single Cadillac. Then it occurred to me that paper mill workers didn't actually get paid like Rockefeller either. Since we were in Appleton anyhow, we drove around on the nearby streets on the off chance that we would find the right car. No luck.

"Shall I drive home now, boys?"

"Could we stop one more place?"

"Where?" she asked.

I didn't want to say it, afraid of her reaction. At last, it was Mark who blurted out the words.

"Gordy's Gun Shop," he said.

Mrs. Borger had an opinion and she wasn't shy about sharing it. "Absolutely not!" she said.

A five-minute lecture followed in which she explained that gun shops were not a place for youths to go without their parents and that we had no business entering one for any reason.

"Under no circumstances shall I allow either of you to set one foot in such an establishment," she said. "I suppose you intend to pursue some sort of revenge-driven foolishness with revolvers strapped to your belts and bandoliers of ammunition wrapped around your shoulders like Pancho Villa. I'm surprised at you boys, especially you, Mr. Finwick."

She glared at us with eyes full of lightning. I kept my mouth shut, afraid that I had just washed all of that good will and confidence right down the toilet. It was Mark who finally spoke. "We just want to ask the owner a question," he said.

"What kind of question?"

Mark looked at me. "Show her, Delmar."

I pulled the hunk of copper and lead out of my pocket and held it up between my thumb and index finger. Mrs. Borger loosened her death grip on the steering wheel and pushed her glasses back up on the bridge of her nose.

"And what, pray tell, is that?" she asked.

"That's the bullet that killed my dad."

Her eyes got damp and a shaky hand went to her mouth.

"We want to ask the gun shop man what kind of gun fired it. The police must not have looked very hard at the crime scene. It took me and Mark to go out there and find it."

"You should give it to the sheriff," she whispered.

"That's what we've been trying to tell you, Mrs. Borger. We don't trust the sheriff."

✳

The gun shop man must have weighed three hundred pounds, with eyebrows like pine cones and a gray and brown mustache that covered up his whole mouth. He studied the bullet under a magnifying glass making quiet, groaning noises as he puzzled over the object. He bounced it in his hand and then put it on a small scale.

"It's a .357 Magnum copper-jacketed soft point. Probably 158 grains." The man shifted his tobacco from left cheek to right and leaned on the edge of a glass-covered gun display case. I looked at Mark and he looked at me. Mrs. Borger looked at the ceiling like she couldn't wait to get out of there.

"What kind of gun fired it?" asked Mark.

"Don't know. There's lots of revolvers made for .357 Magnum. Smith & Wesson, Colt, plenty of others. The only way to know if a bullet matches a gun is to have a ballistics expert match them up as a pair."

"How do they do that?"

"They fire a few bullets from the gun into water or some other soft material that won't ruin the bullets. Then they match up the scratch marks on the outside of the bullet made by the chamber and barrel of the gun. It's like a fingerprint, and every gun has one." The man looked again at the bullet. "It's pretty beat up from impact, but a ballistics expert might still be able to match it to a gun."

I looked at Mark. "Do we have any more questions?"

"Just one," said Mark. "If we did want to see if a gun matched the bullet, who could do it for us?"

"The cops, if it's a criminal matter."

"What if we don't want to talk to the cops?"

The gun shop man squinted his eyes and looked us over.

"What are you guys hiding if you don't want to tell the cops? I'm done helping you if you're running from the cops."

"That's not it at all," I said.

"Well, what is it then?" The man was looking pretty tough with his legs spread apart, leaning forward and his eyes sharp and hungry like a hawk.

I decided to spill it all. Without being mean, I looked straight into those hawk eyes with badger eyes of my own. "My dad is the officer who was murdered last month on Highway 41. We found this bullet out where it happened because the cops quit searching a long time ago. We don't trust them. We think they're hiding something."

Right away the man leaned back and his eyes got soft again. Without saying anything, he went through a door to what must have been an office. A minute later he came back and handed me a scrap of paper with a name and phone number.

"Give this guy a call," he said. "He's with the FBI."

Mark looked at me and nodded.

"Thanks, mister," I said.

When we got outside the door, Mrs. Borger let loose a breath of air that I think she had been holding the whole time.

"Can we go home now?" she asked.

24

Another church confirmation class came and went, and all I could think about during those three hours was how the white bass were probably biting at Doty Park. I skidded to a stop in the driveway, leaned Ike against the garage, and walked in the back door. To my surprise, Mom was not only dressed, she was buzzing around like a bee in a clover field, too busy even to smoke.

"Stir this dough," she said. "I've got to fix my hair."

I didn't argue or even take my jacket off. I just got right to work mushing the brown stuff in a big green bowl. It smelled like peanut butter, and then I remembered that she had promised to bring cookies for the church bake sale that was coming up on Sunday morning. The oven timer beeped.

Mom yelled from the bathroom. "Take out the cookies and put them on a cooling rack!"

"Okay, Mom!"

"Then get another batch ready!"

"Okay, Mom!"

"Remember to flatten them out with a fork and set the timer to twelve minutes!"

"Okay!"

Holy smokes! I was busier than a squirrel in a nut factory. I pulled out the hot pan and scraped the cookies onto the cooling racks. Then I glopped out some fresh blobs of dough and squished them down with a fork, first north to south and then east to west. After shoving those into the oven it was back to stirring again.

Mom popped her head in the kitchen to see how I was doing. "Thank you, honey," she said.

"No problem, Mom."

I had batter in my hair, flour all over my pants, and ten fingers full of everything. I was a cookie-making machine running on full throttle, eating one and making a dozen more all at the same time. Mom looked slightly worried at the big mess, but then her eyes landed on the piles of perfect cookies on the cooling racks and she smiled.

"Take a shower, Del. I'll finish up here. We're dropping the cookies off at church and then driving to Oshkosh to visit Grandpa Asa."

"At the jail? Today?"

"Yes."

Holy Toledo!

❄

The jailer was a barrel-shaped guy barely as tall as my mom. Between his keys, radio, cuffs, and other stuff, he jingled with each step as he walked Mom and me back to the visiting room. We sat on metal chairs behind a metal table.

"Wait here," said the man.

Mom and I looked at each other. She tried to smile but it didn't work out, so she looked away and fidgeted with her ring. From somewhere I heard a man yelling. Then a different man yelling back. I was pretty sure neither one was Grandpa Asa because he was too old to yell that loud anymore.

The door opened slowly, and a different, tall and skinny jailer walked Grandpa into the room and helped him sit in the metal chair. I expected him to be wearing striped pants and a striped shirt, but he wasn't. Instead, he had orange pants and a gray sweatshirt. He looked at us and sort of half-smiled like it was all just a game. He was the same old guy.

"Hi, Dad," said Mom. I could tell she wanted to get up and hug him but the jail people told us that there was no touching allowed.

"Hi, sweetheart, everything okay?"

"Sure."

"Hi, Grandpa," I said a little too quietly.

"Del, how we doing?"

"Good."

That's sort of how the whole visit went, mostly quiet talk with Grandpa being the only one who didn't seem sad. There was a lot of "How's this?" and "How's that?" Asa grumbled about the food and the idiots in the jail cells who kept screaming all the time. We talked about stuff that didn't matter, like how the Packers were doing and about Thanksgiving coming up soon. Mom told him we made cookies for the church and about my enrollment in confirmation class. I could tell that Asa didn't really care about those things, but he smiled a little bit.

Toward the end, Grandpa looked hard at me like he was wondering about the important stuff. I could almost hear his brain spinning with questions about what Mark and I had learned about my dad's murder or whether or not the Eaglewing boots had seen any action. Part of me wanted to jump across that table and tell him all about the bullet. Another part of me never wanted him to find out that I got thumped by Larry Buskin.

"Time's up," said the jailer, and we said some speedy good-byes.

"Hang in there, Grandpa," I said.

"Two more weeks," he said. "Then hot fudge sundaes and I'm buying."

I worked the math in my head about those two more weeks. Grandpa would be spending Thanksgiving Day in jail. I didn't say anything.

❋

Mom didn't say much either on the way home. I guess seeing her dad in a jailbird uniform had yanked something out of her. When we got in the house, she sank into a big, soft chair and lit up a cigarette without even turning on the TV.

"I'm going fishing," I said.

There were no words from Mom.

Before heading out the back door, I slipped three cookies into my jacket pocket. In the garage, I looked for my best fishing pole before remembering that I had given it away. I grabbed one of the old ones and a small box of tackle and made my way to Doty Park. Picking a spot was always the first task. I checked with the fishermen along the riverbank. A few perch and white bass flopped in buckets. A few more hung from metal stringers in the river.

I walked to the bridge side of everyone, tied a swivel to my fishing line, and clipped on a yellow-and-silver Cleo. As I worked my way, casting along the shore, a million thoughts raced through my brain. *Is Mom going to get better? Is Mark going to survive living with his father? How much does Opal Parsons like me? Did Sheriff Heiselmann and the Cadillac Man kill my dad?*

The list of things to worry about seemed endless, and I hadn't even got to Larry Buskin or Grandpa Asa yet. I heard a squeal of happiness from a little kid as he pulled a perch out of the river and flopped it onto the grass. For some reason it made me think about Wolf. I jumped on Ike and stood on the pedals, heading toward the hospital and across the bridge. When I turned the corner behind the library I spotted the guy right away wearing the same ratty clothes and shredded hat. I walked out on the dock.

"Hi, Wolf," I said.

He nodded, tapping his hand on the fishing pole that I had given him. "It works good," he said.

Walking up to his bucket, I saw three decent mooneyes and a rock bass and gave the man the thumbs up signal. "What are you using for bait?" I asked. He held up a pickle jar containing a few small leeches in an inch of water. "Where did you find them?"

"Under some rocks along shore."

"Are you having fish for supper tonight?"

"That's the plan."

"Do you have a frying pan?"

He shook his head before turning away. The thought of Wolf trying to cook fish without a pan bothered me. Then I wondered if he was eating them raw and it bugged me even more. I put my hands in my pockets, felt something, and pulled it out. It was one of mom's peanut butter cookies that I had snatched as I left the house.

I walked up and tapped him on the shoulder. "This is for you." He took the cookie, looked at me with those coal-black eyes, and nodded. He took a bite and his eyes closed as he chewed. A gust swirled around the library building and chilled me right through my jacket.

My mind was made up as I wheeled into my driveway at top speed and skidded to a stop in the garage. The camping supplies were on the second shelf. I rummaged through a wooden box and pulled out a heavy, black frying pan with the number 8 molded into the bottom. I found a box of wood matchsticks and a metal spatula too and threw in the little salt and pepper shakers while I was at it. The old sleeping bags were in an army duffel bag. I yanked one out and shoved it inside a dark-green lawn and leaf bag that we used for grass clippings. Before entering the kitchen I peeked through the screen to make sure Mom wasn't in there.

Quietly, I walked in and opened the food cabinet, helping myself to a half-dozen cans of corn, beans, and soup. From a drawer I found an extra crank-style can opener and dropped it in the bag.

It was a heavy load on my bike, but not much different from delivering Hoot Owls. At the train tracks I ditched Ike in the tall weeds, climbed up and over the rails, and followed the trail to Wolf's hiding place. The first thing I noticed was a wire mesh cage holding mooneye carcasses, drying in the cool sunshine. The fish were lined up like miniature soldiers. The bellies had been slit open and the guts removed, but the heads and tails were still attached. I thought it was pretty nifty how Wolf knew how to preserve fish without a freezer. Finally, I bent down and looked into the hole.

"Are you in there, Wolf?" I asked.

No answer. I looked around and saw nobody as I thought about going inside. It was wrong and I knew it but couldn't resist. On my hands and knees I crawled into the small cave. The air smelled stale. An old blanket and three empty brandy bottles lay scattered on the dirt floor. As I inched in further my right hand touched something smooth and soft. What was that fuzzy thing? A mitten maybe? I picked it up for a closer look in the dim light and reality hit me like the blast from the 12 gauge. I dropped the dead rabbit and jerked my head away, banging it into something hard. Panic surged through me, and all I wanted to do was get back out of that cave, but as I tried to back out my butt hit something hard, and I got the sickening feeling that I could be stuck in there—permanently. At last my knees and hands found traction and got me out of the hole. I jumped to my feet, wiped my nose with my sleeve, and tried to brush the dirt off my clothes. Then I shoved the frying pan, sleeping bag, and everything else into the hole and ran away without even leaving a note.

❈

The smell of grilled cheese sandwiches and tomato soup hit me as I walked through the screen door. Mom smiled and gave a little spatula salute. I tried to smile back but my mind was still in that cave with the dead rabbit. For the first time in my life, I really, really, really needed to wash my hands. I scrubbed them with soap all the way up to my elbows and rinsed them off.

Mom sat in her chair at the kitchen table waiting for me when I came out of the bathroom. Just as I was starting to feel normal again, she hit me with a question.

"Will you say grace?"

"Umm . . . sure, Mom."

"Just a few words of thanks for this food and our family," she said. "And could you please include something about Grandpa?"

Just like at the Parsons' house, it wasn't that difficult. I said the words and ended with "Amen."

"Amen," said Mom. She took a big breath and I could see that her eyes were damp.

Mom scooped tomato soup into my bowl first and then her own. We each grabbed a grilled cheese sandwich off the serving plate. It was warm, greasy, and perfect.

"Did you catch any fish today?" asked Mom. I knew she didn't really care but was trying to make small talk.

"No."

"The Green Bay weatherman said we could get snow flurries tonight."

"He did?"

"Yes, and the *Farmer's Almanac* says it's going to be a cold winter."

"That's good for early ice fishing," I said. My mind was still on Wolf in his cave—the dead rabbit, the brandy bottles, the tattered blanket.

After we finished eating, Mom tapped a cigarette out of the pack, lit it, and blew smoke across the kitchen. Her eyes were on the ceiling.

The smoke stung my nose and eyes and I needed to get away from there. I cleared the dishes into the sink and escaped to the quiet and clean air of the garage. Hoses, rakes, and shovels all hung from hooks, every object in its place just like Dad had arranged things. My head rested up against a wooden ladder that hung on two hooks screwed into the wall. I said one more prayer—a silent one. It started out asking God to help Mom get away from those cigarettes and went on to asking for help getting Wolf out of his hole. After that I got selfish and asked something about Opal Parsons, but you don't need to know everything.

❋

Mom was watching Lawrence Welk on TV when I walked past her toward the stairs. Halfway up the steps I paused. Mom leaned in toward the screen, studying the dancers intently as they swayed and twirled.

"Can you dance like that, Mom?"

She looked in my direction, embarrassed to have been caught in a trance. Then she smiled softly and said, "There was a day when I could dance *exactly* like that. Not anymore."

I looked again at the brightly dressed couple swooping all over the stage. The lady's dress flew weightlessly. The man guided her as easily as if he were lifting a twig. They looked into each other's eyes and smiled, obviously having great fun while entertaining millions of people along the way.

"Could you show me how?"

Mom's eyes grew wide and round. "Why are you so interested in dancing all of a sudden?"

I shrugged one shoulder. "It just looks like fun . . . that's all."

"If you want to learn, I'll teach you what I can. I think the Neenah library has music we could check out. Should I pick up a couple records this week?"

"Sure." I smiled at her and she smiled back. Then I went upstairs to my room.

You know that thing I said to my mom about dancing? . . . "It just looks like fun, that's all"? . . . Well, that was actually a white lie. The Shattuck High Snow-Ball dance was coming up in January and, believe it or not, I had ideas about asking Opal to go with me. Imagine that. A stupid, little, scared minnow like me thinking about asking the prettiest girl in the whole school to the dance. Okay, so it was a long shot, and the thought made me nervous, but I still wanted to try.

❈

After the ten o'clock news and a glass of milk, I lay down on my bed and started reading *To Kill a Mockingbird*. Mrs. Borger said we would be working in teams again on the book reports. If I had my way, Opal would be my partner again—dance or no dance.

It didn't take me very long to figure out that *To Kill a Mockingbird* was no ordinary book, and if you haven't read it you should, and that goes for white and black people both. It was especially good for folks like me who never lived anywhere else except the all-white town they were born in. Neenah was like that—like a white cake with white frosting and white sprinkles spread all over the top. Just the thought of a few colored sprinkles getting mixed in made some folks uneasy, like the cake wouldn't be good anymore.

The story in *To Kill a Mockingbird* was about people in a small, Alabama town during the Great Depression. It talked about day-to-day life, but there was a lot more to it than that. Some of the characters practically popped right off the pages, they were so real. The book was sad in some ways and sort of funny and heartwarming in other ways. It was weird, but while reading through the chapters, I kept seeing the faces of people I knew. I saw Opal and her mom and dad in there. And it seemed like Grandpa Asa and Mark and Mrs. Borger were in it too. Even Wolf, in his hole under the railroad ties, was in the book. With all those real characters mixed up with the pretend ones, my brain was practically spinning with every page.

25

In English class on Tuesday I was excited about getting teamed up with Opal again on my *To Kill a Mockingbird* report. Guess what. It didn't exactly work out that way. Mrs. Borger said that everyone had to choose a different partner this time, and if we didn't have a partner by Thursday, she would assign one for us.

Right away, Kathy Marks asked Opal to be her partner. Then football players picked other football players and cheerleaders picked other cheerleaders and dirtballs picked other dirtballs. Well, pretty soon everybody was partnered up except me.

When Thursday came around, I figured I would be doing the book report on my own. Oh well, that wouldn't be the end of the world, and it sure beat getting teamed up with some grit.

Mrs. Borger faced the class in her usual, drill-sergeant stance and cleared her throat. "If you do not have a partner for your book report, raise your hand."

My embarrassed hand went up about as high as my right ear. I looked around the room. Just as I had guessed, mine was the only one. *I'll just do it alone*, I thought. That's when I saw another hand pop up like the flag on an ice fishing tip-up.

My eyes zeroed in. *Oh no! Not Rhonda Glass.*

"Mr. Finwick and Miss Glass. I shall put you down as partners."

It was done. I had Rhonda Glass as my partner—and it was irreversible. I avoided eye contact and stared at my hands. Rhonda was unusual in many ways. For starters, she was as big as a house. Maybe Rhonda had trouble finding clothes that fit, because she never wore nice-looking pants or blouses. It was always the same baggy dresses that looked like they came from a used tent store and big clunky shoes from military surplus. And her hair—*sheesh*—just a brown, greasy mess on top of her large head, like she never washed it or brushed it or anything.

But maybe the worst part was how she carried herself—head down, never smiling, and dragging her feet as she walked.

Sorry if I sound like a dink. And believe me, as the boy shrimp of Shattuck High, I had no business picking on anybody. But there was a difference between Rhonda's problems and mine. Compared to Rhonda, I had it easy. For one thing, I had friends. I felt sorry for Rhonda, really I did, but I still didn't want to work with her on my book report project.

When the bell rang I glanced at Rhonda and she looked about as nervous as I was.

"I guess we're working together," she said.

"Yeah, I guess." In my brain I was trying to figure out how we could get through it without spending too much time together.

"Where do you usually go to study?" she asked.

"The Science Resource Center," I said.

"I guess that would work."

We decided that sixth hour on Monday was free for both of us. I sure hoped that Mark and Steve wouldn't be there.

※

In case you've been wondering about me and Larry Buskin, there wasn't much to talk about anymore. He avoided me like I had the bubonic plague or something, and it wasn't because I wore the Eaglewing steel-toed boots to school every day. The way I had it figured, Larry knew that other people knew that he was the reason for me being out with a concussion for a week. That's right. In a weird way I think Larry was scared of *me* for once. Maybe he wondered why I never turned him in to the principal, and to tell you the truth, I was still wondering that myself.

Without Buskin to worry about, and with Steve's and Mark's and my suspension behind us, school had turned almost normal again. Mark got back to living with his dad and actually said things were going okay. He wasn't even using the hideout anymore, which was a good thing, because by the middle of November in Neenah, it was freezing cold almost every night. Steve was the happiest of all to be back in school. I guess he had spent the week of his suspension working for his mom, scrubbing, washing, painting, raking, vacuuming, and dusting. She even made him clean the oven.

My life still wasn't simple, but it got calmer than before. At least I had my regular routine again, which included school, goofing off after school, Hoot Owls, confirmation and church and, of course, helping Mom around the house. One day I stopped at Wolf's cave under the railroad ties and dropped off a can of corned beef hash. Then I noticed that for three days in a row the cans hadn't been touched, and I figured Wolf must have moved away. Maybe he hitchhiked to Florida or found someplace with a roof, four walls, and a furnace.

As far as Dad's murder investigation was concerned, it seemed like nobody even wanted to talk about it anymore. Jeepers, was it ancient history already? The newspeople had all but given up on their reporting. The Highway 41 Killer hadn't struck again, and nobody except Mark and I even cared. If you think that didn't bug me, you're wrong.

❀

Sixth hour on Monday was bound to come up and it did. When I walked into the Science Resource Center, Mrs. Schwartz gave me her usual friendly smile. Steve sat alone at a table doing geometry homework, and a couple of tenth graders had their physics books open, solving problems with slide rules. No sign yet of Rhonda.

"Hey, Steve."

"Minnow, did you get your geometry problems done yet?"

"I'll do 'em later," I said.

A section of glass separated the Science Resource Center from the real world of dirtballs, jocks, burnouts, and drama queens. I scanned the masses of people roaming the halls and spotted Rhonda in the distance as she waddled back and forth in my direction. She wore a dress that hung from her shoulders like a burlap sack that was the color of wet cement. Nothing else about her had changed from any other day—army boots, ratty hair, eyes to the floor.

I waved as she walked in but Rhonda neither smiled nor waved back. Maybe she sensed my lack of enthusiasm. Maybe she felt unlucky too. I wasn't exactly a prize around Shattuck High and everybody knew it.

"There's an open table in the back," I said.

"Okay." She shrugged.

I sat with my back toward Steve so I wouldn't have to look at him making idiotic faces and immature gestures.

Unlike me, Rhonda had come prepared. She brought an outline with recommended topics for the oral report as well as her suggestions on which sections each of us should present. She asked me if I had read the book and I had. She asked me what I thought it was about and I said that it was about discrimination against black people. Rhonda nodded, but then explained that it went way beyond that. It was about people who didn't fit in, like Bo Radley. It was about people who behaved differently when they got mixed up in a mob, like Mr. Cunningham. It was about people with courage, like Atticus, and cowardly, ignorant people, like Bob Ewell, and how the forces of society prevented change for the good.

Holy smokes! Rhonda Glass was one smart cookie. On top of that, I actually had fun talking to her. *Heck*, she had all sorts of interesting ideas. We talked and worked together for over an hour and when we were done we had a nifty outline ready to hand in for part one of the assignment.

"I'll type it up," she said. "It'll look nicer that way."

"Thanks Rhonda. You're a natural at this. Maybe you should be an English teacher someday."

I guess it was the right thing to say, because an actual smile popped up on Rhonda's face. "Thank you," she said, and at that moment I realized that she could be pretty if she wanted to be.

26

Thanksgiving Day was my second favorite holiday, after Christmas. I jumped out of bed and flipped on our black-and-white Zenith to watch the Macy's parade in New York City. The gigantic helium balloons had just started floating down the avenues between the skyscrapers as millions of people and thousands of cops crowded around. All the cartoon characters were there—Mickey Mouse, Bullwinkle, Snoopy, Popeye the Sailor Man, and even Underdog, flying with his arms and legs outstretched. Guess what happened to Donald Duck. A gust of wind caught him and swung him into a tree where his wing got punctured on a branch. As you can imagine, that created a fuss on the ground and brought a string of dumb jokes from the announcers.

Like many families, the Finwicks had a long tradition of inviting relatives over for a big Thanksgiving Day dinner. We always had a turkey, stuffing, potatoes, squash, pickles, and the kind of cranberry sauce that came in a can. That was usually followed by about three different pies, all with ice cream. After dinner, Uncle Kermit held court in the living room with his card tricks and Grandpa Ed told war stories in the kitchen. All the while, Aunt Judy would mix up brandy old-fashioned drinks, which kept everybody smiling. That was back when all the relatives were still alive, of course, and as you can probably guess, it was a pretty raucous time.

It all reached a peak in about 1966. The following year we lost Grandpa Ed, Aunt Judy, and my mom's cousin, Felix. A year later, both of my grandmothers died and Uncle Kermit passed away. Now with Dad gone, our house was getting to be like a danged echo chamber. Heck, with Grandpa Asa still in jail, we didn't even have enough bodies to surround a single table.

When nine o'clock rolled around and neither Mom nor Sally had made a peep, I walked upstairs, knocked on Mom's door, and poked my head inside.

"Happy Thanksgiving, Mom."

"Is that today?"

Oh-oh. Not the response I was hoping for. "Yeah, the parade is on TV. You should get up and watch. And shouldn't we put the turkey in the oven soon?"

Mom lifted her head off the pillow like it weighed five hundred pounds. Her bottom eyelids drooped so much that I could see the pink insides.

"What's wrong, Mom?" It was scary. She looked almost as bad as the night Dad died.

No response.

"Should I call the doctor?"

"No. I just want to rest."

"But, what about the turkey?" Okay, I know what you're thinking. That was a selfish, boneheaded thing to say while my mom wasn't feeling well. It just came out, okay? And of course it was too late to take it back.

Mom looked at me like I had just pulled the plug on her batteries. Her head plopped back on the pillow and she closed her eyes.

"I didn't buy a turkey," she said.

"Does Sally know?" Okay, I shouldn't have said that either.

"I think she's going to Kevin's house," whispered Mom. "Sorry, honey, but if you check the freezer there should be something in there you can heat up."

❈

Thank goodness Mark came over. Otherwise I would have spent the day eating TV dinners all by myself. Mom never did get out of bed, Sally disappeared without a word, and of course Grandpa Asa was finishing out his sentence in the hoosegow.

I cooked those TV dinners for Mark and me, and luckily, the main course was turkey. Two slices of breast meat in gravy steamed away in the aluminum tray. The other compartments held mashed potatoes, peas, and something called cranberry cobbler that we figured was supposed to be a dessert. Okay, so it wasn't the way the pilgrims feasted with the Indians, but what the hay. It sure as heck beat leftover broccoli casserole.

I set up a card table in the living room and got us each a glass of milk. All in all, we had a pretty good time, and I know it was a lifesaver for Mark to get away from his dad for the whole day. We jabbered and joked around while eating our meals. Mark talked about girls and teased me about Opal Parsons, which I didn't mind. I talked about fishing and told him he couldn't catch a walleye if the whole world depended on it.

Mark dumped the empty TV dinner trays in the trash, and I made a big batch of popcorn on the kitchen stove and splashed it with salt and melted butter. Then the two of us sat around on the couch with our feet up on footstools like a couple of big shots, drinking root beers from the bottle while watching the Cowboys get waxed by the 49ers on TV. After the football game we played about fifty games of Nok-Hockey until our knuckles were so scraped up that they ached. Somewhere in all of that, I told Mark about Wolf living under that pile of old railroad ties.

"No kidding?"

"Yeah. He fishes behind the library. I'm pretty sure he's trapping rabbits too. Sometimes I leave food and other stuff to help him. I feel sort of bad for the guy."

Mark slugged me in the shoulder. "And you're not even in Boys Brigade."

I smiled.

Well, one thing led to another, and pretty soon Mark wanted to see Wolf's cave. We grabbed our jackets and went out the back door without letting it slam. It was an easy walk and the day was warm. Cars rolled in and out of the parking lot at Theda Clark Hospital. The yellow water of the Fox River tumbled over the dam and the paper mills still churned big clouds of white steam into the sky. The city didn't come to a stop just because it was Thanksgiving.

When we got to Wolf's cave I noticed my cans of food, still sitting there, untouched. Mark poked his head inside. "Anybody home?" he asked.

No answer.

"He could be fishing for mooneyes," I said. "Either that or he moved away. If I was him I'd have hitchhiked to Florida by now."

Mark nodded. "Well, he must be pretty tough if he lasted this long."

We screwed around on the railroad tracks for a while, chucking stones in the river and looking for returnable pop bottles that we could bring back for two cents each. Eventually, the conversation got back around to my dad's murder.

"We should call the FBI man," said Mark.

"Let's wait for my grandpa to get out of jail first."

"It wouldn't hurt to call though. Then when your grandpa is back he can drive us to where we need to go. The way I see it, Delmar, the trail to finding whoever killed your father keeps getting colder every day. Let's call the FBI guy tomorrow."

Mark had a good point about the trail getting colder. And one thing was for darn sure. That crime wasn't going to get solved by itself.

❋

The following day we made the call from a telephone booth on the corner outside the bowling alley. That way Mom wouldn't find out when she looked at the phone bill. She had enough things to worry about without knowing that her son was making long-distance calls to the FBI. Mark dialed the operator and told the lady that he wanted to place a telephone call to Milwaukee. He gave her the phone number and she said we had to deposit five quarters to talk for ten minutes. Mark and I dug the coins out of our pockets and put them in the slot, where each one made a clanking sound that the operator must have been listening for because the next thing we heard was the phone ringing.

I decided to let Mark do all the talking, partly because it was his idea and also because he had a deeper voice and knew how to sound confident around adults.

"FBI, Agent Culper speaking."

"Hello, sir. My name is Mark Marmotti. I'm calling from Neenah, and my friend Delmar Finwick is here with me. His father is the deputy officer who was murdered last month on Highway 41. Are you familiar with it?"

"Yes, I've heard about it." His voice was deep and serious.

"Sir, we're calling you because we need help figuring out what happened and catching the murderer. The local cops aren't getting anywhere."

"Why do you say that? From what I hear, they're on the trail of the Highway 41 Killer and the investigation is still underway. How old are you, by the way?"

"I'm sixteen, sir, and Delmar is fifteen. Sir, the cops are blowing it off like yesterday's news. They haven't found any evidence and they did a lousy job on the crime scene. Besides that, we have a pretty strong hunch that Sheriff Heiselmann is hiding something."

At that point, Agent Culper got mad at Mark. "Listen, kid, you can't just call the FBI because you've got a hunch and you're mad at the cops. You need facts. You need evidence. Otherwise I can't help you. Do you understand?"

"We've got one of the bullets, sir."

The whole conversation changed after that. By the time our ten minutes were used up, we had an appointment with Agent Culper in his office. He told us that we needed to come with a responsible adult, so we signed up Grandpa. We didn't tell him the part about Asa being locked up in the Winnebago County Jail.

❄

Grandpa got out the very next day. He yawned as he hobbled to the car between me and Mom.

"That's the noisiest damned place I've ever stayed," he said. "People yelling, doors slamming, toilets flushing. I barely slept a wink."

"Was it scary?" I asked.

"No. It was noisy, cold, and boring."

"Did you meet any crooks?"

"Of course," said Asa. "We were all a bunch of crooks. I told them I robbed a gas station."

"Why did you say that?"

Grandpa Asa looked at me sort of cross-eyed. "What was I gonna tell 'em? That I was part of the baking soda and vinegar volcano caper?"

"Can we *please* talk about something else?" begged Mom.

"Okay," said Asa. "Let's go get some hot fudge sundaes. I'm buying."

27

Grandpa Asa fixed it so that we could go to our meeting in Milwaukee with Agent Culper on Tuesday. He wrote me a note that said I had to be absent from school all day to visit a sick relative. He wrote Mark a note too, saying he had to have minor surgery on his thorax, whatever that was. On that one he used different paper and ink and wrote left handed so it would look like a drunk guy did it. Then he signed it Robert Marmotti.

It worked, and at nine in the morning on a chilly December Tuesday, we all piled into Asa's pickup and headed south on Highway 41. I had only been to Milwaukee once before, two years ago, when my dad took me to a night game at County Stadium for the Brewers very first season. Dad said it marked the end of the baseball drought in Wisconsin that began in 1965 when the Braves moved away to Atlanta.

As we crossed Big Lake Butte des Morts on the edge of Oshkosh I looked down on the dark water that was already freezing up at the edges. Swamp grass lined the south shore and I could see the abandoned duck blinds, now frozen in place.

Further south we came to Fond du Lac and the big Mercury Marine outboard motor factory. It was a giant-sized building and modern—nothing like the paper mills. Man-made ponds sat between the factory and the highway. We weren't sure, but Mark and I figured that maybe they were for testing the boat motors.

"Wouldn't that be a cool job?" asked Mark. "Buzzing around on speed boats all day long?"

"Yeah," I said. "And you probably wouldn't even have to go to college for it."

"That's radar hill coming up," said Grandpa.

"What's that?" asked Mark.

"You'll see."

Mark and I craned our necks as Grandpa Asa kept his speed right at fifty-five. Sure enough, at a gravel road going east, in a cutout through a shallow hill, a state patrol car popped into view. Another mile down the road, a different state patrol car had somebody pulled over. His cherry-red lights flashed as the officer wrote out a ticket.

As we kept going, we got into a few more rolling hills and finally, the first signs of the suburbs of Milwaukee. Without saying anything, Grandpa Asa pulled over at an exit ramp and stopped the truck.

"Why are you stopping?" I asked.

"I don't like driving in the city," he said. "You're taking over from here."

"What?!" My brain was about to explode.

"You did fine around home."

"That was different! This is Milwaukee!"

"Just a bigger version of Neenah," he said. "You drive. I'll navigate."

The conversation was over and, before I knew it, I was sitting behind the steering wheel with Grandpa on the passenger side and Mark still in the middle. Grinding through the gears and working the clutch pedal, I got it up to fifty-five as we zoomed onto the highway. Now I'll tell you something you probably already know. Your first time driving on a highway feels a lot faster than being a passenger. I gripped the wheel like I was choking it.

"Relax," said Asa. "Just stay in the right lane and keep it at the speed limit."

I did as he said, and after five minutes I did begin to relax. Pretty soon there were houses, stores, and power lines everywhere. A little later we came into Wauwatosa, and the highway went to three lanes. It seemed like everybody was trying to go faster than me, all zooming up in my rearview mirror.

"Don't worry about the cars behind you," said Grandpa. "They'll pass you if they want to get by. Just drive at fifty-five in the right lane."

A huge, brick building on our right seemed to go on for a mile. "That's the JC Penney's warehouse," said Mark.

Suddenly factories started popping up all over the place and some of them even had their own water towers. The Briggs & Stratton water tower to our right showed the same red, white, and blue emblem that was fixed to our lawnmower engine back home. The Roundy's water tower reminded me of the labels on the cans of corn in Mom's pantry. Then there was the biggest one of all—a giant-sized blue octopus water tower with something like two dozen legs and the crazy name,

WAUWATOSA, painted on the side. We sure didn't have anything like that in Neenah, Wisconsin.

"Stay to the right here," Grandpa directed.

We went through neighborhoods where the houses seemed all bunched together with parked cars and trash cans jumbled out front. All I could think was that I wouldn't want to live there. I sure hoped that the old Chevy Apache would keep on going.

All of a sudden, it seemed like we were right on top of County Stadium. The words HOME OF THE BREWERS! were displayed on the huge gray walls of steel and concrete. Underneath, giant cartoonish beer barrel men swung oversized bats and chased after imaginary fly balls. I couldn't believe it. I was driving past Hank Aaron's old stomping grounds.

"Exit ramp coming up," said Grandpa a few minutes later.

I took it. After some left and right turns, Asa pointed me to a parking spot, and I pulled into it like a master.

Mark grinned. "Way to go, Delmar. You're a stud."

I couldn't keep from smiling as I handed the keys back to Grandpa Asa. I used to think of Milwaukee as a scary city. Now, it felt like I owned the place.

We had an hour to kill, so Grandpa pointed us to a hamburger joint nearby. It had a bunch of booths, but they were all filled so we found three stools together at the counter and ordered burgers, fries, and bottles of pop.

"Why do they have two clocks right next to each other?" I asked.

Grandpa looked at the side-by-side, circular, white-faced clocks. "I guess that's just how they do things around here. Maybe one is a backup in case the first one breaks down."

I kept looking around. All sorts of people sat around. White, black, Chinese even. I recognized people dressed as factory workers, businessmen, and nurses. I saw a black lady with a leopard-skin purse and hat to match. I saw a white guy in a leather vest with snake tattoos wrapped around both arms. A Middle Eastern man with a white gown and a turban leaned over the counter sipping tea. At the table right behind me, two guys jabbered about dumpsters in their blue coveralls, and I figured that they belonged to the garbage truck parked outside.

Of all the different colors, clothing, occupations, and everything else that made each person unique, there was one thing they seemed to have in common. Smoking. I'll bet that two-thirds of the people in that joint smoked—even the lady in the nurse uniform. It seemed like everybody was jumping for their last chance in the world to have a cigarette before

Russian H-bombs started falling or something. I was almost used to it from my mom, but Mark kept on blinking his eyes, and even for me it seemed like a lot to breathe in. That combined with the grease smoke rolling off the griddle filled the whole place with a blue haze.

Mark signaled me with his head to check out the man walking in the door. I looked over and saw the bearded guy with gray hair and even grayer skin as he stumbled through the place and plopped down on the stool next to Grandpa Asa. He talked to himself for a few minutes. Then he turned to Asa and mumbled something about a dollar.

Grandpa turned and looked directly at him. "No."

The guy kept babbling and tapped him again on the shoulder.

"I said no!" Grandpa Asa shouted it this time and the man walked over to a booth in the corner and bothered those people for a while.

In the end, a waitress guided him out the door and the poor guy disappeared just as fast as he came in. The world seemed backward all of a sudden. There was a man who needed a hamburger and a warm place to sit more than anybody, and what did we all do? We ran him back out onto the street. I thought again about Wolf.

We gobbled down those burgers pretty quick because of our appointment coming up. Grandpa Asa said we still had a couple blocks to walk. He moved slowly with his cane, but we got there right on time. A guard at the front directed us to sit down until Agent Culper came out. I put my hand in my pocket to check on the bullet. It was still in there.

We watched folks come and go in the lobby of the FBI, and it surprised me when they didn't all look like the people on *Hawaii Five-O*. One pink-faced guy with a potbelly looked more like an accountant than a federal agent. Right behind him a lady hobbled in high heels, and I wondered how long she would last in a shootout.

"Mr. Marmotti and Mr. Finwick?"

I looked behind me where a man in a navy-blue sport coat, white shirt, and striped tie looked down at us. He was thin, but tough-looking, with a chin as big as my fist and eyebrows that jutted out like a canopy. His short hair was blond. We all shook hands and introduced ourselves. Then we followed him to a small room with a table and chairs but no window.

"First of all, I'm very sorry about the loss of your father," said Agent Culper, looking directly at me.

I nodded.

"Let's start at the beginning, shall we? Why are you here?"

Grandpa Asa and I let Mark do most of the talking. He told Agent Culper what a crummy job the cops had done on my dad's murder investigation and how nobody was getting anywhere with it. It was like the cops just expected the Highway 41 Killer to walk in the door and turn himself in or something. Mark went on to talk about our two trips to the crime scene and how we found the place with the matted-down grass by the billboard, where someone could have been waiting, and we told him about the partly smoked cigarette.

Agent Culper took notes and nodded his head as he listened.

Mark paused and looked at me. "Tell him your part, Delmar."

I started out by telling Agent Culper that Sheriff Heiselmann had something against my dad but I didn't know what it was. Then I described the secret meeting that I saw between Sheriff Heiselmann and the Cadillac Man. I told him about how the sheriff kept looking around before taking the yellow envelope and that he put something that looked like money in his pocket.

"I'm pretty sure he was doing something illegal," I said.

The agent took some more notes. While he wrote, I remembered the Winston cigarette dropped by the Cadillac Man at the Neenah lighthouse and how it was a perfect match for the cigarette butt at the crime scene. I also thought about the black plastic button with the white streak that I found under the Fine Dining billboard. Why was I still keeping secrets? I knew it was probably stupid, but I decided to keep those two tidbits tucked away and not even share them with the FBI man.

"Show him the bullet," said Mark.

I pulled it out of my pocket and placed it on the table. Mark explained how we found it. Agent Culper looked at the bullet, then at me, Mark, and Grandpa Asa. He took some bifocals out of his pocket and put them on, then picked up the bullet and studied it closely while rotating it in his fingers.

"It's a .357 Magnum, sir," said Mark.

"Yes, it is. And the deformation is consistent with what we would expect to see from soft tissue penetration."

I got a knot in my stomach thinking about my dad and the soft tissue that the FBI man was talking about.

"We think we need to match it up to a gun," said Mark.

"That would be helpful."

"Maybe Sheriff Heiselmann's gun," I said.

Agent Culper took off his glasses, drilled me with a scowl, and held it until I looked away. That's when he relaxed and leaned back in his chair.

"Gentlemen, let's start with the caliber. It would be unusual for a sheriff to use a .357 Magnum as his service revolver. Most cops use a .38 special or Colt .45."

"But it's possible, isn't it?" asked Mark.

"It's possible."

"And if we got the gun, it could be checked out to see if it matched the bullet, right?"

"Yes, but whoever shot Deputy Officer Finwick has probably disposed of the gun by now."

We all nodded.

"Here's the bottom line," said Agent Culper. "You don't have enough evidence to take action against the sheriff. The bullet is important, but we have no way of connecting it to a person. The stuff about the meeting in the park, although interesting, doesn't lead us anywhere. And that business about the sheriff not liking your dad? Well, those kind of grudges exist in every law enforcement department in the country. My advice is to let it go. Turn the bullet over to the Winnebago County Sheriff's Department, and back off. Let the professionals handle it."

Several seconds passed with nothing but silence in the air. Then . . .

"That's bullshit!" Grandpa Asa's face glowed bright red.

Agent Culper flinched. He sure as heck didn't like getting shouted down, especially by an old man who hadn't said anything the entire meeting. He and Grandpa Asa were nose to nose with neither one blinking. It was like two of the faces on Mount Rushmore in a stare-down.

"Typical—bureaucratic—bullshit!" Asa said.

Culper's eyes went black but he kept his composure. "You don't have a case, sir. And my advice to you and the boys is to drop it and turn your evidence over to the local authorities."

Grandpa's face went from red to purple. His hands formed two fists. His whole body shook. His lips quivered.

"What if we found the gun?" I blurted.

Agent Culper rolled his eyes. "That's not going to happen."

"But, what if it did?" asked Mark.

Agent Culper let his eyes soften and slowly tapped the table with his index finger. "If you *did* find the gun, then we would be having a very different conversation."

The temperature in the room seemed to drop by a few degrees. Grandpa Asa's hands unclenched.

28

Believe it or not, I drove all the way home and we made it. During the two-hour drive Grandpa Asa did most of the talking, and we learned a few new swear words that must have come out of World War I, because even Mark hadn't heard them before.

※

All day Wednesday I racked my brains about what to do next about Sheriff Heiselmann and Dad's murder investigation that was going nowhere.

Let the professionals handle it?

Those words from Agent Culper scratched at me like fingernails on a blackboard. I didn't know what we were going to do with the bullet, but I sure as heck wasn't going to hand it over to *the local authorities*. I needed some new ideas. I needed to talk things over with someone else — not Mark, not Grandpa Asa, and especially not Mom.

The cafeteria lady dumped a huge scoop of cream-style corn on my plate. *Yuck!* At least the pizza burger and apple slices looked edible. I scanned the cafeteria tables until I found her. There was Opal with her girlfriends, talking and laughing. I walked over.

"Hi, Opal."

"Hi, Del." She glanced at her girlfriends. They were staring at me like an insect that had just crawled a little too close to their lunches. Opal ignored them and smiled at me. "Do you want to join us?"

"No," I said. "But when you're done, I'd like to ask you something. I'll be over there."

She shot me a confused look. "Okay."

Ten minutes later, I had devoured my pizza burger and apple slices and because I was still hungry, even gazed down at my cream-style corn.

With enough salt, pepper, and butter almost anything could be transformed. I took a scoop and swallowed it. Half a minute later I had gulped down the whole pile.

"What's up, Del?" Opal sat down, looking like a sunset in her yellow blouse and her orange headband.

"I want your opinion on something."

"What's that?" she smiled.

"I'm trying to figure out who murdered my dad." Opal's smile washed away, replaced by a very serious expression. She leaned in closer, eager to listen.

"I think Sheriff Heiselmann is hiding the truth," I said.

"Why would he do that?"

"Because I'm pretty sure he's involved in the crime."

"What?" Opal's eyes got big.

"Can you keep a secret?"

"Yes."

"For starters, the sheriff hated my dad. And since the shooting, the department hasn't done anything to solve the case. My grandpa thinks the investigators are incompetent."

"What?"

"And after the murder I saw the sheriff talking to a suspicious-looking guy near the lighthouse. They both looked nervous, but then the guy gave him something. Maybe money."

"Go on."

"Mark and I found some other clues. We found where we think the shooter was hiding. We found a partially smoked cigarette there."

"Sorry, Del, but where are you going with this?"

"We found one of the bullets that killed my dad."

"You did?"

"Yes."

"But that doesn't mean you can point the finger at the sheriff, does it?"

"Not really. At least that's what the FBI agent said."

"You talked to the FBI?!"

"Yesterday, in Milwaukee."

"You're really serious about this."

"The FBI agent said we should drop it and turn the bullet over to the cops."

"Maybe you should."

"I can't. I know in my gut that there's something bad going on with the sheriff."

For a minute or two, both of us just sat there in silence. Opal was thinking. Her eyes burned into the tile floor and a wrinkle zigzagged across her forehead that I had not seen before. Suddenly, she looked up with a clear and determined expression on her face. "If you feel that strongly, you should confront him face-to-face."

"Who?"

"The sheriff."

"How would I do that?"

"I'm not sure. Talk to him somehow. Say something that smacks him right between the eyes. Then you watch for his response and hope that it tells you whether he's involved or not."

❈

I didn't sleep very well that night. My brain whirled like a pinwheel in a tornado.

Something that smacks him right between the eyes?

Opal's words kept repeating and asking me for an answer. And that wasn't the only part of the puzzle. The other was figuring out how to get face-to-face with Sheriff Heiselmann in the first place.

I muddled through the day and managed to get most of my homework done during sixth period in the Science Resource Center. After school I looked for Mark and found him hanging out by the football field with his back to the goalpost, chucking pieces of gravel onto the end zone grass.

"What's up, Delmar?"

"Nothing." I picked up my own handful of gravel and sat down with my back against the goalpost too, but facing the opposite direction.

"I'm still pissed off at that FBI agent," said Mark.

"Oh—he wasn't so bad. He just told us the truth. We don't have enough against Heiselmann."

"So what are we going to do about it?"

"I'm going to talk to him," I said.

Mark quit chucking stones and spun around like I had just announced that I had been elected pope.

"Delmar?"

"What?"

"That's brilliant. Have you got the guts for it?"

"Yeah—I think I've got the guts. Now I just have to figure out what to say."

"I'll tell you exactly what to say."

29

During sixth hour the following Monday I met again with Rhonda Glass on our *To Kill a Mockingbird* report. Our grade on the outline had been an A+, a rarity from Mrs. Borger. I was waiting in the Science Resource Center talking to Steve about the warrior robots that we had seen in *Popular Science* magazine. Rhonda smiled at me as she walked through the door. Steve saw her coming, yanked his books to his chest, and shot out of there. From the door he glanced back and made a stupid face like blowing a kiss. I almost gave him the middle finger but decided to ignore him instead.

"I'm excited about the report," said Rhonda.

I shrugged. "Reports are just a lot of work if you ask me."

"I have a new idea."

"What is it?"

"You know how most of the book reports have been pretty much the same with a synopsis followed by an explanation?"

"Yeah."

"That's pretty boring, don't you think?"

"Yeah, most of the oral reports are practically putting people to sleep," I said.

"Right! Here's my idea to liven it up. Instead of just talking, you and I can mix in some dialogue and act out certain scenes from the book. I can be Scout and other female characters and you can be Atticus and other male characters. Then after each scene we don't just tell the class what it means, we get them involved in the discussion. Maybe we can even bring in a student or two from the class at the end to help us act out the final scene." Rhonda flashed her biggest ever smile. "What do you think? Should we try it?"

Holy smokes! I bit my lip and pondered the dilemma. I knew it was good. I also knew that Mrs. Borger would absolutely love it. But acting in front of the class? I just didn't have it in me.

I was about to chicken out and ask Rhonda if we could do our report the regular, boring way when I saw her eyes. I didn't know it before, but Rhonda Glass actually had blue eyes the color of a melting glacier. They were mermaid eyes—Catwoman eyes—Miss America eyes. *Wow* . . . how had I not seen *them* before? Maybe nobody ever had because her head usually hung down as she clomped around in those frumpy clothes. But now, under the fluorescent lights, with that rare smile on her face and her eyes wide open and beaming right at me . . . *criminy*—there was no way in heck I could say no.

"Okay," I said. "I guess we can try it."

It was like I had flipped the on switch to Rhonda's creativity. Other than nodding my head, I didn't have to do a thing. She picked out all the scenes. She matched them up with discussion topics right off our outline. Before I knew it she had the whole script put together and even volunteered to type it again. I thought we were done and was getting ready to leave when she stopped me.

"Have you ever acted before, Del?"

"No," I said honestly.

"To do it well, we'll have to practice."

"Okay."

"And you have to be expressive."

"Okay."

"But more than anything else, you have to really get into the mind of the character. Do you know what I mean?"

"I think so."

"Good."

I looked at her. Was this really the girl who stared at the floor? "How do you know all this?"

"I read things."

"You read things?"

"And I watch a lot of movies—carefully."

I shrugged. "Okay."

"Let's meet at the same time next week," said Rhonda. "I'll get you a copy of the script so you can practice. And I have one more question for you."

I watched and waited.

"What's your name?" she asked.

"Del Finwick?"

"Wrong. Your name is Atticus Finch. It's the most important part . . . remember? You have to get into the mind of the character. You have to *be* Atticus."

I know this is going to sound weird, but all of a sudden, I actually wanted to be an actor.

"See you later," said Rhonda, smiling as she plodded out the door with that *thump, thump, thump* echoing through the halls.

❋

Heavy, wet snowflakes fell as I prepared to walk into the Oshkosh headquarters of the Winnebago County Sheriff's Department.

"You can do this, Delmar," said Mark.

"We'll be waiting right here for you," said Asa.

I took a deep breath, and walked up the sidewalk and into the building, where I brushed the snow off my hair and coat. A white-haired receptionist at the front desk glanced up at me.

"May I help you?" she asked.

"Yes, I called to see when I could talk with the sheriff. I was told that he gets done with a meeting at four o'clock."

"He'll just be a few more minutes. There's a chair right outside his office door."

"Thanks."

Sitting in that wooden chair, I couldn't keep from squirming. I twisted my scarf until it looked like a pretzel. I got up a couple times for a sip of water from the bubbler. I found a copy of *Field and Stream* and pretended to read it but could barely even look at the pictures.

Then a voice boomed through the corridor, and I knew right away it was Sheriff Heiselmann as he shouted orders at someone. He stopped outside his door and I stood facing him.

"Who are you?" he asked, looking at his watch.

"I'm Del Finwick."

It took a few seconds for Heiselmann's brain to process those words. Then, suddenly, his attitude switched to smiling politeness.

"Yes, of course. How are you? Are you doing well in school?"

"I'm fine, sir."

"How's your mother?"

"She's okay, sir."

"And what can I do for you today?"

"I have a couple questions."

"Fine. Fine." He chuckled. "I hope they're easy."

"They should be, sir."

"Well?" Heiselmann looked right at me, leaning forward slightly with his hands behind his back. The fake smile on his face was wearing thin. "I'm waiting."

"Where is the .357 Magnum revolver that killed my dad?"

The fake smile melted away fast. He tried to salvage it a couple of times but it flickered out and eventually became a hard flat line.

"I don't know anything about a .357 Magnum revolver," he said.

I didn't flinch but kept my eyes steady and straight at the sheriff. "And who was the man in the black Cadillac who handed you a yellow envelope at the Neenah lighthouse?"

His eyes gave him away first—darting and flashing. Then it got scary, starting with the big veins in his neck bulging out and turning purple. The redness moved to his cheeks and it looked like tiny rivers of blood forming on a topographic map. The anger stretched out across his whole face until every square inch was on fire. Only one word could describe what was pouring out of Sheriff Heiselmann, and that word was *hate*.

Maybe I should have backed off, but I didn't. Maybe I should have nodded and walked away. Instead, I just stood there, staring hard at the sheriff. I don't know where it came from, but I suddenly had all the power. It was like I was a fox and Sheriff Heiselmann was a gopher. And the funny thing was, Heiselmann knew it too.

Not knowing what else to do, the sheriff finally turned to the receptionist. "This boy has come here by mistake," he said, trying hard to look and sound human. "Please show him the door."

With that, Heiselmann retreated into his office and closed the door slowly with nothing more than a mild thud.

The receptionist looked at me with a sort of wonder in her eyes. "What did you say to him?"

"I just asked him a question."

"Well—it must have been a doozy."

I don't know what I was thinking as I walked through the falling snow to Grandpa Asa's truck. Maybe I should have been happy, but I wasn't. The knot in my stomach from Dad's loss ached stronger than ever. But that wasn't the only thing churning inside me. Mixed in there was something else—maybe pride. Yes, I felt pride for having confronted the sheriff, but there was even more. Then it came to me. Courage. That's right. Courage. At long last I had found some. *Criminy!* It made me feel so big that I figured that maybe my name shouldn't even be Minnow anymore. The truck door flung open.

"Well?" asked Mark.

I lifted my eyes to meet his. "He's guilty as hell," I said.

30

couldn't wait to tell Opal about my meeting with Sheriff Heiselmann, so I taped a note to her locker.

> Hi.
> MET WITH S.H.
> CAN WE MEET AT LUNCH?
>   D.F.

The cafeteria ladies were in a good mood because they were serving Italian Spaghetti and knew that people liked it. As usual, it came with lime Jell-O, carrot sticks, and a half peanut butter sandwich. I had just found a table in the corner when I saw Opal and waved her over.

"That looks good," she said, glancing at my tray.

"It's got all four food groups," I said.

She squinted. "I guess so—if you count lime gelatin as a fruit."

Opal organized the items from her brown bag lunch on the table, including a salami and cheese sandwich, a bag of pretzels, three radishes, and a small carton of milk.

"So, you talked to the sheriff?"

"Yes."

"Well? Let's hear about it." Her eyes grew big like a kindergartener at story time.

I told her the whole thing, starting with Mark coming up with the question and ending with the sheriff turning several shades of red before asking the receptionist to show me the door. By the time I was done, Opal had stopped eating her lunch and had a huge smile on her face.

"You really did it."

I couldn't keep a grin from bubbling up on my own face.

"That took nerve," she said. "I'm proud of you."

Do you know what it feels like to get a compliment like that? Do you remember the lump of pride that I felt in my gut, walking out of the sheriff's office? Well it was back again. I sat there quietly, because there was nothing left to say.

"But what does it all mean?" Opal asked.

"It means Sheriff Heiselmann's guilty," I said. "I don't know if he pulled the trigger himself or not, but one way or the other, he's in on it."

"You still can't prove it, Del. That's the problem."

"I know."

"What are you going to do next?"

"I don't know."

We both sat quietly, nibbling our lunches. When I had finished my spaghetti I picked up the peanut butter half sandwich and used it to clean all the red sauce off my tray before gobbling it down. I looked at Opal in the hope that she could answer the "What next?" question. That zigzag wrinkle in her forehead had returned. I kept my mouth shut so she could think.

At last her eyes met mine. "I have a suggestion," she said.

"What's that?"

"You need to talk about this with someone."

"What do you mean?"

"You need to talk to someone with experience going up against authority."

"Experience pushing back against the cops?"

"That's right," said Opal. "Experience against forces even more powerful than Sheriff Heiselmann."

"But what person has *that* kind of experience?"

"My mom," said Opal.

❁

Opal worked it out so I would come over to her house for supper again on Friday evening. I told my mom I was going to Robby's Hamburgers to hang out with some friends. I know, I know. Another lie, but I had to. Otherwise she would try to stop me from "*fraternizing with the Negroes.*"

Mrs. Parsons had dishes clanking and steam rolling out of the kitchen when Opal and I walked in. Fried shrimp sizzled in a large pan on the stove. Sweet corn boiled in another and something that smelled and looked like pumpkin pie appeared behind the oven door when she peeked inside.

"How are you, Del?"

"I'm fine."

"How's your mama and sister?"

"They're okay." At least the part about my sister was probably true.

"You can sit down right there." She nodded at the chair next to me. "Opal, honey, you can set the table. Just three places. Your father's working late."

"Why does he have to work late, Mama?"

"He's got a machine acting up at one of the mills. He need to stay until it's fixed and you know how that go sometimes."

"Yes." Opal rolled her eyes.

"Dinner be ready in two shakes. You not allergic to shrimp, are you, Del?"

"No ma'am."

"Ever have sweet potato pie before?"

"No."

She smiled and those little wrinkles popped up in the corners of her eyes. "Well then . . . I guess you is in for a treat."

Let me tell you something about Mrs. Parsons's sweet potato pie. Maybe it sounded like a weird creation, but it was delicious and I told her so. The whole meal was full of tasty flavors about a hundred times better than those TV dinners Mark and I ate on Thanksgiving.

"What was it like living in Alabama?" I asked. I was just trying to make small talk, but the question turned out to be more complicated than I thought.

"Well, that depends."

"On what?"

"It depends on which part of my life in Alabama you talking 'bout. You see, I was born in 1933. It was a hard time for most people, and especially for black folk."

Mrs. Parsons went on to tell me all about her life growing up as the daughter of share-croppers on a cotton farm where they all had to work in the fields, even the little kids, and there was almost no chance to build a better life for your family.

"Maybe you've learned about it in school," she said. "The system was rigged for the landowner. They put us up in a one-room shack with a leaky roof and some raggedy clothes and a bag of dry beans and maybe a few chickens. But them beans and chickens was no gift, let me tell you, and when that cotton crop was picked and sold at the market, the expenses were subtracted out, and then, of course, the owner had to take out a profit for his-self. Well, what you think was left for the family after that?"

"Not much, probably," I said.

"Not much is right. And families went hungry. Blacks and whites, but especially blacks. And school? Well, most black children never made it past the fifth grade."

"What was school like?" I asked.

"Well, everything in the South was segregated of course. Bathrooms, restaurants, hotels, even drinking fountains were separated between blacks and whites. The same was true for schools, and the black schools were shabby—especially in the countryside."

"How did you get to be a nurse?"

"I was lucky. Our family moved to the city when the war broke out, and my parents both got jobs at a munitions factory. Because of that I was able to go to high school and go to a black college. Plus, I was lucky enough to meet Sam Parsons. He ain't never went to high school or college but was so good with machinery that everybody needed him. Sam Parsons could fix anything—still can. And that's what got him into Pearson & Greene, and that's how we be following the paper mills all the way up here to Neenah, Wisconsin."

"Tell Del about Selma," said Opal. "I told you why he needs to know."

She nodded and then scooted her chair over next to me. "Touch my head right there." She pointed to the top, left side of her head with an index finger. "Go ahead and press down right there on my skull."

I did as she asked and my finger rose up on something like a knot on a tree. "There's a lump," I said.

"That's right," she said. "And the hair gone on that spot too."

"What happened?"

"That's where a police officer done clubbed me and nearly cracked my skull."

"Why?"

"Because I stood up for something."

"You protested?"

"That's right. I protested for black voting rights."

"You did?"

"Yes, I did. Have you heard of Dr. Martin Luther King Jr.?"

"Yes."

"Have you ever heard of John Lewis and Hosea Williams?"

"No."

"Well they were our leaders on March 7, 1965. I was one of a group of six hundred at the Edmund Pettis Bridge in Selma, Alabama. Have you learned about what happened there?"

"I'm not sure."

"Good Lord! Now honey, I knows Wisconsin be a long ways from Alabama, but this is important to the whole country." Mrs. Parsons looked at me. Her jaw was set. "Now Del, I already aware that you like history, so I reckon you ought to read up on this."

"I will," I said, and I meant it.

"We was beginning a march from Selma to Montgomery, about fifty miles. Both cities were known for their rules making it difficult for black people to vote, and somepin needed to be done about it. Opal was seven at the time and I left her for the day with her grandmother."

I looked at Opal and she looked at me.

Mrs. Parsons continued. "The plan was to have a peaceful march, but when we approached that bridge it be blocked by Alabama State Troopers in their riot gear with helmets on their heads and clubs in their hands."

"What did you do?" I asked.

"We stood our ground." Mrs. Parsons dropped her head briefly. Then she looked toward the wall and blinked several times as she brought her hand up to her cheek. Her chin quivered.

"Are you okay, Mama?" asked Opal.

Mrs. Parsons nodded, pressed her lips tightly together, and then looked me straight in the eyes.

"Like I said, Del, we stood our ground. That was the main thing. We was face-to-face, us and the troopers."

"What happened next?" I asked.

"The troopers fired tear gas and came right at us until they was running us over. It was awful. Keep in mind that this was a nonviolent protest, Del. We was only fixin' to march. But that's when the clubs come out, the policemen went crazy, and the screaming began. Like I said, they didn't just push us back away from the bridge either. They run right over us. It weren't even a fight, Del. It was a beating."

I said nothing.

Mrs. Parsons's lips tightened up. "Do you think the State of Alabama won on that day, Del?"

"I don't think so, ma'am."

Mrs. Parsons nodded. She had a serious and prideful look on her face, sitting up with clear, bright eyes and a perfectly straight back, and

I wondered if that's what Chief Oshkosh looked like when he stood up for the Menominee Indians when the government tried to push them off the land.

"Now, why don't you tell me what's going on between you and the sheriff? Opal tells me you gots your own kinda struggle."

31

As I sat in the kitchen stirring up a glass of orange Tang the next morning, my head was still spinning from my talk with Mrs. Parsons the night before. The whole idea of organizing a protest march seemed both exciting and crazy at the same time. On the one hand, I knew that something had to be done to put pressure on Sheriff Heiselmann and bring attention to my dad's unsolved murder. On the other hand . . . *Gosh! A protest march?* It all seemed so extreme.

While pondering the dilemma, I noticed the afternoon paper on the kitchen table. I grabbed it and started flipping through the pages. On the front was an article about an earthquake in Nicaragua. Page 2 had a story about an airplane crash rescue in the Andes Mountains. Page 3 explained how Australia was pulling all its soldiers out of Vietnam. *Gosh Nixon—take the hint.*

Then, as I turned to the local news section, my eyes crashed into five words that hit me harder than a Mohammed Ali punch.

Fisherman Drowns in Fox River

My eyes scanned the first paragraph, and for a few seconds I couldn't even breathe.

An unidentified man died in a drowning accident below the Menasha dam on Friday. He was swept away by the current while trying to un-snag a fishing line along shore. Local authorities described him as an Indian and believe that he had no permanent residence. Efforts are underway to locate family members. His name is not known at this time.

"His name is Wolf," I said out loud.
"What's that, Del?" asked Mom.

"Nothing." A whirlpool of sadness spun inside of me.

The article was short, only three inches long, yet I had a million questions. What really happened? Where was his body? Were they really trying to find his family?

I grabbed my jacket and, like a zombie, walked outside and opened the garage door. Eisenhower's red reflector blinked like a bear waking up from hibernation. I barely pedaled as the cold wind blew me down Nicolet and around the bend past the Banta Mill.

A yellow torrent roared and churned from the bottom of the Menasha dam. The rapids surged bigger than usual. Standing waves stood steep and jagged like the spiny back of some great serpent stirring up lumps of foam and carrying them toward the mills downstream. Three fishermen worked the shore on the Banta side. I started with the closest one. Had he heard anything about the drowning? Had he seen it? The man just shook his head in somber reverence. The second man, like the first, knew nothing but expressed sadness at the lost soul.

I approached the third man as he fished all by himself amid some concrete rubble at the base of a tree. He was hooking a minnow through the tail and preparing to cast it out on a bell sinker rig. I flipped down Ike's kickstand and approached.

"Have you heard anything about the man who drowned?"

"Yep," he said. "Saw the whole thing." The man hurled the minnow and sinker at least twenty yards and set the rod vertical in a gap within the concrete. He then turned to me and smiled. "Never saw such an idiot."

His comment and manner cut me like a fillet knife. "What do you mean?" I asked.

"It was that same, stupid Indian I've seen fishing around town."

I felt my teeth clamp down tight as the man continued.

"The fool was intentionally fishing for mooneyes, if you can believe that. Just like an Injun to go after a trash fish. Anyhow, he was just downstream from here, wasting his time on them mooneyes when he gets his line snagged on a rock. Most people, like you and me, we'd snap it off and tie on another hook and sinker. Right?" The man looked at me, waiting for an answer.

"Maybe," I said.

"Yeah, well Tonto didn't do that. Get this. The dumb blanket-ass waded out into the freezing water—yanking and tugging—trying every damned thing to get it loose. Next thing I know he slips on a rock and goes off with the current. His head was bobbing and his arms were flapping. He yelled a few times but after a hundred yards or so he just went down for good."

I felt my toes curling inside the Eaglewings on my feet. A surge of blood rushed to my face.

"You didn't do anything?"

"Nope."

"You did nothing?! How could you do nothing?! A man was drowning!"

The man's eyes went hard and dark. He spat a stream of tobacco juice into the river and returned his gaze to me.

"No skin off my nose, kid," he said. "Just another dead pine savage as far as I'm concerned."

My whole body tensed. My toes coiled even tighter in the Eaglewings. My hands transformed into sledge hammers. I stared hard into the man's bloodshot eyes and for those few seconds he and I just stood, face to face, spewing hate at each other.

"Get out of here, shrimp," he said. "Or I'll toss you in the river too."

What happened next was like watching a movie. The camera zoomed in on my right leg as it swung back in slow motion and then surged forward. The nose of the Eaglewing steel-toed boot was a locomotive on the Soo Line barreling at full throttle toward its target. The man's foam plastic minnow bucket exploded on impact, sending water, minnows, and white chunks airborne in every direction. Water sprayed all over everything, including the guy's pants. The result was a circle of wet concrete littered with dozens of minnows flipping around like silver coins.

After that, I just stood there. That's right, all eighty-four pounds of me just stood there, refusing to run. My fists were clenched, the Eaglewings cocked and ready. At first, the man made a sort of growling sound. He leaned in and even took a step toward me. Maybe I would get thrashed or maybe I would get tossed in the freezing river like he promised. Either way I wasn't moving from my spot.

Then a strange thing happened. The man's jaw dropped a little, he looked down at the flipping minnows and sagged. The hardness in his eyes washed away and a look of confusion took its place. The next thing I knew he was on his hands and knees scooping up minnows into the only fragment of his minnow bucket that still held water.

I stepped over to Ike, gripped the handlebars, and flipped up the kickstand. Before riding away, I glared down at the man.

"His name was Wolf!"

32

I walked around on Monday morning with my head in an invisible fog. When I really thought about it, Wolf and I had probably talked to each other for a total of three minutes, yet his death hit me hard, like I had lost a best friend or something. I didn't get it. Part of me was saying to shake it off, but a bigger part of me said "shut up" to the first part.

The lunch lady in the cafeteria plopped a tuna melt sandwich, some chips, and a cookie on my tray. I sat alone and tried to eat the sandwich, but it tasted like cardboard. Something smacked me in the back of the head. I turned around and gazed up at the ugly face of Leon Dinsky, the dirtball who had spotted out Opal on the first day of school.

"Hey, Minnow, can I have your cookie?" he said.

"No."

He reached over the table, no doubt expecting me to do nothing. When his hand touched the cookie my fist came down on it like a hammer forge. It hit his knuckles dead center and crushed the cookie beneath it at the same time.

"Ahh!" he yelled and jerked his hand back as the tray clattered to the floor. All heads turned in the cafeteria and the place went quiet. "I'll get you for this, you little shit," shouted Dinsky.

I stood and faced him, fists clenched and drawn. My toes curled inside the Eaglewings and I felt my jaw muscles tighten.

"How about right now," I said, and I meant it.

For a second or two Dinsky's eyes went blank. He glanced left and right but found himself alone. At last his eyes focused on me again.

"Screw you," he said. He flipped me the middle finger and walked away.

Yeah, Wolf was dead all right. But something, maybe part of him, was still alive inside of me. I looked at my own fists and had to will them to unclench. *Gosh*, I thought. *That wasn't anything like a minnow.*

✳

I was *not* excited for my meeting with Rhonda on Monday afternoon, but I had arranged with Mrs. Schwartz to use the chemistry lab to practice our *Mockingbird* lines and didn't think I should back out. Mrs. Schwartz was eager to help us and said we could rehearse as much as we wanted. Besides, she thought it was a cool idea, acting out our book report. On her desk I saw a copy of the morning newspaper.

"Can I borrow your paper, Mrs. Schwartz?"

"Of course."

I scanned the whole thing, especially the local section, but didn't find anything new about Wolf.

"Hi, Del."

"Oh . . . hi, Rhonda."

"Did you practice your Mockingbird lines?"

"A little."

I returned the paper to Mrs. Schwarz's desk and we settled in at a table in the chemistry lab. *Shake it off*, I told myself as we sat next to each other at a workbench. I offered up a weak smile, but my heart wasn't behind it.

She went first, in the character of Scout and—*Wow!* Rhonda absolutely nailed it. How she pulled it off was like some sort of a miracle. Her performance of the character Scout swallowed me up to the point that I almost didn't feel like pouting anymore. In fact, I wasn't even seeing those baggy clothes and army boots. Through those eyes and expressions, with the southern drawl mixed right in, I was on the front porch of a house in Macomb, Alabama, at a time thirty years before I was even born.

"Holy kamoly," I said. "That was swell." I meant it too. Rhonda was everything that she had coached me to achieve. She *was* expressive. She *did* get into the mind of the character. She *was* Scout.

"Your turn," she said.

I opened my script and cleared my throat. Did I let it rip? Did I give it everything I had? Nope. I just couldn't do it. The words came out about as lifeless and flat as the robot on *Lost in Space*.

"What's wrong?" she asked.

I swallowed and blinked. Then I told her about Wolf and what happened to him. Rhonda's eyes softened and even got damp. She stepped next to me and hugged me hard—so hard that I found my face sandwiched between her breasts and wondered if I was going to suffocate in there. I didn't mind.

"Are you going to the funeral?" she asked.

"Huh?"

"Wolf's funeral. Are you going?"

"I don't know if there *is* a funeral," I said.

❀

I made two telephone calls after I got home from school on Monday. The first was to Rhonda Glass to see if she would come to school early to help me practice acting out my Atticus lines again before our *Mockingbird* report. She said yes and even sounded excited.

The second phone call was to the county courthouse to find out about the funeral plans for Wolf. Yes, he would be buried at taxpayer expense. No, there would be no funeral.

"What about a gravestone?" I asked.

"A small, numbered marker will be provided."

"A number?"

"He has no name."

"His name is Wolf."

"We don't actually know that, now do we."

"I do. I've met him. He's my friend." I kicked the stove.

"If you would like to provide a stone marker at your own expense, you may do so. In the meantime, the state will be marking his grave with the number 648. 'Unknown male' is how he will be entered into the registry."

No, I did not slam down the phone. It took every speck of patience that I had inside me, but I placed the phone down, gently in the cradle.

Then I slammed my fist hard on the countertop. "Jeez!"

❀

My practice session with Rhonda on Tuesday morning went better than I'd expected. I had worked on the lines at home and made myself into a pretty good Atticus. Rhonda Glass made me better.

She listened and smiled. "That was good, but make it bigger and louder. Use your hands. Use your eyes. This is Scout who you are speaking to, your only daughter. Now, look into my eyes and try it again. Really *be* Atticus Finch this time."

Rhonda was right. I needed to really cut loose. I cleared my throat and looked into those sparkly blue eyes. I took a deep breath and went for it.

After I finished reciting my lines, Rhonda stepped up to me with a huge smile on her face. For the next few seconds, there was no talking.

Now, if you're wondering if I liked being kissed by Rhonda Glass, the answer is yes. And it didn't matter that she was a giantess in a burlap sack either. I went lips to lips with Rhonda Glass, the best actress in the history of Shattuck High. Besides, did you hear what she said about me afterward? If you missed it, I'll tell you again.

"You were wonderful."

Yep, that's exactly what she said. And that's when I knew I could be an actor—for real.

✸

I wasn't even nervous walking into Mrs. Borger's English class. I waved at Rhonda in the back of the room. Then I sat down at my usual spot next to Opal.

"Good morning, Del."

"Hi."

It felt a little weird talking to Opal just a couple hours after getting kissed by Rhonda Glass. What I really, really wanted, of course, was to kiss Opal. Could it happen? I still hoped so. Could I get her to go to the dance with me? I didn't know, but I sure as heck wanted to try.

She's the one, I told myself. *The girl I'm going to take to the Snow-Ball Dance.*

✸

Mrs. Borger tapped her ruler on the desk to get the class to shut up and pay attention. After a few boring announcements, she introduced me and Rhonda to give our report.

Did Rhonda and I get through our play acting report without a glitch? Yes, we did. Was it a home run? Absolutely. And when I walked back to my desk, Opal Parsons looked at me with a smile on her face like I was Clark Gable and she wanted my autograph or something.

At the end of class, Mrs. Borger asked me and Rhonda to stay for a few minutes. After the rest of the class had cleared out, she looked at us both very seriously.

"I want to speak to you both about your report," she said.

Rhonda and I glanced nervously at each other. What had we done wrong? Had we broken some rule?

Suddenly, Mrs. Borger couldn't hold back her smile any longer. She reached out her hands and squeezed mine and Rhonda's in her own.

"I'm so proud of both of you."

"Thank you," said Rhonda. I felt my chest get bigger.

"*That* . . . was the best, most creative book report ever given in the history of my twenty years teaching English in this school."

"Thank you," said Rhonda. I had about a ten-pound frog in my throat and couldn't speak.

"I am assisting Mr. Schirmer in a spring theater production here at Shattuck High," said Mrs. Borger. "The play is *Romeo and Juliet* and I want the two of you to try out for the lead roles."

33

I didn't say no to Mrs. Borger, but the whole *Romeo and Juliet* thing scared the crap out of me. Giving a book report in front of thirty people was one thing. Acting out love scenes on stage in front of a real audience was something else completely. And what if I had to put on makeup and wear tights?

I worried about it all afternoon and evening, and when I sat down with Opal for lunch the next day, she convinced me to quit being such a dipstick.

"It's a huge opportunity, Del."

"I'll look like an idiot."

"You'll look great and everybody who is *not* an idiot will admire you. You've got talent, Del. Believe me; you showed that yesterday. You owe it to yourself to try this. Not only that, but you'll be doing a favor to Mrs. Borger and the whole school because I don't think anybody in all of Shattuck High could do a better job than you and Rhonda."

Maybe she was right. Maybe I was just being a dweeb. Maybe the play *was* my big opportunity to get out of everybody else's shadow at school, and it took Opal to make me realize it. Maybe it would even help me shake off my crummy nickname.

"Okay," I said. "I'll audition for Romeo."

Did Opal kiss me? No, but she gave me a big, giant smile about as bright as the sun. After that I knew for sure that I would ask her to the dance.

✳

After all of those nice words from Opal and Mrs. Borger, I was practically floating down the halls. The good feeling stayed with me through geometry class, even though we had a quiz. At the end of seventh period,

I felt so confident that when I had to go to the bathroom, I decided to take my chances in the central lavatory. It was usually the last place I would go, but on that afternoon, I walked right inside.

Can you guess who was already hanging out in the central lavatory? That's right. Larry Buskin and a couple other grits, all leaning against the sinks smoking cigarettes. They had the window cracked open and the cold draft smacked me right out of my happiness. I tensed up and, for a second, thought about running back out the door.

Buskin spat on the floor in front of me. "What's up, Minnow?"

"Nothing." I looked at the row of old urinals that were about as big as bathtubs tipped on their ends but decided not to turn my back on the goons. Instead I went in a bathroom stall, shut the door, and latched it.

Buskin spoke quietly to the other two. "I need to talk privately with the punk." There was a shuffling of feet as the other guys bumped out the door.

Holy crap! This is it! Just me and Buskin in the central lavatory—what a lousy place to get thrashed, and I was 99.9 percent sure that's what was coming next. The only question was whether he would wait until I came out or bust through the latched door and grab me right out of the stall. I looked down at the Eaglewing steel-toed boots with the reinforced shank. They weren't shiny and new anymore after wearing them for a month and smashing one plastic minnow bucket to pieces. My toes curled in each boot.

"I have a question for you, Minnow."

I said nothing.

"I'll wait," he said.

Nuts! There was no way out.

I said nothing, but finished my business, zipped up my pants, and hit the flush lever. For a minute I just stood there, sweating and wiggling my toes inside the Eaglewings. To keep my hands from shaking I put them in my pockets. My right hand touched the bullet. I rubbed it, hoping for a genie, but of course nothing showed up. Nothing, that is, except memories of Dad, and that was enough.

I opened the stall door and stepped into the cave of tile and giant urinals. Each footstep in the Eaglewings seemed to echo off the walls. I stopped a few feet away from Buskin, who towered above me with a cigarette sticking out the corner of his mouth. He pulled it out and blew a stream of smoke at the ceiling.

"I've been wanting to talk to you about something," he said.

"What?" My muscles tensed. It was almost go-time. I stood as ready as I could be.

"How come you never turned me in to the principal that time I kicked your ass?"

I said nothing. My concentration was focused on the Eaglewings and when to flip the switch.

"I would have been expelled," Buskin continued.

I said nothing. My teeth were clenched.

"I think I owe you for that."

Am I really hearing this? "You gave me a concussion," I said.

"I'm sorry."

An apology from Larry Buskin?

"I just wanted to say it. That's all," he said.

I nodded, and for some reason didn't leave, but just stood there looking at Buskin's face. For the first time ever, he looked almost normal, like someone who probably had a family who cared for him and worried about him. Maybe he even had problems like me. Maybe he had problems worse than me. Suddenly, I wasn't looking at a dirtball anymore, and I almost forgot about the Eaglewings altogether.

Buskin flicked his cigarette butt into the urinal. He started out the door but stopped a step short and turned around again. "I heard that you and Marmotti are pissed off at the sheriff about what happened to your father."

I said nothing.

"Don't mess with Heiselmann," he said.

"Why not?"

Larry paused and then spoke. "He's into stuff."

"What does that mean?"

"It means he knows people that you never want to meet." Larry tipped his head forward and raised his eyebrows in a sort of *believe me, I know* expression. Two seconds later he was gone.

❁

Opal and I stayed after school to talk about planning a protest march against Sheriff Heiselmann. I didn't tell her anything about my little chat with Larry Buskin in the central lavatory.

"First, we need people," she said.

I nodded.

"Second," Opal continued. "We need to contact the newspapers and TV stations ahead of time so they can send reporters."

"That makes sense," I said.

"Third, we need a message."

"Yeah," I said. "I was thinking about something like *Justice for Officer Finwick.*"

"That's not enough. We need something stronger—something powerful."

"What do you mean?" I asked.

"We need something that will make people talk and make Sheriff Heiselmann nervous. He needs to feel it like a kick in the ass."

I stiffened and my jaw dropped an inch. "*Like a kick in the ass?*" I had never heard Opal talk like that before. Her face was black ice.

"What can we say?" I asked. "We still don't have any real proof against him."

"You're right," said Opal. "And we can't go around chanting 'Sheriff Heiselmann is a murderer.' But we still have to come up with something that really points the finger at him."

I shrugged. "But we don't have anything."

"Think, Del. There must be something. Even if it has nothing to do with your dad's murder, is there anything that we can say about the sheriff that would make him squirm?"

I didn't say anything. Neither did Opal. We had nothing. Was our march going to be a flop before it even started? Suddenly, out of nowhere, the answer popped into my brain.

"He killed a swan," I said.

"What?" Opal's eyes reflected confusion.

"On the Poygan Marsh," I said. "I saw it with my own eyes. A beautiful white swan. They're supposed to be protected by law, but he killed it anyhow."

"That's it!" said Opal.

"It is?"

"Yes!"

She reached over the table and placed her hand on top of mine. Her smile glowed brighter than ever, and for a second I wondered if it was really meant for me. We were all alone in the hallway outside the cafeteria. *Should I try to kiss her?* It was just an idea, but who was I kidding. This was Opal Parsons and I was Del Finwick. Heck, I could barely even look her in the eyes. I may have been brave about a few things lately; but mostly, I was still just a minnow.

✳

We walked home together, but I didn't even try to hold her hand or walk her up to her door or anything. *God—I'm hopeless*, I thought.

"See you tomorrow," I said.

"See you tomorrow."

I ran the rest of the way home in the darkness, sliding across frozen puddles when they came up. Right away I went to the garage and got down on hands and knees on the cement floor. My hands were nearly frozen as I rolled papers and slid on the rubber bands. My stomach growled but there was no time for supper. It was Thursday, after all. Hoot Owls needed delivering and the people couldn't wait. An envelope with $2.32 found its way to my pocket—right next to the bullet.

34

Friday was the start of our Christmas break and the very next day was to be our protest march against Sheriff Heiselmann.

Opal and I had been working hard in her kitchen to get ready after school. She made phone calls to all three of the Green Bay television stations to let them know what we were doing.

"Did they even sound interested?" I asked.

"Hard to say," said Opal. "They said, 'We will give it our consideration,' whatever that means."

At the same time, I was on the floor making big, sturdy signs out of double-thick cardboard. The message was the same on each one:

SHERIFF HEISELMANN

KILLED A SWAN

I put the words on both sides so people could read them coming and going. We only had Opal, Mark, and me signed up to march, which was a bummer. I had tried to convince Steve to join us, but his parents still had me rated with Jack the Ripper on the bad guy list. I mentioned the march to Eric Staley and Dale Benson, two guys I knew from my neighborhood. They listened politely and everything, but in the end, I might as well have been talking to a couple fire hydrants on the corner. *Oh, well.* I made up a few extra signs anyways, just in case somebody joined at the last minute.

The protest route was Mrs. Parsons's idea, and it was a big one. She suggested that we begin on Highway 41 at the exact spot where Dad was murdered and continue south all the way to the Sheriff's Department headquarters in Oshkosh. Thousands and thousands of people would surely see us with all the traffic going by. Mrs. Parsons agreed to drive us out there and pick us up again when we were done. The whole hike would cover eleven miles and take most of the day. We would need sandwiches, cookies, and drinks. Opal's mom took care of that part too.

By the way, our protest plans never made it to my mom's ears. I thought about telling her, but then had second thoughts, knowing that she might squelch the whole thing. I could have just snuck out of the house, I suppose. Instead, I told her that I was going to confirmation class at the church and then hanging out with Mark at the bowling alley. It was no small lie this time, and I was already feeling rotten about it. In my mind I had to do it. The march was just too important to stop. My only hope was that God would understand, because I knew that Mom never would.

❄

At eight o'clock Saturday morning, we met at the Neenah library. It had snowed overnight so everything sparkled like the glitter on a Christmas card. The bank thermometer told a different story. The rectangle of yellow light bulbs flashed a number that began with a minus sign. *Two below zero. Yipes!* If those kind of temperatures kept up, they would be driving cars on Winnebago by New Year's.

I had on my long underwear, parka, and snow pants. Mark showed up in coveralls with an orange deer hunting coat over the top. Opal wore her bright-blue ski jacket with matching pants. Except for the color of her skin, she could have modeled for a catalog. Just as I was piling the signs into Mrs. Parson's station wagon, an unexpected voice pierced the cold air.

"Hi, everyone."

I turned around quick. *Holy moley!* It was Rhonda Glass, clomping down the sidewalk like a greenish-gray version of Frosty the Snow Man.

"Can I join you?" she asked.

I gulped some air. "Sure, Rhonda. The more the merrier." My mouth said the words, but my brain wondered if she could walk a single mile. To be honest, I didn't even know if we could fit her inside the car. I looked at her feet. Army boots.

"We're so glad you came," said Opal. "We've got plenty of signs." She gave Rhonda a big hug and I was mildly jealous, thinking about when I might get a hug like that from Opal Parsons.

Mrs. Parsons offered Rhonda her hand and a big smile. "Welcome and thanks for coming," she said. "The larger the group the more they gonna take notice."

"She makes us larger all right," Mark whispered in my ear. I kicked him in the leg and shot him a look that I usually reserved for dirtballs.

After Mrs. Parsons dropped us off on the side of Highway 41, a surge of pessimism ran through me. The cold was one thing, but that wicked north wind? *Criminy!* It nearly ripped my face off. We had no sidewalk, no map, and the cars whipped by like cannonballs. On top of that, I remembered hearing somewhere that it was against the law for pedestrians to walk on divided highways. *Good grief!* If we didn't freeze or get hit by a truck, would we all land in jail?

"Let's go," said Opal. "The walking will warm us."

Guess what. She was right. Marching south, the wind pushed us along and stayed out of our faces. It took some muscles to hold up our signs, but they pulled us down the highway like spinnakers.

The giant slide from the old amusement park looked down at us like we were insects on the big, white flatness of the eastern Wisconsin landscape. Billboards on both sides of the road screamed their advertisements for cars, steak houses, and insurance companies. The shoulder of the road itself was a minefield of ice clods, slick patches, and the occasional shredded truck tire. By all accounts, it was an ugly place on an ugly day for marching.

What we had in our favor were passing eyeballs—thousands, millions, billions, zillions of cars and trucks roaring both ways. And, of course, that meant people—and some of those people had to be reading that "Sheriff Heiselmann Killed a Swan." And that had to mean that people were talking. We had to be making a difference. We just had to.

From my position in the rear, I could see my whole, small army. Right in front of me, Opal's scarf whipped every which-way from where it wrapped around her blue coat. In front of her, Mark stalked, predator-style, scanning left and right with his sign over his shoulder like a rifle. Rhonda amazed me most of all by leading the charge. She walked with a wobbly, sort of teetering stride—a human metronome ticking back and forth along on the shoulder of frozen gravel.

"Good job, everyone!" I shouted over the wind.

Rhonda hooted. Mark pumped his sign toward the sky. Then, Opal started singing and the whole group joined in. First off, she led us in several verses of "If I Had a Hammer." From there she taught us a bunch of verses of "This Train Is Bound for Glory," and we ended up marching to "The Marine Hymn" with Mark at lead vocals.

After we were just about worn out from singing, the group settled back into a sort of mindless slog with our heads hanging low. It was Mark who decided to liven things up by signaling people to honk their horns. He walked backward to face the oncoming cars and trucks and pumped his fist up and down.

"Come on, people, let's hear it!"

Well, guess what. It worked, and as long as folks saw Mark yelling and pumping his fist, about one in three of them happily delivered a few beeps in return. And when you're talking about a billion cars, one in three is a whole lot of horn honking. I especially liked the big-throated foghorn sound of the eighteen wheelers. Some just gave us a couple taps, but others let loose with a long-winded blast that practically shook the ground.

That energy got us through the coldest part of the morning. Then a car pulled up on the shoulder of the road. It was Mrs. Parsons in her station wagon with a bag of sandwiches and two Thermos bottles.

"I brought hot chocolate," she said.

She filled four steaming mugs and I don't think anything ever tasted so good. Mark made some wisecrack about wanting to spike it with whisky. Mrs. Parsons ignored him. "You only two miles from the bridge," she said.

"After that, it's Oshkosh," I said.

"That's right, and guess what. A Channel 2 news van is waiting for you at the bridge. You all gonna be on television."

All four of us whooped it up and did a little dance with our signs.

Mark looked at me with a big, stupid grin. "This is pretty cool, Delmar. You better think of something to say."

"Yeah . . . I'll think of something."

After Mrs. Parsons left, we were all still chirping and laughing—practically having an early victory celebration. That's when a Sheriff's Department patrol car drove by real slow. It wasn't Heiselmann, I was sure of that, but the guy had read our signs and his face wasn't smiling. As he went past I saw him pick up the microphone of his radio.

Was I worried? Yes, I was worried.

It was just past noon when we made our way up to the beginning of the mile-long bridge that crossed Big Lake Butte des Morts. Opal had us singing "If I Had a Hammer" again. We high-stepped to the rhythm and pumped our signs like a miniature marching band. Just like Mrs. Parsons had predicted, the newspeople were there. Two newspaper men each had fancy-looking cameras in their hands as they waited by their cars on the exit ramp. A Channel 2 news van was parked behind the others and a reporter wearing a bright-blue jacket with the *Eyewitness News* logo and holding a microphone waved us over. A television camera-man kneeled on the ground and aimed the big film camera at us marching toward him.

"Make it look good everyone," I yelled. "Keep singing."

Rhonda's knees chugged up and down like pistons. Between that, Mark's sign pumping, and Opal's singing, well, I don't mean to brag, but for four Shattuck High kids on a freezing-cold day in December, we were an impressive sight.

We stopped right in front of the TV cameraman and kept the singing and high stepping and sign pumping all going. The camera was just ten feet away and the reporter jabbered into his microphone. Then he walked up to me.

"Are you Del Finwick?"

"Yes, sir." Behind me, Opal, Mark, and Rhonda sang and stomped and waved.

"Can you tell us the reason for your march today?"

"My dad was Officer William Finwick, the sheriffs' deputy who was murdered on Highway 41. The sheriff and his investigators have done practically nothing to solve the case. We're here to demand justice."

"Why do you say that they have done practically nothing?"

"Well, for one thing, they hardly even looked for evidence. Barely tried to find the bullet that killed my dad."

"How do you know that?" asked the reporter.

I reached in my pocket and pulled out the bullet, holding it between my thumb and index finger for the reporter, the cameraman, and the whole world to see. "Because my friend Mark and I found the bullet after the cops gave up. It's from a .357 Magnum revolver."

"I see," said the reporter. "And what is the meaning of your signs? They say 'Sheriff Heiselmann Killed a Swan.' Can you tell us what that's about?"

"It's the truth," I said. "He's a lawbreaker. I saw him shoot a swan for no reason and leave it to die right there on the Poygan Marsh."

Guess what happened next. Two police cars showed up with their red lights flashing. They zoomed in fast and skidded to a stop in the gravel next to the news van. And who do you think got out of those cars? That's right. Sheriff Heiselmann himself and three of his deputies. They approached us, and they weren't smiling. I pocketed the bullet.

"This is an unlawful protest!" shouted the sheriff. Even from a dis-tance I could see the red color burning across his face.

The reporter stepped back, but the cameraman aimed at the sheriff and kept right on filming.

Sheriff Heiselmann moved forward with his handcuffs, gun, and other gadgets clanking with each step. I could tell he was trying to read our signs. Once he figured out what they said, the full eruption of Mount Heiselmann went off. In two seconds, the sheriff was practically on top of me, shouting right in my face. "You have no idea who you're messing with, you little brat!" I felt his hot, stinky breath on my nearly frozen face. His eyes wanted to kill me. He then spun around to face Mark, Opal, and Rhonda. "You will disband and disperse! You have two minutes!"

Nobody moved or said anything.

"I said you will disband and disperse! You have two minutes before you are placed under arrest!" It was like my team of marching protesters had finally frozen solid.

We used up one of our two minutes before anything happened. Then, it was Opal's voice that finally thawed the ice as she started singing the words to "If I Had a Hammer" again.

Mark looked at her like she was crazy. Rhonda looked at her like she was a genius. I looked at her and saw her mother marching over the Edmund Pettis Bridge in Selma, Alabama. I started singing along. Next thing I knew, we were all singing along. Pretty soon, with our feet stomping and our signs pumping, we became a unified force and I almost felt like we should lock arms.

I don't know why, but all of a sudden I thought about Wolf yelling from the freezing rapids below the Menasha dam. I had a vision of him splashing around in the water and finally slipping below the surface. Suddenly, the march was for him too.

"To the bridge!" I yelled out.

Rhonda didn't hesitate. *Thump! Thump! Thump!* She led the way. At that point, there was no quit in us as Mark and Opal moved in right behind her with me bringing up the rear. We made the biggest ruckus we could muster with our singing, stomping, and sign waving. That's how Opal, Mark, Rhonda, and I made our first attempt to cross the Butte des Morts Bridge to Oshkosh right in the face of the sheriff and his deputies.

Opal was right in front of me when she turned and looked back. At that moment, I noticed something about her eyes. They were her mother's eyes.

What happened next was as predictable as the sunrise over the Poygan marsh. The sheriff ordered his deputies to stop us, and they came at a full sprint. The big red-haired guy wanted me first, his hand-cuffs at the ready. I pulled into a crouch, faked right, and dodged left toward the ditch.

"You little bastard," he said, and he followed me with his long legs pumping. I was no sprinter, but I was wily, and I eluded him every time he came close. For what must have been a full minute we played keep-away. I heard Opal scream as another deputy tackled her and cuffed her hands behind her back. Rhonda shoved the cop, trying to get him off Opal, and before long she had her face in the snow with hands behind her back too. Mark didn't run, but he made it difficult on the officer by pulling his arms into his sleeves so they couldn't handcuff him. In the end it took two deputies to wrestle him into the back of their car, un-cuffed, and lock the door.

Through adrenaline and quickness I continued to evade the red-haired deputy on my tail.

"This is a peaceful protest!" I yelled. "We're marching to Oshkosh!"

My luck ran out. It was Sheriff Heiselmann who finally brought me down with a cross-body tackle that sent my body flying and my head thumping into the crusty snow. When I opened my eyes I was face-to-face with him. His eyes bulged and the veins in his cheeks and nose glowed red. His gray teeth showed through snarling lips. I saw a shadow block the sun and suddenly something busted me in the side of the face. The next thing I knew, I was in the back of a cop car with Mark.

"You're going to have a shiner there, Delmar."

I brought my hand to my face and pulled it away with a smear of blood on my fingers. Suddenly, my mind was on a hundred things all at once. What was happening to us? Were we under arrest? Would Mrs. Parsons even find us? Were we all going to jail?

Once I caught my breath I imagined myself behind bars and almost started to cry. But then I looked over at Mark and he sat there with his head held high, steady as the Neenah lighthouse.

"We did it, Delmar," he said.

"Huh?"

"We did it."

Hearing those words helped, and somehow I held it together realizing what we had all just accomplished. We got the sheriff to show his true colors. He had cracked. He had blown his lid, and it was all caught on film.

35

In case you're wondering, Sheriff Heiselmann never did throw us in jail. As it turned out, fifteen-year-olds can be locked up for killing people, stealing cars, or robbing banks, but not for trying to march across a bridge.

Instead, they gave us each a citation for walking on a restricted highway and in my case, a warning about resisting arrest. The deputies called our parents and talked to us about the foolishness of our actions. They told us it was our duty as young men and women to obey the laws of the land and quit causing unnecessary disruption. Through it all, we never saw Sheriff Heiselmann.

Opal's mom arrived first at the Sheriff's Department headquarters. She was angry at the cops and let them know it. "How dare you go around handcuffing minors just for expressing their constitutional rights of free speech?!" Her words echoed through the halls and nobody said a thing.

She walked right up to the group of three deputies and told them that they ought to be ashamed of themselves. Then she told us she was proud of what we had done before glaring again at the deputies. I thought about the lump on her head. She had seen worse than we had — much worse.

Rhonda's dad was next to arrive. He was a scruffy-looking guy who hadn't shaved in a few days. His shoes were untied and one side of his flannel shirt hung lower than the other because the buttons were lined up wrong. The man didn't say a word to any of us, not even Rhonda. He just waved her toward the car and they drove off.

Mom came next and when I saw her face I almost wished they had thrown me into solitary confinement. She wore a blue overcoat, but her pajama pants showed underneath. Her eyes were red and wet.

"You lied to me," she said.

I hung my head and walked to the car.

As Mom started driving away, I thought about Mark sitting there all by himself. "We can't leave Mark," I said.

"He's not my responsibility," said Mom. "His father will pick him up."

"I don't think so."

"Why not."

"His father doesn't care about anything except getting drunk."

"That's Mark's problem, not mine."

As soon as Mom said those words I could tell that she regretted them. We drove toward home on the lake road, neither of us talking. Snow piled in drifts as the wind whipped in off the frozen desert of Lake Winnebago. It was a nasty day on the ice but I sure wished I was out there. Nothing could be worse than the climate I was feeling inside the car.

When we reached the Neenah city limits sign, Mom slowed to a stop, checked her mirrors, and turned around.

"What are you doing?" I asked.

"Going back to get Mark."

✳

As you can imagine, we were the lead story on Channel 2 *Eyewitness News* at six o'clock. That's right—me, Rhonda, Opal, and Mark. Only the real star was Sheriff Heiselmann, and they captured him in living color—red face, purple veins—the whole works. They even caught the part where he punched me. He was on top of me, and as I squirmed to get away, he pulled back his arm and swung it forward, blasting my face.

After the news, the phone started ringing. First, a man at the *Post-Crescent* wanted an interview, and I spent a half hour telling him the whole story. Then a lady called from the *Oshkosh Daily Northwestern* and I did it all again. It was after ten o'clock when the man from the *Green Bay Press-Gazette* called, and I gave him the whole run-down just like the others. After those three, Mom pulled the plug on the phone.

Every reporter I talked to was focused on one thing in particular and it wasn't even the punch I got from Sheriff Heiselmann. It was the bullet. How had a couple of fifteen-year-old kids found more evidence at a crime scene than the entire Sheriff's Department? And why hadn't the kids turned over the evidence?

Even after the ten o'clock news ended, Mark and I kept reviewing every little event of the day. We talked about how the reporters had covered the story and wondered how it would appear in the newspapers the next day.

"Enough is enough," said Mom. She pointed Mark toward the living room couch, and I went to the bathroom to brush my teeth.

I needed sleep more than anybody. My head was drooped like a stuffed bear on the dart board at the County Fair, but there was still one very important thing I had to do before going to bed. I had to hide the bullet.

I snuck into the garage and turned on the light. Every hiding place I looked at seemed too obvious. The workbench drawer. The corner behind the shovels. The stack of scrap lumber. Then my eyes landed on the old, red gas can in the corner that we used to fuel the lawnmower. I lifted it by the handle. It was still half full. The lid unscrewed easily, and I took a sniff to make sure. Retrieving the bullet from my pocket, I dropped it into the can with a *ploink* and screwed the lid back in place.

❋

The very next morning, right after Mark went home, my family started laying into me. We were all in the kitchen, Sally and Mom drinking coffee at the table while I stirred a glass of Tang and waited for two Pop-Tarts to jump out of the toaster.

Sally spoke up first. "Thanks for destroying my life, Del."

"What do you mean?"

"Are you that stupid? Don't you realize that I'm now the sister of a juvenile delinquent? You broke the law and your face was all over the TV, you idiot. And to make it worse yet, Kevin's parents know the sheriff, *personally*. So thanks for wrecking my life."

"You're welcome."

"None of this is going to bring Dad back, you know. Why don't you just quit harassing all of the good people who work in law enforcement?"

"I'm only harassing the sheriff," I said. "Because he deserves it."

As you can probably imagine, none of that went over very well. Sally called me a hopeless jerk and asked my mom why she had to live with a criminal. Mom yelled at both of us, but especially me, and said I should quit harassing my sister. *Holy crickets!* I had to get out of there. It was

Sunday morning—Christmas Eve morning—and I decided to go to church. At least those people would be on my side. Right?

✸

I couldn't have been more wrong. As soon as I stepped through the heavy wooden doors all eyes drilled into me and the whispering started up. I couldn't hear everything, but I detected certain words like "such a shame" and "disrespectful."

Then a scowling old lady with steel hair and a blue hat stepped up to me. "Are you pleased with yourself, young man, besmirching the reputation of one of our finest civic leaders?"

I said nothing.

"Maybe you didn't realize that the sheriff donated his time and fifty dollars to the Ladies Aid Society. He's a good citizen and an honorable man—unlike some people."

"He killed a swan. That's not honorable."

"You're just a mouthy little brat aren't you? What would your father think?"

"I think he would have been proud of me," I said, looking directly into her eyes.

The lady gasped and made a face she had probably been saving for Fidel Castro.

"Hooligan!" she shouted.

I half-expected to see crusaders in armored uniforms storming out of the janitors' closet to slap me around before running me through with a sword.

Then, just in the nick of time, Mrs. Borger showed up.

"Mr. Finwick."

"Oh, hi, Mrs. Borger." I braced myself. What would she think? Would she put me on trial for sorcery?

"I saw you and your classmates on television, and I can't tell you how proud I am of you. That took real courage." She studied my face. "Looks like they got a little rough with you."

"It's just a bruise," I said.

"He deserved it," said the scrap-iron lady under the framed picture of Jesus holding a lamb.

"He most certainly did *not* deserve it!" Mrs. Borger nearly shouted. She took a step toward the blue-hat lady, and for a second I thought I would have to jump between them like a hockey ref.

The two women glared at each other for a while until Mrs. Borger finally spoke. "Like I said, Del, it took courage. And even more courage to show up here, I see." With that comment, Mrs. Borger earned her own gasp. The blue-hat lady made a face and stormed off to the fellowship hall, where she was probably fixing to report that the devil and his English teacher had just showed up for worship.

For the third time since Dad's murder, Mrs. Borger grabbed me by the elbow and marched me down the aisle, to a pew near the front. Both of us were wound up tighter than mouse-trap springs. I could hear Mrs. Borger still huffing and mumbling to herself. It took a few minutes, but we finally settled down and focused our attention on the pulpit.

I don't know how he did it, but Pastor Olson said all the right things again that Sunday morning. The title of his sermon (and I'm not kidding here), was "The Road Less Traveled." It was all about how the right direction isn't always the easy one, and that, sometimes in life, a person has to go against the grain. Sometimes a guy just has to do what feels right, and if it upsets some folks—well, tough cookies.

My own personal road less traveled had stirred things up all right. It was still too early to tell whether or not that road even went in the right direction. Would it make a difference in the long run? Maybe—maybe not. Would it bring back my dad? Nope.

I still needed to get out of the house for the afternoon, so I called Mark on the telephone. Guess what. He was trying to get away too, and from his father's yelling in the background I figured that we had better do something quick. We agreed to meet at his hideout in the swamp. I made two peanut butter sandwiches and bugged out the door.

We showed up at the hideout at around the same time. Mark had bought a Sunday *Post-Crescent* at Red Owl and we opened it to see what they had written about us and Sheriff Heiselmann. On the top of page 2, we found the story, including a headline printed in big bold letters.

Protesters Clash with Authorities at Butte des Morts Bridge

The written part filled up about a third of the page, but it was two photographs that really caught our eyes. One photo showed the four of us marching on the shoulder of the highway with our signs and raising our fists to the sky. The words "Sheriff Heiselmann Killed a Swan" were easily readable, and we must have been singing because our mouths hung wide open. The second picture was an action shot of Heiselmann tackling me as I tried to escape. Snow flew in every direction as the two of us tumbled to the ground. I could see the sheriff's clenched fist and the anger in his face. Lucky for me, I didn't look scared.

As we read the whole story out loud, a feeling of pride surged through me. *Jiminy Crickets!* The whole Fox River Valley was reading about our protests. Now everybody would know that Sheriff Heiselmann killed a swan. Now everybody would know that we didn't trust him. No wonder the people in church were hot under the collar. We had busted the lid off Pandora's Box and there was no telling what the newspeople might dig up next.

Mark felt the same way I did and gave me a solid punch in the shoulder. "We did it, Delmar! Heiselmann's a bug under the microscope now."

"Maybe."

"Maybe nothing. Let's celebrate."

I smiled, not knowing for sure what Mark meant. Then I watched him pull a bottle out from the inside of his coat. He twisted open the metal cap.

Mark took a big gulp from the bottle that sent an air bubble gurgling up through the clear liquid. He blinked hard and grinned before handing it to me.

I worried that I would gag and have to spit it out, but I tipped the bottle and let a little bit drain down my throat. It was like candy—nothing to it.

"Not bad," I said.

"Peppermint Schnapps," said Mark.

Proud of myself, I took a bigger swallow and wiped my mouth on my sleeve before handing the bottle back to Mark. It took less than an hour to empty the quart of flavored booze. I felt warm all over and laughed at everything. *Holy smokes!* Mark was practically Johnny Carson, he was so funny all of a sudden.

I lay back on the bed of frozen mud and closed my eyes. *Whoa!* My whole universe was swirling around me. I sat back up and shook my head.

"What's wrong, Delmar?"

"Everything's spinning."

"Of course it's spinning. You drank half a bottle of booze, you idiot! Son of a bitch, Delmar, you finally got drunk!" We both laughed and punched each other in the shoulder a few times. It was all pretty neat and I felt sort of grown-up for a change. *Look at me.* I thought to myself. *I'm a drinker.* I felt pretty darn cool, even cocky. I joked around about how I wished Mark had another bottle.

Ten minutes later the feeling in my head started moving toward my stomach. Five minutes after that, I was on hands and knees trying to pull my face out of the snow with puke dripping out my mouth and nose and all over the front of my coat. I kept on coughing and gagging even after everything in my stomach had already been heaved up. Without any water to drink, I couldn't get the sickening taste of peppermint-flavored puke out of my mouth. I tried eating snow but it only made things worse. I heaved and hacked and hunched my back until I thought I was going to cough up my own stomach.

Mark laughed at first. "One shot too many, Delmar?" But then he saw my whole body shaking and clammed up. It wasn't funny anymore, even to him. I felt like I was going to freeze to death, and maybe I would have. Then I felt the dull pressure of two arms around my chest. Mark grunted loudly and lifted me to my feet.

The two-mile slog home from the swamp marked a new low point in my dull and stupid life. Mark propped me up the whole way as I wobbled along on sewing machine legs. We must have been a sight to the passing drivers on their way to and from Christmas Eve services at churches all over town. There I was, the proud and courageous protester, now drunk, shivering, eyes half-closed, with streaks of frozen vomit all over my hair, face, and unzipped coat.

I thought we would never get home but we did. Mark cleaned me up as best he could with some shop rags in the garage.

"You're on your own from here, Delmar." He guided me through the door to the kitchen and disappeared.

Using the table for support, I found my way to the sink and drank a glass of cold water. I barely made it to the toilet in the downstairs bathroom before I was puking it all up again.

I felt Mom's eyes on me as I stumbled up the stairs to my bedroom. She said nothing. I woke up in the middle of the night beneath a stack of quilts that Mom or Sally must have placed over me while I slept. My clock radio showed a time of 2:15. My head pounded like a drum at a Rockets pep rally.

"Merry Christmas, jerk," I whispered to myself.

36

Someone nudged my shoulder and I opened my eyes. Mom looked down at me, smiling. "Merry Christmas."

"Merry Christmas, Mom," I said.

"Are you feeling better?"

"I think so."

"Jump in the shower. Breakfast will be ready in a half hour."

Suddenly, I noticed that Mom wasn't in her pajamas. She was dressed in black slacks and a bright-red sweater. Her hair was fixed up nice too. I heard her slow, even steps going back down the stairs.

I looked in a panic for the vomit-stained clothes that I had left in a heap. They were gone. Mom must have put them in the washing machine. I touched my hair and felt the hard splotches of dried puke. It brought back the day before, and for a second I felt sick again. In the bathroom I dreaded turning on the light, not sure what I would see in the mirror. With a flick of the switch I had my answer. My skin was the color of cooked fish. My hair was like a swallow's nest. And the bruise where Sheriff Heiselmann nailed me was an even bigger, purple half-moon under my right eye. I wouldn't be posing for pictures in front of the Christmas tree.

After a shower I almost looked human and felt a whole ton better than before. I got dressed in clean underwear, jeans, and socks and even found my red-and-green plaid shirt.

The whole house smelled like bacon as I walked down the stairs and a platter full awaited me when I got to the table. Another plate held German-style coffee cake with candy cherries mixed in with the breading and white frosting on top. A steaming bowl of scrambled eggs completed the makings of a swell Christmas morning breakfast, just like when Dad was still alive.

"Thanks, Mom." I nibbled on a corner off the coffee cake, trying to put on a good front.

"Sally did most of it," said Mom.

"Thanks, Sally," I said. She forced a little smile.

We opened gifts in the living room, and I was excited to get three new ice fishing tip-ups and a minnow bucket. They made me think again about Wolf. I opened another present and gawked at a pair of felt-lined boots, which I hadn't expected at all. They were genuine Sorels, the brand that had become all the rage among the deer hunting and ice fishing crowd.

"Thank you, Mom," I said.

I watched Mom as she opened her gift from me. She pulled the green object out of the department store box from Prange's, where I bought it.

"It's a frog," she said. She mustered up a sort of confused smile.

Uh-oh, she doesn't like it. "It's a jewelry box," I said. "It's just shaped like a frog."

I showed her how to lift up the top half of the frog box, and then she discovered the pair of earrings that I had hidden inside. They were bright-red simulated rubies in 24-carat gold-plated settings. Between the frog and the earrings, the purchase had set me back a couple months of Hoot Owl money. It was worth it though, because once she figured it out, she really loved my gift. She put the earrings on right away and said the frog would go right on top of her dresser.

Sally liked her gift too. I knew she liked Lifesavers candies, so I got her one of those sets of ten different flavored packs all wrapped up in a box that pretends to be a book. When she opened it and saw all those tubes of candy, her eyes really popped. She thanked me and Mom for our gifts just as a horn honked in the driveway.

"That's Kevin," said Sally. She grabbed her coat and dashed out the door.

With the fancy breakfast behind us and the gifts all opened, Mom lit up a cigarette and sat down in front of the TV. *Gosh*, that seemed like a sad way to spend Christmas day, so I suggested something else.

"Do you want to put on some music and teach me some more dance steps?"

She hesitated for a few seconds. "Why are you so interested in learning to dance all of a sudden?"

There was no way I could lie to her again, especially on Christmas Day, so I blurted out the truth. "I'm thinking about asking someone to the Snow-Ball next month."

That earned me a wink. For over an hour, Mom showed me how to dance the Twist, the Hully-Gully, the Mashed Potato, and the Watusi. I picked it up quick because I've always had good coordination for stuff like that. Besides, Mom really knew the steps and was a great teacher.

Let me just say this. Dancing on Christmas morning with my mom was a hoot and a half, and I was happier than ever to see such a big smile on her face. By the time the last record played out, we were ready for a couple tall glasses of genuine orange juice from concentrate.

"I'm pretty sure most kids at the dance won't know half of those steps," said Mom.

"I'm pretty sure you're right," I answered. "Now I just have to get a date."

After cooling off, we were both still in a good mood, so I asked Mom if she would play a game of chess and she agreed. I set up the board at the kitchen table. She made herself a cup of coffee and we were off to the races. There were a few tricks in chess I had picked up by playing the other nerds in the Science Resource Center. I started with a strategy of getting my horses and bishops out early and lining up some pawns at a diagonal. I captured her queen in about five minutes by using my horse to put her king in check and the queen in danger at the same time. It's an old trick that my mom forgot to watch out for. With her queen out of the way, I moved in on her rooks and bishops and had her whipped into checkmate in fifteen minutes.

"Do you want to play again?" I asked.

"I'll play you in checkers," she said.

I was pretty sure that if I could whip her in chess I could do the same in checkers. Then I learned that Mom was the Winnebago County 4-H club checkers champion when she was a kid. The words "king me" hit my ears four times before I knew what was happening and she went on to trounce me without even breaking a sweat.

It sure was great seeing Mom having fun and smiling for a change.

"Do you think you're getting any better?" I asked.

She shrugged. "I have good days and bad days," she said. "I'll probably need a nap this afternoon."

We both sat and said nothing for a while.

"Who were you drinking with yesterday?" she asked.

Uh-oh. I should have known this was coming. The way I looked and smelled, Mom had me pegged from the moment I got home.

"Mark."

"How much did you drink?"

"Half of a bottle of peppermint schnapps."

"What size bottle?"

"Quart."

Her eyebrows jumped and she let out a low whistling sound. "You keep that up and it'll kill you."

"I know."

"And if it doesn't kill you, then I'll kill you."

I looked at her wide eyed.

"Do you understand?"

"Yes."

"Are you going to do it again?"

"No."

"I don't know if I can believe you. You lied to me on Saturday, didn't you?"

"Yes."

"What do you think your punishment should be?"

Uh-oh. Trick question. I waited to see if she would break the silence, but her eyes were on me like a walleye on a crayfish.

"Well?"

I blurted out the only thing I could think of. "Fifty pull-ups every day for a month?"

She flinched. Then squinted. "Fifty is a lot of pull-ups," she said. "Some people can't do one."

"I can do it," I said. "Not all at once, but over a full day."

"Let's make it three months then."

"Okay," I felt like I had dodged an arrow. Maybe I had a future as a negotiator.

"And for the lying part, you're going to wash all the dishes, scrub all the floors, and clean the bathroom to my satisfaction for three months. Understand?"

I paused to let my heart start pumping blood again. "Sure, Mom."

For the next half hour, Mom rested on the couch watching *I Love Lucy* on television while I sat alone in the kitchen with a stack of old comic books. I had almost finished reading *Tarzan and the Ant Men* when the doorbell rang. It was Mark.

"Hi, Delmar." He looked left and right, then whispered, "How are you feeling?"

Before I could answer, my mom hollered out from the living room. "Mark, could you come in here please?"

For the first time in my life I saw fear in Mark's eyes. He took off his shoes by the door and walked back to see my mom. I stayed in the kitchen and five minutes later he returned.

"What happened?" I asked.

"Your mom threatened to kill me."

"Me too."

"What are we doing today?"

"Not drinking peppermint schnapps," I said.

"Good idea. What else are we doing?"

"Do you want to play Monopoly?" I asked. "We can probably convince my mom to join us."

"Okay."

For almost the entire afternoon of Christmas Day, the three of us played games. We started with Monopoly but moved on to Parcheesi, hearts, Probe, and Landslide. Between games, Mom heated up Swanson TV Dinners and served hot chocolate. It was a blast. Mark, in particular, seemed to be having the Christmas Day of his life. Then the doorbell rang and it got better.

Can you guess who showed up in the middle of the whole party? Mrs. Samuelson and the church ladies.

"Merry Christmas, Dorothy," said Mrs. Samuelson, as she forced her wide body through the door with a tray of cookies the size of a bicycle wheel. Her deep, gravelly voice, refrigerator-sized body, and neon pink face came as a shock to Mark. But when she sat down to join us in a game of hearts and shot the moon on the first hand, the queen of the church ladies instantly became his best friend for the day.

The other ladies, the super-skinny Mrs. Stevens and the pear-shaped Mrs. Weiden, went straight for the kitchen sink, cleaning up every dish that we had dirtied, and saving me a ton of work along the way.

Before long, the conversation found its way to the protest march against Sheriff Heiselmann, which everyone had seen on the Channel 2 news and read about in the paper.

Mrs. Samuelson commenced her rant by standing at the head of the table. "I was *appalled* at the way you kids were treated! And for the sheriff to punch you in the face—good gracious! I've got a good mind to take a rolling pin to that man! And if he touches you again, why, I'll do more than that! Of course, I must forgive him first. But after that, somebody needs to teach that bully a lesson, and if I get the chance I'll take it."

Mark turned his head and tried to hold in his laughter.

Then Mrs. Samuelson put her plump hands on both sides of my face like she was picking up a pumpkin. "And how is your injury, dear?"

"Still a little sore."

"I should say so!" She leaned over and kissed my head as I tried and failed to duck out of the way. The rant lasted a few more minutes. Then she looked at me again with that puffy, pink face beneath the roof of white hair.

"Did he *really* kill a swan?"

"Yes, ma'am. I saw it myself."

Mrs. Samuelson let out a yelp like a wounded dog, and it kicked off another tirade on the subject of animal cruelty that went on for five *more* minutes.

"Are you kids planning another march?" she asked.

"I'm not sure," I said. That brought a bent eyebrow from my mom.

"You *must* march again," said Mrs. Samuelson. "And I shall *join* you next time!"

She turned her excited gaze toward the other church ladies. "Mrs. Stevens, will you march?"

"Yes, of course."

"And you, Mrs. Weiden?"

"I believe I can."

"How about you, Dorothy? Certainly you won't stand idly by. You'll join the march too, won't you?"

"Well . . . I don't know," said Mom.

"How can you not?!" asked Mrs. Samuelson. "That fiend slugged your boy! He killed a swan!"

"Don't forget about Delmar's dad!" shouted Mark.

"An excellent point, young man," Mrs. Samuelson replied, and before Mark could dodge it, she plunked a kiss on top of his head, making him blush like a poinsettia.

"What will it be, Dorothy? Will you march or won't you?"

"I guess so."

37

On Tuesday morning, the day after Christmas, I was amazed at all the letters to the editor written about our protest march on the opinion page of the *Post-Crescent*. I jogged down to the Food Queen, bought a copy of the *Oshkosh Daily Northwestern*, and brought it back home. *Holy mackerel!* Both papers were buzzing with letters that people had mailed in.

Just like at church, some people were mad at us for causing a ruckus.

They're disrespectful! Somebody should teach them a lesson! They should be locked up!

But most of the letters, maybe three-quarters of them, stuck the needle to Heiselmann.

How dare he bully those students!

Who does the sheriff think he is—Adolf Hitler?

Believe it or not, most of the letters were about the message on our signs—"Sheriff Heiselmann Killed a Swan." You'd have thought he had harpooned the last blue whale the way folks carried on. I chuckled at the thought of the sheriff reading those letters and turning red and purple all over again. It was Opal who had figured out that the swan would light people up, and now we had Heiselmann on the defensive. That much was for sure.

It was almost lunchtime and I had just finished scrubbing the floor and washing dishes when the doorbell rang. I had a feeling it wasn't good news, and I was right. I peeked through the curtain. *Holy crap!* A sheriff's department uniform! I opened the curtain wider. *Hellfire!* It was Heiselmann himself.

I jumped into the living room. "It's the sheriff!" Mom crushed out her cigarette and got a sort of *ready-to-fight* look on her face. Together we approached the door and opened it.

Heiselmann put on a Count Dracula smile. "Hello, Mrs. Finwick. I'm sorry to bother you on the morning after Christmas, but I'm here on official business."

"You hit my son." My mom's voice was strong.

He turned off the stupid smile. "That was an accident."

"The hell it was. Look at that eye." Mom pulled me forward, pushed the hair up on my forehead, and tilted my head back to show him the purple ring.

"I'm sorry, Mrs. Finwick. It was completely unintentional, I can assure you. We were just trying to catch him."

"The hell you were. Now, what do you want?" asked Mom. She blocked the doorway, one arm propped against each side.

"It has come to our attention that your son has found a piece of evidence near the crime scene. A bullet. I'm here to retrieve it."

Mom glared at him.

The sheriff then pulled a piece of paper from his pocket. "I have obtained a court order," he said. "You are required, by law, to comply."

Mom turned to me. "Get the bullet, Del."

"He can't have it." My fists were clenched.

"Why not?"

I looked at the sheriff and then back at my mom. "Because he either killed Dad or knows who did."

I could feel the sheriff's anger without even looking at him. Mom put one hand on my shoulder and looked into my eyes.

"You have to give him the bullet."

Very briefly I thought about saying that I lost it, but I didn't want to lie again to Mom. "He can't have it. I hid it."

"Where is it?" asked Mom.

"I won't say."

Mom and the sheriff both gave me the same look of disbelief. Heiselmann took a step forward and the corners of his mouth turned severely downward. "Maybe you'd like another trip to my office?"

Mom went face-to-face with him and took a step forward herself. "Get out of here." Her voice could have scratched glass.

"I won't leave without that bullet."

"You *will* leave. Now!" She closed the door in his face and arranged the curtain to cover every square inch of the window.

Heiselmann yelled through the closed door. "I'll get a search warrant!" We heard him clomp down the steps.

Mom walked to the kitchen and lit up a cigarette. I peeked out the corner of the window and watched the sheriff's car spin its wheels on the slushy street and disappear.

"What are we going to do now, Mom?"

"I don't know."

"Are you mad at me?"

"No."

❋

That meeting with Heiselmann really got to my mom. She didn't know what to do, so she vacuumed the whole house, nonstop, while puffing cigs and dropping ashes all over the floor at the same time. The combination of smoke and noise just about drove me bats. I grabbed my new Sorel boots and ice fishing gear and hiked toward Little Lake Butte des Morts.

It was always neat walking past the steaming mills wedged between Washington Street and the river channel in Menasha. White, man-made clouds swirled like dragon's breath, flashing the sunlight on and off. I admired the old stone towers that marked the corners of the Tayco Street Bridge. In the summer months the bridgetender sometimes waved at me from his tiny room while waiting for boats so he could lift the drawbridge and let them pass through. Once off the island, I took a left on First and knocked on the door of a small house with a bait shop sign hanging from the porch roof.

An elderly lady opened the door and waved me in. "Come in out of the cold," she said.

"Thanks."

"What can I get you?"

"Do you have any wax worms?"

"Yes, but folks are catching perch on mousies," she said.

I pulled a few coins out of my pocket. "How many can I get for sixty-five cents?"

"I usually sell a container of three dozen for a dollar," she said. "But I'm running a sale today."

"Thanks."

She smiled. "How about a cookie? They're still warm."

"Sure."

The old lady disappeared behind a door, and I was left staring at the geezer who must have been her husband. He was sitting by a lamp with his nose buried in a book. His lips moved as he read through thick glasses. Suddenly, his head bounced off the page and looked in my direction like he had just been surprised by a burglar.

"Do you like to read?" he asked.

"Sometimes."

"Do you like poetry?"

"I guess so."

"Listen to this."

He moved his shaking index finger to a bookmark and found the right page. It took him a few more seconds to get started, then he read to me with a deep, loud voice.

The great flood-gates of the wonder-world swung open, and . . . there floated in my inmost soul, endless processions of the whale, and, mid most of them all, one grand hooded phantom, like a snow hill in the air.

He looked at me, smiling. "Do you know what that's from?"

"*Moby-Dick?*"

"How did you guess?"

"It's about a whale."

"That's right! The whale is the snow hill in the air. Sort of poetic, don't you think?"

"Yes."

"Melville had to have courage to write *Moby-Dick* that way."

I nodded.

"Did you know that Melville was writing about more than just a whale?"

I shook my head.

"He was. You might ask your teacher about that."

I nodded.

The man lowered his reading glasses and looked me over. "You're the kid who marched against the sheriff, aren't you?"

"Yes."

"I saw you on TV and read about you in the paper. Looks like you got a shiner for your trouble."

"Yes, sir."

"Your daddy was the deputy who was killed?"

"Yes."

"And you think the sheriff knows something about it?"

"Yes, sir."

"Well, you better be careful. I understand you found some evidence."

"A bullet."

"Hmm—serious business," he said.

The kitchen door clunked open and the lady showed up with a cookie in one hand and a chewing tobacco tin in the other. I took a bite of the cookie and twisted open the tobacco container exposing three dozen squirming white grubs in a bed of sawdust. I handed the lady sixty-five cents and thanked her.

As I was heading out the door, the man stopped me one more time. "Chapter thirty-five," he said. *Your whales must be seen before they can be killed.*

I nodded, not sure what the heck that was supposed to mean.

❋

I returned home at dusk with nine perch, a frozen face, and that old man with the *Moby-Dick* lines still rattling around in my brain. Without asking, I scaled and cleaned the fish on some old newspapers at the kitchen sink. Mom came in as I was setting up the electric frying pan with oil. She opened a can of baked beans and emptied it into another pan on the stove. We ate it all and had ice cream for dessert.

"You're okay, Del." Mom kissed me on the cheek.

Exhausted, I flopped on the couch. My eyes followed the dancers and singers on *The Lawrence Welk Show* but my mind was everywhere else. Would I end up in juvie if I didn't hand over the bullet? Would Mom ever really get better? Would we ever *really* get justice for Dad's killer?

Mom sat in the chair next to me. "Don't forget your duties," she said.

"What duties?"

"Dishes. Floors. Bathrooms."

"Oh . . ."

"Did I forget anything?"

"Pull-ups," I said.

38

Mom had slipped back into her bad habits of spending hour after hour sitting in front of the television and smoking cigarettes, interrupted only by the occasional, slow-motion walk to the bathroom or the refrigerator. I tried to think of ways to get her off the couch, but she was even losing interest in dancing.

"Can we practice again?" I asked.

"Do you have a date yet?"

"No."

"Do you have someone in mind?"

"Yes."

"Who is it?"

"Just a girl I met in English class," I said. The part about English class was true. The *just a girl* part wasn't.

"Is she nice?"

"Yes."

"Well, why don't you call her then?"

"I don't know."

"No sense working on dancing if you're not going to the dance."

Jeez! Why was I afraid to pick up the stupid telephone? I walked into the kitchen and looked up Parsons in the phone book. I picked up the phone receiver and started dialing but set it back down.

"Just call her. What's the worst thing that can happen?" said Mom.

I picked up the phone with conviction and dialed the number again. It rang once, then twice . . .

"Hello. Parsons residence."

"Hi, Mrs. Parsons. This is Del Finwick. Is Opal there?"

"Hello, Del. She be right here."

I heard her tell Opal that it was me. The next voice I heard was Opal on the phone.

"Hello," she said.

"Hi, Opal. How was your Christmas?"

"It was nice," she said. "How about yours?"

"Mine was good too. Did you get any nice presents?"

"Sure. Mostly clothes. I also got some earrings. How about you?"

"I got some ice fishing stuff and Sorel Boots."

"That sounds perfect for you."

"Yeah. It's great."

"That's nice."

For a pretty long stretch I didn't say anything, not sure how to shift the conversation over to the dance. Opal finally broke the silence.

"Is there another reason for your call, Del?"

"Yes."

"What is it?"

"Would you go to the Snow-Ball dance with me next month?" My knees nearly buckled as the question spilled out of my mouth. There it was. All she had to do was say yes, and we could work out the details later.

Silence.

"Are you still there?" I asked.

"Yes."

"What's wrong?"

"I already have a date to the dance. I'm going with Mark."

❋

Lucky for me I had an escape route, and it was the frozen ice of Lake Winnebago. December was the best time for ice fishing, but it didn't matter. I just needed a place to be by myself. Mom drove me to the Fresh Air Camp south of town.

"I'll pick you up at five o'clock, honey."

"Okay, Mom."

When she drove away I felt a little better. Just me and the ice. I strapped all my gear to a wooden sled, checked my compass, and started walking southeast.

That phone call with Opal had really taken something out of me. It was a blow, like the stomach punch that ended up killing the Great Houdini. On top of it all, I was embarrassed. It wasn't easy telling Mom that I had been turned down. It was even tougher knowing that Opal would be going with my best friend.

I needed to disappear from the entire world. The snow crunched beneath my Sorels as I began my trek into the empty frontier of nothingness. I was Lawrence of Arabia on the vast desert. I was Neil Armstrong on the moon. I was an atom, invisible and lost to the infinity of the universe.

Swish, swish, swish. The legs of my snow pants rubbed together like blocks of sandpaper. *Just get over it,* I told myself. *Who wants to go to a stupid dance anyhow?*

Have you ever tried to force your brain to quit thinking about something? It's impossible. I tried changing the subject to sports, hunting, even my battles with Sheriff Heiselmann, but with every try my thoughts returned to Opal and Mark.

Swish, swish, swish.

What had I been thinking, asking a pretty girl like Opal to the dance? What would I say to her in English class from now on? What about Mark? Were we finished being friends? Jeez! I should have known he would ask Opal out eventually. It was obvious that he liked her.

Everything added up to the same conclusion that I already knew. I was a hopeless loser. My nickname was Minnow for a reason. It was the name that I deserved.

Eventually, I decided on a spot a couple miles from shore and unlashed my gear, starting first with the six-foot-long, iron chisel known as a spud. *Chop! Chop! Chop! Chop!* It felt good to harpoon away with a loud grunt behind each blast. Ice chips flew in every direction from the sharpened tip as I shuffled my feet in a circular path around the emerging hole. The final *ploinck* into liquid water sent a miniature gusher into the hole until the water level was even with the ice surface. A few more chops through splashing water finished the hole. I skimmed out the chips and built a pile of slush on the windward side to support the vertical post of my tip-up. With a clip-on lead weight snapped onto the hook, I loosened the spool and dropped it fifteen feet to the lake bottom until the black line went slack. That's where I tied a loop into the line, which I hung on the nail in the end of the wooden cross bar. The whole idea of a tip-up was to use the pull of a fish on the line to send a signal to the fisherman. As the fish pulled down one side of the teeter-totter crossbar, a weight slid down a wire and lifted a red flag all the way up toward the sky.

I repeated the process and within thirty-five minutes had three tip-ups baited with minnows and bobbing gently in the wind. It was time to sit and watch. I scrunched up Indian style, pulled my hat over my eyebrows like a visor, and waited.

Guess what. After all that work of chopping holes and setting up tip-ups, the sick feeling of rejection was almost gone. I had pretty well finished beating myself up after the disastrous phone conversation with Opal. I had decided that my life as a fifteen-year-old wasn't over and my brain actually moved on to other things.

At the top of the list were the protests, the news reports, and the visit by Sheriff Heiselmann and his court order to make me hand over the bullet. The newspapers and TV people sure had shown the world the Genghis Khan side of the sheriff, and all those letters to the editors were just gravy on the mashed potatoes. Yep, he was feeling the squeeze, all right. I could practically see him squirming in his office. Now if only I could put together the rest of the puzzle. If only I knew how the Cadillac Man fit in and who actually pulled the trigger on the .357 Magnum revolver that was used to murder my dad.

With the orange sun sinking low and the wind dying off, the flag on my number 3 tip-up teetered slightly. I knew right away that it was a walleye. They always pull slowly on the line. A northern or white bass will grab the bait and run, flipping the tip-up flag instantly upward. A walleye sucks the minnow into its mouth and barely moves. I walked over to the flag, which was still at half-mast. The line was taut and pulled to one side of the hole. There was no sense waiting; the fish was on. I grabbed the heavy, black line and gave it a yank. *Tug, tug, Tu-tu-tug*, the fish came up and splashed out of the hole. A nice eighteen-incher with greenish gold on the sides and a belly as white and shiny as a porcelain sink.

I rebaited the hook with another minnow and dropped it back down. Not thirty seconds later that same tip-up flag went up again. Holy smokes! Was there a school of them down there? Just like before, I grabbed the line barehanded and set the hook. Moments later, another beauty, slightly smaller than the first, flopped onto the ice and snow.

I hadn't even reached the minnow bucket to rebait when the flag on my number 2 tip-up started moving skyward. I jogged over as the loop in the line slid off the end of my tip-up flag and started slipping down into the hole. I gave it a yank and again felt the familiar *tug-tug-tug* of what I was certain would be my third nice walleye inside of ten minutes. This time the fish was a slab of black-and-gold flecks about fifteen inches long. A sand pike, and a darn nice one.

The action died down as quick as it had started. Three for three in ten minutes. Was anything in the world more fun? I sprawled out on the ice as the light grew dim and the billowing clouds of steam from the mills washed away into gray darkness. That was it—time to go home.

My catch of two walleyes and a sand pike was just two fish short of the limit. They were already frozen into bricks as I slid them, nose first, into a Wonder Bread bag. The frozen tail of the eighteen-incher hung out the open end. I wedged the bag between the minnow bucket and tackle box on my sled and roped everything down again so as not to lose anything on the bumpy ice and pressure ridges as I walked back toward shore in the darkness.

As I guided the sled over the last rough patch, my eyes fell on the frozen beach, lit up by a single overhead light suspended from a telephone pole. A car sat at idle, pumping a twisty tail of exhaust in the yellow glow. It wasn't Mom's car, I could tell that much. Instead, my eyes crashed into the distinctive shape of a long black Plymouth with white doors and a gold star on the side. *Crud!* It was a Winnebago County cop.

Maybe he's taking a break, I thought. Cops loved hanging out in public parks and boat landings. It was probably just a deputy, killing time and having a donut. When my sled runners hit gravel, Sheriff Heiselmann stepped out of the car.

Rats!

"Nice day for fishing," said the sheriff.

I said nothing.

"Did you catch anything?" he asked.

"A couple." I looked around. "My mom is supposed to be here."

"I was just over at your house having a little chat with your mom. We talked for quite a while and straightened a few things out. She said it would be okay if I picked you up and brought you home."

Was this for real? I thought Mom and I were a team. I thought that she hated Heiselmann as much as I did. I looked at his smiling face and saw Dr. Jekyll, knowing full well that Mr. Hyde was just under the surface.

"Come on," said the sheriff as he popped the trunk open with his key. "I'll help you load your gear."

I took a couple steps back toward the lake. There was no way in hell that I was getting into that car. The creep either murdered Dad or he knew who did.

"It's okay," he said. His phony smile was as big as ever. I took a couple more steps back, prepared to leave my sled and make a run for the lake if it came to that.

"I'll just wait for my mom," I said.

Heiselmann held up both hands in a submissive gesture. "I under-stand," said the sheriff. "How about if I get your mom on the police radio and she can explain it herself."

What?

Heiselmann got in the car, leaving the door open so I could hear the radio, and had the dispatcher patch him through with a phone call to my house. I heard the ringing of a phone.

"Hello?" It was Mom's voice.

"Hi, Mrs. Finwick. It's Sheriff Heiselmann again. I'm here with your son at the Fresh Air camp. He wanted to check with you to see if it was all right to ride back to your house with me."

"Yes, of course. Del, if you can hear me, go ahead and ride home with the sheriff. You'll be glad to know that we had a nice discussion and cleared the air about our disagreements. You be sure to thank him for the ride."

Not sure what else to do, I rode home with the jerk. He wanted to chitchat and talk about working together with me and Mom to solve the crime. He said that from this point forward we were a team. I kept my mouth shut and my eyes straight ahead. I didn't know what kind of fancy talk he had used on Mom, but it sure as heck wasn't going to work on me. I had my hand on the door handle when we pulled into the drive-way and immediately jumped out and grabbed my stuff from the trunk before Heiselmann could offer to help.

"I look forward to working with you and your mother," said the sheriff.

I said nothing. Not even a *thanks for the ride.* As soon as my sled runners scraped the floor of the garage, I pulled the door shut and let it slam at the bottom. I stood in silent darkness, waiting for Heiselmann's car to crunch out our driveway and go away.

Suddenly, Mom was all bubbly, if you can believe that.

"He's just doing his job," she said. "We need to cooperate with the sheriff so that he can solve the murder and catch the Highway 41 killer."

"He's a crook!" I shouted. "It's because of Heiselmann that Dad was murdered in the first place. I haven't figured it all out yet but I know he was part of it. You've got to believe me. Jeez, Mom—you don't even know the guy."

"Del, we don't have to like the man, but we have to work with him. Take your coat off and sit down. I'll get you a piece of apple pie."

"Apple pie?"

Mom looked sort of embarrassed. "Sheriff Heiselmann brought it over," she said.

"Jeez, Mom!"

❀

Just when I figured things couldn't get worse, Channel 2 *Eyewitness News* came on the tube at ten o'clock. The lead story showed a reporter standing in front of the Winnebago County Sheriff's Department building. He talked about a press conference held by Sheriff Heiselmann earlier in the day in which the sheriff apologized for the way he and his deputies responded to the protest march conducted by four Neenah High School students on December 23. The television report clicked over to film footage showing Sheriff Heiselmann in his uniform speaking into a microphone at a podium. I nearly puked when he smirked with that idiotic, Jerry Lewis grin into the camera.

"I'm really sorry, folks. I was wrong about the way I responded to those young protesters during their march on December twenty-third," said the sheriff. "Even though they *broke the law* on Highway 41, we should have used it as an educational opportunity. You see, young people are our most valuable resource. They are our future. They need our guidance in matters of this type to understand the difference between acceptable and unacceptable forms of behavior. In this instance, the students should have simply asked for cooperation from my department in advance and we would have been more than happy to help them."

"What?!" I was on my feet, yelling at the TV.

"From this point forward, my department will be assisting the youngsters. We are now a team. We will cooperate rather than confront. If they desire to protest again, we will help them to do it in a safe manner."

I couldn't believe it. "Hey Peckerhead, you're the damned criminal!" I yelled.

Heiselmann tilted his head slightly and licked his lips like some sort of bogus diplomat. Then he continued.

"Not only will we be teaming up with the young people, we intend to do more on the investigation of the unfortunate death of Officer Finwick."

"Unfortunate death? He was murdered, asshole!" I felt the blood rising into my face.

"I have added two additional investigators to the case. In addition, we have learned that Officer Finwick's son, Delmar, has located a bullet near the crime scene, which will be very helpful to the investigation. I have been assured by Mrs. Finwick that the bullet will be turned over to me expeditiously, as required by law."

"Fat chance, jerk!" Now I was the one foaming at the mouth. The sheriff looked so fatherly and concerned that I felt like kicking one of my Eaglewings right through the television set.

"Lastly, I would like to address another subject that has been troubling me. As many of you know, the protest signs used by the young marchers accused me of killing a swan. Well, it's true. This fall, during waterfowl hunting season, I mistook a flying swan for a goose and accidentally shot and killed it. I apologize for this mistake and am prepared to pay whatever fine the DNR chooses to impose upon me for the violation. Thank you."

As the reporter wrapped up the story and the TV switched over to a commercial, my mouth hung open and my eyes blinked rapid-fire. Did I really hear that? What did it all mean? Did that dink really expect me to just hand him the bullet? Was it really that easy for Heiselmann to wash away his evil deeds?

I walked slowly into the kitchen.

"What was that all about?" asked Mom.

"Sheriff Heiselmann was on TV," I said.

"Yes, he said he held a news conference today. By the way, honey, you *will* give him the bullet."

"I'm going to bed," I said. I had had enough. My head and eyes drooped. I was zonked.

"Are you forgetting about the dishes?" I glanced at the pile in the sink that might as well have reached the ceiling. Mom took a long drag on her cigarette and blew a cloud of smoke across the room. "Have you done your fifty pull-ups yet?"

"Not yet," I said.

"Well, you need to. And if I ever hear you use language like that again, you can bump those pull-ups up to one hundred a day."

As mad as I was, I knew when it was time to keep my mouth shut for once. I turned toward the sink and reached for the dish soap.

Have you ever seen the movie *Night of the Living Dead*? It's about zombies that come to life and climb out of their graves. Well—that's what I felt like when I finally finished my last pull-up and hung the dirty dish towel on the oven door.

Did I go straight to bed? No, I did not. There was still one very, very, very important thing to do. While Mom slept upstairs, I walked out to the garage and drained the gasoline can into a bucket until the bullet rattled out. I took the bullet in the house, washed it off, and taped it to a note I had written on a sheet of paper. I addressed the envelope to Agent Culper at the FBI in Milwaukee, put a couple of stamps on it, and walked it out to the blue-and-white official U.S. Postal Service mailbox on Forest Avenue. If I had to turn over the bullet, it sure as heck was *not* going directly to Sheriff Heiselmann.

39

At Shattuck High the next day, I set up an emergency meeting with Opal, Mark, and Rhonda to take place at lunchtime in the cafeteria. Mark and Opal showed up together. They both looked a little embarrassed.

"Sorry I didn't tell you earlier that I had asked Opal to the dance," said Mark.

"I'm sorry too," said Opal. "I should have told you."

I waved it off. "It's okay. I'm not really big on dancing anyhow."

Everybody smiled awkwardly at the same time. Then Rhonda showed up, allowing us to change the subject. I swept the crumbs off a cafeteria table with my sleeve and we all sat down around it. Everybody had seen the sheriff on TV and I added the story about his coming over to my house and giving me a ride home from ice fishing.

You're not going to believe this, but Mark and Opal actually thought that the sheriff's change of heart was a *good* thing.

"It means we're winning," said Opal. "Our goal was to put pressure on the sheriff and it's obvious that we got to him."

"But he's lying," I said.

"I don't know what you're complaining about," said Mark. "We're kicking his ass. He doesn't know what else to do, so now he wants to be on our side."

"I'll never believe that. The guy's a crumb. He hated my dad and he hates me. And if the sheriff didn't kill Dad, then he knows who did. Mark, you know how he reacted when I talked to him at his office."

"Yeah . . . but if he says he wants to be our teammate now, don't we have to give him a chance? If we don't, then everybody is going to start calling *us* the big jerks."

Opal nodded. "Mark's right, Del. We have to give him a chance."

I shook my head, crumpled up my paper napkin, and threw it at the trash can. It bounced off the rim and rolled to a stop on the floor. I was so disgusted that I just left it there.

"Mr. Finwick!"

I turned around and saw Mrs. Borger glaring at me over folded arms.

I walked over and tossed the napkin in the can.

Mrs. Borger walked over to our table. "Are you discussing the sheriff's recent announcements?"

"Yes."

"What do you think?"

"I think he's a stinking liar," I said.

"He came clean about shooting the swan, didn't he?"

"Yes."

"Isn't it possible that he really wants to help you solve your father's murder?"

"No!"

"Why not?"

"Because I know, that's why. I know that he hated my dad."

"Be careful, Mr. Finwick. The sheriff is innocent until proven guilty, just like everyone else. He's making a peace offering. Do you really want to slap the olive branch away?"

"Maybe I do."

"I suppose that's your choice. But, if you turn your back on the sheriff's offer to help, what's next?"

"What do you mean?"

"You've said all along that you want justice for your dad. What will you do next?"

"I don't know."

"Would you like a suggestion?"

"Sure."

"Make him prove his good intentions."

"How do I do that?"

"March to Oshkosh again."

I kicked my foot against the metal table leg. "What's the point? Heiselmann already said that he added investigators to solving the crime. He apologized for killing the swan. He brought my mom a stupid apple pie, for crying out loud. We might as well just give up on the protesting."

"Maybe he wants you to give up," said Mrs. Borger.

There was a long pause. It seemed like nobody knew what to say.

"Will you march with me?" I asked and looked around the table.

"I will." Rhonda's hand shot up.

"Me too," said Opal.

"I'm in." Mark nodded.

"May I join you as well?" asked Mrs. Borger.

I actually smiled. "Sure, Mrs. Borger. You can go too."

❁

The week flew by. I delivered my 232 Hoot Owls in a freezing-cold wind that nearly made an ice statue out of me. Luckily, a few ladies took pity along the way. Mrs. Zweigeldorf invited me in for a cookie and Mrs. Nesput even fixed me a cup of hot chocolate.

The next night was spent making protest signs again. I had run out of sturdy sticks and decided to try knocking on the Johnsons' door, the same place where I had borrowed the metal detector.

Mrs. Johnson answered and told me she didn't have any sticks. Then Mr. Johnson poked his bald head around the door jamb.

"Meet me by the garage," he said.

He came out the side door in just a white T-shirt on a freezing cold night. I could see his arms turning pink as he scrounged through a collection of wood scraps. From the pile we pulled out a half-dozen two-by-twos and a pair of shovel handles.

"Thanks, Mr. Johnson," I said.

"Anytime. They weren't doing me any good. Are you making more protest signs?"

"Yes, sir."

"Good. Shove one up the sheriff's ass for me."

"Yes, sir," I said. "First chance I get."

In case you haven't figured it out by now, I liked Mr. Johnson.

Opal came over to help me make signs, and between the two of us we came up with some new slogans, including *A Murderer Walks Among Us* and *Justice Will Never Give Up!* I liked them both because I figured the messages might make Heiselmann twitchy. But my favorite sign was still *Sheriff Heiselmann Killed a Swan.* It was still just as true as before, and that was the one I planned to carry.

I told my mom we were marching this time and reminded her of her promise. I called up Mrs. Samuelson and the other church ladies too. I posted notices on the school bulletin board and others at the Food

Queen, the Red Owl, and the bowling alley, inviting anybody and everybody. The signs were simple and to the point.

MARCH TO OSHKOSH SATURDAY, JANUARY 6
JUSTICE FOR OFFICER FINWICK!
MEETING 9 A.M. AT NEENAH LIBRARY

Guess who I didn't try to contact. That's right—Sheriff Heiselmann. He may have thought he was part of the team, but I still had other ideas.

Through that whole crazy week I was like one of those jugglers who keeps a knife, ax, and tomato in the air all at the same time. I went to school, pounded the homework, did the dishes, and swept the floors. I scrubbed the toilet as clean as Mom's good china. I was done lying to my mom.

Of course, I did my pull-ups too, and guess what. On my pull-up bar in the basement, I could do all fifty in two sets of twenty-five—one before school and one after. I knew I was getting stronger too. For one thing, the pull-ups came easier, but I also knew because the sleeves of my shirts weren't so floppy any more.

❁

Do you know what else I did every day that first week of January? I practiced lines from *Romeo and Juliet* with Rhonda in the chemistry lab next to the Science Resource Center. Yep, every day during sixth period. It was just the two of us, and just like our practice sessions for *To Kill a Mockingbird*, Rhonda gave me tons of good advice and encouragement. She taught me how to project my voice and how to infuse my speech with emotion. I got pretty good at it too. I even learned how to express my heartfelt feelings for my beloved Juliet. Sure, I was embarrassed at first, but then Rhonda straightened me out.

"It's for the audience, Del. You've got to give them all you've got. Give them a reason to smile and cry. Give them a reason to applaud."

I shook off the embarrassment and really went for it.

This bud of love by summers ripening breath, may prove a beauteous flower when next we meet.

Rhonda leaned in across the Bunsen burner gas valves and smiled. Our noses almost touched. Yep, I was Romeo all right. The star-crossed lover gazing into the sparkling eyes of his darling Juliet. I was really getting the hang of it. And believe it or not, I didn't mind looking into the deep blue eyes of Rhonda Glass either.

❋

A strange thing happened when I left Shattuck High on Friday afternoon. As I walked past the bike racks, all covered in snow, I heard a voice.

"Hey, Minnow."

I glanced left and there was Larry Buskin standing by himself smoking a cigarette. What the heck did he want? I should have kept walking but I didn't. I stopped, turned, and faced him.

"What?"

"You still going on that protest march to Oshkosh tomorrow?"

"Yes."

"Be careful."

"What do you mean?"

"Don't mess with Heiselmann."

I stared at Buskin. He shrugged and took another long suck on his cigarette.

"Why?"

"Like I told you before, he knows some people who you never want to meet. Just avoid him. That's all I'm saying, and you didn't hear it from me."

What was he getting at? I kept right on staring at Buskin. He turned and walked away.

40

Mom woke me up early Saturday morning with a poke in the ribs. "Are we going on this hike or aren't we?" she asked.

I looked at the clock. "Yep, we're going."

She mumbled and rolled her eyes at the ceiling.

"Don't blame me, Mom. It was Mrs. Samuelson—remember?"

"I know, but here's the deal." Mom pointed a finger at me. "If I go on this walk, you have to give that bullet to the sheriff."

"I can't."

"Why not?"

"I already sent it to an FBI man."

She clamped a hand on each hip and blew a lock of hair out of her eyes. "And *how*, might I ask, do you know an FBI man?"

"I met him last month in Milwaukee."

Mom scowled. "Was Grandpa Asa involved in this?"

"Yes."

Mom pushed her open palms toward me like she didn't want to know any more. "Just get dressed and come down for some breakfast." Slowly, she shook her head. "I don't know why I'm even doing this."

❀

A fresh inch of snow sparkled on front lawns and rooftops all over Neenah. The announcer on WNAM said the temperature was nineteen degrees.

At nine o'clock they were all there waiting for us at the library. We made a group of ten this time—me, Mark, Opal, Rhonda, Mom, Mrs. Parsons, Mrs. Borger, Mrs. Samuelson, Mrs. Weiden, and Mrs. Stevens. Honestly, I almost laughed as I scanned my ragtag platoon. There was Rhonda in her army gear and Mark, once again, in blaze-orange deer hunting clothes. The moms and church ladies wore all sorts of garb, from puffy, goose-down coats to red-and-black plaid. Mrs. Stevens standing next to Mrs. Samuelson reminded me of a little brown twig alongside a weather balloon. Mrs. Borger held tight to her purse, looking ready for church in her tan overcoat and white gloves. The mismatched group piled into three cars and headed toward Highway 41.

❀

We parked our cars on the frontage road next to Funland. Fresh snow covered the pretzel-shaped go-kart track. The tires that made the perimeter looked like a hundred chocolate donuts with white frosting. The giant slide looked down on the highway, shiny blue where the snow had slid off the steep parts. Everybody grabbed a sign, and just like last time, Rhonda took the lead.

I had my worries about Mrs. Samuelson, but she managed to keep a steady pace. Instead, it was my mom who turned out to be the weak link in the chain. The past few months had really yanked the life out of her, and I was pretty sure that all those cigarettes and days on the couch hadn't done her any good either. For the first time, her face looked old to me.

Mrs. Samuelson dropped back to walk with her and boost her morale just as my mom was lighting up a cigarette. The mammoth-sized church lady snatched that cigarette from her lips like it was poison and chucked it in the snowbank.

"How dare you!" shouted Mom. "I'm quite sure that kind of rudeness is not in the Bible."

"Cancer sticks!" shouted Mrs. Samuelson. "They're killing you and you don't even know it."

"I'm not asking your opinion," said my mom.

"Come along, Dorothy. March to my beat. One—two—three—four—one—two—three—four!"

Mom scurried forward to escape her tormenter. The other church ladies scared her almost as much, and she kept hustling forward until she had passed all three. Mom slowed down to walk beside Mrs. Parsons but then must have remembered she was black. In the end she settled in alongside Mrs. Borger. I watched her pop another cigarette in her mouth and strike a match.

We were a half hour on the road before it felt like we had found a rhythm. Mark pumped his sign up and down and Opal started singing again. Everyone except Mom marched in time with the beat, and it kept our spirits up for ten or fifteen minutes. Then Mark started giving his horn honking signal to passing cars and it kept us amused for another fifteen.

We were well on our way to the Butte des Morts Bridge when a Winnebago County cop car pulled over with lights flashing. I recognized the deputy who stepped out of the car right away as the red-haired guy who tried to catch me at our last protest march. I remembered him calling me a "little bastard," and those words still stuck in my craw.

He was all smiles, of course, when he stopped to chat. "The sheriff has asked me to give you an escort," he said. "It's for your safety."

"No thanks," I said. "Just leave us alone, please."

That took care of the smiling.

"Sorry, kid. If I had my way we'd mop you up like before. The sheriff says it's going to be different this time. He says we're on the same team. Imagine that."

"Drive ahead of us if you want, but we're not on the same team."

"Watch your mouth, kid. The sheriff is doing you a favor."

We walked, trudged, stumbled, and teetered toward the bridge, getting slower with each mile. Mom ran out of steam and accepted a ride with the deputy but the rest of my team kept moving along. For two hours more we kept it up. Opal energized the team with her singing and Mark got the horn honking started up again. We had our share of detractors too, of course, and a few curse words were hurled our way from open windows, but we did our best to ignore them.

It was well past noon when we saw a crowd gathering up ahead. At least a dozen people and several cars waited for us on the shoulder near the bridge. The *Eyewitness News* truck and other reporters were there again. So were the flashing lights.

As we got closer, I recognized Sheriff Heiselmann. He met us with a stupid gesture of open arms and another phony smile. Then he waved and pointed, directing my group of marchers to a table where two of his helpers had cups of hot chocolate and a mountain of cookies waiting for us.

A reporter spoke into a TV camera, while three others, from various newspapers, jotted notes in steno pads. We moved closer and stopped. One man appeared to be sketching a cartoon, and I hoped he wouldn't show me as a midget. I kept my eyes on the sheriff as he shook hands and slapped backs while making small talk with everyone.

"He reminds me of President Nixon," I said to Mrs. Borger.

She whispered in my ear. "Be polite, Del. This is going to be in the news again."

Mark and Opal led the charge toward the hot chocolate and cookies and everybody else followed. In my mind I sort of wanted to boycott the free treats but the marchers were hungry and thirsty and there was no stopping the stampede. In the end I shrugged and joined them.

Through it all, the sheriff kept working the crowd like a politician. He approached me with an open right hand and I shook it.

"Don't you worry, young man," said Heiselmann. "We're going to catch that murderer. We've got our best people on it."

I nodded. Heiselmann put his arm around my shoulders and we both grinned for the cameras.

"If there's anything I can do for you and your mom just let me know, okay?" Gosh, he almost sounded sincere.

"Sure," I said. He nodded and walked away. I wondered why he didn't ask about the bullet.

One by one Heiselmann introduced himself to each member of our protest group. Everyone was polite until he got to Mrs. Samuelson.

"You'd best watch yourself, sheriff. I've got a number 4 cast-iron frying pan with your name on it."

He shrugged it off with an awkward chuckle and moved on to Mrs. Stevens and Mrs. Weiden.

Like a gopher peeking from its hole, I kept one eye on Heiselmann the whole time. The sheriff roamed easily from person to person and seemed to save the biggest smile for my mom. She smiled back. As you can imagine, that bugged me.

After another round of backslapping, the sheriff moved toward a makeshift podium from which he prepared to give a speech. His polyester smile was back in full force as the news reporters and cameramen lined up to get a shot of Heiselmann with the Butte des Morts bridge in the background. My little army of marchers stood around randomly at both sides of the podium.

The sheriff started off his speech with more glowing words of welcome and continued with comments about what a great country we all lived in. He spoke about the wonderful freedoms offered by the constitution and how those freedoms include the rights of assembly and free speech. Sheriff Heiselmann looked at our group and then spoke directly into the camera.

"I'm proud of our Neenah protest marchers. They represent the best of the United States of America as they seek justice and push for answers to the senseless murder of Deputy William Finwick, one of our finest officers. Today I am proud to say that we are bolstering our commitment to arresting and prosecuting the evil murderer who . . ."

I heard a popping sound from somewhere behind me. A lady, maybe Mrs. Borger, screamed. My eyes darted from person to person. Everyone had the same expression of confusion and fear. My eyes finally landed on Sheriff Heiselmann just as he slumped over the podium and fell sideways into the crusty snow. A bunch of people, including the red-haired deputy, charged to the aid of the sheriff. Others scrambled backward and sideways. Opal pointed at the patch of woods to our west.

Twice more we heard the popping sound and everybody either ran behind the cars or dropped prone to the ground. The red-haired deputy picked up a radio transmitter and called for help. Another deputy pulled a shotgun out of the trunk of his patrol car and ducked behind a brush pile to watch the woods behind us.

I was scared as heck. My heart banged away like a jackhammer inside me. On hands and knees I crawled around in the snow trying to find everybody. I spotted Mom and Mrs. Borger crouched behind the news van. The church ladies and Mrs. Parsons scurried behind the sheriff's car where Opal and Mark had already found refuge. I found Rhonda kneeling next to the fallen sheriff along with the red-haired deputy and a news reporter. Through it all, hundreds of cars continued to zoom both ways on the highway, to and from the Butte des Morts Bridge.

I crawled along the gravel shoulder toward the protection of the row of vehicles. Suddenly, the ground erupted. The spray of dirt and pebbles stung my face and I couldn't understand what was happening. Then my brain woke up and realized that the Highway 41 Killer was shooting again and, this time, he was trying to kill *me*. Instinctively I fell to my stomach and made myself flat. Another bullet sent up a spray of sand and gravel so close that I felt the stones bounce off my face again. I jumped to my feet, then ran behind a patrol car and stayed there.

The sound of sirens came, faint at first but then in swarms. Flashing lights roared in from north and south. Several cop cars peeled off on the side road that led toward the woods. Others skidded to a halt on the side of the highway. An ambulance arrived and paramedics ran to the sheriff. I crawled in that direction.

"Keep breathing," shouted a cop as he unzipped the sheriff's coat and ripped open his shirt. A paramedic cut through the rest of his clothes exposing his bare chest.

The bullet wound in his chest was a ragged mess that left a white bone sticking out. Even the cop had to close his eyes for a moment. "Exit wound," he said.

The paramedic ripped the paper cover off a gauze pad as big as my geometry book. He pressed it against the wound and looked at me. "Push your hands down on this," he said. I did as told. In seconds the white pad was soaked, red with blood. The paramedic rushed to set up a plastic tube and a bottle of fluid.

I heard a groan and looked again at the sheriff. His bloody chest rose and fell, rose and fell. Then all was still. The paramedic felt for a pulse and found none. He pulled my hands away and put his overlapping palms on Sheriff Heiselmann, trying to restart his heart with chest compressions. After a dozen or so pushes, he checked again for a pulse. It was no use.

I reached back in to push the gauze pad back over the top of the wound. If nothing else, it would cover the shredded flesh.

The paramedic touched my shoulder. "It's over," he said. Sheriff Heiselmann was dead. Murdered on the shoulder of Highway 41, just like my dad.

The cop walked away. The paramedic returned his box of first aid supplies to the ambulance. I looked at my bloody hands and felt dizzy, then rubbed them in the snow and on my pants. From my knees I looked across the field at the grove of trees where the gunshots had come from. Police officers with shotguns and pistols snuck around the edges. I forced myself to look again at Sheriff Heiselmann, his face now lifeless and gray. Thankfully, his eyes were closed.

I watched as the sheriff's body was loaded into an ambulance. The red-haired deputy glared at me with bullets in his eyes. "You happy now, kid?"

41

Just like last time, the protest march never made it across the Butte des Morts Bridge. And just like last time, we were all driven in cop cars down to the Winnebago County Sheriff's Department in Oshkosh.

The office was almost empty when we got there. The dispatcher told us that every available officer had been either ordered to the crime scene or had gone there on their own.

Mrs. Samuelson rounded up the church ladies and they prayed in the corner. Mrs. Parsons and Mrs. Borger consoled Opal with hugs and whispers. She had been shaking and crying since the shock wore off. Mark and Rhonda sat like zombies in wooden chairs, saying nothing. Mom found a cup of coffee in the dispatch office and warmed her hands on it, leaning against the wall.

More than anything else, I needed to wash my hands. The dispatch lady directed me to a bathroom. For ten minutes I scrubbed away Sheriff Heiselmann's blood with a bar of soap. When I finally sat down between Mark and Rhonda, my hands were raw. My brain whirled like a dust devil.

Dad, Wolf, and Sheriff Heiselmann . . . all three dead.

One by one, the officers returned. Then the newspeople came in with their tape recorders, cameras, and notebooks. Before the reporters could corner us, a man in a blue shirt and striped tie herded our team of ten marchers into a conference room. He introduced himself as Detective Phelps and said that we would have to wait, without discussing what we had observed, until he could interview each of us individually.

They started with Mrs. Samuelson and the church ladies and moved on to Mrs. Borger, Mrs. Parsons, Opal, and Rhonda. All were interviewed and returned to the conference room. Mark was next, and they talked to him for what seemed like a long time. Then my mom and I were called. Imagine my surprise when FBI agent Culper stood to shake my hand.

"We meet again, Mr. Finwick," he said.

I nodded. Mom looked at me suspiciously.

"Hello, Mrs. Finwick, I'm Agent Culper from the FBI office in Milwaukee. From this point forward, I will be leading the investigation." He placed a small object on the table.

"What's that?" asked my mom.

"That's the bullet that killed Dad," I answered.

❈

Not surprisingly, the murder of Sheriff Heiselmann was the lead news story on every television station in Wisconsin. The red-haired deputy stood in front of a pack of reporters all shoving microphones in his face.

"Was the sheriff the only victim?"

"Yes."

"Have you identified a suspect?" asked a reporter in the front.

"No."

"Do you have a description of the killer?"

"No."

"Do you have any leads?"

"Not much. We found footprints in the woods and tire tracks in the snow. We also recovered a shell casing from a .30-06 rifle. It appears that the killer was waiting in ambush."

"Do you expect it was the Highway 41 Killer who murdered Officer Finwick last summer?"

"That seems likely."

❈

Right after the ten o'clock news, our phone started ringing nonstop. We answered the first few calls, which included everything from concerned neighbors, to reporters looking for interviews, to curious people we had never even met before. When we received a call from some creep yelling "Cop Killer!" into the phone, Mom yanked the cord out of the wall, and I don't mean gently.

Mom glared at me like I was the source of all evil in the world. "You satisfied?" she asked. My mouth swung open but no words came out.

My mom fumbled for a cigarette, but her hands shook so bad that the whole pack fell to the floor. Her eyes closed. Her chin quivered. When she opened her eyes again, the tears poured out. She poked a finger at my face, so close that I had to pull back.

"You are done with this—this—protesting. Done with all of it, and that includes Mark and your teachers and your colored friends—all of it—you hear?!"

Wide-eyed and ready to bolt, I glanced at Mark. He watched my mother's rant like it was expected and normal. He then scooped up the fallen cigarettes and matches and placed them on the kitchen table. Mom gathered up the stuff and stomped upstairs toward her bedroom.

Mark looked at me. "Got any booze?"

I kicked his chair and busted out the lower rung, sending splinters of wood across the kitchen floor. "No . . . I don't got any *booze*, asshole. You think drinking is the answer to everything?"

Mark stiffened. "Screw yourself, Delmar." He walked outside into the January night, two miles from his home, and slammed the door.

❀

Monday was the worst. Donna Krelling, a cheerleader who hadn't said a word to me in my entire life, stopped at my locker as I spun the combination. "Are you happy now, you little punk?" I looked up and saw hatred staring back.

The cafeteria lady with the curly hair and big forehead shot me a look of disgust as I presented her with my tray.

"Well if it isn't the Prince of Justice," she sneered, before slapping a scoopful of scalloped corn on my plate and turning her head away.

Okay, I got the message. One murder had turned into two, and it was my fault. How many more people would have to die to satisfy me?

Kids who never gave me a second glance glared at me, then turned away. Tuesday was almost as bad, and when my gym teacher told me to demonstrate a chest pass, he fired the ball at me like it came out of a musket loaded with black powder.

Remember when I was the little shrimp who everybody ignored? Well, they weren't ignoring me anymore. People noticed me in the halls. People talked about me. I was somebody all of a sudden, and that somebody was mostly despised.

The news stories on TV supported their claim. Reporters shared heartwarming stories of Sheriff Heiselmann, the protector of the county. The man who had cracked down on the burglary ring in Vinland Township. The man who captured the escaped prisoner from Waupun. The man who selflessly donated his time at schools, teaching children about the dangers of drugs and alcohol.

Yep, they lauded the sheriff as a wonderful man. A wonderful man, now dead, and for what? The senselessness of it all had heads shaking everywhere. Only one thing was for certain. That Finwick kid and his protests were somehow at the root of it.

❈

By Friday I had pretty well perfected the weary, head-down foot shuffle of the ultimate loser at Shattuck High. Like a ghost I drifted through the halls. When in class, I kept my nose in a book. Anything to avoid eye contact. Even Opal, Rhonda, Steve, and Mark had somehow managed to elude me, and for all I knew, had faced their own dose of scorn.

"Mr. Finwick! Mr. Finwick, May I see you please?!"

For the first time in four days, I lifted my chin off my chest and looked hopefully through an open door. It was Mrs. Borger. I approached her desk.

"Are you surviving?" she asked.

"Barely."

"I know what you mean. I'm surprised at the reaction I've been receiving."

"I'm not."

"For what it's worth, Mr. Finwick, you've done nothing wrong."

I shrugged.

"I consider your protest march an act of courage and I'm proud of you."

"Thanks."

"Whatever you do from here, I want you to know that you have my support."

"Thanks, Mrs. Borger."

"Will you be attending the funeral this weekend?"

"I guess so."

"Good. I'll see you there."

"Will you be ready for next week?"

"What's next week?" I asked.

"*Romeo and Juliet* auditions! Did you forget?"

Criminy! I *had* forgotten. Did Mrs. Borger really expect me to go through with it? After all of this? After descending all the way to *least-popular kid* status? I could see myself on the high school auditorium stage. I could already hear the wisecracks.

"Do I have to?" I asked.

"You don't have to but you should. You would be doing me, Rhonda, and yourself a favor. I know the two of you would be wonderful."

I shrugged. "Okay." I sure didn't want to disappoint Mrs. Borger. As near as I could tell, she was the only person in the world who still liked me.

42

The funeral for Sheriff Heiselmann was, of course, huge. It took place at a giant-sized, Catholic church in Oshkosh, and thousands of people showed up, including uniformed officers from every county and large city in Wisconsin as well as the four bordering states. The mayors of Oshkosh, Neenah, and Menasha were all there. Family members took up four rows and even the governor showed up in a black Buick to pay his respects.

Just like in school, I felt hundreds of eyes on me as I walked past the casket before sitting with my mom and Sally for the ceremony. Everybody else from the march was there too. Mrs. Borger was there. Opal sat with her mom. The church ladies sat as a group with Mrs. Samuelson, taking up two places all by herself. Even Rhonda came, and she looked like a different person wearing a black dress, lady's shoes, and her hair all done up nice. She sat with Mark, who looked like himself.

I had never been to a Catholic funeral before. It was way different from my dad's. For one thing, I was surprised to find out that four or five priests all had different duties during the Mass. On top of that, they had helpers, mostly teenagers who carried things, held books, and the like. There was holy water sprinkled on the casket and other rituals that I didn't understand. The organ music and singing sounded sad and slow like they should be, and the prayers were mumbled in Latin so we never did know what they said. Just like when Dad died, the church was packed with black-clad mourners filling every pew and officers lined up in the back. I saw the red-haired deputy and he saw me but we both turned away from each other at the same time.

✹

In the days following the funeral, things got worse instead of better. Suddenly, the reality sunk in, and I knew what it felt like to be responsible for somebody's death. Let's just say my conscience was the busiest place in my brain.

Maybe I should have had my mom sew cloth symbols on all of my shirts like they did in *The Scarlet Letter*. I could wear the letter *J* for Jerk on Mondays, and *I* for Idiot on Tuesdays, *S* for Selfish on Wednesdays. There weren't enough days in the week for all the labels I had picked up. The *C* for Coward had been on me so long that it had practically become a tattoo.

Sure, I had made a big fuss about justice. I had pointed the finger at the sheriff, making him out to be a nasty guy. I had broken the law and used the fact that I was a fifteen-year-old kid to get away with it. I had put it all on television because I was so danged proud of everything. But what did I accomplish? I got the sheriff killed and left the real killer still roaming free. Maybe some judge should have just sent me to juvie last fall and saved the whole world a lot of misery.

And what did I have to look forward to? Well, for starters, it was pretty much a certainty that my handful of friends would drift away and never come back. Then there were the hateful stares and mumbled comments. And of course I could look forward to the lunch lady in the cafeteria splashing gruel onto my plate and glaring at me every single day. Heck, she'd probably even find a way to spit in my dessert.

❋

Did you know that if a person tries hard enough, they can be miserable for a pretty long time? For me it lasted for another whole week. I moped around, dragging my feet and staring at the floor every day. I worked hard at not talking, not smiling, and not even making eye contact with anybody. I was more miserable than the hunchback of Notre Dame, and proud of it too.

In the meanwhile, when I wasn't looking, everybody else got back to treating me like Del Finwick. Those who always thought I was okay still did. Those who considered me a worthless little minnow hadn't changed their minds either.

Here are a few of the things that happened during the week following the funeral. Opal gave me the chocolate pudding from her lunch. Mark asked me if I would take him ice fishing. Steve told me he had a new invention to discuss with me. And Rhonda said it was time to get serious about being Romeo. I found out what that meant during sixth hour on Wednesday in the chemistry lab where we practiced the balcony scene.

The raisins in my oatmeal came when Mrs. Borger called me on the phone Sunday morning to *tell* me (she didn't ask) that she was picking me up to go to church.

Crap! I was afraid of that. I had enemies back there. People who were mad at me for protesting even *before* I got the sheriff killed. And there was one enemy in particular who lay in wait, no doubt—a certain gray-haired lady who wore a blue hat.

Mrs. Borger's voice was unswerving. "I'll be there in ten minutes," she said.

Click!

❋

The people in church were mostly nice to me. The man with the wrench-shaped tie clasp smiled and nodded from across the hall. Mr. Kleinschmidt from the JC Penney store shook my hand and asked me how I was doing. A lady in a purple dress who I didn't even know actually stopped just to give me a hug.

As Mrs. Borger and I were fixing to head into the sanctuary and find a pew, the blue-hat lady appeared from behind the coat racks. She shriveled up her face and stared me down over the tops of her glasses. She gripped her purse with both hands like she was afraid I would either steal it or throw her to the floor with a judo move.

"Good morning," said Mrs. Borger.

"Good morning," said the blue-hat lady. She then turned her attention back to me. "Hello, young man."

"Hello."

"Are you happy now?"

Before I could patch together a response, I felt a hard yank at my elbow and was jerked toward the sanctuary by Mrs. Borger. She towed me down the aisle like a raft behind a tugboat until we settled into a pew in the second row. Her ears had turned red and her lips pressed together so tightly that they almost disappeared. She needed to let off some steam, but since you can't do that in the second pew, she let herself cook and simmer instead. By the time the organ prelude was over and we finished singing the first hymn, she had chilled back to a normal temperature.

I was glad when Pastor Olson stepped up to the pulpit in hopes that he would give us something to think about besides the blue-hat lady. According to the bulletin, the sermon title today was "Finishing the Race."

Like always, the sermon was partly about God's expectations for us. The pastor told us that we each needed to set ourselves on a path according to the plans that God had for us. But it wasn't enough just to get started down the path. We needed to find the courage and determination to finish what we started.

That's when Pastor Olson switched over to another one of his stories. I squirmed to fit my butt to the hard, wooden pew and leaned forward.

"How many of you have heard of John Stephen Akhwari?" he asked. Nobody raised a hand.

"How many of you watched the finish of the marathon race at the summer Olympics in Mexico City?"

Lots of hands went up.

"John Stephen Akhwari finished fifty-seventh in the Olympic marathon," he said. The pastor paused and looked around. "John Stephen Akhwari is my hero. Do you want to know why?"

I nodded my head and would have buckled my seatbelt if the church pew had one. The pastor continued with a story about a poor black man who had come to represent Tanzania in the 1968 Olympics. He came with high hopes, knowing that he had a real chance to medal in the twenty-six-mile marathon run. For most of the race he ran with the lead pack. Then disaster struck when his legs got tangled with another runner and he fell. He fell hard—very hard, to the pavement, injuring his knee and shoulder when he hit. The knee injury was bad, possibly even dislocated according to the medical staff, and they told him to drop out. Instead, he asked them to wrap the injured leg in bandages, after which Mr. Akhwari hobbled back to the road and continued along the race route.

In the stadium, over an hour had passed since the winner and every other finisher had crossed the line. The sun had set and only a few people remained in the seats, unaware that one more runner still trudged in the darkness. When Mr. Akhwari emerged from the stadium tunnel, a gasp, and then a cheer, went up from the few people remaining. The man's injured knee had stiffened such that it could barely bend. Slowly he limped the final lap, agony seared on his face. He collapsed at the finish line and was immediately transported to the hospital.

As Pastor Olson talked, the memory returned to me. *Holy smoke! He really was the hero of the race.* I had seen it on TV myself.

Pastor Olson looked around at all of our faces in the pews. He spotted me and smiled. "Do you know what John Stephen Akhwari said to a news reporter when asked why he didn't quit?"

I shook my head.

"He said, *My country did not send me five thousand miles to start a race. They sent me five thousand miles to finish one.*"

Wow!

❋

Mom made fish sticks and peas for Sunday dinner, and for the first time in a long time, we all sat down at the kitchen table together. I made a pond of ketchup on my plate and cut up my sticks into little pieces for dipping.

"What are you going to do now that your days of fame are over?" asked Sally.

I noticed that Mom had paused from buttering her peas to listen to my answer.

"School. Fishing. Stuff like that," I said.

Mom nodded. "Good! You're done with signs and protest marches. No more news reporters and TV cameras. No more interviews for the newspapers. Are we clear on that?"

I nodded.

"Del? . . . Are we clear?"

"Yes."

In my mind, after Pastor Olson's sermon, I wasn't clear at all. The killer was still out there. Did everybody just expect me to give up? The answer, of course, was yes.

Sally got out the box of Neapolitan ice cream from the freezer and three clean plates.

"I'll just use my same plate," I said. When you were the guy washing every dish in the universe, a little ketchup in your ice cream was a small price to pay to reduce the dish count.

Sally put one of the plates back and, with a butcher knife, went about the business of slicing three big slabs off the pink, brown, and white brick. Each slab of ice cream looked like a French flag. I started with the strawberry stripe and moved north toward chocolate.

After doing the dishes I went into the basement and gazed up at the pull-up bar that I had bolted to a wooden beam. Believe it or not, I hammered out thirty-two good ones before my arms turned to jelly. It had to be some sort of record. I dusted off the mirror on a shelf full of forgotten knickknacks and looked at the size of my bicep muscles. My arms weren't scrawny any more. I ran upstairs to the bathroom and stood on the scale. It showed me at ninety pounds. *Holy schmoly!* I was turning into a brute!

Freshly loaded with confidence, I polished off the remaining eighteen pull-ups and returned to my bedroom to practice my lines from *Romeo and Juliet*. The auditions were scheduled for Tuesday. My last practice with Rhonda would be sixth period on Monday in the chemistry lab.

I looked forward to practicing again with Rhonda. Ever since I saw her at the funeral, I had been thinking about her differently. Gosh, she was like a different person with her hair fixed up and wearing that black dress along with the women's shoes with spiky heels. She was going to be a real Juliet all right. And if I could scrape together a halfway decent Romeo, well, we might make a chemical reaction after all. Maybe Del Finwick and Rhonda Glass were going to be the baking soda and vinegar of the Shattuck High theater department.

43

The Snow-Ball Dance came and went. Would you believe me if I said that I didn't want to go to it in the first place? I didn't think so. You know the truth. That's right—while Mark was having a great time, dancing slow and looking into the prettiest face at Shattuck High, I was listening to Wolfman Jack on the radio while washing and waxing the kitchen floor. The worst part came just before midnight when I knew Mark was probably on the receiving end of the world's most perfect kiss—the one that was really meant for me. *Jeez!*

I sucked it up and moved on, and yes, I've had some practice at that. Mom said I needed to quit thinking about murderers and bullets. I figured out that the only way to give my brain a break from that obsession was to keep doing everything else. Here is how I was filling up my days.

Ice fishing
Hoot Owls
Pull-ups
Dishwashing, floor scrubbing, bathroom cleaning
School and homework
Romeo and Juliet practice
Rocket games
Helping Grandpa Asa
Confirmation class and church

Yep, everybody around me could see that I had moved back to my regular life of activities that a fifteen-year-old kid was supposed to do. In the eyes of most, I had become a good citizen again.

But had I really washed my hands of the whole thing? Had I really caved in and just given up? Well, let me put it this way. My dad was still dead. His killer was still out there. The marathon runner in Pastor

Olson's sermon was still limping toward the finish line in my brain. *Jiminy!*—what would you do?

❊

Steve showed signs of life again for the first time in three months. It's not that I had lost track of him completely, but after the volcano prank, Mark and I had pretty much written him off. Steve's parents had branded us as untouchables, so we were both surprised when he called us at our homes and asked us to meet with him before homeroom in the Science Resource Center. He wanted to show us the plans for his latest invention.

I looked around for spies as Steve opened his spiral notebook to the first page of his just-hatched scheme. The pencil sketch showed a kite flying over a baseball field with three stick figures holding the string.

"It's a kite," I said.

Mark cranked up the sarcasm. "Congratulations, Steve! You invented the kite. Oh, I almost forgot, it's been invented already."

"Shut up, butthead." Steve was no fan of Mark's wise cracks.

I waited as Steve turned to the next page to an engineering drawing. It showed the kite in explicit detail and directions on how to build it.

"What do you think now?" he asked.

Mark and I looked at each other. We were still clueless. The drawing showed a pair of crossed sticks supporting a diamond-shaped sheet of plastic and a tail hanging down. It was a kite like any other kite as near as we could tell. We both looked at Steve like he was going loony.

"Don't just look at the picture," he said. "Look at the scale—the size."

We looked again and our eyes finally focused on the numbers.

"Wait a minute," said Mark. "This thing is huge!"

I took a second to study the dimensions. The measurements on the paper showed the kite to be sixteen feet long and ten feet wide, almost twice the size of my garage door. The struts were made of two-by-two lumber and the tail was forty feet long and constructed of rope and empty beer cans, according to the materials list.

Steve turned the page. The next drawing showed the words that would be printed on the giant kite in huge, block letters.

BLUE JAY

SLAYER

Mark grinned like a drunken cowboy. "Another road trip?"

Steve glanced at Mrs. Schwartz and turned to the next page. I leaned in, trying to figure out what was different. Then I saw it. Steve's kite drawing included a box with a release latch and a trapdoor. A second string ran parallel to the main kite-flying string. With a pull of that second string, whatever was in the box would tumble out and fall to the ground.

Mark's face lit up. "We're going to bomb the Menasha Blue Jays?"

"At their baseball game," Steve said.

My head snapped to vertical. "Baggert's gonna freak!"

"Damn right!" said Mark. "He deserves it."

"What if we get caught again?" I asked. "All they have to do is follow the twine to where we're holding the kite."

Mark looked at Steve. "Well?"

Steve's face reflected confidence. He turned the page. Mark and I studied the lines, which showed the twine passing through a maze of left and right turns on the ground, guided by hoops that were held in place by tent stakes going into the ground.

"Once we get the kite in the air we maneuver ourselves behind houses and bushes. Then we set up the stakes and hoops and string the twine in a maze ending at our getaway car. The plan is to let out more and more string until the Blue Jay Slayer drifts into position over the baseball field. When it flies over a good spot, hopefully over the Menasha bench, we pull the second string opening the bomb doors."

"Then what?" I asked.

"Then we scram," said Mark. He grinned like Elvis Presley.

Steve flicked his eyebrows. "Can we use your grandpa's truck again?"

"No," I said.

Mark punched me in the shoulder. "Come on, Delmar, don't be a wuss."

I swallowed hard and raked my hair with my fingers. "Okay, I'll talk to him."

The bell rang. We were all late for homeroom.

❋

Ever since we returned from Christmas break, *Romeo and Juliet* audition posters had been taped up all over the school. The day finally came. Auditions would be held after classes in the auditorium. For the first time in a while, I was having second thoughts, feeling a little self-conscious about tryouts. I waited until exactly four o'clock before walking into the auditorium. When I saw the people, my brain nearly exploded.

Including me, fifteen kids had shown up to audition. That seemed about right. The shocker was the ratio—fourteen of them were girls.

They giggled and gabbed in two separate groups. One circle was made up of the *thespians*. They were the kids obsessed with a single-minded desire to become famous actresses in places like Hollywood or New York City. You could pick them out right away because everything they said came with a hair flick and a hand gesture. They also shared the common goal of marrying David Cassidy. I had seen the pictures taped inside their lockers.

The other circle of girls were from the *popular* crowd—the cheerleader types, all good-looking, and all dating big, strong, athletic guys.

My entrance into the room triggered a pause. At first, every girl glanced hopefully. This was followed by recognition and sour-faced disappointment. I'm not sure who they were hoping for, but it sure as heck wasn't Minnow Finwick in his green flannel shirt and Eaglewing steel-toed boots.

For a second I thought about making a full retreat, like the British troops at Dunkirk. Then I heard a familiar voice.

"Hey there, Del."

Sitting in the middle of the back row of the auditorium was Rhonda. She wore the same nifty outfit as she had worn at the funeral. Her hair was fixed up nice again too, with a shiny silver barrette holding everything in place. She smiled for me and her face practically sparkled.

"Hi, Rhonda." I snuck into the seat next to her.

The door behind us swung open and the two circles of girls on the stage once again took a pause of anticipation. This time the reaction was different—all smiles, hair flicking, and head-tilting adoration.

I turned to look. "Great," I whispered to Rhonda. "It's Heckmeyer."

Norwood Heckmeyer stood six feet tall, with wavy black hair and dark-brown eyes. He had a dimpled chin like Kirk Douglas and a crooked smile like Elvis.

I looked at Rhonda. "I'm doomed."

She gave me a backhanded whack in the chest that just about knocked the wind out of me. "Shut up, Del. He's all fluff. You'll kick his ass."

"Yeah? Look at those girls." The swoonfest continued from the stage. Marjorie Bickersly took a pose with arms extended as if anticipating a hug form Shattuck High's best-loved hunk. Kelly Swoop fluttered her eyelids.

"They all have one problem," Rhonda said, smirking.

"What's that?"

"They don't get a vote."

Mr. Schirmer and Mrs. Borger walked in from the wings. Schirmer clapped his hands and directed everyone to take seats in the first three rows. I had seen him during study hall. The guy always reminded me of a turtle with his bald head and jutting upper lip. He wore a light-blue shirt with a dark vest and stood totem-pole straight.

"Quickly, people!"

Rhonda and I moved down to the third row. When everyone was settled, he explained how the auditions would take place. As expected, we would each speak and act out several lines from *Romeo and Juliet* that we had been given in advance. What I didn't realize until then was that Norwood Heckmeyer and I would each be auditioning seven different times because, apparently, there just weren't enough boys willing to try out for a role in which the actor might have to put on face powder and eyeliner.

The whole thing took just over an hour, and guess what. Not a single one of those *thespians* or *populars* possessed one-tenth the talent of Rhonda Glass. I knew it, they knew it, Mrs. Borger knew it, and I was pretty sure that Mr. Schirmer knew it too. When Rhonda spoke, something more than words came out of her. I don't know exactly how to explain it, but she seemed almost hypnotized into actually thinking that she was Juliet. She could have been standing in her pajamas up there, and it wouldn't have fazed her. She gave her audition with Norwood instead of me but, compared to Rhonda, he came across all herky-jerky and fake.

Rhonda said I did fine, but I wasn't so sure. Without Rhonda across from me, I felt sort of awkward. The usual rhythm wasn't there. It was a weird feeling saying words like "this bud of love by summers ripening breath" while looking into some of those heavily made-up faces. Most of the girls looked right past me, like I was a cardboard Romeo propped up with a stick. Marjorie Bickersly was the exception. She looked down on me like she was being forced to talk sweet to a worm.

I persevered and got through it. Mr. Schirmer thanked everyone for coming and told us that the resulting decisions would be posted outside the auditorium door first thing in the morning.

"See you tomorrow, Rhonda," I said as I shouldered my backpack.

"Bye," she said. "You were good today."

"I was okay," I said. "But *you*—you were slammin!"

It was true. Rhonda had a gift for acting—pure and simple. I wondered where her life would take her and hoped that the role of Juliet would be just the start. What could stop her, after all? Then I thought about that kooky father of hers and answered my own question.

44

I went to school early to check the audition results before homeroom. Here is what I found posted on the auditorium door.

Romeo: Delmar Finwick
Juliet: Marjorie Bickersly

Nothing could have been more backward. I couldn't let it stand. I made a dash to Mrs. Borger's classroom, took a sharp left turn, and came to an abrupt stop at her desk. Right away, I saw the sadness in her eyes.

"You didn't pick Rhonda," I said.

"I'm sorry, Mr. Finwick. But fourteen girls tried out and we could only choose one."

"But you were there. You saw her. None of the others were even close."

"It wasn't to be," she said. "Mr. Schirmer had different ideas."

Mrs. Borger placed both hands in her lap and looked at the empty desktop, then back at me. "Theater is a very subjective business, Mr. Finwick, and Rhonda is not the only disappointed student this morning. Many factors were considered in the selection. Mr. Schirmer and I talked at length, but he had the final say. It only makes sense. He's the head of our drama department and the director of the play."

"Where can I find him?"

"His room is C254."

I checked my watch. Still ten minutes until the homeroom bell. I charged back into the halls and slithered through the crush of bodies. (Sometimes it helps to be the size of a minnow.) Out of breath, I blasted into C254.

Mr. Schirmer clasped his hands together and smiled brightly when he saw me. He projected his voice across the room. "Thou art Romeo, Mr. Finwick!"

"I guess."

"My heartfelt congratulations on the achievement. I must say, you went into it as a considerable underdog, and yet you prevailed. Well done."

"Sure, but what about Rhonda? She's the one with all the talent. You saw her. You heard her. Gosh, Mr. Schirmer, if anyone in this school is a natural born actress, it's Rhonda Glass. She should be Juliet. She deserves it."

Schirmer's smile disappeared as his forehead compressed into a geometric pattern of wrinkles. He lifted his hands together with each finger touching its mirror opposite. "Indeed, Miss Glass is a strong talent and perhaps she will find a leading role in a future production," he said. "I'm hopeful that she will accept a minor role in this play."

"She should be Juliet."

"She simply wasn't right for this role."

"What do you mean, wasn't right for this role?"

"The character of Juliet must project a certain appearance, a certain elegance. Do you understand what I'm talking about?"

"You didn't pick her because she's fat?"

His eyebrows practically banged into the ceiling. "It was a factor in our selection."

"That's not fair."

"Perhaps not."

There it was, the plain truth. Fairness didn't matter. Schirmer was just doing his job. He was casting the role of Juliet to fit a stereotype that the audience expected to see. The role of Juliet went way beyond talent. It demanded a slender beauty. Rhonda Glass never had a shot.

"Maybe I'll quit. I'm the wrong size too, you know?"

"That's your choice," he shrugged. "There's always Norwood Heckmeyer."

I had one more thing to say, and it might have got me my second suspension of the school year. Somehow, I held it inside and walked slowly to homeroom. The bell rang. I was late again but didn't care.

❋

All day at school I looked for Rhonda. I saw Opal and Mark having lunch together and asked them if they had seen her. Neither had. After the final bell, I finally went to Miss Elmore, the school secretary.

"Excuse me. Have you heard anything from a student named Rhonda Glass today? I'm trying to find her."

"She went home sick before first period."

"What was wrong with her?"

Miss Elmore looked at me like I was a Russian spy. "Why do you care? Are you a relative? If not, then I can't help you."

"She's my friend."

"I can't help you."

"She's my girlfriend." Even I was surprised to hear the words come out of my mouth.

"Your girlfriend?" Miss Elmore gave me a stern look and folded her arms in disbelief. "What's your name?"

"Del Finwick."

"Oh yes," she said with narrowed eyes. "I've heard about you."

"I need to help her. She got some bad news this morning and I'm afraid she's going to do something stupid. Something terrible. Was she crying when she came here?"

"Yes, she was."

"Can I use your phone please?"

"Come to my desk."

Miss Elmore looked up Rhonda's phone number in a file cabinet and jotted it down on a slip of paper. She dialed the number and waited. She drummed her fingers on the desk and looked at me like I was a criminal. At last, a voice responded on the telephone.

"Hello, Rhonda? . . . This is Miss Elmore, the secretary at Shattuck High School. Are you doing all right? . . . Del Finwick is asking about you. Would you like to talk to him?"

Miss Elmore handed me the phone.

"Rhonda, are you okay?"

"No."

"Why not?"

"You know why not."

"Will you be back in school tomorrow? I need to see you."

"No."

"Why not."

The phone clicked off. *Criminy!*

I thanked Miss Elmore, ran for the door, and kept on running over a mile to the Emerald Gardens apartments. From the phone book and a map of Neenah, Grandpa Asa helped me figure out how to get to Rhonda's house. She lived on the south side of town, pretty close to the big radio tower. We marked it on the map and I ripped it from the phone book. Asa handed me the truck keys and I was off at a sprint.

The engine groaned but finally started. I let it warm up for a minute, then killed it twice in the parking lot before finding the rhythm of *clutch-shift-clutch release*. At last, I got it moving and followed alongside the railroad tracks on Harrison Street. A stop sign at Cecil forced me to work the clutch again, but I caught it just right and even burned some rubber. With a left turn at the foundry, I saw the giant electromagnet lifting scrap iron off the rust-colored mountain. Through an open door the glowing molten iron appeared the same color as jack-o-lantern light, and a smokestack coughed up a cloud of sooty air.

Rhonda's house was a little green bungalow with a couple pieces of wood siding missing and varnish peeling off the front door. I rang the bell and a dog barked from somewhere inside. After a minute, the door creaked open. Rhonda stood there in a frumpy gray sweatshirt and pajama pants.

"Hi," I said.

"Hi." Her face was puffy red and her eyes watery. A stack of empty pizza boxes sat on the living room floor and the place smelled like rotten vegetables.

"Do you want to go to Robby's?" I asked.

"Not really."

"Are you here all by yourself?"

"Yes."

"Let's go somewhere so we can talk."

She looked away.

"Please. Let's just go for a drive."

"Okay." She grabbed her coat and army boots.

We cruised down Commercial past the Eagles Club and Red Owl. I zigged right at the Butterfly Bar and randomly wandered through the neighborhoods, past Horace Mann Junior High, Wilson School, and Green Park. We drove past the rocket-shaped climbing tower at Riverside Park and past the war cannon. Crossing the bridge to the island we rumbled by the hospital, Food Queen, Roosevelt School, and Atlas Tag. We drove past my house on Fifth, and I showed her where Opal lived and the home of Leroy Kazmynski, the Green Bay Packer who gave me the autographed football. Then it was on to Doty Cabin from a time when Neenah wasn't even a city yet. I told her the story of how the governor got the name Neenah from the Indians, and Rhonda even smiled a little.

Eventually, we landed at Robby's, the fast-food joint I had suggested in the first place. It was right there, on the island, just a baseball's toss from Menasha. They served burgers, fries, and milkshakes in a little joint with chrome-edged countertops and a red-and-white tiled floor—better than five-star dining to a couple of sophomores.

Rhonda told me that she came from a long line of high school dropouts, and her dad wanted her to keep the tradition going.

"My dad said, 'That theater bullshit don't pay,'" she told me. Rhonda's dad wanted her to hire on at the knitting factory, where she could sew the sleeves onto sweaters for the rest of her life.

"That's grandma work," I said. "Your talent is acting."

"My dad says I'm kidding myself."

"Your dad is full of crap! What do you think of that?!"

Rhonda tried to conceal a little smile. She twisted her face and took a sip of her milkshake, which I took as my signal to continue my rant.

"Not only were you the best actress in that audition, you're probably the best in all of Neenah High School, including the juniors and seniors at Armstrong. There will be other opportunities, you know, and Mrs. Borger will *always* be on your side. So will I."

"I tried," she said. "I'm just not pretty enough."

I paused, not sure what to say next. It was true. Mr. Schirmer said so himself. *Juliet must project a certain appearance, a certain elegance.* Yep. Those were his words.

What I did next I'll never forget for as long as I live. I leaned over and kissed Rhonda Glass right on the lips. Yep, Right there at Robby's Hamburgers, in front of everybody.

"You're prettier than you think," I said.

She tried not to smile but couldn't help it.

"Don't give up, Rhonda. Don't quit school."

"I have to," she said.

I needed a different tack. A message. Something powerful. Then I remembered what Pastor Olson talked about in church.

"Have you ever heard the story of John Akhwari in the Olympic marathon?" I asked.

❋

We found our way to the bowling alley, where I spent my last dollar on Royal Crown Cola and popcorn. After that we took a drive to Kimberly Point and looked out at the lake with the moonlight reflecting off the ice. The truck cab was toasty warm as the engine blew a stream of hot air on our feet.

"Do you think I should turn down the Romeo role?" I asked.

"No quitting allowed," she said. "Remember?"

"Will you still help me practice?"

She slid over on the truck seat, put her arms around me, and we started lesson one.

45

The week flew by. Rhonda returned to school and decided to accept the minor role of Lady Capulet in *Romeo and Juliet*. I was excited for her until I learned that her character sought revenge against Romeo and wished him dead.

❀

On Thursday afternoon, I had Hoot Owls to deliver and flew out the side entrance by the cafeteria so I could hurry home and get a jump on them. I had taken my chances locking Eisenhower to the bike racks behind the East Wing and was glad to see that the dirtballs hadn't vandalized anything. As my fingers touched the handlebar grips an arm reached out from behind the janitor's shed and grabbed the back of my bike seat. I snapped my head around.

Damn! It was Larry Buskin.

"What's new, Minnow?"

"Nothing."

"The sheriff's dead. That's something."

I turned and tried to walk away but Buskin wouldn't let go of his grip on Eisenhower.

"I've got a message for you from the guy who killed your dad and Heiselmann."

"What?" I spun around.

"He says you need to chill out. Knock it off with the protest marches and anything else that draws attention to the murders."

I just stared into Buskin's eyes and said nothing.

"The guy told me that if you keep digging into this thing, the next person to die could be you or a member of your family."

"Yeah, sure. What do you know about anything?"

Buskin pulled a plastic bag out of his coat pocket. Inside were pills. Red, blue, white, yellow—a whole cornucopia of addictive junk. There were smaller baggies inside the big one. Some with white powder. Another with candy-sized bundles made of tin foil—*Jeez!*

"You're a drug dealer?"

Buskin shrugged.

"And you have connections with the killer through drugs?"

He nodded.

"What kind of connections?"

"You promise not to rat me out? We're both on thin ice, you know."

With each word I felt like I was sinking deeper and deeper into quicksand. "I promise."

Buskin looked around the parking lot and poked his head behind the shed.

"Okay, Minnow, listen up. You were right about the sheriff all along. There's a drug supplier at the root of all the shit, and he's not nice. If anybody gets too close, they die. Your dad must have known too much, so the guy killed him. Somehow, the sheriff got tangled up in it and was forced to protect him. He must have been blackmailed or threatened like he's doing to us now."

"The sheriff was protecting the killer?"

Buskin nodded. "He had to make sure the investigation didn't lead anywhere. Then you got involved and it changed everything."

"So I was *right* to suspect the sheriff?"

"Yeah. Then the killer decided to get rid of him too. And now? Shit. Now, I'm getting pulled into this mess. And to be honest with you, Minnow, I'm surprised that *you're* still even alive."

I nodded and thought back on the bullets that hit the ground right beneath me.

Buskin put his hands up, palms forward. "That's all I got. I gave you the message. From now on, you and I gotta lay low. It should be easy. Just do nothing—understand?"

"Do nothing?" I repeated.

Buskin nodded slowly. Then he turned and walked away.

Jeez! Now what?

❁

After my chat with Larry Buskin my head was all scrambled up with a confetti storm of thoughts. My Hoot Owl route couldn't wait, so I hurried home and cranked it out. Once finished, I bombed back across the bridge and wheeled toward Emerald Gardens in the darkness. My stomach was barking by the time I finally locked Ike to the lamppost and rapped my frozen knuckles on 118. I could hear Grandpa Asa maneuvering slowly between stacks of newspapers and other junk. The door swung open.

"I was hoping it was you," said Asa. I waded into the maze with my head still spinning. We talked about the weather. We talked about Neenah basketball and whether or not we were good enough to go to the state tournament again this year. We talked about world news.

"They signed a peace treaty in Vietnam," said Asa. "It's about time we got out of that mess."

I nodded my head.

"Won't bring back all those dead boys though, will it?"

I shook my head.

"Looks like some of those Watergate crooks are finally getting locked up. You reckon they'll ever pinch Nixon?"

"I don't know."

Asa was so hungry for a visitor he might have talked all night. While he jabbered nonstop, my brain was stuck on the Highway 41 Killer and his threat to murder my family. For a second I thought about spilling it all to Grandpa Asa, but I quickly changed my mind. It was all on me to keep my family safe, and all I had to do was do nothing. *Jeez!* It sounded so backward that my plan was now to do nothing. Doing nothing was the coward's way out. Doing nothing meant the bad guy had won.

"Is something bothering you, Del?"

"No—I just remembered some homework that I still needed to get done."

"Well, you better run home then."

"Yeah—but I also had another favor to ask you."

"Spit it out."

I explained Steve's plans to build the Blue Jay Slayer and bomb the baseball field at Menasha High and asked if he would let me use the truck as a transport and getaway vehicle.

"You mean to tell me that after we all got busted for the volcano, you want to try *another* goofy stunt?"

"Yes, sir," I said.

"Do you realize that you could be suspended again?"

"Yes."

"And you think I should get involved by letting you use my truck."

"It would be a big help."

Asa scratched his head and tried to look angry, but he couldn't hold the look for long. "Okay, you can borrow my truck."

"Just so you know, I still won't have my license yet," I said. "I won't turn sixteen until May."

"I don't give a rat's ass about a license. We're on a mission, boy. We're gonna bomb the Menasha High baseball field." A trace of pink color came up in Asa's cheeks and ears, and for a second I saw a fifteen-year-old kid behind those gray eyes.

It was almost nine before Asa finally hinted at ice cream. I scooped up two bowls full. Neither one of us had eaten any supper.

❋

After finishing my homework in my bedroom, I walked downstairs and clicked on the Channel 2 news. For several days after Heiselmann was killed, the murders had been the lead story. They had made it sound like the cops were nipping at the killer's heels, following clue after clue on the manhunt. It seemed like an arrest would be coming any day. Tonight the lead stories were about flu prevention and snowplow maintenance. Not a single peep about the murders or the Highway 41 Killer.

The cops were getting nowhere again, and what was I going to do about it? Not one damn thing.

46

I didn't sleep well that night.

Do nothing. Do nothing. Do nothing.

Those words stung like a spear in my gut. I felt as weak and helpless as the first day of school, when I let Leon Dinsky spot out Opal and didn't do a single, solitary thing about it. Whatever happened to the idea of finding some courage? And what about Pastor Olson's sermon about "Finishing the Race"?

Criminy . . . I was so confused that I had become paralyzed—and that's exactly what the killer wanted.

In homeroom, Steve surprised me by inviting me to go to the Neenah Rockets basketball game that evening with him and Mark. Apparently, we had been removed from his parents' forbidden list— proof positive that they knew nothing about our bombing mission with a giant kite. Anyhow, the game was scheduled to take place at the Armstrong High Field House on the other side of Highway 41, and Steve even volunteered to drive, having just turned sixteen and passing his test. He would pick up Mark first, then me.

"Can you go with us?" he asked.

"Okay," I finally answered. At least it would take my mind off my conversation with Larry Buskin.

We walked into the field house to the sounds of the pep band and at least a thousand noisy fans. Steve, Mark, and I each bought a box of popcorn and wiggled into the bleachers. Steve always picked on a player from the other team by shouting his number along with some sort of wisecrack when the band wasn't playing. Mark almost got tossed out when his paper airplane landed on the court. Mr. Schultz came after him from the left aisle but Mark snuck out on the right. Steve and I watched the last five minutes of the game without him. The Rockets managed to beat the Kimberly Papermakers 54–47, keeping our hopes for another state tournament alive

Guess what I spotted in the parking lot after the game. A black Cadillac.

Was it the same car? Heck, there had to be a dozen of them in the county. I looked to Mark and Steve but they were too busy jabbering. Slowly my legs carried me off in the direction of the Caddy and then I saw something that stopped me like my feet were locked in cement. There it was, the melon-sized dent in the rear bumper. That was it! I had to find out who owned that Cadillac.

"Come on, Delmar!" Mark yelled.

I turned and faced him. "Are we going to Quick's?"

"Yeah."

"Can I join you there in a few minutes? I just remembered that I need to meet someone."

"Meet someone? What are you talking about?"

"Just go," I said with a wave. "I'll be there in a few minutes."

"Whatever."

It worked. I knew Mark and Steve couldn't resist stopping at Mr. Quick's, where the upper classmen hung out. Located just a few blocks from Armstrong High, Quick's was a magnet for juniors and seniors, or any kid who had a car for that matter.

Their departure left me in an awkward spot, just standing by myself in the parking lot, staring at the field house door. I decided to watch from a few cars away. I pulled my stocking cap down to the tops of my eyes and pulled my chin inside my coat collar.

Ten minutes passed and the lot got quiet with only a half-dozen cars still scattered here and there. I stood behind the bed of a Ford pickup and kept watching. My eyes drifted to the dark patch of woods that bordered the west edge of the Armstrong parking lot. It would be a perfect place for the killer to set up another ambush. *Jeez*, I thought. *Should I run for my life*? I decided that if the killer was going to shoot me from the woods, he would have done it already. I stayed put and waited for whoever would be walking up to the black Cadillac.

When a tall kid with scraggly hair came through the parking lot, he gave me a funny look since I was standing right next to his truck.

"You got a problem?" he asked.

"No." I took a few steps away from the truck. He gunned the

engine, spun the tires, and crunched across the frozen slush onto Tullar Road.

Now I was really alone and completely exposed. *What kind of spy stands out in the open of a big, empty parking lot?* I shuffled my feet and even took a few steps in the direction of Quick's before stopping myself. I wished I had a bottle of pop, a book, anything to keep my hands busy, to look like I belonged there. Then I decided to do something really stupid. I moved closer. *If I'm going to do this I might as well get a good look*, I thought.

I peeked through the windows of the Caddy but couldn't see anything. I looked at the yellow Wisconsin license plate. Even in the dim light I could read number M52-928 and repeated it over and over again. In my mind, the *M* stood for murder.

My stomach tightened up like a wrung-out towel when I spotted someone emerging from the bluish light of the field house door. Have you ever been so scared you wondered whether or not you were going to pee in your pants? That was me as I stood out in the open waiting to meet the man who may have killed my dad and wanted to kill me next. I lowered my face, pretending to look at the ground and kept my hands in my coat pockets.

Get out of here, said my quavering gut. *Don't chicken out now*, my spine yelled back. Right or wrong, I stood and waited, right alongside that black Cadillac.

Crunch, crunch, crunch, crunch . . . The man in the black pants and black coat approached until he was a snowball's toss away. My eyes were on him even though I wasn't facing him directly. He turned and looked at me and the cone of yellow light from overhead reflected off his face. I studied it—fat nose, brick for a chin, forehead that jutted out like a shelf, shading his eyes. It was the same guy all right. The guy who had delivered the yellow envelope to Sheriff Heiselmann at Kimberly Point in September.

His voice came deep and threatening. "What do *you* want?" he asked.
I shrugged. "Just waiting for a ride."
"From who?"
"My dad."

A thought suddenly popped into my head. *Check his coat buttons.* My eyes drifted down to the man's dark coat. Three buttons held it closed at the front. Each one was black with a white streak running through it. I focused in on the neck where the coat hung open. Sure enough—the top button was missing.

"Do I know you?" The man's voice was louder now.

He took a few steps toward me and if ever there was a time to run, this was it. Still, something told me to stand firm. I lifted my chin up out of my coat collar as I turned and faced him directly. My toes curled inside the Eaglewings on my feet. We were eye to eye.

That's when two things happened at once. The first was a sound, the thud of the field house door followed by two men talking as they walked together toward the parking lot. The second was a look of recognition in the Cadillac Man's face. He knew me. He hated me. He wanted me dead. His face went cold and dark. His teeth showed through a narrow slit. He took a step forward and I took a step back. His eyes fired cannonballs. Mine shot back with peas.

The walking men kept coming. *Crunch, crunch, crunch, crunch* . . . Their feet were now on the parking lot itself, headed toward one of the few remaining cars in the distance.

"Hey, you still here?" The friendly voice came from one of the walking men.

The Cadillac Man drilled me with a final glare from his granite face that carried a message—*I will kill you.*

Just as quickly, he turned and gave a friendly wave. "Hey, fellas."

"See you next Tuesday," said one of the men.

The Cadillac Man pulled his car keys out of his pants pocket and something shiny fell to the ground at his feet. He quickly tossed his gym bag onto the passenger side seat, got in, and drove away, turning north on Tullar. My heart hammered like it was going to bust right out of my ribcage. My knees went weak. I watched the other two men as they walked past me. Both of them also carried gym bags.

Who are these guys, and why are they here later than everybody else? How do they know the Cadillac Man?

As soon as they disappeared in their cars, I reached down to see what had fallen out of the man's pocket. The overhead light reflected brightly off the shiny object. I picked it up. A metal whistle. The clues all clicked together—a gym bag, a whistle, another meeting with the men on Tuesday. Suddenly I remembered the doodle of a basketball player on the yellow envelope.

Holy catfish—the Cadillac Man is a basketball ref.

I pocketed the whistle and took off running, but not toward Quick's. I ran behind Armstrong and straight into the woods. By moonlight, I followed the trail for a few minutes, then charged into the brush, bushwhacking to the south and west. Somehow I had to find my way to

Quick's without being seen. The Cadillac Man was hunting me. Of that I had little doubt. Did he want me dead? Of that I was certain. Somewhere, he lay in ambush and I refused to make myself an easy target. I finally emerged from the woods into somebody's backyard. I had been running on fumes and fell to my knees for a breath. I looked back to where I came from and saw the shadows of my footprints, clear as day in the moonlight.

Criminy . . . is he tracking me?

That was it for the woods. I bombed through the neighborhood side streets where I wouldn't leave footprints. At last, there it was—the Mr. Quick's sign in the distance. I made a dash down Gillingham, waiting for the sound of a rifle and the impact of a bullet. I flung open the door and charged inside.

"How did you get so sweaty, Delmar?" asked Mark through a mouthful of fries.

"I ran," I said.

I ordered a 7 Up and slumped into my chair. As much as I wanted to tell Steve and Mark, I couldn't. No telling friends. No telling cops. Not even agent Culper at the FBI. I know it sounds crazy, but for the safety of my family, that was my plan.

47

For the second night in a row, I barely slept. Visions of the Cadillac Man with a knife in his hand kept running through my mind. About a hundred times I heard doors thump and stairs creak. I imagined him with a ladder climbing up to my window. A few times, I even peeked outside to check. *Jeez!* I was driving myself crazy. At last, my tiredness grew bigger than my fear and I dozed off.

After I got up, it was more of the same. I checked to see that the curtains were all pulled shut. I worried about the sound of every car on the street. Heck, even the thought of bringing in the mail had me skittish. *Doggone it!* I was scared of everything.

Enough was enough. Right or wrong, I had to get out of the house, so I picked up the phone and called Rhonda. No—she wasn't doing anything. Yes—she would meet me at the bowling alley to practice my lines for *Romeo and Juliet*.

❋

Third hour on Monday found me alone at a back table in the Science Resource Center with a pencil and blank sheet of paper. Step one was to find the creep's name. Somewhere in the universe, there had to be a list of Wisconsin high school basketball refs. *Should I talk to the basketball coach? Should I ask my gym teacher?* Since my plan was to keep things to myself, I did neither. Instead, I made a dash to the Neenah Library after school and picked up the Sunday *Post-Crescent* from the newspaper rack. Just as I had expected, the sports page listed all the upcoming games and it showed a full slate for Tuesday night. Neenah played at Kaukauna, Hortonville was at Appleton East, Kimberly was at Oshkosh North, and Appleton West traveled to Fond du Lac. I would start north, at Kaukauna, and work my way south.

I flew out the door and rode Ike through downtown Neenah like I had a Russian MiG on my tail. Once past the curving red bricks of the Bergstrom mill, I crossed the tracks and slowed to a walk at Emerald Gardens.

✹

"I might be late," I said to Grandpa Asa as we clanked spoons into dishes of Rocky Road.

"Where did you say you were going?"

"Kaukauna," I said. "The Rockets play the Ghosts at 6:30. I might make a couple other stops along the way."

It was the truth. I didn't tell him that I would be driving a hundred miles and covering three counties. Asa flicked his eyebrows and tossed the truck keys on the table. I scooped them up.

✹

The last thing I needed was for Mom to thwart my plans, so I parked the truck three blocks from our house. I would drive it to school and take off for Kaukauna from there. With luck, nobody would recognize me.

Breakfast for my mom was a cigarette and coffee as she sat at the kitchen table. *God.* She was getting so skinny that her pajama top practically slid off her bony shoulders. Even the skin on her face seemed to droop and around her cheeks and forehead, her skull showed right through. I placed my empty Froot Loops bowl in the sink and finished off a glass of Tang before washing both dishes right away. It had become a habit to keep dishes from piling up since I still had two months left on my sentence as the kitchen slave.

I grabbed my coat and walked toward the side door. "I won't be home for supper because I'm going to the basketball game tonight," I said.

"Okay, honey." Mom gave me a quick wave as she turned to the next page of *TV Guide.*

Sally glared at me with one of her patented, hands-on-hips, looks. "The Rockets are at Kaukauna tonight. How are *you* planning to get to an away game?"

"Steve just got his license," I said.

That shut her up, and it wasn't even a lie. I was out the door.

❋

Somehow, I made it through all my classes, but when the final bell rang, my nerves started twitching. Fretting about driving all over the Fox Valley without a license had something to do with it. But the scariest part was knowing I was heading off, by myself, in pursuit of the Cadillac Man. A bowling ball rose up from my gut and I swallowed it back down. He knew what I looked like. Worse than that, he knew that I knew what he looked like. I figured out that there was a special kind of fear reserved for certain situations, and I was heading into a doozy. Both me and the Cadillac Man wanted to see each other, only he wanted to see me in a very special way. *Dead!*

Getting through Neenah was adventure enough. I was still about as coordinated as a three-legged dog when it came to working the clutch and managed to stall out twice at stop signs. Finally, I cranked the wheel toward the Highway 41 northbound ramp and worked through the gears. The traffic was "a dog's breakfast," as Grandpa Asa used to say. About a hundred people honked at me while I tried to merge into the mess of cars and trucks. *Cripes*, I must have driven on the shoulder for a quarter mile before somebody finally let me in. A guy who looked like a bear passed me and flipped the middle finger. *Holy mackerel!* I hunkered down in that right hand lane with my nose straight ahead and the speedometer at 55. Once I got past Appleton, Highway 41 took a big sweeping turn to the east. A green sign popped up that directed me to the Kaukauna exit. *Whew!*

The road into town took me over a bridge, crossing the Fox. I saw the big paper mill churning out steam. I saw the dairy where they made the cheese spread that we always ate at Christmastime. A couple of trucks rolled by carrying big green Badger farm wagons that were common all over the countryside. Grandpa Asa had told me that Kaukauna made farm machinery and, sure enough, there was the proof.

As I rolled into the small downtown, I realized that I had no clue where to find Kaukauna High School. I checked my watch—only five o'clock. I was way early. Worse yet, I was way hungry. In my pocket I had six bucks of Hoot Owl money. I spotted a pizza joint, parked the truck, and walked inside. The menu had every kind of pizza, from onion to anchovy. A waitress, not much older than me, walked over. To say that she was good looking would be like calling Pete Rose a decent hitter. *Gawd!* She was a knockout, with her sparkly blue eyes, perfect smile, and short, blonde hair that curled up on the ends.

"What can I get you?" she asked.

I stammered and pushed my nose into the menu. "Umm—what's good?" I finally asked.

"The pizzas are all good," she said. "The Supreme is the best."

A ten-inch Supreme was listed on the menu at $1.60. Along with a pop it would be right around two bucks.

"Sounds good to me," I said. "I'll take the ten-inch Supreme and a root beer."

She smiled brightly as she wrote it down. *Does she like me?*

"Can you tell me how to get to Kaukauna High?" I asked.

She smiled again. "Sure." She grabbed a napkin and drew me a map with a little house symbol representing the school. "Are you going to the game?"

"Yeah, I drove up from Neenah."

Her eyes snapped wide. "You've got your driver's license?"

"No," I said honestly. "I turn sixteen in a few months, but my grandpa still lets me drive his truck."

She looked out the window.

"It's the turquoise Chevy," I said.

Her face lit up in disbelief as she walked away to place my order and returned with my root beer.

"Is Neenah good in basketball this year?" the waitress asked.

"Pretty good."

She nodded. "Well, you're sure to beat the Ghosts tonight. What else do you do for fun?"

My mind rattled through a long list of tenth-grade answers that included fishing for bullheads and dancing with my mom.

"I'm playing the lead role in *Romeo and Juliet*," I said.

It was the golden ticket.

"You are?!" She looked back to make sure the boss wasn't looking, then sat down across the table from me and leaned in close. "I'm playing the lead in *A Midsummer Night's Dream*," she said.

For five minutes we talked. She told me about her dream to be an actress in Hollywood and that she hoped to study theater in college, if she could afford to go. She hoped to visit Broadway and loved everything by some guy I had never even heard of named Arthur Miller. But she also liked Shakespeare and was envious that I got to be in the famous love scene on the balcony. I tried to be cool about it and didn't tell her that the balcony scene was the part I feared most.

"When is your performance?" she asked.

"April."

"Mine's not until the end of May."

"Are your parents excited?"

"Not really. How about yours?"

"Nope."

A man and woman came into the restaurant and the girl glanced in their direction.

"I better get back to work," she said. "My name's Jan, what's yours?"

"I'm Del."

She smiled again and walked away.

Wow! She liked me all right. Too bad she didn't go to Shattuck. I watched her move from table to table, filling water glasses and delivering pizza. She smiled at me every time she walked by.

The pizza came way too soon and my conversation with the pretty girl from Kaukauna washed away with a flood of hungry customers demanding her attention. She only stopped at my table one more time and it was to drop off the bill.

The total for my pizza and pop added up to $1.90. Then I saw the message underneath.

Good Luck, Romeo! Come and see me again sometime!

I paid at the cash register and then returned to place a dollar bill under my root beer glass. Just like James Dean I kept my cool and strutted out the door to the turquoise Chevy Apache pickup. I propped myself up high on a pillow and looked up at the window of the pizza place, giving a casual wave on the off chance that she was looking. I started the engine with a roar and worked the clutch pedal. The truck lurched forward and stalled out.

Jeez!

❀

When I got to Kaukauna High School, the first thing I did was drive around the parking lot looking for the black Cadillac. I saw two yellow school buses with black letters that said Neenah School District on the side. I even saw a couple of seniors who I recognized as friends of my sister, but no black Cadillac.

I was just about to leave when I decided to spend the fifty cents to go inside and see for myself who was refereeing the game. The Rocket and Ghost players were all doing layup drills on opposite sides of the court. Kaukauna had a pretty good crowd, and their orange-and-black colors were everywhere, on banners, signs, and pompoms. Even their cheerleaders were dressed in Halloween colors. On the other side, several dozen Neenah fans all sat in a bunch waiting for the game to start.

A pair of refs in their black-and-white striped shirts walked to the scorer's table at courtside. One guy had a bald head and a beer belly. The other was a twenty-something dude with blond hair. No sign of the Cadillac Man. The first stop on my list had flamed out and there was no sense staying longer. As the Kaukauna band played the first notes of the "Star-Spangled Banner," I walked out the door. Appleton East was my next stop—if I could find it.

I stalled the engine again. "Dammit all!" How was I going to impress girls if I couldn't even work the clutch? Southbound on 41, my hands gripped the wheel and my eyes searched for the College Avenue exit in Appleton. I found it, pulled off the highway, and stopped at a Mobil station.

"Do you know how to get to Appleton East High School?" I asked the man in the gray shirt with the winged-horse patch on his pocket.

"Are you really old enough to drive?"

I took a breath and tried again. "Do you know how to get to Appleton East High School?"

The man spat a shot of tobacco juice into a mason jar. He picked some dirt out from under his fingernail. Then, finally, he told me how to get to East High.

Long story short, I wasted forty minutes—another total bust. Their game was almost at halftime and none of the refs was the Cadillac Man. I knew I had to hurry to get to the third basketball game on my list.

Oshkosh North was a long ways south, and when I crossed the Butte des Morts Bridge I couldn't help thinking about all the trouble that I had already caused. I pulled off at the other side and found a Sinclair. Inside the small office an inflatable green dinosaur hung from the ceiling—a prize, no doubt, to get kids to talk their parents into spending more money.

"Can you tell me how to get to Oshkosh North High School?"

"Why do you want to go there?"

"Basketball game," I said.

"It started over an hour ago."

"Could you just tell me how to get there, please?"

The man drew me a map on a paper towel like those used for wiping dipsticks. I ran for the truck, and when I feathered the clutch it grabbed just right.

Once again, it took a while to get there, search the parking lot, and poke my head in the door. Another bust. Two refs and another at the table, but no Cadillac man. I sprinted again for the truck. Was there enough time to get to Fond du Lac? I spun the wheels on the icy pavement and backtracked to Highway 41.

I checked my watch at the Fond du Lac city limits sign. It was already five minutes past nine. *Shoot!* The game was probably over. As long as I had come all that way, I stopped once more at a gas station where an orange-and-white Gulf sign glowed against the black sky. A young man provided the directions I needed, and guess what. He didn't give me any crap for once.

Five minutes later I was waiting at the parking lot entrance watching an endless stream of cars leaving. By the time I drove in, there were only twenty or thirty cars left. I scanned them all in search of a black Cadillac. Nothing.

Good grief! What a waste!

I sat in the idling truck and finally decided there was nothing else to do but go home. I pulled out and drove past the front of the school. Then a second driveway appeared, leading to another small parking area. My eyes scanned the lot and spotted a dark car in the shadows. I couldn't tell for sure if it was the black Cadillac, and I was afraid of driving in there to check. Lacking any better ideas, I parked on the road, turned off the truck, and waited.

It didn't take long, maybe five minutes, before a man wearing dark clothes and carrying a gym bag left the building and got in the car.

Son of a bitch! It was him all right.

The Cadillac Man drove slowly out to the road, where he turned away from me. Under the illumination of a street light, the big dent in the bumper showed itself. I started the truck, worked the clutch perfectly, and followed. As he made his way to Highway 41 I kept reminding myself to stay far back. A crook like this guy was sure to be on the lookout at all times. If he caught me following him there was no telling what he would do. Most likely he would try to ditch me. Worse case, the psycho would slow down and put a bullet through my windshield.

He turned north on 41. At least it was the direction home. I memorized the tall, skinny shape of his red taillights. From a quarter-mile back I kept him in my sights.

Oshkosh came and went without the Cadillac Man taking an exit. We crossed the Butte des Morts Bridge and a weird mix of sadness and anger surged through me as we passed the place on the road where Sheriff Heiselmann was killed. I wondered what thoughts floated through the mind of the Cadillac Man. Did a creep like that even feel guilt?

We drove on and passed the billboard on the highway where Mark and I found the bullet and the cigarette—the place where he killed my dad. My grip tightened on the steering wheel. We passed the giant slide and kept going. We passed the Cecil Street exit in Neenah and he didn't slow down—just a steady pace of sixty miles an hour.

Suddenly his right taillight blinked red as the car approached the exit to Neenah's Main Street. *Holy crap!* It was the same exit I would normally take to go home. The same exit that passed by Dad's grave. I slowed way down and turned off my headlights because Mark always said that was the best way to run undetected from the cops.

On Main Street the black Cadillac turned right and I let it get a couple blocks ahead. We crossed the little bridge over the slough and past the Hafemeister machine shop. Was he heading to my house? Was he going there to kill me? What about Mom and Sally?

Holy hell!

The Cadillac's red blinker came on just before the railroad tracks and doused my worry about Mom and Sally. I approached slowly and watched the taillights as they cruised toward Emerald Gardens. Was the creep going after Grandpa?

I turned and followed with my headlights still turned off. The black Cadillac continued in front of Emerald Gardens but neither slowed nor stopped.

Whew.

He took another right turn and then a quick left into a driveway. I stopped the truck and waited. The Cadillac Man lifted the garage door and pulled his car inside. He emerged from the unattached garage and entered the side door of a small, two-story house. I watched as a light came on in what must have been his kitchen. Five minutes later the downstairs light flicked off and an upstairs light came on. The creep was in his bedroom. Five minutes after that, all the lights went dark.

"Gotcha!" I said out loud.

I put the pickup in reverse and slowly backed away until I was no longer visible from the yellow house. Through downtown Neenah I rolled with the headlights back on. I rolled past the mooneye spot by the library. I turned left on Oak across the Fox River and drove past the hospital before parking three blocks from home.

I snuck into the house like a burglar, drank a tall glass of milk, and tiptoed upstairs into my room. The house was quiet. My bed felt warm. I had a secret bigger than the sky.

48

Somehow I had slept. The buzz of my alarm clock brought me back to consciousness, and I remembered everything.

Jeez! Now what?

No time for a shower, I pulled on yesterday's clothes, grabbed a Pop-Tart, and stirred a glass of Tang. *Now what? Now what? Now what?* Whatever was next would be up to me. I'm not sure why, but I went back upstairs to my closet and found the X-15 Instamatic Camera that Mom and Dad had given me for my birthday. I looked at the film indicator and saw that I still had twelve pictures left. I shoved it in my pocket, shouldered my book bag, and headed out into the predawn cold.

Asa's truck was right there where I had left it on Seventh. It started right up like it had been waiting for me. I worked the clutch perfectly.

Yes!

The Chevy chugged over the bridge, past the library, through downtown Neenah, left at the tracks, and into the parking lot of Emerald Gardens. Since it was too early to wake up Asa, I put the keys on top of the front wheel.

The big part of my brain responsible for my own survival kicked in and told me to cross the tracks and zig east toward Shattuck. Then a different, pea-sized corner of my brain told my legs to walk toward the Cadillac Man's house instead. I approached the place just as the orange sun popped over the edge of the tracks. A Soo Line engine blasted its whistle and I nearly crapped my pants.

The two-story house appeared as plain as could be in a neighborhood that most people had probably never even seen. Was it too ordinary for a killer? Was I wrong about the Cadillac Man? Then, just as quick, it seemed perfect for him. Every snake needed a hiding place, and the more hidden the better.

The Cadillac Man's house sat wedged between the railroad tracks and the slough. Most of the windows revealed nothing, with shades shut tight and no gaps to peek through. The mailbox was plain and black, standing out by the street—no name, no decoration, not even a number on the post. I was tempted to take a look inside but didn't dare. Instead, I pulled out my Instamatic and started snapping pictures, beginning with a shot of the house from the street. Then I moved around to the side by the garage and snapped another. Looking left and right, I scurried around his neighbor's house and snapped a few pictures from the rear.

My legs felt numb and my heart clanged inside me like an alarm-clock bell as I finished up my recon mission. I retraced my footprints in the snow, pocketed the camera, and got back on the street. Just then, a neighbor man pulled out of his driveway and stabbed me with a disapproving look. I kept my eyes pointed straight down the street and held my breath, forcing my legs to walk slowly. The man drove away and I exhaled. When the yellow house was out of sight, I took off running.

I entered Shattuck almost forty-five minutes before homeroom bell and made my way to the Science Resource Center. The place was empty, too early even for Mrs. Schwartz. I settled into my usual table in the back corner and ripped a sheet of paper out of a spiral notebook. With a dull number 2 pencil, I wrote three words at the top of that page.

OPERATION SNAKE DEN

I woke before the sun on Saturday morning and turned on the kitchen light. The dishes were clean, the toilets scrubbed, and the floor shone with a new coat of wax. All of that I had done ahead of time so nothing could stop me from executing my secret plan. I poured milk over the top of a bowl of Froot Loops and waited for them to get soggy. In the meantime, I converted a spoonful of orange Tang into a glass of instant nutrition and flipped on the kitchen radio, setting the volume low so as not to wake Mom or Sally.

The man on WNAM spoke in his usual boring monotone, rambling on and on about the Lake Winnebago spearing report. It had been a lousy month of February, with only a few sturgeon taken due to cloudy water. That was okay with me. The fewer sturgeon that they speared, the better my chances of seeing one while diving for lures in the river.

The radio announcer wrapped up his report with a warning.

Be careful out there, folks. People are taking their shanties off the lake, and those open spearing holes are big enough to swallow a car.

True enough, I thought. I clicked off the radio and focused on the mission at hand, opening my folder for Operation Snake Den at the kitchen table.

From the left pocket, I pulled out my notes and the photographs that I had just picked up from the film development counter at Camera & Card. I had examined every possible entry point to the Cadillac Man's house. With a red Magic Marker, I drew a circle around the basement window on the back side.

From the same folder, I pulled out a newspaper clipping that showed the times and locations of high school regional basketball tournament games coming up on Saturday. Games were scheduled through the afternoon and evening, beginning at one o'clock. It would be a busy day for basketball referees all over the state of Wisconsin.

I had to get out of the house early, before Mom woke up and gave me more work or, worse yet, sent me to confirmation class. Ripping the side out of a brown grocery bag, I made a note and left it on the kitchen table.

GONE FISHING. BACK FOR SUPPER.

Another lie. Another brick paving my road to hell.

Grabbing my coat and hat, I faced two pairs of boots at the door. Common sense told me to step into the felt-lined Sorels. They would be warm and cozy in my hiding place, the practical option for sure. But my eyes locked onto the Eaglewings, and they appeared to be looking back. Ever since the minnow bucket incident at the Menasha dam, it seemed like they were juiced with an electric energy that was hard to explain. Maybe they were my version of Batman's cape and brought out what little courage was hiding inside me. I stepped into the Eaglewings, laced them up, and slipped out the door.

Eisenhower stood at attention in the garage when I walked in. That red reflector blinked and waited. The spokes practically hummed. It was D day, after all.

The pillow case of tools and my Kodak X-15 fit neatly in Ike's front basket. The light was still dim as I stepped onto the driveway and reached for the garage door. Then I froze. My eyes flashed to the stack of scrap lumber. Did I dare? Beneath the top layer of pine boards I knew that the Model 12 shotgun lay concealed in its case.

Do I bring it?

Call me a liar if you want to, but Eisenhower made the decision for me. It wasn't so much a tug as a gravitational pull away from that gun. My grip tightened on the handlebars and my body leaned away from the open garage door. I took the hint. Yep, breaking and entering was one thing. Bust in with a gun? Cripes—even juvie wouldn't have me. I pulled down the garage door and jumped on the pedals.

At Food Queen I swapped fifty cents of Hoot Owl money for a pack of Twinkies and a bottle of orange pop. After that, Ike hauled me and my supplies over the bridge and through town to where the railroad tracks crossed.

The Cadillac Man's house was only visible as a hazy silhouette through a patch of ground fog hanging over the slough. I pushed through the thorny bushes that bordered the Soo Line tracks and laid Ike in the goldenrod before settling into my hiding place behind a clump of sumac. I couldn't see much behind all those branches, weeds, and fog. *Just as well*, I figured. Concealment was the main thing, and my sense of hearing would have to serve me until the fog lifted. H hour would arrive in its own due course.

I checked my Timex. At 7:35, it could be a wait almost as long as the duck hunting opener, but determination was on my side.

The first hour passed without a single car leaving the Cadillac Man's street. I had to peek a couple times as trains went by. During all of that rumbling and clanging it was dang near impossible to hear anything else. Hour two brought one more train and a flock of chickadees. At the start of hour three, I saw a cottontail rabbit hop so close to me that I almost touched it. One more train went through, and by 10:30 the fog had lifted, and the yellow house glowed in sunlight. I ate my Twinkies and drank my orange pop. If anything was going to happen, I figured it would be soon.

Hour four brought one train and two flocks of geese but still no movement from the Cadillac Man. By the time the noon whistle sounded at one of the mills, I was hungry, antsy, and sick of sitting in slush. *Jeez!* Lieutenant Columbo on TV never had to squat with a wet butt.

Just as I was grousing about everything, the noise finally came. *Clunk!* I craned my neck and leaned forward, eyes wide, heart booming. The garage door rattled open. I heard an engine start and saw white exhaust fumes drift out the open door. The black car emerged, and the Cadillac Man got out to close the garage door. It was him all right. The snake was leaving his den. I hunkered down and watched through the brush as he drove away. Everything fell silent. H hour had arrived at last. According to my math, the Cadillac Man would be gone for at least four hours. If he had two games he could be gone all day.

I must have looked suspicious, climbing out of my hiding place with a pillowcase full of burglar tools. Too bad the fog had burned away. I walked quickly between two houses and behind the Cadillac Man's garage. From there I paused and listened before moving toward my target—the basement window.

49

On my hands and knees I realized that it was time to break things, and in my case that meant breaking everything at once—the window, my promise to Mom, the law. I had done some crazy things in my life, but never anything like this. It was crime, pure and simple—burglary, larceny, breaking and entering—the cops had a hundred names for what I was doing, and they were all as illegal as heck. Do you know what the engine on a Harley-Davidson sounds like? That's what my heart was doing as I crouched by the Cadillac Man's basement window and started in with a pry bar.

For three whole minutes I pried, dug, and scraped at the edges of that window. I switched to a screwdriver, then pliers, and finally started stabbing between the sash and frame with a putty knife.

What's this thing made of—titanium?

After five minutes had passed, I decided that enough was enough. I leaned back on my elbows and pulled back my right leg. The heel of my size 4 Eaglewing blasted into that small window like a wrecking ball. The sound of breaking glass was louder than a car crash.

Am I caught? My eyes darted left and right. Had the neighbors heard me? Some puke came up in my throat, but I swallowed it back down. I listened for sirens but only heard the hum of the foundry and distant rumbles on the Soo Line tracks.

Breathe in . . . breathe out . . . breathe in . . . breathe out. My heart slowly beat down. It was time to go inside. With the glass gone, opening the window was a simple matter of reaching inside and twisting the latch until the sash flopped open. I left my tools outside and crawled through, carrying only my camera. By dangling myself through the opening, I was able to shimmy down to the concrete floor. After spending several hours in the bright sunlight, I thought the basement looked as black as a cave. A sliver of light from underneath a door on the main level revealed the location of the stairs. Like an idiot, I took off the Eaglewings at the top of the steps so I wouldn't mess up the house—a decision that I was bound to regret.

The plan was to find anything that would prove that the Cadillac Man had murdered my dad. At the top of my list was a .357 Magnum revolver that would match up with the bullet that I had sent to Agent Culper. I walked into the kitchen and couldn't believe how normal everything looked. Dishes dried in a rack next to the sink. A folded towel hung on the oven door handle. A clear-glass cookie jar sat, half-full, on the counter. I took off the lid and grabbed one for my aching stomach.

As I chewed the chocolate chip cookie, I walked up to a picture on the wall, an old-fashioned painting of people walking in a big city, probably New York. The frame was gold and expensive looking. Why would a murderer have a fancy picture like that? I told myself to get serious and focus on the mission.

The thought of opening drawers gave me the willies at first. I needed to look for the gun, but what else might be in there—knives, brass knuckles, maybe somebody's cut-off finger? I pulled the first one open slowly. What I found were pens, pencils, and paper. I pulled open another drawer and found napkins and hot pads. A third drawer contained measuring spoons and a telephone book.

Jiminy Christmas! Is this guy a killer or isn't he?

I moved on to the living room and it was fancier than expected. A grandfather clock ticked loudly with a brass pendulum that swung back and forth behind a glass front. The crest of the clock had lots of intricate carving, topped off with an eagle. Its wings were spread apart, ready to fly, and the head gazed fiercely at the ceiling. The couch and end tables were old and fancy too, with swirly carved wooden legs and everything stained and varnished to a dark, blackish shine. Two more old-fashioned pictures hung on the walls. One was of a sailing ship fighting storm-tossed waves on a green ocean. The other showed a lady in a long blue dress gazing out at a field of flowers. What kind of a snake den was this? It was more like the home of somebody's rich grandma.

I moved over to the coffee table, where several magazines lay fanned out. Most were different copies of the same thing—*Antique Collectors Digest*. A single copy of *The Sporting News* lay at the bottom of the pile. On a small side table I found a *TV Guide*, just like Mom always read, and a bowl of mixed nuts. I helped myself to a cashew and moved on to the next room.

The bathroom was plain and boring, with a medicine cabinet stocked with the usual junk—cough drops, aspirin, a bottle of Pepto-Bismol. The sink and bathtub were spotless. The toilet had one of those fuzzy seat covers and looked brand new. I looked at the towels hanging by the sink.

Embroidered yellow flowers?

The stairs to the second floor creaked like old bones as I tiptoed from one step to the next. It sent a chill through my scalp. I turned the brass doorknob on my left and had a funny feeling that the fancy house tour was over. I don't know what I expected—an arsenal of guns, a torture chamber—maybe a skeleton swinging from a noose like the covers of the western comic books. What I found was more of the same, another room right out of *Better Homes and Gardens* magazine. The bed was made, the dresser uncluttered. A fancy stained-glass lamp sat on the end table.

I stood to the side as I pulled open the closet door just in case it had been booby trapped. The explosion never came. A couple dozen shirts and sweaters hung there in perfect order, like the pages in a book. A few still had the plastic from the dry cleaners wrapped over the top. Two black-and-white striped referee shirts filled the slots along the right side and two pairs of black shoes rested neatly on the floor.

I poked my head behind the shoes and found a white, cardboard box. Beneath the lid, the box was full of papers, neatly separated into sections by cardboard dividers. One section was labeled "Taxes." I pulled out a 1040 form and looked it over. I said the words out loud.

"Taxpayer's name. Howard W. Shulepick."

There it was. The name of the son of a bitch who murdered my dad. I paused and repeated the name, memorizing the spelling. Satisfied, my eyes drifted further down the page. Earned income—$938.

What?! A kid could practically earn that much.

I nosed deeper into the files and found about a million receipts from antique furniture places and auction houses in big cities like Chicago, Philadelphia, and New York.

Holy Kamoly! Shulepick had paid $5,200 for a pair of mirrors. The clock with the eagle was another $26,000, and get this: the painting called *Blue Lady* was bought for $85,000 all by itself. I took a photograph of the *Blue Lady* receipt with my Instamatic and continued snooping through the file box.

I waded through some boring junk like homeowners insurance and heating oil receipts. Then guess what I found. News clippings. They were all piled into a plain folder labeled "Jobs," and at the top of the stack was the front page of the *Post-Crescent* on the day after the murder of Sheriff Heiselmann. I dug down further and found another front-page article about the murder of my dad.

A tornado swirled inside me, and I didn't know if I should scream or punch the wall. It was bad enough that he killed Dad, but to call it a *Job* and save the newspaper like a souvenir? It boiled my blood.

"I'll kill him," I whispered to myself. It felt good to say the words, even though I knew it was all just talk, with the Model 12 still sitting back home. The thought of my Eaglewing steel-toed boots passed through my mind, and I wished I hadn't left them at the basement steps.

Were the papers enough to nail him? I wasn't sure, and it bugged me. What I really, really needed was that gun. There was one more room to check out and something told me that it held the key to putting Shulepick away for good. I took photos of the remaining forms, receipts, and news clippings with my X-15 and shoved the file box back in the closet.

There was only one other room on the second floor. I tried turning the door knob but found it locked. I eyeballed the gap around the edge of the door and tried peeking through the old-fashioned keyhole. No luck.

Maybe I can jimmy the thing.

Then I remembered that my sack of tools was still outside by the busted basement window. I pulled out my Old-Timer pocket knife with the lifetime guarantee and slipped the two-inch blade into the gap. I wiggled it and heard the bolt click before turning the knob and swinging the door open.

It took a couple seconds for my eyes to focus. Then . . . "Judas Priest!"

It was no bedroom; that was for sure. Granite-topped counters lined one whole side of the room. Tanks of oxygen and propane-fed Bunsen burners larger than anything I had seen at Shattuck High. Glass flasks and beakers of every size lined the shelves. On another shelf, the finished product. Baggies of white powder. Smaller baggies of brown crystals. A quart jar half-full of tiny blue pills, each triangular in shape. Another jar held little red ones, and there were whites in another. That's when I remembered Larry Buskin's words about the sheriff being mixed up with a drug supplier.

Drug supplier? Criminy! He's making the stuff!

I pulled out my X-15, pushed a new flash cube into the top, and started clicking pictures of the drug laboratory. The creep was killing people all right, and it wasn't just with guns. I opened a few drawers and found them loaded with more chemistry supplies. On the countertop, an ashtray held three cigarette butts burned down to the filters. I leaned in close and, sure enough, the tiny blue letters spelled out the word *Winston*. I pocketed one, another clue, but still not the keystone that I wanted.

My eyes focused on a bright-colored rectangle on the floor. *An oriental rug? In a chemistry lab?* Something about it just didn't add up. On a hunch I lifted a corner to look underneath and my eyes caught the reflection of a brass ring attached to what appeared to be a small trap-door in the floor. I pulled the ring slowly, again fearing a booby trap. When the thing flopped all the way open I saw only one object—a handgun case. I pulled it out and opened the latches. There it was— shiny black with wooden grips. I read the numbers out loud that were inscribed on the barrel.

"3—5—7"

Sure as heck, it was the .357 Magnum revolver that the Cadillac Man had used to kill my dad. In my shaking hands I held the key. The experts would match it to the bullet. Of that I was certain. Howard W. Shulepick's days were numbered. I was sure of it. Maybe it would be life in Waupun Prison, or maybe he would fry in the electric chair. Either way—I had him. I would call Agent Culper as soon as I got home. I wouldn't even wait until Camera & Card developed the pictures.

Just then, I heard it. The sound of car tires crunching through the packed snow. I peeked behind the window curtain.

Holy crap on a cracker! The Cadillac Man! He was back!

50

My first instinct was to bolt for the front door, but the Cadillac Man hadn't wasted any time and was already approaching with keys in hand. I dashed toward the basement, tripping over my Eaglewings as I flew down the steps. I nearly tumbled but caught myself on the banister before running toward the shaft of light on the back wall.

Ach! Something stabbed my right foot. I looked down. My stockinged feet stood on shards from the busted window. I reached down and pulled a dagger of glass out of the bottom of my left foot. The blood gushed out, instantly soaking my sock.

It didn't matter. *Get out! Get away!* Adrenaline had taken over and my brain had shifted to survival mode. I threw both the revolver and my X-15 out the open window and reached for the top rim of the cement blocks underneath, only to find that they were sloped and my hands couldn't get a grip.

What? Two months of pull-ups wasted because I couldn't grip the stupid window sill? I looked around for something to stand on. The kitchen door clunked shut.

No noise. No noise.

I spotted an old dresser and gave it a shove toward the window. The scraping sound echoed off the concrete walls.

Crud! I glanced back at the door. A shadow passed over the crack of light but just as quickly moved away.

In silent panic I lifted the dresser off the ground and monkey walked it beneath the window. Another knife blade of pain shot through me— the left foot this time, and a sort of warm stickiness now saturated both feet.

Will I escape only to bleed to death?

The sounds of footsteps seemed to move back and forth upstairs. The floor let out a rusty hinge sound. I glanced again at the crack of light underneath the door to the kitchen. Another shadow came and went, then came back. Was he listening?

I stood perfectly still, sensing the hammering of my heart inside of my sliced-up feet. Placing one knee on top of the dresser, I hoisted myself up. My bloody feet and socks nearly slipped on the varnished top as I tried to push my head and arms through the small rectangle of sunlight.

Jeez! Climbing in had been so easy. My arms and elbows were wedged and useless on both sides of my body. In desperation, I tried launching myself up and out by jumping off the top of the dresser.

It worked. My body shot through the opening up to my waist. At the same time, the dresser tipped back and crashed to the floor with a BAM!

It was panic time. I wiggled and squirmed like a rabbit trying to squeeze through a knothole. I heard the loud thud of the basement door flying open followed by the thunder of feet charging down the wooden steps. The top half of me was through the window, but my belt buckle had hung up on the sill. I swept my arms wildly. I was swimming in soggy snow, clawing like crazy with nothing to grip.

God . . . Help me!

At last, my arms found the dead grass underneath the snow. I yelled and tensed with an enormous tug that pulled the rest of me up and out the window.

For a microsecond I thought I had made it, but before I could stand and run, something clamped onto my foot like the grip of the devil himself trying to pull me back down into that dark hole. I snapped my head around. The hand gripped my ankle like a noose. Tendons strained through the skin and the knuckles were volcanoes. Attached to the hand was a muscular arm and above the elbow were those black-and-white stripes. It was me against that powerful arm, yanking, tugging to get me back into that hellhole. I kicked the hand with my free foot but couldn't shake it.

Then, without even thinking, my body replicated something I had seen on the *Wild Kingdom* TV show. It was the crocodile roll. I spun once, completely over and back to my belly. It loosened the grip so I spun again—another full 360—and broke free, leaping forward and looking backward at the same time. In the second that I paused, I got my second look at a hate-filled face right out of a horror movie.

I jumped to my feet and ran away like a leg-shot deer leaving a trail of blood. My instincts steered me toward the brush by the Soo Line tracks where Eisenhower lay waiting. But then I heard the house door crash open and looked back. The Cadillac Man was on my tail, arms and legs churning like Bob Hayes.

"Dammit!"

There was no time to retrieve Ike. I needed a plan B and I needed it fast. Emerald Gardens was just two blocks. *Jeez!* If I could make it there.

My stocking-footed sprint was no match for the Cadillac Man. Glancing back, all I saw were black-and-white stripes, a bright-red face, and two layers of teeth.

He'll twist my head off!

I reached into my gut and found another gear. My strides became explosions of pain. My face was on fire.

The killer was just twenty yards back when I yanked open the side door of Emerald Gardens, slammed it shut, and turned the latch. I ran through the dark hallway and seconds later heard him banging and clawing against the locked door. A brief silence followed. Then BOOM! The Cadillac Man slammed the full force of his body, like a battering ram, at the door. BOOM! CRACK! He hit it again and something in the door frame gave way at the same time. SMASH! He stormed into the hallway, and at almost the same moment I flew out the other side and into the parking lot.

I charged to Asa's truck and reached under the fender to the top of the front tire. There they were—the keys, right where I had left them. I jumped in, slammed the door, and hammer-fisted the lock button as the Cadillac Man flew out of Emerald Gardens, looking left and right. He hadn't seen me. I cranked the engine. It groaned twice, then roared to life. I looked up again and locked eyes with Howard W. Shulepick. His whole face was one enormous snarl the moment before he charged.

I slowly engaged the clutch and revved the engine at the same time. *Don't stall! Don't stall! Don't stall!*

The tires gripped the pavement, and I lifted my left foot completely off the clutch pedal while gradually upping the throttle. He grabbed my driver's side door handle at the same time that my tires screeched and produced a cloud of white smoke.

The Cadillac Man yanked and pounded at the door handle as he ran alongside the truck. He tried to punch out the glass but hit the metal edge instead. For a second I thought I had lost him. Then I looked at the side mirror and it was filled with black-and-white stripes. *Good grief!* I was dragging the creep.

I steered toward a snowbank and sideswiped it with an impact that shook the whole truck. It worked. The next thing I saw in my mirror was the Cadillac Man skidding to a stop on his belly.

Yes! I shook a clenched fist like a gladiator. Then—*Uh-oh*. What was that in his hands?

The explosion of the bullet through the truck's windows sent a million, gravel-sized bits of glass into the cab. The rear glass was gone. The front windshield had shattered into a spider web. BOOM! Another shot rang out, only louder this time. The second bullet hit the windshield just a few inches to the right of my head and shattered it even more. BOOM! BOOM! BOOM! BOOM! More glass shattered. The truck kept going and I was still breathing, apparently not hit.

In my side mirror I watched him turn and run. Was he heading back toward his house? It was my chance to get away. Suddenly I remembered the .357 Magnum as a way to fight back. The sickening realization struck that I had left it laying on the ground as well as my X-15 instamatic camera.

My brain shifted to survival mode. About a million thoughts ran through me like a cloud of bugs under a street light. Run for home? No . . . he'll kill Mom and Sally. Run for Mark's house? Nope . . . same problem.

Wait a minute. Drive to the police station!

I zoomed up to the stop sign, and turned right on Main with ideas of racing through downtown. I was met by the flashing lights and dropping crossarm of the railroad crossing barrier.

"No!" I shouted, as a single, red-and-white locomotive engine blasted its whistle and rolled slowly across Main Street. "Hurry, hurry, hurry!" I yelled. The engine had barely passed when it came to a dead stop.

Clang! Clang! Clang!

I had to get out of there, so I threw the shift lever into reverse and looked over my shoulder only to see a little old lady in a blue sedan right on my bumper. *Holy mackerel!* I was wedged!

I checked out the window. No sign yet of the Cadillac Man.

"Come on! Come on! Come on!"

Clang! Clang! Clang!

The locomotive finally rumbled back and out of the intersection. I ground my teeth and bit my lip.

"Come on! Come on! Come on!"

The crossarm started rising, and like a maestro, I working the shift lever, clutch pedal, and throttle. The truck inched forward. CLUNK!

Killed it! A fresh flood of panic poured through me as I pushed in the clutch pedal and fired up the engine again.

"Come on! Come on!"

The truck lurched forward a few feet and CLUNK!—*Dead again.* I checked through the shattered window and there it was, the black Cadillac, charging toward me like a dragster. I fired up the engine and put all my attention on those two foot pedals.

"One Mississippi—Two Mississippi—Three Mississippi." It caught. I hammered the throttle and screamed over the tracks.

As I roared east on Main with my stomach halfway up my throat, I whipped past a couple cars and decided to take my chances right down the center of the yellow line. Cars veered left and right to get out of my way. I screeched the tires, making the big sweeping turn around the curved, red-brick wall of the Bergstrom mill. My eyes darted to the side mirror.

Nuts!

The maniac was right on me. The truck tires screeched through a sharp right and then a sharp left as I ignored every stop sign. With the spire of the clock tower in front of me, I pushed down the accelerator determined to make the green light. Just as it turned yellow I barreled through safely, then checked the mirror again. The black Cadillac never slowed down, flying through on the red light, barely missing the stream of cross traffic.

Suddenly I realized that I couldn't stop no matter what or the Cadillac Man would put a bullet in my head. The idea of going to the police station was out. I had no weapons to fight back. My only hope was to ditch him.

My face was skewed low and to the right, nearly laying on the dashboard as I looked through the only patch of glass that hadn't been shattered by bullets. The whole truck shuttered as I scraped another snowbank turning right on Oak. The rear end fishtailed with a hard left on Division.

I roared past Shattuck and screamed around another right turn on Reed when the idea hit me. With no way of shaking the bastard on dry land, I would take my chances on the lake. I bombed around the corner at Lauden Boulevard and nearly tipped the truck onto two wheels, turning right at South Park before angling left on Bayview. He was still right on me so I jumped hard on the gas. Another left and right turn brought me to the ice and gravel beach of the Fresh Air Camp.

An infinity of ice lay in front of me on Lake Winnebago. It was no skating rink. The spring ice had begun rotting away and was anything but smooth. Remnants of snow drifts and pressure ridges stood in my path. From the way the sunlight reflected, I could tell that it was covered with slushy puddles and laced with cracks. A smattering of sturgeon spearing shanties showed themselves near the east and west shores. Directly in front of me, to the south, lay the flat line of nothingness — an empty horizon. It might as well have been the Arctic Ocean. Thirty miles of ice between me and Fond du Lac. I set my sights on that flat horizon and cranked up the throttle.

Slush sprayed up on both sides as I launched Asa's truck onto the lake and headed for the gap and makeshift bridge across a pressure ridge of jagged ice.

KACHUNK! KACHUNK! I was on and off.

A quick check of the side mirror showed the black Cadillac splashing through puddles and slush beds close behind me. I wondered if he would shoot again by hanging his left arm out the window like in the gangster movies. The black car bounced and lurched, fishtailing one way and then the other.

Asa's truck had two advantages over the Cadillac — ground clearance and snow tires, and I intended to use both to my advantage. While the Cadillac Man bumped over the steel planks of the ice bridge, I hammered the throttle and bucked through a three-foot drift as thick as mashed potatoes. I would forge my own path. Shulepick could either chase me all the way to Fond du Lac or give up. Either way, I was pretty sure I could ditch him.

51

With one eye on the speedometer and another on the ice, I brought the truck up to forty-five miles an hour, heading south. The slush was really flying as the Chevy Apache bucked and swayed like a wild bronc. Every once in a while I scraped a heavy drift with the muffler, and it dragged my speed back to thirty. I know, I know. I was plowing a trail for the creep but there was still no way he could keep up with me in that low-riding sedan. For every mushy snow drift that bogged down the truck, at least a dozen smaller ones scraped at the bottom of the black Caddy. In the first five minutes he had fallen back by the length of a football field. If I just kept going at the same pace, I was certain to lose him.

Visibility was a problem, of course. With my shot-up windshield I was constantly lining up my eyeballs with the top of the dashboard, where I looked through a small patch of unshattered glass just above the wipers. I spotted some wooden sticks poking out of the ice and realized that they marked an abandoned sturgeon spearing hole. Those big, rectangular holes became my biggest hazard. Cut by chain saws, they usually measured six feet long and three feet wide. I steered clear.

Garlic Island came into view a couple miles ahead near the west shore. I would skirt it on the left, keeping my southbound bearing toward Fond du Lac. I looked back and saw my enemy at about three football fields back. Pretty soon he would be nothing but a speck.

But wait. Something was different. The Cadillac wasn't splashing through puddles or swaying back and forth anymore. What was going on? *Had he given up?*

Through the busted-out rear window of the truck cab, I heard a gunshot. The crazy man was shooting at me again. I ducked my head but wasn't too worried because he was way beyond handgun range.

Suddenly, another shot rang out, and at the same time a bullet clanged into the truck.

Dang it!

Another shot sounded and the clang announced another direct hit on the Chevy. Shulepick was shooting a high-powered rifle—probably the same one he used to kill Sheriff Heiselmann.

I ducked my head further and looked around for options. A second pressure ridge of cracked and buckled ice appeared, coming out from the west shore near the island. A thought popped into my brain—one that would allow me to shake off the Cadillac Man once and for all. I angled the truck toward the crack and looked for a crossing point. Slabs of ice as big as cars were tipped vertical here and there, but other stretches looked more like rough snowdrifts laced with trash-can-sized ice chunks. I turned the steering wheel and kept my head low as I bucked toward a likely crossing point. The sound of two more rifle shots clinched my decision to take the chance. I picked the least rough of the possible crossings, dropped my speed to thirty, and went right at it.

KABUMP-BUMP-CRUNCH-KABUMP! I was up and over.

"Try crossing that—Jerk!"

I looked back out at the Cadillac Man. He was following me again, bumping . . . swerving . . . splashing. I cranked the speed back up to forty-five, then decided to bump it to fifty. The Chevy seemed to handle it okay. I looked back again, satisfied that I had ditched him at last.

"See ya in prison—Peckerhead!"

Now that I knew he couldn't follow me across the ridge, it was just a matter of finding a place to drive off the lake. Otter Street in Oshkosh would work. Asylum Bay would be coming up even sooner. From there I would simply find a pay phone and call Agent Culper. Between him and the local cops, they could nab Shulepick, maybe right off the lake, and toss him in the slammer. Then we could go back together and gather the evidence that I left in his backyard.

By the time I turned my eyes back forward in the tiny clear patch of my windshield it was too late. The sticks and twine marking an abandoned spearing hole were right there in front of me.

"Dammit!"

I jumped on the brakes and pulled hard left on the steering wheel. The truck threw up a huge spray of slush like a water skier making a bank turn. My front wheels barely missed the big rectangle of open water. Had I dodged it?

THUMP! . . . BUMP!

The thump was the rear wheels falling in the hole. The bump was my head hitting the metal dashboard of the Chevy Apache pickup. I felt a warm trickle running around my nose to my chin. A salty taste found my mouth. I brought my hand to my forehead, pulled it away, and gazed at a bloody mess. My eyes drooped and my head fell sideways. I slapped my own face, trying to shake off the cobwebs.

"What happened?"

Looking out the window, I saw the horizon at a thirty degree angle to the truck.

"I'm stuck."

The truck was still running, so I gave it some gas. The engine revved but the truck didn't move. On the passenger side, my rear wheel was completely submerged and churning the lake water like a washing machine. I was stuck all right. I was more than stuck. Grandpa's truck teetered on the brink—ready to take the plunge to the bottom of Lake Winnebago.

I pushed hard on my door, but it wouldn't open since the bottom edge was wedged in the lake ice. I cranked open the window instead and climbed out, feeling instant pain as the jagged ice bit into my feet. I looked down at a barefooted left foot stained pink and the right covered with nothing but a bloody sock. I gazed forward, spotting Garlic Island on the horizon. I turned back toward the northeast and saw a black car fishtailing and splashing in my direction. My survival instinct woke up pretty quickly after that.

Holy smoke! He'll be on me in two minutes.

The nearest shore was a mile due west—Garlic Island, a mile to the south. Between the two stood a tiny cluster of three spearing shanties, one black, one white, and one purple. By my reckoning, they were a quarter mile away. I took off at a wobbling trot toward the black one. With each step, my cut-up feet got worse, but at that point it didn't matter. Every so often I stopped to snort blood out of my nostrils. The average zombie looked better than me.

I was almost at the shanty when I heard another gunshot behind me. I looked back just in time to see the Cadillac Man in his referee shirt bracing a rifle on the hood. A flash of light was followed by another crack from the muzzle of the rifle. This time a sharp pain stung my right leg.

"Aahh!"

I glanced down and saw blood soaking into my jeans. I was hit, but how bad? A closer look showed me that the bullet had grazed the edge of my thigh—just enough to put a three-inch rip in my jeans and plow a shallow trough through my flesh about as wide as a pencil. The sting quickly turned into throbbing pain. I turned again toward the black shanty, limping as fast as I could while changing directions every three or four strides. The gunfire continued and I wasn't sure whether or not anything hit me, so I just kept going.

At last I ducked behind the black shanty, breathing hard and trying to figure out what to do next.

I cupped my hands to yell toward the other two shanties. "Help! Is anybody there?! I need help! Is anybody there?!"

No response.

My attention shifted to the door on the black shanty. As expected, it was locked. The other shanties would be locked up just the same. I was a coyote in a trap, just waiting for the bullet that would finish me off.

Waiting for my doom was not an appealing option, so I looked around on the edges of the shanty for something heavy. What I found was a wrench, probably used in cranking the shanty down to the ice level. I grabbed it and quickly went to work on the padlock. It only took about six hits before the combo lock popped open. I ripped it off, went inside, then shut and latched the door.

On the inside, everything was dark except a big rectangle of eerie green light coming up from the gaping hole in the floor of the eight-by-six-foot shanty. I opened a sliding shutter that exposed a peephole to the outside. With my eye to the opening, I saw the Cadillac Man striding toward me from where he had left his car on the other side of the pressure ridge. He was just a couple hundred yards away, carrying the rifle across his body like a soldier. Unless I came up with something, I would be dead in three minutes.

A weapon! A weapon! I need a weapon!

I dropped to my knees and groped with my hands on the floor of the shanty. Two wooden spear shafts stood upright in the corner but the spearheads themselves were gone. I remembered Dad telling me that a good sturgeon spear cost as much as fifty dollars and that nobody left them in their shanties overnight.

Using the two shafts, a wooden bench, and a length of rope, I rigged a barricade to keep the Cadillac Man from busting in on me. I figured it would hold him back for a little while, maybe a minute. Then he would either kick in the door or shoot right through it. I checked the peephole again. There was no mistaking him in that black-and-white striped shirt, only a hundred yards away and walking directly toward me. I breathed in and out.

It was a weird feeling knowing that I was going to die. Believe it or not, it didn't seem real. I felt like an actor in a play that had a script with a tragic ending. I didn't freak out and I didn't cry. Instead, I sat there and waited quietly.

All of a sudden it occurred to me that Howard W. Shulepick was going to get away scot-free. After killing me he would simply push my body in the hole and shove it underneath the ice. My cold, dead corpse would eventually drift away with the spring thaw. No evidence, no witnesses, no funeral, no nothing.

At first, that knowledge only made me mad. Then it made me think. How far away were those other shanties? I peeked through a crack along the edge of the door and saw them both. The white shanty was about eighty yards away. The purple one was closer—just a strong football toss. Could I swim my injured body under the ice in freezing cold water and find the underwater opening to that purple shanty? I lined up the location of the target with the glowing-green rectangular hole and made a mental note of the direction. My thoughts drifted back to my experiences diving for fishing lures. I started taking long deep breaths of air to charge my lungs with oxygen like I did in the murky waters of the Fox.

I shook off my coat and kicked that last remaining bloody sock into the hole.

Deep breath . . . Exhale . . . Deep breath . . . Exhale . . . Deep breath . . . Exhale.

Crunch . . . crunch . . . crunch . . . crunch. The footsteps announced Shulepick's arrival. A shadow crossed the crack of light around one edge of the door. The whole shanty rattled as he yanked at the knob. He rattled it harder and then bashed his whole body against it. My barricade held.

Deep breath . . . Exhale . . . Deep breath . . . Exhale.

One more shoulder hit and the top hinge came loose. It was time to swim or die, so I stepped over the hole, pointed myself toward the purple shanty, put my arms and legs together like a toothpick and dropped straight in.

The freezing cold water felt like it would kill me all by itself. I had heard people describe falling through the ice as a shock like a million needles pricking your skin from every side, and that's pretty close to what I felt. But do you know what? The fear of not finding the opening to the purple shanty scared me even worse. I swam the underwater breast stroke in the direction I had pointed myself.

Arm pull . . . leg kick . . . glide . . . arm pull . . . leg kick . . . glide.

The bottom side of the ice was a puzzle. Every frozen bubble and crack lit up by the sunlight overhead.

Arm pull . . . leg kick . . . glide . . . arm pull . . . leg kick . . . glide.

My lungs were almost tapped out, but I didn't panic. From my practice in the Fox River I knew I could keep pulling myself forward.

Arm pull . . . leg kick . . . glide . . . arm pull . . . leg kick . . . glide.

That was it. I had moved on to uncharted territory and my head and lungs were ready to explode. It would be mind over matter.

Arm pull . . . leg kick . . . arm pull . . . leg kick.

A rectangle of shade appeared just ahead.

Arm pull . . . leg kick . . .

Alarm bells clanged in my brain as I slid under the black shadow of the shanty, found the hole, and splashed up into pitch darkness. I gasped and coughed and gasped again. My hands held the floor of the shanty as I felt a certain sense of accomplishment. My lungs and body basked in the chance to breathe again. I was alive. Then a million needles surrounded me again, reminding me that if I wasn't shot, I would probably freeze to death.

It was time to use my pull-up muscles, and in one swift movement, like a leaping fish, I yanked my body out of the water and lay dripping on the floor of the shanty. Spasms of shivering came next, and there was no stopping them.

Tapped out of energy and shaking like a paint mixer, I knew the Cadillac Man would be busting into this shanty next. I slapped my arms against my chest and shoulders, trying to slow down the shivering. What I really, really, really needed was a weapon. I felt around in the corners and edges of the shanty, finding two metal folding chairs and a pair of wooden shafts.

Dammit!

I was no better off than at the other shanty. I groped around and found what felt like a small knob. I turned it and a panel opened up to a secret cubbyhole in the back wall. Inside I felt something hard.

Could it be?

I lifted out a four-tined spearhead as big as a pitchfork and gazed at it in the backdrop of green light from the hole. It had twelve-inch tines welded to a sturdy crossbar and a round, tubular socket for a handle. I touched the tip of one of the points and pulled my finger away quick. The spear was sharp all right. I pulled out one of the wooden shafts and fit the tapered end into the tubular socket of the spearhead. Lashing them together was no easy matter with stone-cold hands.

Crunch . . . crunch . . . crunch. Howard W. Shulepick had arrived.

With my teeth I held one end of the rope while working the other into a half hitch and pulling it tight with both palms pressed together. I quietly slid into the back corner of the shanty, where I assumed a crouching position and held the huge spear toward the door. The palm of my right hand held the butt end of the smooth, wooden shaft. My left palm created a guide halfway up the shaft. My whole body shook and so did the spear. Could I do it? Maybe. Just maybe. I would have one, single chance. My body shook. My brain waited.

Crunch, crunch, crunch . . . click.

BOOM! Splinters of wood flew into my face as a section of the door as big as my palm was blown away, letting in a jagged bar of sunshine. I held as steady as I could. The door swung open, and all I saw was the silhouette of a man holding a gun against the backdrop of pure white light. The Cadillac Man either hadn't expected to see me or didn't consider me much of a threat, because the rifle was held muzzle-up, in a one-handed grip. For one long second, neither one of us moved.

It was now or never and I surged forward with everything I had—arms, legs, fingers, toes, back, and stomach . . . every muscle in me tightened to drive that spear forward, and when it hit its mark I kept on charging with a scream that I had been saving since the night Dad was killed.

The force of my thrust drove the Cadillac Man backward, and his rifle flew from his grip. I surged forward following the spear—driving, driving, driving that spear into the chest of my father's killer. All the while I screamed and yelled, not stopping until all ninety pounds of me were standing over him, forcing that spear as deep into his chest as I could push it. Four circles of blood grew into the white stripes of the Cadillac Man's referee shirt. He growled and reached for the rifle, but I stomped his hand and kicked it away. I practically climbed to the top of that spear shaft, pushing down with all of my weight until the tips of all four tines were through him and poking into the ice on the other side.

For a long time I stood over that spear, as the horrible reality sunk in. The referee shirt was, by that point, completely soaked in blood, every white stripe now bright red. Through it all, the Cadillac Man's legs kicked and his arms flopped and flailed at the air. There were moments when his eyes locked on mine and he made punching jabs toward my face.

Then blood started coming out of his mouth and nose. I had seen enough war movies to realize what it meant. The spear had passed through the man's lungs and they were filling with his own blood. He coughed and spat. I started feeling sick to my stomach and even guilty about what I had done—about what I was doing.

"You worthless little maggot!" He snarled the words through bloody teeth.

Those words flipped a switch in me and brought back an image of Dad lying dead in the gravel on the shoulder of Highway 41. I climbed that spear and pushed down hard.

"You killed my dad," I said between grunts.

I repositioned my arms so that both palms were on the very end of the spear shaft and called on the remaining strength of my pull-up muscles to bear down as hard as I could on the murderer. I heard myself groan. My teeth ground together so hard it's a wonder they didn't turn to dust.

I knew it was over when his face went white as pulp and his eyes turned to glass. For a couple more minutes, I just stood over him with all of my weight on that spear. Only when I could no longer grip the thing did I finally let it go. I fell flat, shivering like crazy.

I found enough strength to lift my head and looked all around me at the vast emptiness. "Can somebody help me?" I asked. It came out weak—lost to the wind and sky.

I looked down at the bullet wound in my leg, still bleeding. The patch of blood was soaking one leg of my pants and starting to leak over to the other. A weird sort of hopelessness passed through me like a ghost. I tried crawling toward shore but couldn't move. Was it over for me too? After everything—after marching to the Butte des Morts Bridge—after Dad and the sheriff getting shot to death—after Larry Buskin's help—after finding the Cadillac Man at the Rockets game—after Operation Snake Den? After all of that, was it really over for me? I slumped into the slushy snow and closed my eyes.

Have you ever read a story called "To Build a Fire," by Jack London? Well I have, but only about five hundred times. As I drifted off to die on the ice that story played through my mind like a movie.

Day had broken cold and gray, exceedingly cold and gray. . . . The Yukon lay a mile wide and hidden under three feet of ice.

I tried to lift myself but fell flat.

The old-timer had been very serious. . . . No man must travel alone on the Klondike after fifty below.

After all of that, was I going to let the stupid cold kill me?

He pictured the boys finding his body the next day.

"No! Not that way!"

Then the man drowsed off into what seemed to him the most comfortable and satisfying sleep he had ever known.

"No!"

The dog whined loudly. . . . It crept close to the man and caught the scent of death.

"No! No! No!" I scared myself with my own yelling. Where had *that* voice come from? Something inside me wasn't ready to die.

I rolled over onto my belly and tried to stand again but couldn't. On hands and knees, shivering, soaking wet, and bleeding, without boots, socks, gloves, or coat, I started out on the long crawl toward shore.

❊

It must have been late afternoon when I slapped my palm three times against the door of a small house.

The next thing I remembered, a man was dragging me inside. A woman appeared and started throwing quilts and blankets over me. While she was doing that I heard the man yelling something about an ambulance into the phone. The quilts kept coming until the pile must have been ten deep. There they left me to lay on the kitchen floor. All was quiet until I heard them whispering.

"Do you suppose he'll die?" asked the woman.

"Don't know," said the man.

I remembered nothing more. I was off the Yukon trail. I had built a fire. I knew that much.

52

I woke to the inside of a hospital room with a tube stuck in my arm connected to a bottle hanging from a hook. The clock said twenty past three. The window was dark, but I was alive.

I threw off the bedsheet and about a dozen heating pads fell to the floor. A big, giant bandage was wrapped around my thigh where the Cadillac Man's bullet had plowed a furrow.

I wasn't cold anymore. Gosh—I was sweating.

"About time you woke up." My eyes landed on the scowling face of the largest nurse I had ever seen. She grabbed my wrist like it was a frying-pan handle and checked my pulse while looking at her watch, then wrote something down on a clipboard.

"Where am I?"

"Mercy Hospital in Oshkosh."

"Does my mom know I'm here?"

"She was here. The police were here. The FBI was here." She rolled her eyes and gave her head a shake of annoyance.

"Do they know what happened?"

"Everybody knows. Another death, thanks to you." The nurse dropped the clipboard loudly on the table and walked out.

The sun came up and shot a yellow beam of light through the window, really brightening things up. The nurse situation got better too. A young, pretty one named Miss Kittleson took over for the day shift and unlike that sledgehammer from the night before, she liked me. Heck, it was more than that. It was as if I had just won the Olympic Marathon. Her eyes sparkled like the sunrise on Poygan, as she pulled up a chair.

"I heard the story this morning," she said. "Was he the Highway 41 Killer?"

"Well, he killed my dad. I'm sure of that."

She just shook her head and beamed at me. We were Clark Kent and Lois Lane. She took her time taking my pulse with her soft, thin fingers. "Would you like some water or juice?"

"Apple juice?"

She hustled out the door just as my mom walked in—without a cigarette—believe it or not. She smiled and kissed me on my cheek. "Thank God you're alive," she said.

"I'm okay, Mom."

"They said that you almost died."

"Almost."

"I can't lose you, Del. Not after losing Dad."

"I can't lose you either, Mom."

Mom started crying and I did too. And it wasn't the little sniffle and wipe-away-a-tear sort of crying. We sobbed and shook as we held each other. I sure hadn't made life easy for my mom. *Cripes!* How many times had I lied to her? She was the one person who really loved me, and not just a little bit either. Mom really, really, really loved me, and if you think that sounds sappy, then too bad for you.

After a few minutes, Miss Kittleson came back with my apple juice, but when she saw us, she placed the juice on the table and scrammed.

Two cops came next and asked me questions for more than an hour. One of them was the red-haired deputy who had called me a "little bastard" when he was trying to cuff me at the Butte des Morts Bridge. The other one was Agent Culper.

Both guys had already been to the scene on the lake and had put two and two together by themselves. All the same, it took an hour to spill the whole story. I told them almost everything, starting with spotting Sheriff Heiselmann talking to the Cadillac Man at the Point and ending with me driving a sturgeon spear through Howard W. Shulepick's chest. They looked a little skeptical when I told them the part about swimming underwater from one ice shanty to another. When I was all the way finished, the red-haired deputy asked me a question I didn't expect.

"How many laws do you think you broke yesterday?"

I didn't answer but started tallying them in my head. Trespassing, busting into Shulepick's house, damaging property (the window), theft (the cookies), driving without a license, speeding, running stop signs, busting into a fish shanty (two counts), driving with a broken windshield, abandoning a vehicle. All of that and I hadn't even gotten to the part where I killed a man. I swallowed hard and kept my mouth shut. The cops could do the math for themselves.

"How old are you, Del?" asked the red-haired deputy.

"Almost sixteen."

❀

After two days in the hospital, they let me go home. That's when the newspeople got their first crack at me. The most ambitious ones waited outside the hospital. The rest were loitering in front of my house. They jabbed their microphones right in my face as I hobbled up the steps.

"Can you tell us how you were shot?"

"Why did he chase you?"

"Why did you drive on the lake?"

"Is it true that you killed him with a spear?"

As a gift to my mom, I kept my mouth shut. I just waved and offered a smile from my dashboard-bashed face. Then I walked in the house, shut the door, and unplugged the phone.

Mom saw me staring at the sink full of dishes. "Your kitchen duties have been temporarily suspended," she said.

❀

Somehow the newspeople still got the story. The cops blabbed, I suppose. After that, we had more visitors. Opal and Mark stopped over. It kind of bugged me, the two of them holding hands as they sat on our couch.

Opal was polite as we made small talk about school. Mark didn't say much until Opal got up to help my mom with dishes in the kitchen. When they were busy talking, he slid his chair over next to me. For a whole minute neither one of us spoke. Finally, a smile came to his face as he leaned over and slugged me hard in the shoulder.

"What's that for?" I asked.

"That's for killing the bastard."

There was a knock at the door. I could see Steve's face pressed against the glass, and Mark let him in. For a few minutes he asked me how I was doing, and we talked about what happened between me and Howard W. Shulepick.

After that, he got down to the serious business. For the next half hour we yakked about our plans for the giant kite and the bombing mission over Menasha's baseball field.

The parade of people kept coming. Pastor Olson, Mrs. Parsons, Mrs. Borger, and even Mrs. Eckert, our down-the-street neighbor, walked over with a plate of cookies. For years she had ignored me. I guess things were different now that I had made the front page of the *Post-Crescent*.

Neither I nor Mom was a bit surprised when the church ladies showed up just short of suppertime.

"Dorothy! We heard! Where's the boy!?" Mrs. Samuelson charged right past Mom and plopped a big bowl of potato salad on the kitchen table.

I limped into the kitchen. "Hi," I said.

She attacked me with outstretched arms, placing a pork-chop hand on either side of my injured face and burying my head between her giant breasts as she rocked me back and forth. "Oh my . . . poor dear . . . poor, poor dear." To tell you the truth, I didn't mind that experience.

Mrs. Stevens and Mrs. Weiden hugged me too and made their own deliveries of lime Jell-O with pear halves and a pan of chocolate brownies. Mrs. Stevens went straight to work, dusting the window ledges and cabinet shelves, a move that clearly bugged my mom. She couldn't say anything though because, as everybody knows, when people bring you food they can do what they want. Mrs. Samuelson, for one, had no intention of leaving until she had heard the whole story. She pushed my butt into a chair at the head of the table, put two chocolate brownies and a glass of milk in front of me, and ordered me to proceed.

It took over an hour, but I told them just about everything. By the time they went home the church ladies had as much information as the cops and ten times more than the *Post-Crescent* or *Eyewitness News*. Mom finally succeeded at guiding the women out the door.

"Thank you, ladies. See you again soon."

Clunk! Click! . . . Clunk! She shut and latched the door and would have thrown a barricade over the top if she had one. That last clunk, by the way, was her head falling back against the wall with her eyes closed.

53

Grandpa Asa died on Easter Sunday. Mom said it was old age but I saw two ladies at the funeral whispering to each other and looking at me like his death was all my fault. *Crud!* Were people still keeping score on me?

Let me tell you a few things you probably didn't know about my Grandpa Asa. For starters, he defeated that big jerk, Kaiser Wilhelm, in World War I, and if you've ever read history, you know it wasn't easy. Then he married my grandma and raised a great family that included my mom, all the while working at the foundry making manhole covers and sewer grates so he could buy a house on the island and put food on the table. When he went to Emerald Gardens, he sold his house to Mom and Dad for like a thousand bucks or some cheap amount so they could raise their family, and that included me.

You already know that he treated me nice and gave me ice cream every time I came over. And you already know that he let me drive the truck when I was just fifteen and bought me the Eaglewing steel-toed boots when I needed them. You even know that he went to jail because of me. He had confidence in me when I didn't. He was a grown-up I could talk to after Dad died and when Mom could barely get out of bed. Yep, and if I ever do anything right in my life, I owe a great big part of it to Grandpa Asa.

His funeral, of course, was nothing like my dad's. There weren't any police cars or news reporters. There were hardly any people at all. Pastor Olson and the church ladies came, of course, and Mrs. Samuelson did an outstanding job of hugging and consoling Mom, Sally, and me. After that it was just Mark, Steve, Rhonda, Opal, Mrs. Parsons, Mrs. Borger, and a few neighbors from the island.

When we got to the graveside part, Pastor Olson said some nice words that made me feel better. He said that we weren't the only ones looking on. Some of the people who loved Asa the most were already waiting for him in heaven. Grandma Lydia was waiting for him, along with his brothers and sisters, old neighbors, folks who worked at the foundry, even people he may have helped during the war.

When folks wandered off to their cars I paused and looked back at Asa's grave. The only thing left was a tiny American flag standing upright in a metal stand and two men leaning on their shovels by that old burr oak.

❀

Speaking of graves, Wolf eventually got a proper gravestone with his name on it. Yep . . . between Mark, Opal, Rhonda, and me, we managed to scrounge up enough money. The stone said:

WOLF

AMERICAN INDIAN FISHERMAN

DIED JANUARY 15, 1973

I asked Pastor Olson if he would say a few words when we put down the new marker, and so he came with us. We were a small group, just the pastor, Mark, Opal, Rhonda, and me, but the words were nice, and the little ceremony was a million times better than leaving Wolf under that stupid little post with the number 648.

While everyone was walking back to Pastor Olson's car, I got down on my hands and knees and dug a little trench by Wolf's gravestone. In there I placed a few fishhooks, a couple of split shot sinkers, and a slip bobber, along with a few feet of monofilament line, and covered it all back up. I wasn't sure if mooneye fishing was allowed in heaven, but I figured on taking the shot.

❀

The lilacs were blooming as I drove the Chevy Apache out to the lighthouse on the point. The truck was mine now since Grandpa Asa had left it for me in his will. I even had my driver's license, having passed the test on my very first try right after my sixteenth birthday. The truck was all fixed up too. Grandpa's insurance had paid for new glass all the way around, and Mr. Johnson helped me plug and paint most of the bullet holes. (We left one unfixed in the rear bumper just for the heck of it.)

I parked the truck near the lighthouse and sat down at a picnic table with the bright sunshine warming my back and reflecting off Lake Winnebago. A dozen fishing boats rocked back and forth in the waves. Across the lake, the pale bluffs of High Cliff Park stood there like they had since the glaciers. To my left, across the Fox River, my eyes rested on the greenery of Doty Island, my home base, and for the first time in a long while, the earth seemed to be spinning on its axis at a normal speed.

Mom was doing better. She had cut down to a half pack of cigarettes a day and had even joined the YMCA. She swam there three times a week, if you can believe that. Sally graduated from Armstrong and the ceremony was coming up in just two days. She got accepted into college at Stevens Point, and her boyfriend decided to follow her there. Pretty soon it was going to be just me and Mom, and I guess that was okay with all of us.

In case you're wondering, I never did play Romeo in the school play. What, with my injuries and the cops and newspeople and everything, it just seemed like too much. I asked Mrs. Borger and Mr. Schirmer for a reprieve and they were cool with it. They only had one back up — Norwood Heckmeyer — but, boy oh boy, was he ever happy.

Then another funny thing happened. About a week after I quit the Romeo role, Marjorie Bickersly came down with mono (you know — the kissing disease). Well, guess who got picked to play Juliet? Yep — after all those bends and turns, Rhonda got the part. I'm pretty sure Mrs. Borger did some serious arm twisting to make it happen because, as we all know, Mr. Schirmer could be a dipstick sometimes. Anyhow, things all worked out, and I never saw such a big smile on Rhonda's face. I went to the play — twice — and her performance was out of sight. And when everybody came out for their bows at the end — guess what. Rhonda got the biggest applause of all. Heck, little kids were asking for her autograph and everything.

If you think all of that was crazy, wait until you hear this part. Norwood Heckmeyer asked Rhonda to go to Spring Fling, and she accepted. Ever since, those two were transformed into Shattuck High's hottest couple. Rhonda ditched her frumpy clothes and got her hair fixed up nice. She even started wearing tight sweaters and they looked pretty good on her too, if you know what I mean.

Mark and Opal were still dating. I probably shouldn't say this, but I was still a little jealous. Opal was the first girl who sort of liked me. On top of that she was pretty, fun, and smart, and it was really cool hanging out with somebody so different from every other kid in school. Like my mom says, things and people are always changing. She said it was true for the whole world, and it was definitely true for Shattuck High.

Mrs. Parsons still liked me. Sometimes on my Hoot Owl route she would invite me in for a piece of corn bread or whatever just came out of the oven. You know what she liked to talk about most? You guessed it: history—and not just about the civil rights movement either. Mrs. Parsons wanted to learn everything there was to know about the Fox, Winnebago, and Menomonie Indians. She said that ever since I told her about the people who lived here for thousands of years, she couldn't get them out of her head.

And do you know what else she told me? She said that she still wanted to walk all the way across the Butte des Morts Bridge with me one of these days. She said "it must be done," and that she was going to hold me to it. "It's a matter of principle," she told me.

In case you're wondering, the Blue Jay Slayer was a giant flop. Mark and Steve and I finished building it, complete with the sign, a twelve-foot tail made of empty beer cans, and the pull-string-operated bomb hatch. The plan was to load it up with about a million red-and-white ping pong balls and shower the Menasha baseball team as they came out on the field. It would have worked too. We had everything set up and even got it in the air with all three of us pulling hard on the twine. It all worked perfectly for about a half of a minute. Then a gust of wind came out of somewhere and sent the kite spinning in circles until it finally crashed, head first, right onto the street. There was nothing left to do but pick up the pieces and watch all of those ping pong balls roll away with the wind down two city blocks. At least the little kids in Menasha got an extra Easter egg hunt out of the deal.

Of all the people who changed at Shattuck High, guess who changed the most. Larry Buskin. You're probably not going to believe this, but he and I sort of became friends. Remember how Larry helped me follow the trail of clues to the Cadillac Man? Remember how he warned me to be careful? Well, some of those things probably saved my butt.

But at the same time that I was getting all sorts of praise for getting the Highway 41 Killer, Larry was getting into deeper and deeper trouble. Yep, when the cops finally connected the dots and chased down the people in Shulepick's file box, they eventually got to Larry Buskin and took him down hard. Six months earlier I would have cheered. But, all of a sudden, something about it didn't feel right anymore.

I went to the sheriff's office to explain things to them, but they were no help. In the end, I called up Agent Culper again at the Milwaukee FBI. To make a long story short, he worked with Larry and helped him, but he still had to spend a month in juvie. When he came back, Mrs. Borger asked me if I could tutor Larry in a couple of classes. I said I would, and guess what. Larry Buskin got a B- in Geometry and a C+ in American History.

And do you think the grits and dirtballs messed with me after that? No, they did not. They didn't yell curse words at me. They didn't try to get my lunch money. They didn't bug me in the halls. Heck, I even started using the central lavatory again.

As a cloud passed over the sun, I blinked my eyes and focused once again on the fishing boats bobbing out on good old Lake Winnebago. Suddenly, I remembered why I had driven down to the point in the first place. I pulled on my dive goggles, retied my crummy tennis shoes, and tightened the string on my swim trunks. There was only one fisherman on shore, and he was way down at the south end of the park. I climbed down the rocks and into the water crab style, feet first, using both arms for balance. The chilly water brought up goose bumps. Through my goggles, I viewed a familiar, green glow.

On Saturday morning I was up eating Pop-Tarts and drinking Tang before Mom or Sally had made a single peep. I loaded a folding card table and my box of lures into the truck and drove to the Fox Point Shopping Center. The flea market was the same disorganized jumble of vehicles and tables that I remembered from last fall. Folks were set up in two rows, selling everything from dishes and dolls to carburetors and cuckoo clocks.

I spied an opening next to an elderly lady with a table full of fresh-cut flowers of every color and type.

"Hi," I said. "Can I set up by you?"

"Certainly," she said. "Lovely day, isn't it?"

"Sure is."

"Whatcha got there?"

"Used fishing lures, mainly."

I set up the card table and spread out my junk the same way I had last fall. Spoons and spinners in the first row, plugs and plastic worms right behind, with the sinkers, hooks, swivels, and bobbers in the third row. My prices were handwritten on pieces of masking tape stuck to the table and, just like last year, they ranged from a nickel to fifty cents.

Then I pulled out my second box, removed the lid, and placed the contents to one side of my fishing lures. The Eaglewings reflected the bright morning light off the reddish-brown leather from the fresh coat of polish I had applied the night before. Agent Culper had rescued them for me from Howard W. Shulepick's house. The toes were a little scuffed, but otherwise round and rock hard. I tied up the laces so they would look their best.

Just like last fall, folks wandered through at a steady clip. A thirty-year-old blond-haired guy with a sunburned face bought three Little Cleos and a Spinno-King.

"I fish a lot on Haystack Reef," he said. "Need to replenish my supply."

A farmer wearing coveralls and a seed-corn hat bought up all the hooks, sinkers, and swivels.

"Heard they're catching bullheads out by the tissue mill," he said.

With others picking up an item here and there, my fishing stuff was nearly gone by ten thirty, and I had nine bucks and seventy cents to show for it. *Holy smokes!* That was more than a month of Hoot Owl money, and it only took a few hours.

"You're almost sold out," said the flower lady at the next table.

I shrugged and smiled. "I guess it's my lucky day." I didn't ask her how she was doing, because I could see that she hadn't sold much.

"My grandson could use some boots like that. Are they good quality?" she asked.

"Very good," I said. "Genuine Eaglewings, with the steel toe and the reinforced shank and less than a year old."

"Don't they fit you?"

"They fit me just fine."

"Aren't they comfortable?"

"They're very comfortable."

"Then why are you selling them?"

Now *there* was a question. Why *was* I selling them? I opened my mouth but nothing came out and I closed it again. Then I just said what I believed.

"I used to need them, but I don't anymore."

The lady smiled. "You mean you had a job to do, and now the job is done?"

"Something like that."

"What size are they?"

"Size four."

"How much are you asking?"

"Three dollars."

"Hmm . . . well, that's probably a good price." She picked up one of the shoes and tried to squeeze the rounded toe. She worked her mouth a little and put the shoe back down. "But I don't have three dollars," she said.

❈

I arrived home with the card table, two empty boxes, and a pile of fresh-cut flowers.

I poked around in the highest shelf in the kitchen cabinets and found two vases. Arranging the tulips, irises, and daffodils was easy, just a matter of following the lady's instructions. When I was done, both arrangements looked dang-near perfect. I even poked some white flowers called baby's breath around the edges like the woman had showed me. I put a little card on one of them for my mom with a note thanking her for loving me. The second bouquet was for Sally for her graduation, and I wrote some sappy words on her card too.

The last bouquet was the most impressive of them all. The flea-market lady had fixed it up with some big, orange lilies and tied it all together with a pink ribbon and tissue paper around the outside. "Keep them in a cool place," she had told me. I slid the flowers into the refrigerator, then checked the time on the kitchen clock. *Half past four.* I would have to leave soon.

I took a quick shower, combed my hair with Vitalis, and slapped some Old Spice on my face. I put on some clean black pants, a white buttoned shirt, and a blue clip-on tie. I wiped off the black leather shoes that I had only worn to funerals and put them on over black socks. Last of all, I grabbed my camel-colored, corduroy jacket and looked at myself in the bathroom mirror.

"Not bad for a Minnow."

I smiled at my own dumb joke and tweaked the tie a little to make it look real.

By now I suppose you're wondering why a nerdy, scared of everything, little shrimp like me was putting on fancy clothes with flowers waiting for me in the refrigerator.

Do you remember what Grandpa Asa told me once about making my own luck? And do you remember that girl named Jan who I met at the pizza restaurant in Kaukauna? That's right—the one playing the lead role at the end of May in *A Midsummer Night's Dream*? The one with the sparkly blue eyes and the perfect smile and blonde hair that curled up on the ends? That prettiest girl in the world who wrote "Come and see me again sometime!" on my check?

Still wondering?

Well, okay then—now you know.

Acknowledgments

A host of people provided encouragement, guidance, and support. My sincere thanks to the following:

My wonderful parents, Jack and Mary, who gave me fond memories of growing up in Neenah, Wisconsin, and much more.

My dear Carmen, who helped me clear countless hurdles and never wavered in her belief in me.

My daughter, Kavya, and son, Curtis, for cheering me on.

Bev Larsen, Chuck Ladd, Anne Hollenbach, Shirley Brander, and Sachin Gore, for helping me scrub the first draft.

Raphael Kadushin, Sheila McMahon, Amber Rose, Dennis Lloyd, Sheila Leary, Jennifer Conn, Casey LaVela, and Scott Mueller through my association with the University of Wisconsin Press, who brought it all together—for real.